TH.

Tom Knox is the pseudonym of the author Sean Thomas. Born in England, he has travelled the world writing for many different newspapers and magazines, including *The Times*, the *Guardian*, and the *Daily Mail*. His first thriller was translated into twenty-two languages; he also writes on art, politics, and ancient history. He lives in London.

For more information visit tomknoxbooks.com

By Tom Knox

The Genesis Secret
The Marks of Cain
Bible of the Dead

TOM KNOX

The Babylon Rite

HARPER

Harper
An imprint of HarperCollins*Publishers*
77–85 Fulham Palace Road,
Hammersmith, London W6 8JB

www.harpercollins.co.uk

A Paperback Original 2012
1

A catalogue record for this book
is available from the British Library

ISBN 978 0 00 734402 4

Set in Meridien by Palimpsest Book Production Limited,
Falkirk, Stirlingshire

Printed and bound in Great Britain by
Clays Ltd, St Ives plc

MIX
Paper from
responsible sources
FSC™ C007454

The Babylon Rite is a work of fiction. However I have drawn on many real historical, archaeological and cultural sources for this book. In particular:

The ancient Knights Templar preceptory of Temple Bruer, Lincolnshire, England, has long had a reputation for evil and hauntings. In the nineteenth century, a local antiquarian, Reverend Oliver, discovered medieval skeletons entombed in the walls; he concluded that these victims had been tortured, and then buried alive.

The little church of Nosse Senhora de Guadalupe, in the Algarve, southern Portugal, was the private chapel of Henry the Navigator, one of the first great European explorers. The meaning of the sculpture in the ceiling has never been explained.

The Moche culture (pronounced *Mot-Chay*), which flourished in the deserts of north Peru in the fifth to ninth centuries AD, is perhaps the most peculiar of all pre-Columbian civilizations. One of the stranger aspects of Moche religion was a complex ritual known as the Sacrifice Ceremony.

Acknowledgments are due to the many writers on whose work I have drawn for this book. They include Steve Bourget, Wade Davis (especially), John Hemming, Juan Atienza, Ed Vulliamy, Daniel Everett, John Simpson, Johann Reinhard, Michael Wood, Malcolm Beith, David Grann, Steve Monaghan and Peter Just, David Carrasco, Steve Simpson, Marcello Spinella, Hugh Schultes, Martin Carver, Albert Hoffman, and many others.

My trips around north Peru would have been almost impossible without the assistance of the Real Peru travel company, and the Explorama lodges along the Upper Amazon. Thanks are also owed to the unknown but very helpful man who helped to dig my alleged four-wheel-drive out of the forest of Pomac in Lambayeque, Peru. And thanks to Jenny Green for showing me the best and worst of Mexico, and to Mikel Babiano Lopez de Sabando, for assistance with Spanish translations.

In particular I must thank all the many fine archaeologists and other scientists, who, for the last twenty years, sometimes at great personal risk, have unearthed the remains of the Moche culture, and pieced together the beliefs and rituals of a truly extraordinary civilization.

This book is dedicated to my brother Ross, for his endless good humour, for his stoicism and his equanimity, and for generously sharing with me his very small cup of masato beer, made from chewed manioc and human spit, in Belen Floating Market, Iquitos.

'It seems that a new knightly order has recently been born in the Orient. They do not fear death; instead, they long for death.'

Saint Bernard of Clairvaux, in praise
of the Knights Templar, AD 1135

1

Trujillo, Peru

It was a very strange place to build a museum. Under a Texaco gas station, where the dismal suburbs of Trujillo met the cold and foggy deserts of north Peru, in a wasteland of concrete warehouses and sleazy cantinas. But somehow this sense of being hidden away, this strange, sequestered location, made the Museo Casinelli feel even more intriguing: as if it really was a *secret* museum.

Jessica liked coming here, whenever she drove down to Trujillo from Zana. And today she had remembered to bring a camera, to gather crucial evidence.

She opened the door at the rear of the garage and smiled at the old curator, who stood, and bowed, as courteous as ever. 'Ah, Señorita Silverton! You are here again? You must like the, eh, naughty pottery?' Her shrug was a little bashful; his smile was gently teasing. 'But I fear the keys are in the other desk . . . *Un minuto*?'

'Of course.'

Pablo disappeared into a room at the back. As she waited, Jessica checked her cellphone, for the fifth time today: she was expecting an important call, from Steve Venturi, the best forensic anthropologist she knew.

A week ago, she had arrived in Trujillo – taking a break from her studies amongst the pyramids of Zana; she'd brought with her a box full of fifteen-hundred-year-old Moche bones. This package had in turn been despatched to California, to her old tutor in UCLA: Venturi.

Any day now she would get Steve's answer. Was she right about the neckbones? Was her audacious insight *correct?* The anxiety of waiting for the verdict was increasingly unbearable. Jess felt like a teenager awaiting exam results.

She looked up from the silent phone. Pablo had returned from his vestibule flourishing two keys, one big, one small. As he offered them, he winked. *'La sala privada?'*

Jessica's Spanish was still pretty mediocre, and for that reason she and the kindly curator normally conversed in English – but she understood *that* phrase well enough. The private room.

'Si!'

She took both keys from Pablo and saw how he noticed her slightly trembling hand. 'It's OK. Just need a coca.'

Pablo frowned. *'La diabetes?'*

'I'm OK. Really.'

The frown softened to a smile. 'See you later.'

Jess descended the steps to the basement museum. Fumbling in the darkness, she found the larger key, and opened the door.

When she switched on the light it flooded the room with a reassuring glow, revealing an eccentric and exquisite treasure trove of ancient Peruvian ceramics, pottery, textiles and other artefacts – gleaned from the mysterious cultures of pre-Colombian Peru: the Moche, the Chan Chan, the Huari, the Chimu.

The light also shone on a dried monkey foetus, grimacing in a bell jar.

She tried not to look at it. This thing always creeped her out. Maybe it wasn't even a monkey, maybe it was a dried sloth, or some human mutation preserved as a gruesome curio by Jose Casinelli, forever offering the world its sad little face.

Briskly she walked past the bell jar, and bent to the glass cabinets, the vitrines of pottery and treasures. Here were the stone pestles of the Chavin, and here the exquisite burial cloths of the Nazca in faded violet and purple; to the left was a brief, poignant line of Quingnam writing, the lost language of the Chimu. She took out her new camera and adjusted the tiny dial to compensate for the poor-quality light.

As she worked, Jessica recalled the first time she had come here, six months ago, when she had begun her sabbatical: researching the anthropology of the pre-Columbian Stone Age in north Peru, making a comparative study of religious cultures across ancient

America. Back then she had been almost a total ingénue, unprepared for the shock she was about to encounter: the high weirdness of pre-Inca Peru, most especially the Moche. And their infamous 'naughty pottery'.

It was time to visit the *sala privada*.

Taking out the smaller key, she opened the creaking side-door. A further, darker, tinier room lay beyond.

Few people came to the tiny Museo Casinelli, fewer still entered *la sala privada*. Even today a distinct aura of embarrassment surrounded the principal contents: the Moche sex pottery, the *ceramicas eroticas*. They were certainly too shocking and explicit to be shown to children, and conservative Peruvian Catholics would regard them as obscene works of the devil and be happy to see them smashed. Which was why they were kept in this dark and private antechamber, deep inside the secret museum.

Jess knelt, and squinted, preparing to be shocked all over again.

The first row of pots was asexual, merely distressing: on the left was a finely-crafted pot of a man with no nose and no lips, fired in exquisite black and gold. In the centre was a delicate ceramic representation of human sacrifice, with dismembered bodies at the foot of a mountain. And over here was a man tied to a tree, having his eyes pecked out by a vulture. Carefully, she took a photo of the last example.

Disturbing as these ceramics might be, they were just normal mad Moche pottery. The next shelves held the real deal: the *ceramicas eroticas*.

Working her way along them, Jess fired off dozens of photos. Why did the Moche go to the trouble of crafting erotic pottery like this? Sex with animals. Sex with the dead. Sex between skeletons. Perhaps it was just a metaphor, maybe even a joke; more likely it was a dreamtime, a mythology. It was certainly repellent, yet also fascinating.

Jessica took some final photos, using the camera flash this time, which reflected off the dusty glass of the vitrines. As she concluded her task, her thoughts whirled. The Museo Casinelli had done its job, as it always did; and the feeling was very satisfying. It really *had* been a good choice of hers, last year, to come out to north Peru, one of the final frontiers of history, maybe the last great *terra incognita* of archaeology and anthropology, full of unknown cultures and untouched sites.

Jessica shut off the lights and retreated. Upstairs, Pablo was trying to text something into his phone. He abandoned the effort, and smiled at her. 'You are finished?'

'Si! Gracias, Pablo.'

'Then you must go and have some *glucosa*. You are my friend and I must look after you. Because you are the only scholar who comes here!'

'That's not true.'

'Well. It is nearly true! I had some visitors last week, they were quite uncouth! Philistines seeking out . . . thrills. And they were unpleasant. Asking stupid questions. Everyone always asks the same stupid questions. Apart from you, Señorita, apart from you!'

5

Jess smiled, returned the keys, and stepped out into the polluted grey air of Truijllo.

The city greeted her with all its noise and grime. Guard dogs howled behind fences of corrugated iron; a man was pushing a glass trolley full of quails' eggs past a dingy tyre shop; a blind beggar sat with a guitar on his lap – it had no strings. And above it all hung that endless grey depressing sky.

It should really all be lovely, Jessica thought, here at the equator. It should be tropical and sunny and full of palm trees, but the strange climate of north Peru dictated otherwise: this was a place of clouds and chilly sea-fog.

Her cellphone rang; immediately she reached into her bag. She'd expected it to be Steve Venturi but the screen said it was her boss at the dig at Zana, Daniel Kossoy, who was also the overall leader of TUMP, the Toronto University Moche Project. And, as of last month, also her lover.

'Jess, hi. How's Trujillo?'

'All good, Dan. All fine!'

'Where are you now, then?'

'Museo Casinelli. Just left—'

'Ah, the sex pots!'

'The sex pots. Yes.' She paused, wondering why Danny was ringing. He knew she could handle herself in the big bad city. Her silence invoked his real purpose.

'Jess, have you heard anything from Venturi? I mean, we're all on tenterhooks up here. Were you right? About the vertebrae? It's like being in a cop show – the tension and excitement!'

'Nothing yet. He did say a week at least, and it's only been eight days.'

'OK. Well. OK.' A brief sigh. 'OK. Keep us informed? And . . .'

'What?'

'Well . . .' The pause implied unspoken feelings. Was he about to say something intimate, something personally revealing? Something like *I miss you?* She hoped not; it was way too soon in their miniature romance for any such declaration.

Briskly, Jessica interrupted, 'OK, Dan, I gotta go. I'll see you in Zana. Bye!'

Pocketing her phone, she walked to a corner to hail a taxi. The traffic was intense: fuming trucks loaded with charcoal growled at the lights; mopeds weaved between dinged Chevrolet taxis and crowded buses. Amongst the urgent chaos, Jessica noticed one particular truck, speeding down the other side of the road.

Going way too fast.

Jess shook her head. Peruvian driving wasn't the best. It was normal to see trucks and buses tearing down highways as if they were the only vehicles in the world, taunting death. But this was something different.

She stared: perplexed. The truck was *speeding up*, accelerating, leaping over a kerb, horribly dangerous. Somewhere a woman screamed. It was heading straight for – straight for what, *what was it doing?* Where was it going? It was surely going to plough into the grimy houses, the tyre shop, the tired glass kiosk of the quails eggs seller—

The Texaco garage.

The truck was heading straight for the garage. Jessica gazed – rapt and paralysed. The driver leapt from his cabin; at the last possible moment someone grabbed hold of Jessica and pulled her to the ground, behind a low wall.

The crash of glass and exploding gasoline was enormous. Greasy fireballs of smoke billowed into the air. Jess heard dire screams, then frightening silence.

'Pablo,' Jessica said to herself, lying, shaking, on the cracked Trujillo sidewalk. 'Pablo . . .?'

2

Rosslyn Chapel, Midlothian

Everything you could read about in the guide books was here, in Rosslyn chapel, the great and famous fifteenth-century chapel of the Sinclairs, ten miles south of Edinburgh. The bizarre stone cubes in the Lady Chapel, the eerie carvings of exotic vegetation, the Dance of Death in the arches, the inverted Lucifer bound in ropes, the Norse serpents twined around the Prentice Pillar. And all of it was lavished with alluring detail, teasing symbolism and occult hieroglyphs, creating a splendid whirl of conspiratorial intrigue in weathered old stone. Right next to a gift shop, which sold special Sinclair tartan tins of Templar shortcake, baked with special Holy Grail motifs.

Adam Blackwood sighed. His last assignment as a full-time feature writer for the *Guardian*, and it was on the mighty commerce of nonsense that was Rosslyn Chapel.

'You OK?'

It was his friend, and long-time colleague, Jason the Photographer. With the usual sarcastic tilt in his south London accent.

Adam sighed.

'No, I'm not OK. I just lost my job.'

'Tchuh. We all lose our jobs.' Jason glanced at his camera, adjusting a lens. 'And you're not dead, are you? You're just thirty-four. Come on, let's go back inside the chapel, this shop is full of nutters.'

'The whole *town* is full of nutters. *Especially* the chapel.' Adam pointed through the glass door at the medieval church. 'Everyone in there is walking around clutching *The Da Vinci Code*, looking for the Holy Grail under the font.'

'Then let's hurry up! Maybe we'll find it first.'

Adam dawdled. Jason sighed. 'Go on then, Blackwood. Cough it up. I know you want to *share*.'

'It's just . . . Well I thought that at least this time, *my very last assignment*, I might get something serious again, just for the hell of it, a serious news story, as a parting gift.'

'Because they like you so much? Adam – you got *sacked*. What did you expect? You punched the fucking features editor at the *Guardian* Christmas party.'

'He was hassling that girl. She was *crying*.'

'Sure.' Jason shook his head. 'The guy's a wanker of the first water. I agree. So you're a great Aussie hero, and I'm glad you decked him, but is it really so surprising they snapped? It's not the first time you've lost it.'

'But—'

'Stop whingeing! You did a few decent news stories, amongst the dross. And they're sacking journos all over the world. You're not unique.'

This was a fair point. 'Guess not.'

'And you got a bloody pay-off. Now you can bog off to Afghanistan, get yourself killed. Come on. We still got work to do.'

They walked out of the shop into the forecourt. And stared once more at the squat stone jewel-box that was Rosslyn Chapel. A faint, mean-spirited drizzle was falling out of the cold Midlothian sky. They stepped aside to let a middle-aged lady tourist enter the ancient building. She was carrying a dog-eared copy of *The Da Vinci Code*.

'It's under the font!' said Adam, loudly. Jason chuckled.

The two men followed the woman into the chapel. The Prentice Pillar loomed exotically at the end. A young couple with short blonde hair – German? – were peering at the pillar as if they expected the Holy Grail to materialize from within its luxuriously carved stone, like a kind of hologram.

Jason got to work. Tutting at his light meter, taking some shots. Adam interviewed a Belgian tourist in his forties, standing by the grave of the Earl of Caithness, asking what had brought him here. The Belgian mentioned the Holy Grail, *The Da Vinci Code* and the Knights Templar, in that order.

Adam got an initial glimpse of how he might write the piece. A light but sardonic tone, gently mocking

11

all this lucrative naivety, this cottage industry of credulity that had grown up around Rosslyn Chapel. A feature that would explore how the entire town of Roslin, Midlothian, was living off the need of people in a secular age to believe, paradoxically, in deep religious conspiracies. No matter how absurd and embarrassing they might be.

He could start it with that GK Chesterton quote: 'when people stop believing in God, they don't believe in nothing – *they believe in anything*'.

Adam turned as a baritone voice resonated down the nave: one of the more pompous guides, holding a fake plastic sword, was pointing at the ceiling, and reciting some history. Adam listened in to the guide's well-practised spiel.

'So who exactly were the Knights Templar? Their origins are simple enough.' The guide levelled his plastic sword at a small stone carving, apparently of two men on a horse. 'Sometime around 1119, two French knights, Hugues de Payens and Godfrey de Saint-Omer, veterans of the First Crusade, got together to discuss over a beaker of wine the safety of the many Christian pilgrims flocking to Jerusalem, since its brutal reconquest by the Crusaders of Pope Urban II.' The guide's sword wobbled as he continued. 'The French knights proposed a new monastic order, a sect of chaste but muscular warrior monks, who would defend the pilgrims with their very lives against the depredations of bandits, and robbers, and hostile Muslims. This audacious idea was instantly popular: the new King Baldwin II of Jerusalem agreed to the knights' request, and gifted them a headquarters on the Temple Mount, in the recently captured Al-Aqsa Mosque. Hence the full name of the Order: the Poor Fellow-Soldiers of Christ and of the Temple of Solomon, or, in Latin, *Pauperes Commilitones Christi Templique Solomonici.* Ever since then, the question has been asked: was there also an *esoteric* reason for this significant choice of head-quarters?' He hesitated, with the air of a well-trained actor. 'Naturally, we can never know. But the Temple Mount very *definitely* had a mystique: as it was located above what was believed to be the ruins of the first Temple of Solomon. Which,' the guide smiled at his attentive audience, 'is thought, in turn, to be a model for the church in which you stand today!'

He let the notion hang in the air like the fading vibrations of a tolling bell, then trotted through the rest of the story: the Templars' rise and supremacy; the twenty thousand knightly members at the very peak of the Order's strength; the great, Europe-wide power and wealth of the 'world's first multinational'. And then, of course, the dramatic downfall, after two proud centuries, when the French king, coveting the Templars' money, and envying their lands and status, crushed them with a wave of violent arrests and ferocious torture, beginning on one fateful night.

The guide flashed a florid smile: 'What was the date of that medieval Götterdämmerung, that Kristallnacht of kingly revenge? Friday the 13th, 1307. Yes, *Friday the 13th!*'

Adam repressed a laugh. The guide was a walking

store of clichés. But entertaining, nonetheless. If he'd been here for the fun of it, he'd have been happy to sit here and listen some more. But he had just seen something pretty interesting.

'Jason . . .' He nudged his friend, who was trying to get a decent shot of the Prentice Pillar.

'What?'

'Isn't that Archibald McLintock?'

'What?'

'The old guy, sitting in the pew by the Master Pillar. It's Archibald McLintock.'

'And he is?'

'Maybe the most famous writer on the Knights Templar alive. Wrote a good book about Rosslyn too. Proper sceptic. You never heard of him?'

'Dude, you do the research, you're the hack. I have to worry about lenses.'

'Very true. You lazy bastard. OK, I suggest we go and interview him. He might give me some good quotes, we could get a picture too.'

Advancing on the older man, Adam extended a hand. 'Adam Blackwood. The *Guardian*? We've actually met before.'

Archibald McLintock had sandy-grey hair and a demeanour of quiet, satisfied knowledge. Remaining seated, he accepted Adam's handshake with a vague, distracted grasp.

An odd silence intervened. Adam wondered how to begin; but at last the Scotsman said, 'Afraid I don't recall our meeting. So sorry.' His expression melted

14

into a distant smile. 'Ah. Wait. Yes, yes. You interviewed me, about the Crusades? The Spear of Destiny?'

'Yes. That's right, a few years back. It was just a light-hearted article.'

'Good good. And now you are writing about the Chapel of Rosslyn?'

'Well, yes,' Adam shrugged, mildly embarrassed. 'We're kind of doing another fun piece about all the . . . y'know . . . all the Dan Brown and Freemasons stuff. Templars hiding in the crypt. How Rosslyn has become so famous for its myths.'

'And you want another quote from me?'

'Do you mind?' Adam flushed, painfully aware he was disturbing a serious academic with all this fatuous, astrological absurdity. 'It's just that you famously debunked all this rubbish. Didn't you? What was that thing you said? "The Chapel of Rosslyn bears no more resemblance to the Temple of Solomon than my local farmer's cowshed is modelled on the stately pleasure dome of Xanadu."'

Another long silence. The tourists whispered and bustled. Adam waited for McLintock to answer. But he just smiled. And then he said, very quietly. 'Did I write that?'

'Yes.'

'Hm! A little piquant. But why not? Yes, I'll give you a quote.' Abruptly, Archibald McLintock stood up and Adam recalled with a start that the old man might be ageing but he was notably tall. Fully an inch taller than Adam, who was six foot two.

'Here's your quote, young man. *I was wrong.*'

'Sorry?' Adam was distracted: making sure his digi-corder was switched on. 'Wrong about . . . what?'

The historian smiled. 'Remember what Umberto Eco said about the Templars?'

Adam struggled to recall. 'Ah yes! "When a man talks about the Templars you know he is going mad," You mean that one?'

'No. Mr Blackwood. The *other* quote. "The Templars are connected to everything."'

A pause. 'You're saying . . . you mean . . .?'

'I was wrong. Wrong about the whole thing. There really *is* a connection. The pentagrams. The pillars. The Templar initiations. It's all here, Mr Blackwood, it's all true, it's more strange than you could ever realize. Rosslyn Chapel *really is the key.*' McLintock was laughing so loudly now that some tourists were nervously looking over. 'Can you believe it? The stature of this irony? The key to everything was here all along!'

Adam was perplexed. Was McLintock drunk? 'But you debunked all this – you said it was crap, you're famous for it!'

McLintock waved a dismissive hand and began to make his way down the medieval aisle. 'Just look around and you will see what I didn't see. Goodbye.'

Adam watched as the historian walked to the door and disappeared into the drizzly light beyond. The journalist gazed for a full minute as the door shut, and the tourists thronged the nave and the aisles. And then he looked up, to the ancient roof of the Collegiate

Chapel of St Michael in Roslin, where a hundred Green Men stared back at him, their faces carved by medieval stonemasons, into perpetual and sarcastic grins.

3

Rosslyn Chapel,
Midlothian, Scotland

'OK, I'm done. Got it all.' Jason stood and stretched. 'The upside-down angel thingy, Mary Magdalene by the fire extinguisher. And a cute Swedish girl bending over the tomb of the Earl of Orkney. Short skirt. Plaid. You all right?'

'Yes . . .'

Jason theatrically slapped his own head. 'Sorry. Ah. I didn't get a shot of your old guy – what was his name?'

'Archie McLintock. Professor McLintock.'

'So,' Jason capped his lens. 'He give you any good quotes?'

Adam said nothing. He was wrapped in confusion.

The silence between the two men was a stark contrast to the hubbub of tourists coming into the building: yet another tour guide was escorting a dozen Japanese sightseers into the nave and pointing out the Templar sword on the grave of William Sinclair, 'identical, they say, to the Templar swords inscribed on Templar tombs in the great Templar citadel of Tomar!'

'Hey?' said Jason, waving a hand in front of Adam as if testing his friend's blindness. 'What is it?'

'Like I said. Just something . . . a remark of his.'

'Okayyy. Tell me in monosyllables?'

Adam stared hard at the carving of the Norse serpents at the foot of the Prentice Pillar, and there, on the architrave joining the pillar the famous inscribed sentence. *Forte est vinum fortior est rex fortiores sunt mulieres super omnia vincit veritas*: 'Wine is strong, a king is stronger, women are stronger still, but truth conquers all.'

Truth conquers all.

It was all true?

'Well . . .' Adam exhaled. 'He admitted, or rather confessed, that he had been wrong all along. That it was all true. The Templar connections. Rosslyn really is the key, the key to everything. The key to history. That's what he said.'

Zipping up his light meter in one of the many pockets of his jacket, Jason gazed laconically at Adam. 'Finally gone gaga then. Doollally tap. Too much tainted porridge.'

'You'd think so, wouldn't you? Yet he sounded sane I . . . I just don't know.'

'Mate. Let's get a beer. What's that shit they drink up here? Heavy. A pint of heavy.'

'Just a half for me.'

Jason smiled. 'Naturally.'

They walked with a mutual sense of relief out of the overcrowded, overwarmed confines of Rosslyn Chapel into the honestly dreary Scottish weather. For one last second Adam turned and looked at the church, landed in its green lawn, a greystone time machine. The gargoyles and the pinnacles disturbingly leered at him. A chime, an echoic buzz, a painful memory resonating.

Alicia. Of course. *Alicia Hagen*. His girlfriend. Buried in a Sydney suburb with the kookaburras in the trees and the sun burning down on the fake English Gothic church.

Anxiety pierced him. Now he had lost his job, would he go back to brooding? He needed to work, to take his mind off the past; he had emigrated from Australia to put distance between himself and the tragedy, and that had succeeded – to an extent – but he also needed to *occupy* himself. Or he would recall the girl he had truly loved, who died so pointlessly, so casually. And then he would feel the sadness, like a g-force, as if he was in a plummeting plane.

Adam paced quickly into the car park. The local pub was just there, on the corner, looking welcoming in the mizzle and cold.

'Maybe I'll have an entire pint. And a few chasers.'

'Good man,' said Jason. 'We could—'

'Watch out!'

Adam grabbed at Jason, and pulled him back. Jason spun, alarmed.

'Whuh – Jesus!'

A car shot past, inches from them, doing seventy or eighty miles an hour: an insane speed on this suburban road, skidding left and right, but the driver's intention was disturbingly obvious.

'Christ—'

They ran after the vehicle, now heading straight for a high brick wall flanking the curve of the road.

'*Fuck—*'

'*Jesus—*'

'*No!*'

The impact was enormous. The car smashed straight into the wall with a rending sound of sheared metal and shattered glass. Even at this distance Adam could tell that the driver must be dead. A head-on crash with a wall, at eighty miles an hour? It was suicidal.

They slowed as they approached the car. The crash was enveloped by an eerie silence. Shocked onlookers stood, seemingly paralysed, hands to their mouths. As he dialled his phone urgently for an ambulance, Adam leaned to see: the windscreen was entirely smashed on the driver side, the glass bent outwards like a massive and obscene exit wound: the driver had indeed gone straight through.

Chunky nuggets of glass lay scattered bloodily on the pavement. Shards of metal littered the kerbstones. The driver was clearly dead, his blooded body half-in, half-out of the car.

Jason already had his camera out.

Adam didn't need a camera to record his memories;

he would not forget what he had seen. The driver had been *smiling* as he raced past them: smiling as he drove straight into the wall.

And the dead driver was Archibald McLintock.

4

Pan-American Highway, north Peru

Every second or third time Jess closed her eyes, she experienced it again: the truck slamming into the garage, the dirty black pornographic fireball, the terrible aching crash of glass and silence and screams. She opened her eyes. Enough of this: she had to stay alert: because she was driving, taking the road north out of Trujillo, the Pan-American Highway.

Pan-American Highway was a very grandiose name for what was, in reality, just a dirty, narrow, trash-littered blacktop, slicing through the wastes of the Sechura Desert. The route was long and monotonous, punctuated only by the odd strip of green as a river descended from the Andes, and the odd desultory greasy township, where drivers paused at gas stations to refuel their huge trucks, full of Chinese toys and pungent fishmeal, being ferried south to the factories of Trujillo and Chimbote and Lima.

One such truck was headed her way now: arrogantly dominating the road. She swerved to give it room, catching the ammoniac scent of the fishmeal as it swept past, shaking her pick-up.

Who the hell would drive a truck into a gas station in Trujillo? She winced, once again, at the images: like grainy internet videos projected on a wall. She didn't want to watch but she had to watch.

Jessica lifted the truck a gear, and replayed in her mind the terrible moment, and her questionable reactions. Should she have done something else? Anything else? *What exactly?* After the fireball had subsided, she had wrenched herself free from the man holding her down, the man who had saved her life, and sprinted over the road, shouting Pablo's name.

But the smoke had been so thick, and so hot, and so *burning*. Unable to get near, she'd choked and stumbled in the violent blackness. Then the police had swept in, sirens shrieking, nightsticks waving. Fearful of further explosions, they had angrily pushed people from the scene, down the road, away from the burning carcass of the building and the truck. So there was nothing she could have done for Pablo, and she had done nothing. But the guilt abided.

And then she'd seen it. Tossed a hundred metres by the wild explosions was an entire Moche pot, miraculously unharmed, lying on a greasy verge next to a burned plastic oil canister from the Texaco garage.

The pot was unusual: a spouted jug in the form of two toads copulating. This was maybe all that was left of the Casinelli collection, yet she couldn't bear to pick it up.

After that, she'd done her duty: weeping, occasionally, in her hotel room at night; giving her evidence to the police by day. Dan had called many times, very attentively, and she had been grateful to hear a consoling voice. Now, a week later, she was heading back to work. Determined but rattled.

Her hands trembled for a moment on the steering wheel of her long-term rented Hilux. She needed a break, and she definitely needed a cooling drink, a Coke, some water, even an Inca Kola, even if it did taste like bubblegum drool. Anything would do. Slowing down, she drove past a row of shanty slums, houses of reed and plastic, people living in the middle of nowhere.

It was barely more than a hamlet, and a pretty impoverished one at that. Adobe bricks lay drying on the roadside, like hairy ingots of mud. The settlement was surrounded by a cemetery so poor it had hub cabs for gravestones, the names daubed thereon in red paint. She knew what to expect in a desert village like this: restaurants where the chicken soup cost twice as much if the chicken was plucked; dire and rancid *tamales* served on plastic plates.

But she had no choice. This was north Peru. It was always like this, everywhere, a satanic part of the world: no wonder the civilizations that emerged here had been so insane. The landscape was evil, even the sea could not be trusted: one day serving up endless riches of anchovy and sea bass and shark, the next offering El Niño or La Niña, and wiping out entire civilizations with drought or flood, leaving rotten corpses of penguins strewn across the beach.

The image of the burning garage filled her mind once more: she thought of her dead father and she didn't want to know why.

'Señorita?' a dirty barefoot kid looked hopefully at her gringa blonde hair as she climbed out of the Hilux. *'Una cosita? Señorita?'*

'Ah. *Buenas* . . .' Jessica deliberated whether to give the kid a few *soles*. You were not meant to. But the poverty gouged at her conscience. She handed over a few pennies and the lad grinned a broken-toothed grin and did a sad barefoot dance and gabbled in Quechua, the ancient language of the Inca: *Anchantan ananchayki! Usplay manay yuraq* . . .

Jess had no idea what he was saying. Thank you kindly? Give me more, Yankee dogwoman?

It could be anything. She barely understood Peruvian Spanish, let alone this Stone Age tongue. Braving the boy with a half-hearted smile, she headed for the nearest cantina advertising the inevitable *pollos*.

Inside it was, of course, dingy: a few plastic tables, the whiff of old cooking oil. Three men in cowboy hats were sharing one dirty glass of maize beer served from an enormous litre bottle. The men glanced at her from under their hats, and turned back to the shared liquor. The first man poured a slug, and guzzled, and tipped a little on the dirt floor, making an offering to

Pachamama, the mother bitch of the earth, with her dust that ate cities.

'*Agua, sin gas, por favor?*' Jess said to the tired woman who approached, her hand was scarred with an old burn. The woman nodded, loped off behind a counter, and returned with a bottle of mineral water. And a chipped glass. A chalkboard on the wall advertised ceviche, the national dish: raw fish. Jess shuddered. What might that be like out here in the desert? Rancid, rotten, decomposing: six days of dysentery . . .

Her cellphone rang. Daniel, again. Click. 'Jess, you're OK?'

'Dan, I'm fine! You don't have to keep ringing me – I mean, I'm glad you do but I'm fine.'

'Where are you now?'

Jess squinted out of the little window, at the thundering fishmeal trucks heading Lima-wards. 'Pan-American, about sixty klicks south of Chiclayo. I'll be in Zana in an hour.'

'OK. That's good. Great. So, uh, do they know any more about the truck? The driver?'

'No, not really.' Jess drank a cold gulp of the water, refreshing the memory she would prefer to leave undisturbed. 'The cops think, now, it may have been just some guy with a grudge. Apparently he was sacked by Texaco a week before, he was working off his notice. No one really knows. But Pablo paid the price.'

A sad brief silence. 'Jesus F. Poor Pablo. Still can't get over it, the museum was totally destroyed: all the Moche pottery, the best collection outside Lima!'

'Yep.'

One of the men in the cowboy hats brushed past Jess, opening the door to the noisy highway. He turned, for a second, and glanced at her from beneath the brim of his hat. The glance was long, and odd, and obscurely hostile. The image of the eerie Moche pot, with the toads copulating, filled her mind. But she shook the stupidity away, and listened to Dan as he went on.

'Jess, I do have, however, some pretty good news. It might cheer you up. We got results. From your friend the bone guy.'

Her alertness returned, even a hint of excitement. 'What? Steve Venturi? The necks? He called *you*?'

'Yes. He kept trying to reach you, apparently, but you were in the police station. So he called here and I picked up this morning and . . . well bone analysis confirms it all, Jess. You were *right*. Cut marks to the neck vertebrae, coincident with death. Made with the tumi.'

'The cuts were made deliberately?'

'Yes. No question.'

'Wow . . . Just. Wow.' Jess felt half-bewildered, half-exhilarated. Her theory was expanding, but the concept was still a little sickening. She pushed away her glass of water. 'So we finally know *for sure*?'

'Yep we do, thanks to you . . .' Dan's voice drifted and returned, with the vagaries of the Claro Móvil signal, across the vast Sechura.

'Wait, Dan – wait a moment! I'll take it outside.'

Jess stood, and left a few soles, on the table. She

needed the fresh, dirty air of the Pan-American. The two remaining men in cowboy hats watched her depart, their gaze fixed and unblinking. As if they were wax statues.

Outside she breathed deep, watching the traffic: the SUVs of the rich, the trucks of the workers, the three-wheeled motokars of the poor.

'Go on, Dan.'

'This is it. The sacrifice ceremony really happened. You were spot on. *They really did it, Jess.* The Moche. They stripped the prisoners, lined them up, and ritually cut their throats, hence the strange cut marks on the neck bones. And then they probably drank the blood, judging by the ceramics. Extraordinary, eh? So the scenes on the pottery depict a real ceremony! I'm sorry I doubted you, Jessica. You are a credit to UCLA Anthropology. Hah. Steve Venturi actually called you his *prize pupil.*'

Jessica felt like blushing. She watched as a turkey vulture descended from the sky, and pecked at a fat-smeared piece of plastic, half-wrapped around a lamppost. A dog came running over to investigate; the animals squabbled over it. A shudder ran through her: surely another aftershock, from the explosion.

'Jess, are you still there?'

'Sorry, yes, I'm still here.'

'There's something else. Something else you need to know. More good news.' His pause was a little melodramatic.

'Dan, tell me!'

29

'An untouched tomb.'

'Huaca D?'

'*Yes.*' He paused. 'And you'll be there to see it, when we go in tomorrow. If you want, of course!'

Jess smiled at the endless desert. 'Of course I want to be there! An untouched tomb. Yay!'

Saying her goodbyes, she closed the call, and walked to the truck with renewed vigour. Her moments of fear and self-doubt had passed; she was already dreaming of what lay inside the tomb. An untouched Moche tomb! This was a fine prize; this would be perfect for her thesis. Now perhaps they would get to the heart of the matter: the ultimate Moche deity. The identity of the mysterious god, at the heart of the Moche's mysterious religion, was one of *the* great puzzles of north Peruvian archaeology.

And maybe the solution was coming into reach.

Jessica started the truck and pulled away. Above her, unseen, the turkey vulture had won the day; with a flap of grimy wings it swung across the sky, carrying its prize.

5

Braid Hills, Edinburgh

The hotel was overheated, and reeked of beer from last night's raucous wedding, which had kept him awake until three.

As he packed his bag, Adam wasn't sad to be leaving. He'd done his job here in dark, wintry and rather depressing Edinburgh. The *Guardian* had run his Rosslyn Chapel story, with a gratifying double-page spread and some nice quirky photos by Jason. The paper had also taken a small but judicious personal addition, by Adam, to its unsigned obituary of Dr Archibald McLintock, expert and author in medieval history – *'in his last days I met Professor McLintock once again, and he was as courteous and enlightening as ever . . .'*

Yet even as he stuffed his dirty shirts into his suitcase, Adam felt a nagging sense of unease. Of course the suicide of Archie McLintock had been upsetting, but it was also those last words the professor had used, in the chapel.

It's all true, Rosslyn is the key.

Adam had, with some reluctance, omitted their brief and eccentric encounter from his article on Rosslyn. The professor had obviously been mentally unbalanced at the end, and Adam had not wanted to trash McLintock's memory by using those uncharacteristic quotes, which made the man look a fool. Not so close to his death. But the unanswered questions were still out there.

Frowning, Adam gazed through the bay windows of his second-floor bedroom. The hotel was a converted Victorian villa, with creaky corridors, wilting pot plants, a conservatory where old ladies ate scones; and a very decent view across the medieval skyline of Edinburgh Old Town, down towards the docklands of Leith.

That view was already darkening. Two o'clock in the afternoon and the onset of night was palpable, enshrouding the city like a sort of dread. Down there, on the Firth of Forth, vast swathes of winter rain, great theatre curtains of it, were sweeping westwards – past Prestonpans and Musselburgh, past Seafield and Restalrig.

A Nordic doominess prevailed even in the names. Alicia Hagen. Norwegian.

Adam hastened his packing, zipping up the suitcase with a rush of vigour, sealing any morbid thoughts inside, with his dirty washing. Jobless now, he could not waste time. He had done his last article for the *Guardian*, his pay-off was being wired into his account, now he really should *bog off to Afghanistan*. Or at least go right back to London, and look for more work.

He turned to the phone on the bedside table, and picked up. The receptionist greeted him cheerily, and gave him the number for a taxi. He re-dialled the cab firm. 'Yes, Waverley Station. Straight away?'

Straight away turned out to be impossible: he'd have to wait twenty minutes. But that was OK: his train wasn't leaving until four thirty.

Strolling to the window, he lingered. Edinburgh Castle brooded on the skyline, dour and clichéd and impressive. The dark Scottish streets glistened in the smirr.

Then his own phone rang. Adam took the call, though he didn't recognize the number. An Edinburgh prefix . . . 'Hello.'

The answering voice was young, and female, and rich with Scottish vowels. 'Hello, is that Adam Blackwood of . . . the *Guardian*?'

'Yes.'

'You wrote the piece about my father?'

'Sorry?'

A short, distinctive pause. Then, 'My name is Nina McLintock. Archibald McLintock was my father. I'm sorry to bother you but . . .'

'Go on. Please.'

'Ach, it's just . . .'

She sounded distracted, maybe even distraught. Adam felt a sudden rush of sympathy. He blurted, 'I'm so sorry for what happened, Miss McLintock, it's so shocking. I mean I was there, I spoke to your father just moments before, before the suicide, I actually saw the crash . . .'

Even as he said this Adam chastened himself. It felt like a silly boast, or something presumptuous, and using the word *suicide* was just graceless. But the girl seemed encouraged by his words, rather than offended.

'Call me Nina. Please call me Nina. I want to talk with you. You saw it all. The police told me, you spoke to my dad just before.'

'Yes, but I—'

Nina McLintock was not for pausing. 'So you know! My father was not in any way depressed. He was happy. These last weeks he was really happy. I know my dad. He wasn't suicidal. Just wasn't.'

The first raindrops rattled on the window.

'I think he was murdered.'

'Sorry?'

'Murdered. He was killed. I'm sure of it, but meet me and I'll tell you why. Tell you everything.'

6

The Hinnie Tavern, Edinburgh Old Town

The Hinnie was one of those Edinburgh pubs that seemed to contain a slightly rancid, off-putting darkness, in the heart of the Old Town, under the louring stone bulwarks of the castle, down a tiny medieval wynd so obscured and sooted by history that only the initiated knew those ancient, uninviting steps led down to an equally ancient, uninviting pub.

Glum drinkers stared into glasses of The Famous Grouse. Old men ignored each other at the bar, drinking pints of 80 Shilling. Another young man gazed aggressively at Adam, with the stare of an antlered male stag on a hillside in the rutting season: *fuck you*.

Adam raised his glass and toasted him, staring right back, making the boy visibly seethe. *Come on then*, Adam thought, *I am descended from some of the worst English criminals in the history of transportation. My grandfather killed dingoes with his bare hands. You think you're harder than me?*

Adam felt guilty about his temper, but he also had a pleasing confidence in his physical capabilities, which sometimes came in handy. He recalled the day they beat up the Lebanese boys in Cronulla, gave them a hiding for nearly gang-raping his sister's friend when the police wouldn't do anything. *Too racially sensitive, mate.*

His father, of course, was – or at least had been in his prime – exactly the same. A bit of a drinker, a bit of a bruiser. Almost liked a fight; he and Adam used to wrestle and box when Adam was a lad. So the propensity must've come from Dad.

Don't let anyone push you around, son, unless they have a gun. Then go get a gun. That was what his dad used to say. Dad was a real larrikin, a true Aussie, albeit descended from centuries of English cutpurses and high-waymen. Mum had been very different.

'Hello?'

Startled from his thoughts, he looked up – to see a young woman, standing directly opposite, extending a delicate white hand.

Nina McLintock.

She didn't look anything like he had expected; she had remarkable pale skin, and lush dark hair. She was also petite and slim and wearing dark clothes and a white shirt or blouse: she looked like a figure in a mono-chrome photo. The only thing that told him this was sandy-haired Archie McLintock's daughter was the eyes, they were the same intelligent grey-green. The sad eyes he had seen in Rosslyn Chapel.

'Recognize you from the paper. I'm sorry I'm so *late*.'

He lifted hands as if to say no worries.

She hastily explained, 'We've got this Facebook page. For my dad. Seeking info. Look. Ach. Sorry. Do you mind if I get a drink first?'

She was obviously a local: the barman, who had stared at Adam as if he was a large and ugly centipede, smiled at her shouted request and brought her drinks over. An action almost unheard of in a British pub.

Nina smiled, introspectively. There was true sadness there, which made her look quite beautiful – and a little haunting, Adam thought.

'This is your local?'

She nodded and shot down her Scotch in one gulp. Then she turned to her glass of Tennants, which seemed a bit too big for her very small hands, but she managed to down a quarter of it anyway. Then she said, 'I've got a flat down the road, in the Grassmarket. I like it here, the fact it's so rough. The fights can be fun. You know in Scottish we have five hundred words for fight: a *stramash*. A *fash*. A *brulzie*. All different.'

He gazed at her pint glass.

'Yes. And I'm a recovering teetotaller.' Her eyes twinkled. 'I tried to be sober. But my God, the boredom. Like Byron said, *Man, being reasonable, must get drunk*. I like Byron. You?'

'Uh . . .'

'Sorry I talk too much. Drink too much and talk too much. Too quickly.' She set her pint down. 'Sorry . . .'

And for a moment the vivacious energy seemed to leave her.

Adam said, 'What's this about a Facebook page, then?'

'My sister. Hannah. Teaching in London, lecturer. She and I both believe it wasn't suicide. So we've set up a Facebook page, asking for help. 'Cause the police won't do anything. Muppets. They say the car was fine, not tampered with. And I don't buy it. Hence the page.' She turned slightly as if to address the pub. 'Adam, my father was *not* mad. Not a nutter. *I don't believe it.*'

'You really want to talk about this?'

'Yes! I want to know what *you* think. You spoke to him last.' Her eyes fixed earnestly on his. 'What was he like? His mood that day?'

'OK well . . .' Adam hesitated. 'I suppose you could say he seemed pretty happy when I met him. However, he did say something very odd. Which might imply he was – ah – a little unbalanced. Sorry.'

'What? Nina leaned close, but not angrily. '*What did he say?*'

Adam felt uncomfortable. 'I mean, well, all his life he wrote those academic books, very scholarly works, sceptical, rigorous, highly respected. But then, suddenly, in Rosslyn that day he said to me: oh it's all true, there really is some truth here. Rosslyn, the Templars, the Norse elements. He appeared to reverse everything he believed. I was quite shocked.'

'You weren't the only one! *He said exactly the same to me*. A few weeks ago.'

Her face was flushed. 'On the phone. He made this strange, passing remark. That his whole life's work had been pointless, that he had been wrong about the Templars, there really was a deep deep secret. Some mega-conspiracy. Yet he laughed when he said it. I thought he was talking blethers—'

'Sorry?'

'Thought he was talking nonsense. Thought maybe he was drunk. 'Cause he was fond of a dram. The McLintock genes.'

'So what convinced you? And how does that lead to . . .'

'My thinking he was murdered? Loads of things – his behaviour over the last year or two, for a start. About eighteen months ago he just disappeared, went off on some crazy walkabout. Spain, France, South America even. We had no idea where, or why, he told me and Hannah nothing. When he came back he was richer, quite a lot richer. I mean he was never poor, but he was never rich either, writing books about how there is no Holy Grail and all your favourite fairy tales are pathetic and gibbering nonsense does not necessarily make you loadsamoney, y'know?'

'I can see why.'

'But now suddenly he *had* some money, he bought a flash new car, he indulged himself in antiques. Bought a TV maybe bigger than Canada. And he gave me some cash, and also Hannah, and I'm told there is more cash coming, in the estate: but where did all that come from? And . . . another thing. He got so happy by the end, he was a changed man. He'd been depressed for a while but when he got back he was happier, more enthusiastic, like he really had discovered something. And then, right at the *very* end . . .'

The dark pub seemed to have become even darker. The atmosphere smokier, though no one was smoking. She leaned close, whispering. 'Two weeks ago, almost the last time I saw him, he was anxious. Still happy, but anxious. Like he was being menaced, or chased. Or at least watched.'

Nina drank a quick half-pint of Tennants, then said, 'He didn't say much, at first. He was jokey. Offhand. But I'd had enough, and finally I confronted him. I said, "Dad, what is going on? You've got all this money, you went away, you seem different, moody, happy one minute, weird the next. Now you say there are people watching you." And I badgered him. I wouldn't take no for an answer. I insisted, and finally he said, "OK, it's true, I have discovered a secret, an extraordinary truth, a revelation . . . but it must remain with me. Don't go after this secret *unless you want to die, unless you want to get yourself killed"* . . .'

'He was drunk when he said this?'

'A bit. Maybe. A wee bit, aye. *But also quite coherent.* He wasn't rambling. And then soon after that he gets himself killed.'

Adam sat back. Nina finished her beer. She sought his gaze with her own.

'So. Will you help me? Adam? Will you help me find the truth? The cops are divvies.'

'How can I help you?'

'Come with me to his flat. Find all his notes! He was a diligent note-taker. You know. 'Cause he was an author. Then we can see what he had found.'

'Why do you need *me*? Surely you are his executors, you and Hannah?'

'No. His wife is. Second wife. Mum died a decade back. Car accident. He remarried five years ago, some Irish woman. I've tried to like her but she's – she's just an idiot. Guess she's got her own issues, but life is too short, I can't be arsed. Besides, she thinks it's suicide and she hates all this Facebook stuff. But *she's away tomorrow night*: we can break in.'

'Break in?'

'And find the notes. You're an investigative journalist. You must know how to do all this. Find the secret that can get you killed, that got my *father* killed. What do you think, Adam?'

Adam said nothing. He was trying to reconcile two conflicting thoughts. The first was: that this girl reminded him of Alicia. It was unmistakable: she had the same intelligence and vivacity mixed with the same damaged quality. Even the poetry quoting was similar. And anything that reminded Adam of Alicia was bad news, set off sirens in his mind, red lights strobing danger.

But against this was set another, opposing desire: to learn more, to get the truth, to be a journalist. Everything in his training was telling him: This is it: this is a Real Story. Adam was jobless and directionless, and if he wanted to make a living he could not afford to turn down a cracking story when it was given to him like this.

He sipped the last of his beer. 'Where did your father live?'

7

The Huacas, Zana, north Peru

'Are you ready?'

Jess felt a trace of annoyance amidst her professional excitement. 'Of course!'

They were standing at the entrance of Huaca D, the latest adobe pyramid of the Moche era to be opened by the TUMP team. She had a notebook in her hand. 'So. Tell me again. How do we know this is an important tomb?'

Dan shrugged. 'Various indications, such as grave goods in the outlying chamber. And the disarticulated skeletons.'

'Sorry?'

He explained briskly. 'The skeletons are slaves, or maybe concubines who were forced, during the funeral rituals, to have their limbs amputated, in a gesture of servility to the noble. Remember, we discussed the funeral sacrifices. They indicate the prominence of the inhabitant of the tomb.'

Jess remembered as she scribbled, the ghastliness of the notion making her sway a little in the burning Sechura sun.

For once the clouds had parted and it was fiercely hot: out there beyond the huacas the villagers of Zana were tilling their fields, bending to cut the reeds of sugar cane, white towels of turbans on their heads to ward off the sun. Otherwise the landscape was empty. Drifting, and empty, and dying.

'OK?'

She nodded. Dan smiled, and there was a definite but discreet warmth to his smile. The smile of a boyfriend. Jessica welcomed his discretion, and reticence: no one else in TUMP knew she and Dan were having a relationship – not yet. And Jessica wanted to keep it that way. Because she wasn't sure what she *felt* yet. Dan very definitely wasn't her normal type: she usually went for young bohemian guys, unshaven and unreliable, casual and sexy. Musicians and artists. She'd been quite promiscuous at university. But now suddenly she'd gone for the older man. Why? Maybe she was emotionally a late developer, even as she was professionally precocious: maybe she was finally filling the father-shaped hole in her heart. Wasn't that what daughters who lost a dad at an early age were meant to do? Seek out the missing male security figure?

The wind was stifling, the sun relentless. Dan was sweating in the heat, showing damp sweat patches under the arms of his grubby T-shirt. Yet she still felt a stir of attraction: he was quite rugged in an older and scholarly way. And his expertise itself was attractive: a man doing something well. He was a very gifted archaeologist – quite famous in his field.

As if aware of her scrutiny, he looked up: 'Do you not have a flashlight? You'll need it in the tomb, Jess. If you want to see to take notes.'

'I've got it. Don't worry. I've got everything.' She glanced behind her at the waiting huaca, the ancient pyramid of crumbling dust, and lifted her notebook. 'Tell me again what we know for sure about the age. When does the tomb date from?'

'From the very last gasp of Moche civilization. Eighth or ninth century, when they evolved into the Muchika. Essentially they're the same people, same culture, same bizarre civilization, but with dwindling resources.'

Jess nodded and wrote in her notebook, then said, 'How do we know there haven't been any *haqueros*? Any graverobbers? How do we know the tomb is sealed?'

Dan didn't answer, he was distractedly patting his pockets, apparently making sure he had some kit on his person. This was typical for Dan – the classic intellectual scientist, always elsewhere.

Jess took the time to gaze around at the strange town that had been her home for six months. In a part of the world singularly blessed with hideous towns, Zana, an hour's drive south of Chiclayo, and even deeper into the Sechura Desert, was still a shocker.

The streets were mostly paved with mud, or mud

and sewage. The houses were concrete or adobe hovels, painted dirty white or a hopelessly sour pastel. Most of the buildings were one storey, but they didn't have proper roofs, just ugly amputated concrete pillars bristling with steel cables that pointed at the empty air, waiting for the day when the family got rich enough to afford a second storey. These amputated houses gave the city an odd appearance, as if some dreadful god of pre-Columbian Peru – the mysterious Decapitating Demon of the Moche – had come along and swept a chainsaw across the town, levelling the buildings, chopping off anything too ambitious.

Turning back to the huacas, the prospect hardly improved: it seemed impossible that such ugly, if sizeable, heaps of mud, stretching almost to the horizon, could be so archaeologically important. Yet they were. These were the Moche pyramids, great sacred sites brutally eroded by fifteen hundred years of desert wind and El Niño rain. Once they would have been lofty, painted ziggurats dominating the flats and cornfields, full of warriors, priests and bloodthirsty nobles. Now they were muddy lumps, fabulously unexcavated muddy lumps, the precious knolls that had persuaded Toronto University Archaeology to locate its Moche Project in Zana.

In just two seasons of digging, Dan and the guys had opened only three of the many huacas, and already they'd found two senior Moche tombs, both undisturbed, one of which had provided the damaged neck vertebrae which had afforded Jessica her insight.

46

So it was exciting to wonder what else lay out here in the endless heaps of dry soil and potsherds.

At last, Dan lifted his eyes from his kit. 'Sorry, Jess? Did you say something?'

Jessica smiled. 'I said: how we do know the *haqueros* haven't been here? The graverobbers.'

'Well, we don't, not absolutely,' he confessed, his long grey hair falling over his dark brown eyes, 'But we're extremely optimistic. We're guessing the reputation of Zana, as a *bruja* town, a town of sorcerers, has protected these huacas. Most of the people here are emancipated African slaves, thought to possess magical powers – that's probably why the other tombs were untouched, in which case, why not this one also? *And* the doors are also intact. Anyway, we can talk later. Shall we do it?'

'Yes!'

'Turn on your headtorch.'

Dan was already buckling the chins strap of his helmet, with its halogen headtorch. Jess followed him.

The path around the southwest incline of Huaca D led to a low, excavated entrance. The smell emanating from the dark mudbrick tunnel beyond was earthy, and homely, and yet tanged with something else: something warm and maybe fetid. Something alien.

Stooping, they entered. Nina felt the brush of the mud roof on her helmet, and it was a distinctly satisfying sensation. At last she was *inside a huaca: a real-life Moche adobe pyramid! Fifteen hundred years old!*

Their uncomfortable crawl through the narrow adobe

passage took several minutes: this was one of the biggest huacas in Zana. As they inched their way along, the mudbrick walls narrowed, tapering on either side, and above. A few minutes later, she and Dan were virtually crawling, abject and animal-like, on hands and feet. The darkness was intense.

Jessica hated the dark. It always reminded her of her father, and his last days. Specifically it reminded her of being in his hospital room at night, with the lights low, near to his death, as his cancer conquered him. She had been just seven years old and hadn't understood what was happening. But she had nonetheless imbibed some emotional association: darkness equals death, equals a terrible nothingness, an inexplicable nullity. Yes, she hated the dark.

The darkness in the huaca was made worse by the claustrophobic conditions. The air was clammy and over-warm, lacking oxygen. Jess sweated. How could Dan be sure the pyramid wouldn't simply collapse on top of them, smothering them in ancient mud, their mouths filling with suffocating soil, an avalanche of crumbling adobe? And then more darkness.

They moved on. Two more minutes of crawling became three. The passageway zigzagged, perhaps as a deterrent to graverobbers. The darkness was now pure and solid, cut through only by the beam of her head-torch: it illuminated Dan's white T-shirt, as he led the way, crawling and crouching. The white of the T-shirt was turned a dirty orange: grimed with fifteen-hundred-year-old mud.

'Here.'

Panting with relief, Jess saw they were entering a taller antechamber. She could stand; though Dan, with his lanky six feet four, still needed to hunch over.

Two other team members were waiting for them, kneeling in the dust. Jay Brennan and Larry Fielding. They said hello, and made poor jokes about the loveliness of their surroundings. Jess smiled as best she could, but she was too distracted by the floor of the antechamber.

'My God.'

Here were the disarticulated skeletons, half-excavated. These were the sacrificed concubines or servants of the lords buried further within. From her research, she knew what these signified. The Moche believed their aristocrats required servants in the afterlife just as they did in the present life: so when the slaves were sacrificed to accompany their master their feet were chopped off. So that they couldn't run away in the hereafter.

The idea was absurd, yet also appalling. Jess stared at one long skeleton, probably male, judging by the narrowness of the pelvis. It certainly had no feet. It looked like a pretty tall skeleton for a slave.

Recalling her thorough lessons in forensic anthropology from Steve Venturi at UCLA, she knelt and examined the ankle bone where it had been severed. Something was not quite right about it. Jess steadied her torchlight over the bone, examining the angle of the blow, as a voice echoed above her.

'Right. This way.'

It seemed she didn't have time to linger. She was a guest on this trip, conspicuously the anthropologist amongst proper archaeologists, so she was lucky to be here at all, and in no position to ask for a delay.

They moved down the last length of darkened passage to the sealed tomb. The air grew hotter, the coarse mud walls even rougher: they had only recently been excavated. The weight of the great adobe pyramid above them was palpable, and oppressive.

'There.'

Dan pointed. A slab of rock blocked the passage, illuminated by their collective headtorches; the slab was the height of the passage itself – maybe one and a half metres wide and tall.

Jess asked the obvious and probably stupid question. 'How do we move that?'

'Brute force,' said Dan. 'The mud is ancient, it gives way. It's surprisingly simple, you can dislodge the portals by hand. The rocks aren't thick, they're more like large slates.'

'But – the roof?'

'These adobe pyramids are secure, they won't collapse. They erode in the sun and rain, but they've lasted fifteen hundred years: they don't collapse from the inside.'

Jess felt her excitement surging. What was beyond this ancient portal? Already they had found a trove of mutilated skeletons. This was an important tomb, from the mysterious end of the Moche Empire, the desperate time of the Muchika. They were headed for the dark heart, the airless core of the pyramid.

Jay was muttering behind, in the depths of the gloom. His colleague joined in, giving voice to his concerns. 'You know. The air is, ah, pretty bad down here, Dan.'

'But what can we do? We haven't got any oxygen tanks at the lab, have we?'

'Nope. We finished the last on Monday.'

The frustrating debate continued, then Dan lifted a hand. 'So, either we call a halt and wait a week for a new delivery, or we advance. Guys?' His headtorch illuminated their white faces one by one.

In turn, everyone nodded. The decision was made.

'Then let's do it!'

Reaching up, Dan began tugging at the door. There was just room for his fingers to grasp an edge, and pull. He pulled once. Nothing. He pulled again. No movement.

Jess came up beside him, kneeling in the dust, to help. Still nothing.

'Another go, come on.'

As one they tugged, and then the door seemed to shift, a few millimetres; then decisively, with a cloud of soil and choking dust. *But something was wrong*. This dust was red—

It was *pouring* from somewhere, from some hidden channel, some broken vessel above; draining like a tipped-up load of vermillion sand over Jessica's face and hair and mouth. She was being *smothered* in thick red dust with a weird smell. She screamed out loud, in terror.

It was a ghastly childhood dream – of being stifled at night, feeling cold hands that throttled; it was a dream of being her father in his last moments, in hospital, misting the oxygen mask, drowning in pain, staring hapless and terrified at the nurse and the kids and the oncoming darkness – until his own seven-year-old daughter had wanted to thrust a pillow right over his face and end it for him—

And then the scarlet dust filled her mouth, and she could scream no more.

8

The Bishops Avenue, London

There were murders and there were . . . *murders*. That was the unspoken agreement between Detective Chief Inspector Ibsen and his detective sergeant, Larkham. A plain old murder was just that: a murder. A robbery gone nasty, or a domestic gone awry.

But a . . . *murder* was different. It required a microsecond of hesitation before the word was enunciated, or a subtle drop in voice tone, barely half a note, a third of a note. 'Sir, we have a . . . *murder.*'

This one was, by all accounts, very much a . . . *murder*. Ibsen could tell from his DS's demeanour. DS Larkham had already seen the corpse, which had been discovered six hours previously: his already-pale English face was paler than ever, his voice subdued, his normal cheeriness quite dispelled.

Their large police car was slowly rolling down The Bishops Avenue, one of the richest streets in London.

Ibsen gazed out at the enormous houses, the fake Grecian villas looking faintly surreal in the drizzle. One resembled a vast temple from Luxor, inexplicably transported to the wintry north of the capital and fitted with six burglar alarms. The next house appeared to have *sentries*.

'Who the fuck lives in houses like this?' said the driver, giving voice to all their thoughts.

'Kuwaiti emirs,' said Ibsen. 'Billionaire Thai politicians. Nobody in winter.'

'Sorry, sir?'

'Look – hardly any cars. A lot of these people have houses all over the world. They come here in summer, it's dead in December. Makes it a good place to commit a crime. In winter.'

'Well, our *murder* victim lived here.' Larkham grimaced. 'Even in winter.'

'What do we know about him?'

'Nephew of the Russian ambassador.'

'Ouch.' Ibsen winced at the complications. 'This is an official residence?'

'No, sir. Just a rich family. Father's into oil and diamonds. Oligarch.'

'Has someone told the Foreign Office?'

'Already did it, sir.'

DCI Ibsen gazed, with a brief sense of pleasure, at Larkham's keen face. Here was an ambitious policeman, a bright young man who had skipped university to go straight into the force, already a DS in his mid-twenties, with a very young family. He'd been Ibsen's junior for just six months, and he was obviously itching for Ibsen's job, but in a good way, just so he could move on up. Ibsen preferred to have someone nakedly and brazenly ambitious than a schemer who subtly politicked.

Larkham yawned; Ibsen grinned. 'Nappies at dawn?'

'And feeding at four a.m. Feel like I've done a shift already.' He stifled his sleepiness and asked, 'Does it get better?'

'It gets better. When they reach the age of reason. About five or so.'

Larkham groaned; Ibsen chuckled. 'OK. Tell me again. We've got statements?'

'Yes, sir.'

Larkham repeated what information they had gathered so far. The first statement came from a passer-by, who had heard two raised male voices as he walked past the house at eleven p.m., though they didn't sound violent . . .'

'And the other statement?'

'From a neighbour, an au pair in the house next door, at one a.m., approximately the time of death, according to Pathology's very rough initial guess, sir. She also heard the raised voices of two men. She says these voices were shouting, aggressive, possibly violent, possibly drunk.'

'But she did nothing?'

'Very young lady, sir, Just nineteen. Croatian.'

'Ah.' Ibsen understood this. Bishops Avenue was the kind of place where rich important people went to be seriously undisturbed in big houses. A teenage au pair living in a strange big house in a strange new country would be reluctant to cause any bother.

'Here we go, sir.'

The car parked outside a large building fronted by two-storey-high white Doric pillars. A big car in the driveway was covered with some kind of tailored sheet. Ibsen stared: he had never had a car expensive enough to require special protection from the English winter.

'The body?'

'This way.'

They were greeted at the door by the Scene of Crime Officer, wearing a paper suit which zipped up at the front. Other forensic and attending officers came out of the building, carrying evidence bags, and walked to a large steel van, parked behind the sheet-covered car.

'There's a lot of blood,' said the SOCO through his paper mask, with the air of a host at a house party greeting his latest guests.

'Can we see?'

'You need to nonce up first, sir.'

Stalling at the doorway, Ibsen and Larkham slipped on their plastic gloves and paper masks and translucent overshoes, like politicians visiting a fish factory. Then they stepped through the enormous pillared hall into an enormous pillared sitting room. Ibsen resisted the urge to swear, as he surveyed the crime scene. Then his resistance crumbled.

'Fucking hell.'

The victim was young, blond, and handsome: maybe twenty-five or thirty at most. He was lying supine on the floor near a large antique desk. A phone and a notepad sat on the desk, to the left of a laptop, which was lightly smeared with blood.

Opposite the desk stood some speakers, and a vast black television: ultra-expensive kit.

The face of the young Russian was slightly turned towards the desk, as if in his last moments he had tried, but failed, to make a desperate call. He was dressed in a neat blue shirt, probably bespoke, from Jermyn Street; and fashionable jeans – perhaps Armani. The new collection. The jeans were loosened at the top, half-unbuttoned.

Ibsen, who cultivated a sincere interest in clothes, would have liked to give an opinion of the kid's foot-wear, but that was impossible, as the cadaver had no feet.

Someone had sliced off his feet. The raw stumps were an obscenity: the victim resembled a casualty of some industrial scythe. The body was also missing his right hand: blood had spurted from the severed wrist all over the rich Turkish carpet, making the rich red of the wool richer and purpler. The angle of the brutal amputations was unusual. Ibsen stopped to have a closer look, squinting, clutching his face mask to his mouth, and found there was even a deep grinning cut mark to the right side of the neck, as if the murderer had tried to slice off the head as well, but had given up. Perhaps the killer had got bored, or maybe the victim died of blood loss before the decapitation could be completed, rendering it pointless.

Crouching by the body, Ibsen went through the PMI calculations. How long *had* the body been here? Forensics would strip the corpse, and check for livor mortis – pooling of the blood at the bottom of the body – and for rigor mortis, and algor mortis, and get a scientific answer; but Ibsen's instinct told him Pathology's first guess was good: this body was pretty fresh. You could smell the new blood. Twelve hours at most. That made the overheard violence, at one a.m., very likely the time of death.

'He dragged himself in here?' Ibsen gestured at the long, lurid smears of blood along the parquet floor.

'Yes,' said the SOC officer, Jonson. 'Seems he was chopped up in the kitchen, then the killer dragged the body in here, or he dragged himself, trying to reach the phone.'

'The feet and hand?'

'Found 'em on the kitchen floor. Gone to Path.'

Ibsen walked through the hallway into the white-and-steel kitchen. At the far end a set of French windows gave on to the lawn. The doors were open to the cold and the drizzle. Bleak, leafless trees bent over the vast lawns; a tennis court, padlocked shut for the winter, lay at the far end of the grounds.

The streaks of blood stretched from the sitting room through the hallway into the kitchen to a larger pool of blood where the butchery must have been committed.

Larkham came alongside.

'Prints?' asked Ibsen. 'In the mud, the garden?'

'Nothing yet, sir, but we have found . . . this. Incredibly.'

Larkham was holding a clear plastic bag, inside which was a very large, viciously serrated Sabatier kitchen knife, smeared and gummed with blood. The murder weapon, without question.

The DCI gazed at it in astonishment. 'The killer just left this?'

'Lying on the kitchen floor. By the fridge, sir. And look—' With a pencil Larkham pointed to the black resin handle of the knife. Perfectly visible was a large red thumb print: a patent print. The lottery win of evidential police work.

For the briefest moment, Ibsen felt like celebrating: this was so easy, a *patent* print, on the murder weapon, an open door to solving the case. But another second told him this was too easy. *Way too easy.* The door closed, revealing a darker truth. He regarded the puzzle, gazing at the fridge and the blood and the knife. What did he have? Something. Definitely something. He considered the missing right hand. The cut to the right of the neck. The *left*-hand thumb print on the handle. The strange oblique angle of the amputations themselves.

Ibsen took out his own pen and pointed at the knife. 'That's not the killer's print. I bet that's the *victim's* print.'

Larkham's face expressed wide and sincere puzzlement.

'Don't you see? The murderer has, so far as we can tell, left no other clues, no boot prints, no blatant trace

59

evidence. A truly professional job, then, despite the torture . . . despite the butchery.'

'So?'

The French windows creaked in the cold wet wind, and blustered old dead leaves into the kitchen.

'Would he just leave behind a murder weapon with a big fat print on it? No. So he discarded or ignored the knife for a reason. *Because he must have known the print on the blade belonged to someone else.* So it would provide no evidence against him.'

'Ah . . .'

'Now think about the corpse,' Ibsen continued. 'The slice to the neck was on the right, like someone left-handed, reaching around, *trying to cut his own neck.* This is a left-handed thumb print on the knife. Likewise, the cuts to the leg are distinctively angled, as if the severing blade was wielded in a particular direction. By someone crouching, doing it to *himself.*'

'Sir?'

'The kid was living here alone, right?'

'Uh, yes, sir.'

'Remember the desk. The notepad and the phone were to the left of the laptop. *He's left-handed.* He did the amputations himself. Therefore my guess is . . . the thumb print is from the victim's own hand.'

Larkham stared moodily at the garden, at the grey enormous lawn. 'That means, it means . . .'

'Yes. That means the killer forced the victim. To cut off his own feet. And his own hand. And even to slice into his own neck. He kindly left the victim with one hand intact, his best left hand, so he could do this to himself. Check the corpse for prints: I wager the thumb print will match.'

For the faintest second, the coolly ambitious Detective Sergeant Peter Larkham of New Scotland Yard looked as if he was going to be sick.

9

Morningside, Edinburgh

Nina McLintock and Adam Blackwood halted at the corner of Springvalley Terrace. The night had cleared and it was now piercingly cold, with a keening wind off the Firth of Forth, and the street was wholly deserted. Glittery with silent frost.

'It's in that block there,' Nina said. 'Stepmother's flat. He moved in with her a coupla years ago.'

Adam followed her anxious steps, looking up at the severe windows as he went. The terrace comprised one of those sandstone tenements which in England would have been considered lower class, if they existed at all; in Scotland these large, sombre blocks of Victorian apartments had a posh ambience, especially here in Morningside, the upmarket inner suburb of Edinburgh.

A burst of noise behind them – drinkers falling out of a shutting pub – hurried the two of them around the curving pavement to the front door of the tenement block.

'How are we going to—'

'I know where he kept his spare key. He was a bit of a lush. If you get home drunk a lot, you learn to hide a spare key.'

Adam nodded. He could empathize with that, all right. He remembered his own days of drinking: the fights and the forgetfulness. Locked out of his home in Sydney. After Alicia.

'Here.' Nina thrust a hand through some railings, and scrabbled in the soil of a small front garden. 'Just here, under the rosebush. Second rosebush on the right.'

She rummaged under the dead roseless plant while Adam glanced up and down the street, increasingly fretful. This didn't look good. Two people loitering on an empty street at one in the morning, digging in a stranger's garden.

He strove to repress his greater anxiety: the unnerving two-way logic of what he was doing. Either Nina was deluded and he was painfully wasting his time because he was so pathetically desperate for a story; or she was *right*, and Archie McLintock had been murdered. Which meant a murderer.

'Quick!' He could hear footsteps, somewhere. Round the curving corner, coming their way.

'Got it.' Nina stood, brandishing two very muddied keys.

The footsteps were louder now, right behind them. It

was one of the drinkers from the pub. Tall, shaven-headed, wearing a dark coat. The man abruptly paused, under a streetlamp, to light a cigarette, scratching a match into flame. Adam stared, even as he tried not to stare. There was something odd about the man's hands, cupped around the cigarette: they were decorated with large tattoos. Tattoos of skulls. Was he really just a drinker? Or a murderer?

The secret that can get you killed.

This was nonsense; Adam calmed himself. Just a drinker . . .

Flicking the match, exhaling smoke, the man continued, passing by. He gave them a fraction of a glance, and a trace of a boozy smile, as he loped on down the road.

Adam and Nina stared at each other in the cold and frosted lamplight. She shook her head. *'Come on.'*

Wiping the mud from the keys with the sleeve of her big anorak, Nina turned and paced to the front door. The first key slotted in; they stepped inside. The hall was dark and hushed with tragic silence, it *felt* like the shrouded hallway of someone who had recently died. Adam's hand reflexively moved to the wall, but Nina shook her head and whispered, *'No light switch.'* Instead she used the light on her mobile phone to guide them, warily, up four steep flights of stairs.

Faint noises echoed. A soft Edinburgh voice floated up from somewhere; he heard a TV turned off. The muffled noises of posh tenement life.

'37D.' The effete beam of her mobile phone just picked out the number on the doorway and she lifted the second key to the Yale lock.

Then a shrill voice from below sent a rush of schoolboy fear through Adam. As if he had been caught, in the most flagrant way, by a headmistress.

'What is it? Who is it? I'll call the police!'

Light flooded the stairwell.

'Crap,' Nina said, very quietly. 'It's the landlady. Sophie Walker. *Say nothing*.' She stepped to the banister and stared down. 'Oh, God. Sophie, *hello*, I'm so sorry to scare you – we didn't want to wake anyone – it's just . . . you know . . .'

The woman was briskly climbing the stairs. She was about fifty, with a hint of hippyishness: wearing a Greenpeace T-shirt under a thick purple cardigan, and supermarket jeans and sandals. Her stern face softened as she ascended.

Because Nina had started to cry.

It was probably an act, Adam reckoned, but if so it was a brilliant act. The grieving daughter of the beloved father. How could *anyone* object to Nina returning to her dead father's apartment, no matter the unusual circumstances?

'I know Rosalind is away, and this is a terrible intrusion,' Nina sniffed. 'I just wanted a few wee photos. Of my father. Please forgive me.'

Sophie Walker crooned with sympathy as she came over and hugged Nina. 'Oh please. Nina. Don't you worry, please sweetheart. I'm so awfully sorry about what happened – and of course I understand.' The landlady flickered a glance at Adam.

Nina explained, her voice tremulous, 'This is Adam. He's . . . he's a good friend who's been helping me. Y'know, deal with this. But I know it's late and this must appear crazy.'

'I lost my own father last year, I entirely understand, it's such a *terrible* thing – it always hits you more than you expect. The only reason I was so paranoid is because of the break-in. Before. But you know about that.'

Nina lifted her face. And gently detached herself from the hug. 'Yes. He told me, of course. Were you frightened?'

'Not me, no! But he was so upset. You know they took all his notebooks, don't you? His precious notebooks from his trip.'

'Yes.'

'But why did he refuse to go the police? Very odd. And then of course that man – the argument – anyway that's why I'm so paranoid.'

'Which argument? There were lots, Sophie. His mood swings at the end.'

'In the flat, a few days later. With the American. I heard the voices.'

Adam watched the two women, bewildered, unable to gain a purchase on the conversation.

Nina sighed. 'Was he really *that* upset?'

'Oh I think so. Oh yes, he was very unsettled. First a break-in, then the arguments. A colleague perhaps? Anyway.' The woman hugged her arms around herself, her purple cardigan tight around her chest. 'Look at me, this is not the time for chatter. I'm so sorry for everything Nina. If you ever want to . . . you know . . . just call. I've been through it. You have to give yourself space, let yourself grieve.' She gave Adam another glance, this time entirely unsuspicious. 'It's such a raw night, I'll be going, and I'll let you . . . get on with things. Goodbye. And call me!'

'I will Sophie, I will. Thank you.'

The two women hugged again. Then Sophie Walker disappeared down the cold tenement stairs, heading for her ground-floor apartment. Without a word Nina, swivelled, turned the key in the lock, and she and Adam entered the flat.

It was very cold and truly dark inside, the apartment exuding a maudlin scent of beeswax polish. Adam flicked a hallway switch, which engulfed them with sudden light.

'You never told me any of this. A break-in? An argument? Surely this is relevant?'

Nina's reply was fierce: she turned and gazed at him with her green eyes wet and wide. 'Because he never told me. Any of it.'

10

East Finchley, north London

'Er, dad, what are you doing?'

'Nothing, son, nothing.'

Mark Ibsen was flat on his back on the living room floor in their small house in East Finchley. His wife was Sunday shopping with his younger daughter Leila. His son was unimpressed with his dad's answer.

'Dad. You're lying on the floor.'

'Luke. I'm fine. Haven't you got some Xbox thing you can go and play for seventeen hours on your own, like normal kids?'

'It's more fun watching you, Dad.'

DCI Ibsen sighed, and gazed up. He was trying to conceptualize the final hours of Nikolai Kerensky, their murder victim. So here he was, theoretically lying on the kitchen floor of the big house at 113 Bishops Avenue, with no feet. And one hand. Blood gushing everywhere. The killer was – what? – looming over him with a gun, or another knife, some sort of weapon? The blood would have been everywhere.

Why slide from the kitchen into the sitting room? Fully sixty yards? In deep agony? Slowly bleeding to death?

Maybe the killer fled, therefore allowing Kerensky to make a desperate bid to reach a phone.

Ibsen glanced up at the kitchen window of their small terraced house. Weak winter sunlight was shining through the bottle of Tesco's lemon-scented washing up liquid poised on the kitchen window sill.

He tried to imagine his kitchen as five times the size, with big French windows flung open to a massive garden, windows through which the killer had presumably made his ingress and egress. But how did the murderer do that without leaving any signs whatsoever? It was a true puzzle: they had no trace evidence, no fibre evidence, no hint of forced entry, no shoe marks in the muddy garden, no eye witnesses, nothing.

And why would the murderer flee halfway through his task? No one had disturbed him at his grisly business: it was a cook returning the following morning who had discovered the mutilated corpse of Nik Kerensky. The only 'witnesses' to the incident were those passers-by and neighbours who heard unusual noises – and did nothing.

'Can you shift the cat, Luke, don't want to squash him.'

'He's too fat to pick up! Mum gives him all the leftovers.'

'Try?'

With a manful effort that made his father proud, Luke picked up their enormous cat Mussolini, and moved him to a nearby stool.

His route cleared, Mark Ibsen slowly dragged himself across the hallway, into their living room, again trying to quadruple the distance in his mind, and conceptualize the pain of having severed feet and a severed hand as he did this. At what point did the killer force Kerensky to try to cut his own neck? Why did he stop doing this? When did he loosen Kerensky's trousers? Was that the prelude to some hideous castration, or was there a sexual element?

The hint of a glimpse of an idea caught the light of Ibsen's mind, like a jewel momentarily illuminated. *Gay sex*. Gay sexual murders were often the most brutal. Was Kerensky gay? All they knew, so far, was that he was a bit of a playboy. They had yet to receive the toxicology and serology reports but friends had spoken of drugs and nightclubs.

Now he had reached his immediate goal. Their IKEA dining table had been laid out exactly as the antique desk in Bishops Avenue had been laid out: notepad and phone to the left, laptop to the right.

'Have you finished, Dad?'

'Nearly.'

Ibsen was lying on his back on the living room floor. Their ceiling needed painting. He let his thoughts coalesce to a quietness, then hoisted himself on one theoretically amputated arm – the blood theoretically spurting everywhere – and reached for the phone. But he didn't make it, of course – they already knew no phone calls had been made from the house that night – so Ibsen fell back, in his mind smearing blood on the laptop. And then he theoretically died. The last blood jolting from his horrible wounds.

'Dad, open your eyes. It's scary now.'

'Sorry, lad.' Mark stood up, and tousled his son's hair; then stared at the laptop on his dining table, slightly smeared with marmalade from breakfast.

The laptop.

The laptop.

The laptop.

Grabbing his mobile, Ibsen stepped urgently into the hall, calling Larkham's mobile. 'It's Ibsen.'

'Sir?'

'You're at the Yard?'

'Yesssir. We don't all get Sundays off—'

'Nor do I, I've got an idea. Have we checked the laptop yet?'

A telephonic pause.

'Sir?'

'Has anyone checked the laptop, seen if it was used?'

'Ahh, no.' Another pause. 'We're getting round to it eventually, sir. Tomorrow, probs. Course it's been fumed for prints but all we've got is Kerensky's as he reached for the phone like you said . . .'

'But maybe he wasn't reaching for the phone! Maybe he was reaching for the laptop!'

The next pause was tinged with sarcasm. 'Visiting Facebook, sir? As he bled to death?'

'Have you got the laptop there?'

'It's in the hard evidence bags, sir. Downstairs.'

'Grab it and meet me at the house, Bishops Avenue. Now.'

'But the chain of evidence, sir?'

'We'll fix it. Bring it!'

After leaving his son with the neighbours, it took ten minutes for Ibsen to drive his Renault to Bishops Avenue, a brief journey which comprised a vast social ascent.

The murder mansion was now decorated with so much police tape, fluttering in the cold winter wind, it was as if there was a small regatta taking place inside. Two constables guarded the large double front door.

'DCI?'

'Morning, constable. Wife OK? Kids?'

Their chat was desultory. Because Ibsen was still working through the logic in his mind. The laptop. *The laptop*. The sitting room with the big TV and speakers . . .

'Ah, Larkham!'

The detective sergeant had arrived, driving himself from New Scotland Yard. As Larkham stepped out of his car he held up a large clear plastic ziplocked bag containing a laptop.

'Let's go inside.'

'Sir.'

Another constable opened the door. Ibsen gazed

around a marbled hallway which shone with the polished gleam of wealth.

The victim's father, the oligarch, was apparently staying in a hotel in town, having flown in from Moscow, shocked and grieving. The man was understandably avoiding all the horrible police work: the house had been gridded and marked and powdered to uninhabitability, and it stank of cyano fumes.

They stepped into the sitting room.

A young forensic photographer was just finishing her UV work on the carpets, seeking hidden blood stains. Nods were exchanged as she quit the room, leaving them alone, though the DCI could hear more forensics officers in the kitchen.

'All right, put the laptop on the desk, where it was, and boot it up.'

With carefully gloved hands Larkham turned the laptop on, and Ibsen bent close to the screen. He sought Kerensky's last browsing history, for the night he had died. He searched and scrolled, and scrolled a little more. And stopped. 'There. Look.'

Larkham leaned, and looked. 'Jesus. Porn sites! Hundreds of them.'

'Not just that. Look at the timing. All through the evening, Larkham . . .' Ibsen checked the times again. 'All through the evening in question he did this, surfing porn. Gay porn by the look of it. Justusboys. Hungdaddy. Grindr. Then – look – here – at about eleven p.m. He clicked on—' Ibsen moved closer to the screen, tapping keys with his gloved fingers. 'Redtube. And it seems like . . . He watched a movie. Yes. He watched an online porn vid. This one.'

Another key click.

The two men watched the little video buffer into life on the laptop. An older man was seducing a younger man in a doctor's room. It was a patient/doctor porn scenario, a young jock being stripped and 'examined'. The actors proceeded to vigorous sex, laughing and panting.

'Nice.' Larkham blushed faintly. 'So he liked gay porn so much he watched it from about four in the afternoon to eleven p.m. the night he died.' The young sergeant frowned. 'He liked it so much that after his killer had forced him to cut off his hand and feet and practically his damn head he dragged himself from the kitchen, to go and watch some more gay porn as he was dying, with the killer standing over him – there. One a.m.! He's online again. Surfing! What the fuck?'

'There was no killer.' Ibsen shook his head. 'See, here, the computer.' A click of two keys minimized the porn video, and revealed the tray of icons at the bottom of the screen. 'There's a wi-fi connection, surely, with those huge speakers. Turn them on.'

Obediently, Larkham crossed the room and found a remote. With his gloved left hand he pressed a button. A red light at the bottom of the wall-high speakers flicked green, and a wireless symbol turned orange. The faint yet unheard hum of large electrical appliances, switched on and waiting, somehow filled the room.

'Now,' said Ibsen, 'let's play the video he watched at one a.m., as he was lying on the floor, dying. Here it is . . . on Boundstuds.com. Big Daddy's Dungeon Party. I'm guessing this is not Teletubbies.'

The video buffered for two seconds, then burst noisily into life. The sound from the speakers was intensely loud. On the laptop screen a man in a leather coat, a leather mask and a leather jockstrap, was whipping a chained and naked young man, whipping him hard. The boy screamed. The man shouted abuse. The noise filled the entire house – and beyond.

Ibsen turned the video off.

Larkham was staring at the speakers. 'So that's it. That's what our witnesses heard? They heard the *first* porno video at eleven p.m., and the second, the violent one, at one a.m. They didn't hear any intruder. Sir, that's it. That explains it!'

A constable entered the sitting room, breathless and flushed. 'Is everything OK, sir? We heard – er – strange noises – ah—'

Larkham laughed quietly. 'No, it's fine. It's all good.'

The constable looked between the two officers, bemused. 'OK then . . . sir. I'll leave you to it.'

Ibsen stepped gently over the stained carpet and gazed towards the distant kitchen, speaking quietly. 'That's why we have zero evidence for a killer, why we have the victim's prints on his own murder weapon. Because there was no murderer. *There was no murder.* It's autoerotic. It's a damn suicide. Kerensky watched gay porn all night, for some reason, then for some reason we don't know this drove him to mutilate himself, so he went into the kitchen – and hacked off his own feet and his right hand.'

Larkham crossed the room and stood beside his boss. 'Then he even tries to cut his own throat, but realizes you can't 'cause it's virtually impossible. Without a chainsaw. But he is dying, anyway, and he wants a final high. Autoerotic as you say, sir.'

Ibsen walked back into the middle of the enormous sitting room. 'Exactly. He drags himself from the kitchen, because he wants that last amazing thrill. And then he reaches the desk. But he's lying on the floor weak from blood loss. Desperately he reaches up for the laptop, turns it on, smearing blood on the keys. And he watches . . .'

'Big Daddy's Dungeon Party.'

A throbbing silence filled the room. Ibsen expected to feel a rush of vindication, even triumph, but instead he felt only a tinge of disappointment. So: it was not a murder but a bizarre suicide, a truly bizarre suicide. He'd solved it, and probably deprived himself of a fascinating case.

'Er, sir?' Larkham was pointing.

'What?'

'Look at the screensaver.'

Ibsen swivelled to look at the computer. As the laptop had been left to its own devices, the screensaver had come on: the entire screen was filled with a single image.

It was a human skull. The skull was adorned with a

crown, and the neckbones were festooned with pink pearl necklaces and a red-and-blue Barcelona football scarf. Lodged between the stained brown teeth of the skull was a fat cigar, trailing smoke.

Ibsen frowned. 'That's a little weird.'

Larkham shook his head. 'It's not just weird, it's fucked up. This whole thing is totally fu—'

But he was interrupted. A young woman was standing at the sitting room doorway, in gloves and a paper suit, her frizz of blonde hair just visible under a paper bonnet. She was clutching something in another clear plastic bag.

Ibsen just about recognized her. 'Sergeant . . . Fincham?'

'Yes, sir, Forensics. Are you the SIO?'

'Yep. DCI Ibsen. What's that?'

'Something you ought to see, maybe.'

She walked over to him, carefully stepping around the blood stains on the Turkish carpet, and dropped the bag on the desk for him to examine.

Inside the plastic bag was a glass. It was smeared red, on one side in particular. The concept thrown up by this made Ibsen's stomach churn.

'Where and when did you find this?'

'Just now, sir, it had rolled under the cooker.'

Larkham squinted. 'Christ, is that blood?'

The woman nodded. 'Almost certainly. Human blood. Congealed. Nearly dried. Maybe two days old . . . ?'

Larkham pointed. 'Look at the way it's smeared down

one side, like it has been . . . drunk from. It's been used.'

Ibsen didn't need to have this pointed out. Before he died the victim had drunk a cup of his own blood.

11

Tomb 1, Huaca D, Zana, north Peru

She could hear voices in the redness.

'Jessica. Jessica!'

Someone was pulling her; sideways. She coughed, and coughed again. Spluttering the dust from her mouth, rejecting it, puking it up.

'Give her the water!'

Another voice. Larry. She opened her eyes but all she could see was the redness. She shut them tight again. A cold sudden splash of water dragged her back to reality.

'Jessica!'

It was Dan: she could sense his touch, his fingers wiping the dust from her face with a cloth. Washing out her eyes and her mouth. Again she peered, and this time she saw.

She was still in the passage chamber at the entrance to Tomb 1 of Huaca D. Beams of light pierced the floating clouds of red dust, beginning to settle: beams cast by the headtorches of her friends and colleagues, Larry, and Dan and Jay, who were staring at her: dark shapes behind the beams.

'Jess. *Jessica*. Are you OK?'

Her voice was a dusty croak. 'I think so – think so, I . . .' Faltering, she choked up some phlegm, and spat it on to the passage floor.

With a shudder, Jess grabbed the cloth from Dan, and started rubbing the dust from her own face, and hands, and her shoulders. *Get rid of this filth.* She was covered in the stuff, hundreds of pounds of it must have fallen from the vault above, raining down on her head.

'It's cinnabar powder,' said Dan. 'Just cinnabarite.'

Urgent and repulsed, Jess pared the disgusting powder from under her fingernails. The powder had a definite scent, not quite pungent, but organic, and dirty, and soiling. Like something excreted by insects.

So it was cinnabar? Powdered ore of red mercury, used on corpses as decoration since the early Stone Age.

And then the anxiety came rushing back.

'Hold on. Cinnabar is mercury,' she said, 'it's a *poison*—'

Dan spoke, his voice softened by affection. 'Yes, Jess . . . That's why you got a dumping. The Moche put it in some of their tombs as a booby trap to ward off graverobbers. It's triggered by opening the door.' His headtorch was bobbing as he nodded. 'It was lethal millennia ago, but it's inert after so long: really – there is no risk, Jess. It's just a shock when it happens.' The headtorch turned, its beam circling like a lighthouse beam in the sea fog, through the floating red dust. 'Larry?'

Larry Fielding's laconic voice emanated from the reddened darkness. 'Yeah,' he laughed. 'It happened to me at Huaca de La Luna in Trujillo. Few years back, when Tronna first sent us here, we were tryin' to get into Burial 5, you know, the famous one, with the princess.' A chuckle. 'Freaked me out. Like being in a little avalanche. But I was fine!'

'But I passed out?' Jessica said shakily.

'Seems so,' said Dan. 'Only a few seconds, though – just the shock, I should think.' A heavy pause. 'Look. If you wanna go back we totally understand. Larry can help you, you can come back later.'

The idea of scuttling back to the TUMP lab for a shower, then waiting, lamely, to hear what they had found, was surreal. And she definitely didn't want any indulgent treatment from Dan, just because they were having an affair: secret or otherwise. Her defiance resurged. They were still here. At the door to Tomb 1 of Huaca D. What was beyond that door? She urgently wanted to be here the moment it opened, like Lord Carnarvon in the Valley of the Kings, like every explorer in human history, she wanted to say: *I was there*.

'No way!' Her voice had regained its edge.

'Go, girl!' Larry laughed.

'OK, then.' Dan was deciding. 'OK, let's get this done.

81

A few more minutes and we'll be in the tomb.' Slowly, he shifted left, in the fetid confines of the dark passage, and began tugging once again at the rock doors to Tomb 1. The slates shifted as he spoke. 'You know, this is actually a damn good sign. The Moche only used cinnabar as a deterrent for their most precious graves. That's right, Larry, right? What did you find in the Huaca de la Luna?'

From down the passage came the reply. 'Oh, wow. The lot. A main skeleton: the warrior priest, buried with his tumi. Decapitated llamas, that was nice, and tons of grave goods – a headdress made from desert fox bones, this fantastic wooden club . . .'

Dan was still working at the door. A faint crack of blackness could be seen – beyond. The tension was thick in the air, replacing the crimson powder of lethal cinnabar. Jessica guessed that all of them were feeling it, the rising tide of excitement.

Jay spoke up. 'Didn't you find blood on that club?'

The door was definitely opening. Larry replied, 'Yeah, it was covered in this . . . like . . . black stuff. Horrible. We did immunoanalysis. It reacted to human blood antiserum only.'

The door was opening further. Larry added, 'It had been used so often, to kill people, ritually, that the blood had soaked through the wood. Like jam in a sponge. Yuk.'

They were seconds from entering Tomb 1, Huaca D.

Dan interrupted, his voice strained by exertion. 'Looking back, ah, you know, with what we know from

Jessica and Steve Venturi, I reckon – ah—' He was pushing at the door now, and it was opening easily. 'I reckon that, ah . . . the mace must have been used in the sacrifice ritual. When they were done drinking blood, they just lined victims up, hit them with the club, bludgeoned the brains away – so all we need to do is know why: who they did it for, who they, ah . . . worshipped. OK . . . ah . . . I think I think we're in. *I think we're in the tomb!'*

Even the veteran professional calm of Dan Kossoy was affected by the excitement: he said nothing more. But the beam of his headtorch told the story.

The door was open.

Jessica breathed the ancient air exhaling from Tomb 1. It seemed to be respirating, releasing a long ancient sigh of relief, or submission. This was nonsense, of course. It was just some ventilation, air blowing through the entire huaca, now that the door was fully open, the desert wind whistling through, probably from their entrance to some further concealed exit – air sucking from one end to the other.

The smell was tainted with an old putridity, something ancient, and distant, and incorrigibly dead.

Jess looked around. Was she the only who had noticed this disgusting odour? No. Jay had a sleeve over his mouth. But Dan Kossoy seemed entirely unfazed.

'It's an unbroken Moche tomb all right. A big one. I know that singularly lovely perfume. Come on. Let's go see.'

One by one they crouched and waited to pass through the portal of Tomb 1, Huaca D. Jess felt, for a fraction of a moment, like a Second World War POW in a movie, waiting to use the secret tunnel to escape from the Nazis. The difference was, they were going *further into* the imprisoning evil.

The first thing she noticed was the size of the tomb: it was huge, big enough to stand in, and it stretched deep into hidden darkness. Mud steps led down. So that was how it worked. The Moche must have dug down, to make this vast tomb, then built the adobe pyramid over the pit.

Her feet crunched on something. What? She shone her headtorch down on the floor.

A thousand glittering corpses sparkled back at her: the desiccated carapaces of beetles, iridescent, still showing their sinisterly gorgeous colours: purples and lurid greens and deep dark blues.

'Skin beetles! *Omorgus suberosus.* Flesh-eating Coleoptera. The Moche worshipped them – they worshipped skin beetles and blowflies. We see them on ceramics. Familiars of the unknown god, perhaps? Hmm.' Dan Kossoy was standing close to Jess as he said this. Very close. The beams of their headtorches crossed like battling swords as they both stared at the floor. She felt his hand reach for her hand and grasp it discreetly, giving a brief, secret, affectionate, reassuring squeeze. Then he pointed. 'And here, these are fly puparia. Thousands of them. But . . . my goodness. Look. Here – totally staked out.'

84

Jessica gazed. The dead beetles formed a kind of stencil or silhouette: and they surrounded a skeleton of a smallish human figure.

Protected by the sealed door, the corpse had rotted slowly, free of any covering. The body must have been totally naked for there were no clothes, no adornments, no headdresses or weapons or grave goods: it was stark naked. And it was, as Dan said, staked out.

Hoops of metal fastened the wrists and ankles to the floor. Worst of all: the skull was screaming, locked in a rasping howl of pain, yellowy teeth grimacing. This person, this adolescent or young woman or man, had died in agony.

'Dan!' It was Jay, calling. 'Dan, come and see!'

They ran over. Another skeleton was staked to the floor along the side of the tomb, near the adobe wall.

'Another girl, it looks like.' Jay said. 'No feet. Chopped off. Must be a human sacrifice, right? And here. Birds? Avian skulls. Vultures – must be vultures.'

Jessica knelt by the skeleton. It was adorned with a necklace of some sort; she shone her flashlight. The necklace was maybe copper, and decorated with small, symbolic commas embossed into the metal. She had seen these before, many times, in Moche art. They were called *ulluchus*. No one truly knew what they were: stylized drops of blood, maybe; perhaps blood of the primary deity.

But who was the god who demanded these strange rites? What kind of ancient faith demanded this horror?

'Dan!' Another shout across the tomb. This time it was Larry.

The finds were coming fast. The tomb was littered with many skeletons, filled with precious grave goods: it was a rich and wonderful prize. Wooden weapons mouldered in the gloom. Broken vessels, in the shape of naked prisoners, squatted in the dust, next to little copper bottles for coca taking, and endless broken potsherds with the strange comma-shaped blood drops, more ulluchus, and then – quite wonderfully – a spray of tiny pink coral cylinders, still pretty after fifteen hundred years, where a glorious headdress had rotted away. This was a high-status tomb, a tomb of nobles surrounded by sacrificial companions.

One especially high-status skeleton, possibly a princess, with a great owl headdress, featured another severed ankle, like the skeletons outside. Why? It was inexplicable. This couldn't be a sacrificial hobbling to prevent a concubine or a slave from fleeing in the afterlife: this was a noble. Why would *she* have this bizarre amputation? And how did it fit with the puzzling aspects of the other severed limbs?

The puzzle was too hard. Jess felt the throb of a headache as she walked carefully between the skulls and the ribcages.

In the gloom of the Tomb 1 she could hear the others enthusing over this grand discovery. The worry of the last hour was gone; Larry and Jay and Dan were chattering excitedly.

'Brilliant, just brilliant, this is excellent . . .'

'We need to grid this, today – and we need Kubiena boxes.'

'I'll go back and grab the cameras.'

Part of her was pleased for them: Jess could understand the excitement. But she just couldn't share the elation. Because she couldn't shake the primary image from her mind: that terrible first skeleton staked out in the mud floor, surrounded by the purple and green shells of a million skin beetles.

The anguished, frozen, terrified howl of the skull told her one thing: the victim had surely been tied to the floor, then fed alive to the insects.

12

Morningside, Edinburgh

'You're *sure* he didn't tell you any of this?'

'Absolutely. Nothing. Nada.' Nina gestured, angrily, chopping the air. 'A break-in! And he was upset! So that explains why he felt menaced. Or watched.'

Adam gazed down the silent hallway. The McLintocks' apartment was so very hushed. Several doors gave off the hallway, which was decorated by black-and-white prints of old Edinburgh. Auld Reekie. The medieval city with its Luckenbooths and witch-burnings, the Stinking Style and the royal gibbet.

From somewhere he got the peculiar sense of a clock, somewhere, having stopped. It was a silence comprised of tension, and absence. But maybe it was simply the tension: they were, after all, in someone else's flat, which they had entered with illicit use of a stolen key.

'So, what now, Nina? I don't quite see why we're *here*. If the notebooks are gone then we might as well quit. Get out. No?' He searched for her reaction. He was happy to continue but he didn't want to take pointless risks.

Her gaze was narrowed by contempt, or something close to it. 'Ach. Hell with that. We search! There may still be something? Clues!'

She was already unzipping her large blue quilted anorak; as she dropped the hood, her hair loosened, and shimmered. He gazed, unwittingly recording the details: he couldn't help it, all those years of journalistic training made him do it – this was the stuff that made an article come alive. Details. Description. Details. With her very twenty-first-century anorak now discarded, standing petite and slender in black jumper and grey jeans, she looked like a young and comely widow; yet she also looked as if she was dressed for a break-in. Dark clothes and raven-dark hair. Quite hard to see.

'Let's try the sitting room. And his study. Study first.'

He followed her gesture.

'Here. Dad's study. They had one each.'

The door opened; they entered the study. The light switch was dimmer style: Nina carefully calibrated the dial – finessing it so they had just enough light to search. Not strange blazing light at the windows, not at two a.m.

The study was definitely the man's private space in a shared apartment. The decor was austere. Scottish rugby paraphernalia – team photos and faded rosettes – adorned the walls. A medieval globe in a corner. A large photo of Nina stood proudly on the big wooden desk. A slightly smaller photo – Adam guessed it was the older sister, Hannah – was positioned beside it.

Sitting next to the photos was a strange ceramic object, a piece of pottery; it looked old and exotic. Adam had once been to Mexico City, and this item definitely looked Aztec, or at least Mesoamerican.

He picked it up, and turned it in his hand. Deciphering the painted image on the jar. It showed a man with no hands and feet praying at an altar. The image was so disquieting he almost dropped the pot.

'What the hell?'

She nodded. 'Yes. It's odd, isn't it? He brought it back from South America last year.'

'After his trip?'

'Yeah. Creepy, huh? There's a couple more in the kitchen. Just as sinister.'

Adam replaced the pot on the desk, took out his phone camera and grabbed a couple of shots of the jar.

'You think it's relevant?'

'No. Yes. Who knows? We need to hurry up—'

'OK, I'll do the desk.'

Adam felt like a burglar, or an undercover cop. He got the distinct feeling he should have worn gloves. *Leave no prints.* If anyone caught them doing this it would be ghastly.

He leaned towards a shelf. As he did, a car passed, very slowly, at the rear of the tenements. Was it parking? The blood ran a tiny bit colder in his veins. Adam stared at the far wall of the study: the wall was mainly glass and gave on to a kind of fire escape, and the darkness of chilly Edinburgh beyond. But the car passed on.

Slowly, he sorted along the shelves, turning over books, and peering in a box of cufflinks, fruitlessly.

Leaning down, he pulled at a drawer. For several minutes he rummaged, but there was nothing here. Just files of paperwork. A cancelled mortgage. A cheque book stub. Then floppy disks, and old cassette tapes with handwritten labels. *Arwad. Damascus. Aleppo. A* brief history of technology in one drawer, and little else. He'd had enough: he didn't even know *what* he was looking for. 'Nina. This is pointless. How about the living room? Let's look at it laterally, different kinds of clues?'

She stared in the half-light. Then she nodded; together they prowled out of the study, and walked along the hallway. The door to the dark living room creaked, and squealed. Another dimmer switch was turned. But a quick glance around the room gave Adam no hope they would find anything here, either. It was just another nicely furnished, middle-class living room, with feminine touches.

The large windows were single-glazed: the flat was cold. Adam was glad he had kept his coat on. He wondered how Nina could stand the cold without her anorak: maybe all that alcohol was providing insulation.

She walked across the room to bookshelves stacked with volumes, and began pulling down books, one by

91

one, her small, empty rucksack by her side. Adam paused, and cast another glance at the walls, where abstract art was juxtaposed with framed photos.

There was Archibald as a young man, probably receiving his doctorate: he was wearing a scholastic gown and smiling, and clutching a scroll of paper. Next to it, his wife – or so Adam guessed – photographed as a very young woman: attractive and smiling in some sunlit, foreign place. Deserty beige rocks and red sand formed a background. Taken in Morocco, perhaps?

The rest of the decor similarly implied shared yet divergent interests, in history, art, architecture. More prints of medieval Scotland hung above the scoured and unused fireplace. A lurid Victorian penny dreadful engraving of *Sawney Beane, the Scottish cannibal,* decorated one far corner.

A final photo of Archie and a woman, also framed, stood aslant on a small antique writing table. Adam walked over and examined the photo. The woman was definitely an older version of the young traveller in Morocco.

'Your stepmother?'

Nina was furiously paging through books and didn't hear him, or ignored him.

'Nina.' His voice was a hiss. *'Nina!'*

She swivelled, eyes narrow and green in the half-light. 'What?'

'Is this her? Your stepmum?' He lifted up the silver-framed photo.

A grimace. Yes, that was her.

Adam returned the photo carefully to its allotted place.

'Tell me about her.'

'Why?'

'Because.' Adam shrugged. 'If you want my help, I need to know as much as possible. Context.'

Their hunt resumed. '*Context*?' Nina flung the word down as if she wanted to stamp on its neck. 'OK. Sure. Ach. I'll give you context. But while I'm doing it – help me.'

'How?'

She indicated the wide shelves, the many hundreds of volumes. 'He used to write in books, annotate them. He was notorious for it. Scrawling on every page, and he had a real fishwife's scrawl, like Byron! So, see if you can find . . .'

'What?'

'Somethin'. Anything. *Please?*'

Adam obeyed. He walked to the shelves and reached and began flicking through the volumes.

'No.' Nina hissed, staring at him.

'Sorry?'

'Jane Austen? That'll be *hers*. He never read fiction, hated it. He used to read novels then throw them down after a chapter and say, *It's all a pack of lies!*'

Adam replaced the paperback of *Pride and Prejudice*.

Nina was wearing a sad, remembering smile. 'Look for history and biography. Science. Up here. On the higher shelves. Those are *his*.'

Adam selected a fine, leatherbound edition of Bede's

History of the English People. He flicked through the pages, which were, sure enough, scribbled with spidery marginalia. But the notes were almost illegible: not just faded, but very small – and very badly handwritten, in ancient fountain pen.

He wasn't remotely convinced of this detective work, but he didn't want to argue with Nina. Returning Bede to his slot on the high shelf, Adam tried again, with Runciman's *History of the Crusades*. And as he flicked and scanned the aromatic, scholarly pages, he asked, in a low, careful, wary voice, 'Tell me where they met.'

'Some academic conference, five years ago.'

'Where?'

'London. She teaches law there, that's why she's away so much. Like now. But she's back tomorrow for the funeral.'

Adam nodded, absorbing the information, as he scanned the books, reading the little margin notes – *see pp 235-237 Geertz; Tyndale/KJV?* A thought unsettled him. 'How do you know she won't come back tonight? Late tonight?'

Nina shrugged, examining another paperback. *The Trial of the Templars*.

'Nina. You don't actually *know*, for sure, do you?'

She shrugged again.

Adam spat the words, 'Christ's sake. She could be here any minute!'

Nina didn't reply. But her eyes were locked on Adam, and widened by fear. Because a *muffled crash of glass had just sounded from the study.*

Adam lifted a finger to his lips. She turned, half-crouched, by the bookcase, and her green eyes stared at the wall as if she could see through it. The uncertain silence returned. Then a doorhandle squealed distinctively.

Her words were quiet and fierce. 'Jesus. Who is *that*?'

Adam pressed his ear to the wall: he could hear the mouselike squeak of metal: a metal doorknob in a glass and metal door.

'Someone's on the fire escape, back of the study . . .'

She shook her head. 'No, Adam. *They're already in.*'

She was surely right: he could *sense* the human presence, another heartbeat in the apartment. And now he strained to hear a footfall. And yes, there it was: the almost inaudible creak of floorboards, of someone stealthily moving around.

Adam grabbed Nina's hand, which was damp with sweat, and hissed, 'We have to get out! This could be, this could be anyone – the murderer, anyone!'

In an agony of fear they stepped to the door. As quietly as they could.

The presence – the intruder, the murderer – was moving around the study. Searching for what? The fear mixed with fierce anger somewhere in Adam's soul: it was the old eagerness for action, maybe even violence, to resolve things. He could hear his father's drunken boasts: never let a man frighten you, never show your fear. Take him on and beat him.

Maybe Adam could tackle the intruder: he lingered over the thought for a moment. But sanity quickly chased him back to reality. The man could easily have a knife. Even a gun. Any resistance might be suicidal.

No: they needed to flee. Adam pulled Nina to the open door, which gave into the darkened landing; he indicated with an urgent nod what he planned – they should run down the hallway to the front door and escape – before *he* opened the study door to the hallway and trapped them inside by standing between them and the only exit.

The floorboards creaked again. The intruder was moving across the study, *coming their way.*

Adam got ready to run, but even as he tensed for action he felt Nina disappear – she wrenched herself free and ran to the door at the *other* end of the landing. What was down there? A bathroom? A kitchen? What the hell was she doing?

He stared at her, quite desperate. Then he stared at where she had been, at the half-open door through which she had disappeared. What should he do now? Run away and leave her? But of course he couldn't leave her – what if the man found her and . . .

She was back, hefting her rucksack: she had something inside it. He turned and pointed at the door and whispered the word *now!*

Together they ran. Uncaring of the noise, they raced down the hallway, flung open the front door, which creaked on its hinges, and slammed it behind them. The stairwell was dark again, but their indifference was pure and driven. Just get out fast. *Just get the fuck out.*

Panicking and hectic, they raced down the steps.

96

Adam heard a noise above them, surely the intruder, alerted, sprinting onto the landing.

Just keep running and don't look back. They had made the last flight. They were at the main door, and now they were outside, in the cold air, still running.

At the end of Springvalley Terrace Adam halted for a second, and turned. He could sense they were being watched and the feeling was so intense he *had* to turn and see.

Someone was standing at the window of the McLintocks' flat. It was a very distinct figure, moment-arily framed by the light: a thin tall man, wearing dark clothes, with close-shaven hair.

Was it him? The man he had seen, passing by an hour ago, with the tattoos? The figure suddenly shrank from the window, apparently aware he had been spotted.

Nina grabbed his hand.

'Run!'

13

Interview Room D,
New Scotland Yard, London

The girl really was exquisitely beautiful. Detective Sergeant Larkham had told him so on the phone, almost warned him – *she's a real looker, sir* – but nothing had quite prepared him for the reality. She was like an artist's idea of an English beauty. Golden waterfalls of hair, misted blue eyes, a pure and rose-dawn complexion. And she had been crying for about seven minutes.

The girl stared at him. Ibsen snapped himself out of his reverie, and went over his notes. Her name was Amelia Hawthorne. She was twenty-three, an aspiring actress, privately educated, a graduate of RADA. And she had been Kerensky's girlfriend for the last two years.

He repeated the question. Were you in love with him?

Amelia Hawthorne sniffled, tearfully, in the quietness. 'I'm sorry. I am. I know. It's just the way Nik died – I . . . I still . . . I still . . .'

Larkham leaned in. 'We understand, Amelia. It's a total shocker. Horrible.'

'But that's *exactly* why we need to know,' Ibsen repeated the point. 'Your boyfriend cut off his own feet, and his hand. It's an appalling suicide. So we need to know all the facts. All of them.'

'Yes. Yes, I know. I get it.' Slowly, the girl seemed to source some resolve, she sat a little taller, visibly preparing herself. 'OK. Go on, then. Ask me.'

'You say you met him two years ago?'

'Yes.'

'At a nightclub.'

'Yes. Anushka's.'

Ibsen flicked a glance at his notes. 'And that is . . .'

'A club in Mayfair. It's down near Nobu. *Everyone* went there . . . back then . . . I mean, you know, two years ago . . .'

Ibsen had never heard of the place. He had also never heard of several other places the girl had already mentioned. In truth, he felt a little at sea in this world of beautiful young actresses and billionaire Russian playboys.

Larkham interrupted.

'It's a nightclub just off Berkeley Square, sir. Well pricey. Two hundred quid for a bottle of bubbly.'

'Really? Prefer something more upmarket myself.'

The DS smiled; Ibsen turned to the girl. 'So you met him at this high-class night club – and you started dating?

She scoffed. 'Dating?'

'I mean, you started a relationship. You were stepping out?'

'Please. We started *fucking*.'

Ibsen leaned nearer. 'OK, then. You began a sexual relationship.'

'That first night. Yes.' She stared at her exquisitely manicured nails. 'Because I liked him. I liked Nik from the start, liked him a *lot* . . . Y'know, everyone said he was probably just another . . . Eurotrash wanker, like all the Russians, with their hookers in furs, all that awful crap. But he wasn't.'

'No?'

'He was witty and smart. As well as fit.'

'And extremely rich?'

'Yeah, sure. He was rich. But, you know, everyone was *rich*.'

She gazed at Ibsen with those slightly contemptuous blue eyes and he wished, for a second, he had worn his better suit. The one from Hugo Boss.

'Why else was he different? Explain.'

'He was clever and really . . .' She sighed. '*Adventurous*, really *interesting*. Not, like, totally desiccated like some of them, all those boring Chelsea boys banging on about their stupid fucking Ferraris. He used to go places, Asia, Africa . . . He read books, he would read to me, talk to me . . . and he went to the theatre, he loved London, art, *everything*, but he also liked fun, partying.'

'Drugs?'

She halted.

Ibsen pressed the point. 'Did you do drugs?'

No reply.

DCI Ibsen briskly reached pulled some folders out of his briefcase and laid them on the table. The folders contained the serology and toxicology reports on Kerensky, N, white male, 27. Instinct had told him the latter report would come up trumps, but it hadn't. The hair tests showed just a trace of cocaine usage, probably from days before the death. Serology showed a small amount of alcohol in Kerensky's blood, but he hadn't been blind drunk when he killed himself. How then had he summoned the courage to do his self-mutilations? How had he managed the pain? Gastric examination showed he had eaten nothing more than bar snacks that night: nuts and crisps.

'We have a hair test, Miss Hawthorne. We know he used cocaine. Did *you* do drugs with him?'

Total silence.

Larkham was leaning against the window. 'You're not under *arrest*, Amelia. We're not going to arrest you if you confess to doing a little gak? Some charlie?'

The girl looked at her fingernails again. Then gazed up and said, 'All right. All right, *yes*. He liked drugs sometimes. He liked sex too. And vodka. Taittinger. Everything. Caviar. Fucking sevruga. I told you, he was a party animal, and yet it wasn't, like, *frivolous*, it wasn't just for the sake of it . . .'

'What—'

'He *knew* he was going to take over his father's business and I reckon he just wanted to get it all out of his system . . . see the world and do it *all,* do the lot, have his fun, and then he would sober up.'

'Tell me more about the drugs.'

'It *wasn't* heavy. Really. *No smack.* Maybe a little toot. Before dinner. That's all. You know? Maybe he dropped some E or mcat with his friends. But nothing heroiny, not with me. He was into new shit, new experiences, but not necessarily *drugs . . .'* She looked straight at Ibsen.

He sensed the direction of her thoughts. 'Did you know he was bisexual?'

The actress pushed her ringlets from her eyes. 'Yes.'

'But you didn't mind?'

'He was basically, like, straight. But . . . but that was another of his . . . *things.* Try everything twice, that was Nik's motto. So. Yeah. I knew. We had a few threesomes. It was funny . . . just fun. We *are* young.'

Ibsen waited. Her frown darkened.

'But then it kinda changed. Towards the *end.* The last few weeks. He got . . . *out of control.'*

The moment intensified. Larkham stared at the girl. Ibsen said, 'How?'

'He wanted . . . *things.* Y'know, in bed.'

'Things?'

'Kinkier sex.'

'In what way, precisely?'

Her lips were trembling. 'He wanted *anal sex.* He wanted it . . . *that way* . . . all the time. I didn't mind for a while, though it's not my . . . not my scene – but then it was bondage. Heavy stuff. Ropes. Candle wax.

Jesus. Every night, night after night. And he wanted me to go with other men, groups of men, in front of him. It was too much, it got way too much. That's why we split, just before . . .'

'Were you doing drugs at this point? Together?'

'No! That was it. There were no drugs, it was like he had changed *inside* . . . he'd met new people. It changed him. Like someone converted him. Changed him.'

'Who?'

'I don't know.'

'But you mentioned new people. Who?'

'I don't know.'

'Think.'

'OK. OK, there was . . . there was an American, maybe.'

'Sorry?'

She took a long breath. 'It was the very last time I went to Soho House, two weeks ago, to meet Nik, talk about our . . . about the *problems*. In our relationship. But there was an American there. Older. Thirties. Maybe even forties, this really fucking eerie guy, tattoos, vulgar, aggressive, clever but . . . aggressive. Not Nik's style at all. But Nik seemed to be in love with him, worshipping him like he was some . . . *deity*. This hero. Yet he was just a fucking *villain*, as far as I could tell.'

'You know his name?'

'No.'

'Was he Nik's lover?'

'Jesus, I hope not.'

'Did you ever see him again?'

'Who?'

'This American.'

She stared straight at Ibsen. 'I never saw *Nik* again. *That's what I'm telling you*. The last time I saw Nikolai alive was then: Soho House, two weeks ago. That was *it*. I'm telling the fucking *truth*.'

Ibsen sat back. He believed her. So they needed to find this American. But how? He felt the irritation inside himself, as something just out of reach.

'Tatts,' said Larkham, from the sill where he was perched. 'You said he had tattoos?'

The girl turned, the light from the window gentle on her face. Ibsen could imagine her on stage. Spotlit.

'Yeah. Serious tattoos. He had a skull tattooed on his hand. Both hands maybe . . .'

Larkham and Ibsen immediately swapped glances. Ibsen reached for another document, a print from Kerensky's laptop. The skull screensaver.

'Skulls like this?'

The girl took the barest moment to look at the print-out, and she shuddered visibly.

'Skulls just like that.'

They concluded the interview ten minutes later. Two hours after that, Ibsen was back home, in the chaos of domesticity, talking football with his son, trying to use his wife's intelligence.

Jenny was good at this stuff. She worked as a nurse, but she had a first-class degree in psychology from Bristol. The nursing was a choice. The psychology was a talent.

Ibsen cooked the dinner – rib-eye steaks and rocket salad – while Jenny stood at the kitchen door, a big glass of Merlot in a cradling hand. And while he cooked he told her about the case.

Her wise grey eyes narrowed as she listened to the details. 'Jesus. His own hands and feet?'

'One hand, both feet, yup.'

'. . . That's just ghastly.'

'Yes. And all the sexual stuff. Any idea? How could anyone *do* that? What's the psychology?'

'Let me think . . .'

He knew her well enough to see this as a good sign. She was engaged and intrigued. But she needed time to ponder.

They ate the dinner, and Jenny walked the dog because she wanted the fresh air. When they went to bed, Ibsen tried to read an entire page of an Ian McEwan novel, but failed. Yet again.

He was woken at six a.m. He thought in his half-dreaming sleepiness that it was a fire alarm, then realized it was his phone, ringing merrily.

Jenny was breathing in deep sleep, beside him. He picked up, his hushed voice was sodden with tiredness. 'Hello?'

'Sorry, sir.'

It was Jonson: the SOC officer from Bishops Avenue.

'DS. Ffff . . . What time is it?'

'Far too early, sir. Sorry to disturb you. But we have another suicide, and we think it may be linked.'

'Linked?' Ibsen's weary brain tried to engage the

gears. 'How can they be linked, I mean, how do you know?'

'This one also tried to cut his own head off, sir.'

'What?'

'And this one succeeded.'

14

Huaca El Brujo,
Chicama Valley, north Peru

'Gracias.'

Jess waved in gratitude to Ruben, the gateman at the temple complex. He waved back, and lifted the wooden barrier for her Hilux. His little motokar, his three-wheeled ride home, was parked by the kiosk. It had *Jesus es Amor* stencilled in purple letters on the transparent plastic roof.

The day was hot yet clammy: typical muggy Sechura weather this close to the coast. She turned in her seat as she passed the kiosk and the gate. From here, looking west, she could see the Pacific, a line of dull sparkle, where the big dirty waves crashed on the lonely shoreline.

The only interruptions to the desert flatness were the bumps. The sacred huacas.

Changing down a gear, she accelerated towards the pyramids. Another kilometre in her pick-up brought

107

her to Huaca Cao Viejo, known to the locals as El Brujo. The Sorcerer.

It was, like most Moche ruins, an unprepossessing site: a large adobe pyramid, very weathered and eroded – somewhat like a vast, ghastly, and collapsing chocolate sundae – maybe thirty metres high and a hundred metres wide. Beyond and around it were other, smaller pyramids, stretching down to the coast, half a kilometre east, where the waves made a distant thunder, where dead dogs lay on their vile bleaching spines and howled at the sullen sky.

It was a bleak and grisly location, yet the nothing-ness felt necessary, even soothing. Right now Jess needed the calm grey nullity to salve her anxieties; the events in the huaca last week still jangled uncomfort-ably in her mind. The cinnabar, the skeletons, the flesh-eating beetles, the unknown god. How did it all fit together?

There was no easy solution. So she needed to focus on the issue at hand.

Swerving sharp and right, she parked the car on the ruins of the old Spanish church. Notebook and camera zipped briskly in her rucksack, she opened the car door and inhaled. The humid air was distinctly flavoured by the sea: salty, and tangy, maybe slightly rancid. Weighing the keys in her hand, she wondered whether to lock the pick-up; then locked it, feeling stupid as she did so. There probably wasn't another human being, apart from Ruben, for ten kilometres. It was just her and the crying seagulls.

A quick walk brought her to the muddy steps of El Brujo, which she ascended to the First Enclosure. Scraps of burned wood and old paper scribbled with Quechua spells and curses, littered the beaten earth *en route*. This was not unexpected. Probably some *curanderos* – some local shamans – had been here, performing their strange ceremonies in the depths of the desert night. The local villagers still revered the spiritual power of these huacas, hence the local name for the huaca – the Sorcerer. The descendants of the Moche still came to this horrible place to partake of whatever power the sacred pyramid possessed.

Jess strode close to the largest wall, and knelt to take photos. Here, in red and gold, and white and blue, were the great treasures of El Brujo: long wall murals showing fish and demons and seahorses and manta rays and dancing skeletons, and the sacrifice ceremony.

As they now knew, beyond doubt, this ceremony *really happened*. And this mural described it: precisely.

Jess scrutinized, and scribbled her notes. How was it enacted? First, it seemed, the Moche warriors performed some kind of ritualized combat. The main object of this brawl was to grab the opponent's hair. When a man had his hair seized, he fell to the ground: submissive, and willingly doomed. All of these stylized combats took place *within the community.* DNA analysis showed this. The fights weren't with enemies, but *between friends and relatives, between brothers and uncles.* The sole purpose of the fighting was to produce endless victims: for the sacrifice.

She snapped and clicked. And scribbled again in her notebook.

The ritual proceeded from here, with minor variations. The defeated warriors were stripped naked, and bound by ropes at the neck, like slaves being walked to the African coast. After that, as the next murals showed, the prisoners were taken *inside* the precincts of the temple. That could be here at El Brujo, or in Zana, or Sipan, or Panamarca, or the Temple of the Moon in Trujillo. At the peak of their empire the Moche had many great temples, stretching for hundreds of miles along the coast.

Jess scrawled, and then paused, thinking about Tomb 1 of Huaca D. She remembered the insect shells shining gaudily, like discarded fairground trash, in her flashlight, gathered grotesquely around a staked-out corpse.

What was the link between that discovery and El Brujo? Maybe there wasn't one. And yet maybe there was.

They now knew the sacrifice ceremony had really happened. They also now had a sense the Moche really fed people to insects: hence their reverence of insects, depicted on the pottery as flies dancing around prisoners and skeletons. What, then, about the severed ankles and wrists of the skeletons they had also unearthed in Huaca D?

A few days ago Jess had sent another sample of these bones to Steve Venturi. Now she waited for his second verdict. If Venturi confirmed that her hunch was right on the amputations, then the clues began to form a narrative. But what narrative, precisely?

Jess pulled out her cellphone, and squinted at the little screen, in the dusty light, wondering idly when Steve would ring, or maybe Dan. But naturally there was no signal, not out here in the wilderness. She wouldn't be disturbed by good or bad news, by any news at all, for the next few hours.

This was good, maybe. Fewer distractions meant she could concentrate on the task at hand: recording the murals.

Another scramble, up another flight of mud-brick steps, brought Jess to the Second Enclosure, where another large mural showed the concluding rites of the sacrifice ceremony.

Finding an angle to best catch the light, she took her photos of the row of prisoners, painted in vivid red. But the sea-wind was brisk up here on the higher levels and it kicked at her hair, which fluttered over the lens. Irritatedly she pushed her hair back, and considered what she was seeing.

The meaning of this penultimate mural was plain enough: the third stage of the ceremony, the procession to ritualized murder. But why did the prisoners have erections? The murals definitely showed them sexually aroused. Were they really aroused by the proximity of death? Turned on by their own approaching slaughter? It was yet another great puzzle of Moche culture: the sexualization of death; yet here it was, daubed in lurid red on the wall of a temple. Naked men waiting to die – with erections.

What was that noise?

That rattling?

She swivelled, alarmed – but it was just the homeless wind, catching at a flap of canvas. *Flap, flap, flap.* She was very definitely alone, with just the lamenting seagulls for company.

The final flight of cracked adobe steps brought her to the top of the pyramid, where the breeze was truly stiff, but the view spectacular, straight out to sea, beyond the other huacas. A faint thread of green, to the distant north, showed where the feeble Chicama River reached the Pacific.

She turned back to her work. And the Final Enclosure. Here the murals were most eroded, yet most unsettling. After being paraded and tortured – stabbed and whipped – the condemned men, still with their inexplicable sexual arousal, were brought into the highest and most sacred patio, quite open to the sky. And there, at last, the prisoners' throats were cut with the great sacrificial tumi knife, in a complex and stylized interaction. The same figures were always involved in this mass murder: the Warrior Priest, the Bird Priest and the Priestess. It was presumed that these were Moche nobles and priests, wearing special clothes and jewels.

At the same time as the throats of the victims were cut, the ordinary citizens gathered to watch. And then the people held hands like children, and slowly danced around the dying men, playing ring-a-ring-a-rosy; they sang and chanted and danced as they watched the blood being drained from the men's deftly-opened throats.

The blood was probably siphoned through little silver pipes – or toucan bones – and poured into the great chalice. This cup of sacred blood was then given to the Bird Priest, who drank the hot blood of the victims even as they died very slowly in front of him.

Jess shuddered. It was, frankly, appalling. And yet the sacrifice ceremony was not the end of the Moche terrors. Nor was it the worst.

Here was an image, often encountered in Moche sites, that no one had entirely deciphered. It was called the Decapitator, and it was thought to be one aspect of the high but unidentified Moche deity. Whoever this god was, here he seemed to be worshipped in the form of a massive tarantula, because tarantulas severed the heads of their victims. This great painted spider, with his lurid bulging eyes and his multiple octopoidal arms, nearly always held a severed head in his hands. And a tumi knife. But here he was lording it over a frieze that stretched right away around a central room, painted on the external wall at about waist height.

And the frieze showed women coupling with pumas, maybe even being raped by pumas. What the hell did *that* mean? It was truly, and richly, disturbing. It was almost too much. Jess felt a need to calm herself. *This is just archaeology!* There was no need to be spooked.

And yet she *was* a little spooked; it was so lonely out here. She *really* wanted a signal on her cell. The urge to talk to a friend, to talk to Dan, and hear his comforting reassuring scholarly voice, was strong. It didn't even matter what they talked about, just a voice would be good, a voice plucked from the air – literally a voice in the wilderness.

She had so few friends in Peru. Apart from Dan, there was just Laura working down in Nazca, and Boris her old tutor in Iquitos. Both of them hundreds of miles away. Yes there were Larry and Jay at the dig, but they were more colleagues than chums, though she liked them a lot.

That left just Dan. And he was also her boss.

Part of Jessica liked the loneliness, the solitude. She'd always been a loner – ambitious, dedicated, trying to be the girl her father would have wanted. That was why her relationships had, hitherto, been so casual. Just sex and friendship, nothing serious. No attachments. Nothing to get in the way of the work.

But now her essential loneliness, her drive, was emphasized by her situation: she was *literally* alone, in a frightening desert, surrounded by Decapitator gods and murals of dying men.

She shivered. Remembering herself as that tiny girl in the hospital room, watching her father, slipping into his terminal unconsciousness, in the darkness of the night. She shivered, and closed her eyes. Her hand was definitely trembling as she took her last photos. Maybe her diabetes was getting worse. But she carried on anyway. Because she had just one more photo to take.

The final shot was one of the most revolting of all El Brujo's secrets, contained in the very last mural at the end of the wall. In this strange final mural the builders of El Brujo had positioned a real ankle bone in the *painted* ankle of the depicted priest. The bone slotted into the wall was human, as they knew from tests. The mural was, in other words, a kind of collage made from *real human remains*.

The wind dropped, even as her thoughts raced. *Could this be it?* Could this be the answer: the way in to the Moche culture, to their mysterious worship? Maybe this humble bone was a symbolic and universal key.

The bone was positioned exactly where the mural showed an ankle, of a priest. Why? Perhaps because the bone was a deliberate *clue*. It was emblematic advice to anyone who saw the Moche murals of the Sorcerer: *Look, all this is true. All this happens. We really do all of this.*

She nearly dropped the camera. Jess stared, appalled, at her own trembling hand. She definitely needed sugar.

Snatching up her stuff, she paced across the patio, past the puma room, past the murals; she took the muddy steps as fast as she could, and then at last she was on the flats and running to the Hilux. Jumping in, she reached straight for her soda, guzzled it and waited for the glucose to correct her blood sugar.

But as she sat back in relief, a terrible, long-buried shard of memory finally worked its way to the surface of her mind.

She remembered her dad before he died. The way his hands used to shake.

15

The Inner Circle,
Regent's Park, London

It was DCI Ibsen's second visit to the scene of crime – if it was a crime – but he still had to fortify himself. Indeed, as he passed the fluttering police tape and walked towards the off-white SOC tent which entirely covered the car, he experience a greater, nauseating apprehension than he had during his first visit to the scene, six hours before.

The Mini was parked along the Inner Circle, in the middle of Regent's Park. Ibsen glanced left and right as he approached the tent.

Down there was the boating lake, and the bandstand. A row of bare willows looked stark against the chilly grey waters and the overcast sky. On the other side of the road lay the Regent's Park open-air theatre, Queen Mary's Rose Gardens, flower beds and fountains, and empty footpaths making sad diagonals across the lawns.

On a winter's night, like last night – which was

when the incident must have occurred – this was definitely a good place to choose: if you wanted somewhere very quiet, in central London, to slice off your own head with a chainsaw.

'Sir?'

'Constable.'

The uniformed man quickly stooped and unzipped the entrance, allowing Ibsen inside.

It was even colder within the tent than without. Letting his eyes adjust to the soft, suffused daylight inside, Ibsen leaned and gazed through the driver's side window of the car.

The cadaver was still here, though it was about to be moved: a headless corpse sitting in the front seat. The clothed body was in rigor mortis, and it was also twisted, tormented, locked in a shouting grimace from the sheer stunning pain induced by auto-decapitation.

The head had tumbled off the body onto the passenger seat. It lay there on its side, gory with dried blood, looking unreal. It looked, momentarily to Ibsen, like a fake head from some execution scene in a TV series about the Tudors; a ludicrous wax head in a basket.

Behold the head of a traitor.

And yet: it all was too horribly real. The guy really had parked here, and got out his chainsaw, and sawn his own head off. The noise must have been tremendous, Ibsen surmised: the buzz of the saw, the grinding of steel on bone, the glottal scream of reflexive pain, the final rasp of blood-frothed air from the severed

117

windpipe, and then . . . nothing. Did the chainsaw keep buzzing until it ran out of fuel? Presumably so. It had already been removed from the stiff cold grasping fingers – and taken away by Forensics.

They now knew the chainsaw was an unusual, pricey model, a Unifire Rescue Saw, stocked by only one shop in London, and they consequently already knew it had been bought just yesterday, by the victim, the suicide: Patrick Klemmer.

Leaning close to the driver's side window – for some reason the only window not liberally splashed with blood – Ibsen stared in at the headless body.

What did they already know of Patrick Klemmer?

He was a rich kid. Another *very* rich kid. Twenty-seven years old, heir to a large fortune; his retail billionaire German father had gifted him a two-million-pound flat in London – just across the park, in Cumberland Terrace.

In other words, it seemed that young Patrick was, like Nikolai Kerensky, a European playboy: Patrick Klemmer's particular *thing* was sex parties. He organized them for a living, as much as he needed a living: themed orgies and swinging sex parties – erotic masques for bored, affluent young Londoners, people perhaps not unlike himself. The business, for all its scandalous nature, was a proper business: their initial investigations showed Patrick Klemmer was doing well, making a good profit.

So why had he killed himself?

Ibsen marvelled once more at the flamboyant spray

of arterial blood across the windscreen. And the blood hadn't just spattered the windscreen, it had sprayed the passenger window, the ceiling, the rear seats. There was one elegant Art Nouveau signature of blood even on the rear window.

Enough. Ibsen checked his watch. Pathology would be here to take away the body in a few minutes. He had just wanted to see it one more time.

Unzipping the tent, the DCI stepped out into the damp and chilly December air and breathed, deep and longing.

The constable on duty gave him a sympathetic nod. 'Doesn't get any prettier, does it, sir?'

'No,' Ibsen agreed. 'It certainly does not.'

'Any idea why, sir? I mean, like, a *chainsaw*?'

Ibsen gazed at a pair of grey Canada geese flapping laboriously across the blank white sky. 'If you wanted to cut your head off, that's virtually the only way to do it. A chainsaw, with one bold movement. Either that or fall onto the saw. Almost any other method and you lose consciousness, or blood, too quickly, before you can complete the task. Some people have managed to guillotine themselves, under falling sash windows with blades attached, for instance, but that's very complex and difficult. Or you could hang yourself from too high a drop, and wrench the head off, but that needs mathematical precision, the drop and bodyweight and so forth.'

'Er, yes, I see, sir.'

'Sorry. A surplus of information?'

'Not at all, sir.'

Ibsen smiled, politely. 'Please ask Path to give me a call when they get here. I'm going over to Klemmer's flat now, Cumberland Terrace.'

'I can get Jim to give you a lift, sir, he's just—'

'No bother, Constable. It's a walk in the park.'

Ibsen turned and made his way through a gate into Queen Mary's Gardens. The fountains had been switched off. A few couples patrolled the deserted flower beds. The darkening afternoon was dank and uninviting – even without the knowledge that there was a headless corpse somewhere in the vicinity.

As he walked, a strange but sudden sense of dread made Ibsen hurry along in his polished Barker brogues. It was odd. Most odd. As if he was being pursued by something he could not properly see. He actually glanced behind, into the twilight, as if he expected to see – to see – to see *what*?

This was foolish. Ibsen cogitated as he paced. *Solvitur ambulando.* Solve it by walking. He often found walking good for working out puzzles. These deaths, they had to be linked: two rich kids, two bizarre and brutal suicides with an underlying motif of sexuality. But: what, and how, and why?

Perhaps the young man's apartment would yield the answer. Ibsen was nearly there: ten minutes' brisk strolling had brought him to the Outer Circle; crossing the road brought him to the impressive entrance of Cumberland Terrace, another of the vast white-pillared mock-palaces that comprised the Nash Terraces, two-hundred-year-old Regency apartment

120

blocks overlooking the park. A beautiful and very expensive place to live.

Klemmer's big, first-floor flat was busy with activity: three policemen were in the kitchen, another in the master bedroom. But Ibsen walked straight into the luxuriantly modernist sitting room and gazed at the view from the vast, floor-to-ceiling sash windows.

The vista stretched right across the Regent's Park, to the minaret of the Regent's Park mosque, the green heights of Primrose Hill, and to the south, the millionaire townhouses of Marylebone, where the houselights were flickering on, rich and yellow.

Imagine living with a view like this, every day. This kid had *everything*. Youth, brains, education, all the money he could need, even a thriving business. And this magnificent home.

Why kill yourself?

'Sir.'

Ibsen swivelled. It was DS Larkham.

'I was about to call, sir. You should take a look at this. I've been going through Klemmer's laptop. His pictures.'

Ibsen followed his eager junior into a large bedroom. He glanced at the wardrobes: wall to wall. A beautiful suit, just returned from the dry cleaners, judging by the clear plastic wrap, hung from one door. He couldn't help wondering as to the exact make of the suit. It looked properly canvassed, with hand-sewn buttonholes, and real hornbutton cuffs. Savile Row, probably. Gieves & Hawkes perhaps?

121

And then he realized something much more interesting. Why would someone intent on suicide collect a beautiful bespoke suit from the dry cleaners? So that he could look smart at his own funeral?

This didn't fit. The suicide was apparently an impulse. Yet the man had bought a chainsaw, so it *wasn't* an impulse. Yet it must have been an impulse, otherwise why the suit? Was it, therefore, truly a suicide?

'Sir. Here we go—'

Another computer, another batch of files: this time photos.

Briskly, Larkham paged through the snaps.

'They're from his sex parties, I'm guessing,' Larkham explained. 'But there's no full-on scenes. Just people drinking and laughing, the odd kissing couple. Maybe he needed photos like this for his website, to attract punters.'

'So what's the interest for us?'

'Here.'

Larkham gestured. Ibsen tilted the laptop to get a proper look. This latest photo was slightly different from the others. It showed a happy group of partygoers sitting around a dining table. They were lifting up champagne glasses and toasting themselves; they looked drunk and young and exuberant.

'I still don't see it.'

'Bloke at the far end.'

The DCI made a second pass. The photo had obviously been taken at the end of a big boozy dinner. There was a slight sense of dishevelment. The men had removed their dinner jackets, and rolled up their white sleeves. The tall, faintly smiling man at the far end had what looked like tattoos on his arms. Ibsen felt the buzz, at once.

'Christ.'

'Yep. And it's a high-res shot, and I already enlarged the tatts. *Look.*'

Larkham clicked the photo editor and the enlarged section of the photo offered up the crucial detail: the man's tattoos comprised a pair of elaborate and grinning skulls.

Ibsen gestured intently at the photo. 'Trace all these people. *All of them.* We need to speak to every single person. They *must* know something.' He paused. 'And they might not realize what danger they are in.'

Larkham nodded and pulled out his phone. DCI Ibsen walked, pensively, to the large windows and gazed out over the dark, twilit park. Once again he got the strange, foolish, infantile sense that something dreadful was out there. Watching.

16

Lothian & Borders Police Headquarters, Edinburgh

Nina was dressed again in black: she had come straight from her father's funeral.

Adam hadn't had a chance to ask her how it went, whether or not she had spoken with her stepmother. He had been sitting in his overheated hotel room, digesting an overcooked hotel breakfast, wondering quite what to do, thinking about the previous night's events in Archie McLintock's flat when he had got a call from Nina. *I'm going to see the police again, try and get some sense out of them. After the funeral. Will you come with me?*

Then he'd know at once what to do: help her. He wanted to help her as much as he wanted to get at the root of this peculiar, and now menacing, situation.

But the police – as Nina had lucidly predicted when they walked into the stumpy, redbrick, 1970s-style divisional headquarters of the local cops – were somewhat obstructive, or at least very obviously uninterested.

The Detective Chief Inspector, who gloried in the splendidly Italo-Scottish name of Lorna Pizzuto, had practically rolled her eyes at her colleague as Nina and Adam had walked through the door. As if to say: *here she comes again, the nutter who thinks her dad was murdered.*

And now Adam sat in his plastic police chair, feeling uncomfortable.

Nina repeated her earlier question. 'Have you examined the car? Properly?'

Detective Pizzuto put a hand to her forehead as if she was warding off a migraine. 'Yes, Miss McLintock. As we told you last Tuesday, and indeed last Wednesday, we have taken it apart, piece by piece. There is absolutely no evidence of any tampering, the car was almost new, the wrapping was barely off. The brakes were perfectly functional.'

Nina leapt on this statement, her green eyes fierce. 'But what about that? A new car? How did he afford a new car?'

Lorna Pizzuto sighed. 'That is not our proper *concern*, Miss McLintock. We can't investigate a man's entire life and finances, no matter how tragic his demise, if we have no due cause. We have neither the manpower nor the remit.'

Adam felt the need to say something. He was starting to feel sympathy for the *police* – and that was unjustified by the facts. The man with the tattoos. The break-in at the flat. *A secret that gets you killed.*

'But Detective, you now have direct evidence of an intruder? Last night?'

'Yes. And we'll investigate this. But, I have to say, burglaries like this, are not exactly unknown.'

Adam rejected this. 'It's just another crime? How can you be so dismissive?'

Pizzuto interrupted. 'Because you're not *listening*, Mr Blackwood. These particular burglaries are horribly common. What I mean is: criminals actually wait for the obituaries. That's how it goes. You can surely imagine it, some thief reads about the death of Miss McLintock's father in the papers. Then he thinks: ah, look at this, Morningside, rich district, well-known author, just died, there'll be money, antiques, distracted relatives, or even a nice empty home, so easy to crack. It's cruel but true.'

'But the description? The man I saw?'

'The tattoos? It sounds like some local lowlife. We're on it. We will, however—' her direct and honest gaze switched to Nina, '—have to talk to Rosalind McLintock, the householder. She – your stepmother – will need to know that you both were, ah, shall we say, clandestinely on her property?'

Nina waved a hand at the idea, 'S'all right. I told her. Go ahead and talk to her. *Knock yourselves out.*'

The detective permitted herself the faintest smile. 'We will.'

There was another hiatus. Adam seized the moment to ask his own questions, again. 'What about the previous break-in, the one we heard about? The stealing of the notebooks?'

The junior policeman spoke up, for the first time. 'It wasn't reported.'

126

'What does that mean?'

'To be frank, we don't know it even happened.'

'But the landlady, what's her name . . . Sophie Walker. She said Archibald was freaked. Scared.'

'Yes,' the junior policeman persisted calmly. 'But it's just hearsay. She heard it from him. He didn't report a break-in, so we have no evidence of a break-in. And of course, unfortunately, we can't interview him now.'

Adam felt as if he was trapped in a maze of impermeable logic. Everything the police were saying was entirely reasonable and rational. Yet he felt frustrated. But maybe his frustration was illogical: maybe *he* was the irrational person here. Him, and Nina?

Pizzuto took over. 'Again, we will ask Rosalind McLintock if she knows anything about the theft of,' her eyebrows drifted upwards, by a sarcastic fraction, 'the theft of these "notebooks", and this "break-in".'

'Don't bother.' Nina spat the words. 'I asked her today. Again. Says she knows nothing.'

The two police officers exchanged a wearied frown.

Adam had one last go, trying to remember his training in news journalism in Sydney. Always ask the obvious questions. Get straight to the heart of the matter.

'He seemed happy that day. In Rosslyn. Why would he kill himself?'

Pizzuto eyed Adam. 'You mean he was smiling? Cheerful?'

'Yes!'

'But you said yourself, Mr Blackwood, he was also behaving "oddly". Saying strange things. No?'

'Yes, but—'

'We have it on tape. "He seemed a little unbalanced, he was behaving oddly". I'm sorry to be so brutal but these are your words.'

'So why, then? *Why* did he do it?'

The detective sighed. 'Please. As you must know, that's not our territory. You know that, as a journalist. And if I may explain something, because you might be unaware, as an Australian, Britain has differing legal systems. Remember you are in Scotland, not England. There is no coroner here. We have something roughly similar: a procurator fiscal. She, or he, will gather evidence. If anomalies or grounds for further investigation are found there may be a Fatal Accident Inquiry, where these issues can be aired. But, I have to say,' she turned to Nina, giving her an expression of genuine sympathy 'if you want my honest opinion, and I feel you deserve it, Miss McLintock – then there probably won't be an FAI. Why? Because this was a suicide. All the evidence points that way.' She raised a conspicuously wedding-ringed hand, preventing Nina from interrupting, and continued. 'I know this is distressing, Miss McLintock. No relative, and certainly no child, wishes to hear that their parent may have killed themselves. Suicide is a tragedy *for the survivors*. You will have feelings of deep guilt and confusion, as well as grief. Guilt that you didn't spot the clues as to his moods, guilt that you didn't do something. You feel helpless. It is only natural to hope, paradoxically, for a different explanation. Murder is easier to deal with, emotionally, for close relatives, than suicide, however odd that sounds. I've seen it before. But, again, all the evidence we have – and I am a fairly experienced police officer – tells me this was a suicide. I am sorry. But there it is.'

The discussion was over, it seemed. DCI Lorna Pizzuto was already standing, putting documents in a briefcase, then offering a handshake.

Nina accepted the gesture, in a way that said eloquently, *I still don't believe you.*

Their walk to the door of the police station was short and silent. Outside, Adam inhaled the Edinburgh air, on busy Craigleith Road. The cold winter breeze was malted, carrying the distinctive tang of the breweries nearby. Yellow Edinburgh buses queued at the junction. He thought, inadvertently, and piercingly, of Alicia, crushed by a bus: King's Cross in Sydney. How easily it happened, how easily death just took you, flippantly, crazily; with no logic, no logic at all.

It was an interlude of sadness and of awkwardness. Adam didn't know what to say, or do. Believe the police, or believe Nina? Carry on, or go home? He didn't want to think about Alicia, he didn't want to brood.

'You believe *them*, don't you?' Nina said at last.

'I . . .' He wondered whether to lie and decided against. 'To be honest, I don't know.'

'Come on.' She took his arm. 'Let me show you something. It wouldn't mean anything to the cops. But it might just mean something to you.'

She was already hailing a cab. He followed, bemused.

Ten minutes of light Edinburgh traffic found them in Grassmarket, climbing another set of tenement stairs to another flat: Nina's own.

The flat was pleasant but spare, chic but austere. The flat of someone who wanted to live quietly and unfussily, or of someone who expected to be moving again soon. He sat down at her request in a leather chair. What was she going to show him?

She returned with two mugs of tea, in Rangers Football Club mugs.

'Nice flat.' He didn't know what else to say.

Nina looked around the living room, appraisingly, as if she were an estate agent estimating the value. 'Yeah well.' She shrugged again. 'I can only afford it because I sold up in London. Sold my ill-gotten gains.' She sipped her tea. 'I used to work in the City. But the job was so intense I quit.'

He gazed at her, wide-eyed; she laughed, ruefully. 'Ach. You didn't take me for a banker, did you?'

'Well . . .'

'You're right. I wasn't. Took me five years to realize it. I don't know what the hell I am but I'm pretty sure I'm not one of nature's bankers. But I made a bit of cash so I'm set. I guess. For a while.'

It occurred to Adam that, stupidly, he hadn't ever asked her what she *did*. Her job: the most basic and essential of questions. The darkening whirl of drama meant he had neglected the primaries of his craft. Get the facts, all the facts, especially the most basic: age, job, race, marital status and hair colour if you are writing for a tabloid. *Pretty Nina McLintock, 27-year-old brunette, spoke of her father's death . . .*

'What do you do then, now?'

'Charity work. Atoning for my sins.'

'What kind of charity work?'

'Scottish Shelter. For homeless people. I help them raise and make money, because I know how to handle money.'

'Full time?'

'Three days a week. The pay is dreck but that doesn't matter, right now. Anyway, I've taken some time off, since Dad.'

'Of course.'

Nina set the tea on the table. 'Enough. Look at us! Reduced to bourgeois chit-chat.' Her smile was terse. 'Let me see if I can engage you. *Re-engage* you? Do you want to see what I've got?'

'Yes, please.'

She stood and crossed the room to a cupboard. Opening a large drawer, she pulled out a plastic shopping bag. Then she dropped the bag on the coffee table between them. It was apparently stuffed full of small slips of paper.

Adam stared.

'Remember last night?'

'Not something I'm going to forget.'

'Remember I ran into the kitchen—'

'Of course.'

'I went to get *this*.' Nina gestured at the bag. 'Receipts. Hundreds of receipts. Maybe thousands.'

131

He didn't understand, though he could see the dim outlines of where this was going. Then he realized. 'Your dad's receipts.'

'Exactly! You were a freelancer once, right? You *understand*.' She barely waited for his affirmative reply, then hurried on: 'Dad was meticulous about this stuff, tax returns, claiming expenses. All that. As I was searching his desk, last night, I suddenly remembered that he kept all his receipts in a big bag in the kitchen, he'd chuck them in there automatically, whenever he got home.'

Adam felt the pleasure of something unfolding, reverse origami. 'I get it. All his receipts from last year, you can see exactly what he did, where he went?'

'I've already looked at a few. And . . . in here—' she tipped the bag over, and dozens of little slips and chits and invoices rustled onto the table, '—is an exact record of where he went on that trip around Britain, and Europe, and everywhere, last year.'

'So?'

'He went to Tomar in Portugal. He went to Rosslyn again and again. He went to Temple Bruer. He went to the Dordogne.'

'Rosslyn, Temple Bruer . . .'

'Yup. He went to a whole bunch of sites connected with the Templars. A long, long trip. And then he went to *South America*. Because he really was on to something. He must have been. He did *intense* research! My dad was not a lunatic. He was a scholar, a serious man, and he did serious research last year. And it's all here, all the clues we need. We just have to piece together the damn puzzles, follow this paper trail. And then we can find out what he discovered.'

Adam gazed at the litter of paper and he recalled McLintock's words. *It's all here, it's all true, it's more strange than you could ever realize.*

The Templars are connected to everything.

17

TUMP Lab, Zana, north Peru

'So, darling, tell me your theory.'

Dan Kossoy was sitting on his usual stool, in the centre of the main lab in Zana, virtually the only clean modern building in the town. His grey T-shirt expressed support for the Hamilton Mastiffs ice hockey team, his wise brown eyes expressed sincere interest in his anthropologist's latest conception. But he'd used the word *darling* – and it was the first time he'd ever used it.

The lab was quiet except for the low buzz coming from the big fridges, which stored the Moche bones, cradled in soft yellow polystyrene foam – like holy babies in swaddling.

'Jess? Your theory. Tell me! You have my unusually undivided attention!'

'Why? Because we are sleeping together?'

He shook his head and looked genuinely hurt. Jessica

immediately regretted her flippancy. Dan was a decent and kindly man; that was why she liked him. He didn't deserve sarcasm, however frivolous.

'Sorry, Dan. That was glib. I just . . .' She took her seat, on a stool next to his; then she pushed the blonde hair back from her eyes and looked at him. 'To be honest, the situation between us is kinda weird. I don't normally do this sort of thing. Us, I mean. Sorry. I want to know that you are taking me seriously as an *anthropologist*, a *scientist*, not just because we are . . . going out. Does that make sense?'

He gazed at her; his warm hand rested on hers, briefly, then withdrew. 'I understand. There are ethical questions.To be entirely honest,' he sighed, 'I have never got involved with anyone like this, before. I haven't even had a girlfriend since my divorce, Jess. I was a monk in the desert! Then you walked in to the laboratory . . .' He smiled, earnest and affectionate. 'But please, do trust me, I can detach our relationship from the science. I promise. Now tell me your theory.'

Jess cleared her throat. 'For what it's worth, I now believe that, in opposition to our accepted understanding, virtually all the representation on Moche ceramics and in their murals are essentially depictions of *real events*. Not just the sacrifice ceremony. All of them.'

Dan stared at her. 'And what makes you think this?'

'The bone in the ankle at the Sorcerer.'

'Sorry?'

'You know it. El Brujo. The human bone, in the mural of the ankle?'

Dan nodded.

'Ah. Yes. And so?'

'I think it's a clue. The Moche are telling us something. Think about it! You put a real human ankle bone in a *representation* of an ankle. What does that say?'

'They ran out of paint?'

She didn't smile. 'It says this is all meant to be taken literally. *When we show you something, we mean it.*'

Her lover looked distinctly unconvinced. 'OK. The bone. What else?'

'Flesh beetles. We see beetles and flies on pottery, dancing around skeletons and prisoners who are waiting to be killed. Now we have a staked-out prisoner, fed to beetles.'

He shrugged. 'I suppose . . . it's just possible. But even if it was the case we can't know whether he was fed to them alive or dead.'

Jess nodded, despite her frustration. She needed to stay lucid and plausible to persuade the world, beginning with the leader of TUMP. 'But, Dan, he was definitely in agony, right? He died in some great pain, judging by the skull, right? Which is odd, and telling.'

'Hmm.'

'OK, OK maybe it's a question of interpretation. But look at it this way: even if we discount that example, *there are so many others*. Such as the other prisoner. Skeleton 1d. The one at the side of Tomb 1? Now think of the context – the avian crania nearby.'

'Vulture skulls. Yeeeeees . . .'

'They were positioned around the *head* of that victim, who was staked out. As if they had been there, pecking at him, as he died. *The eyes.* Just like *this.*' She reached in her inside pocket, unfolded a printed photo of the pot from the Museo Casinelli, and held it out to him. Dan frowned and scrutinized the photo: of the bottle in the shape of a skeletal man, half-dead, half-flayed, and tied to a tree with his eye being pecked by a vulture.

'You think he died like this?'

'Of course.'

'But this man is tied to a *tree,* Jess, not staked to the ground, and he could just as easily be a dream figure, symbolical, some mythological—'

Jess shifted on her stool, repressing her impatience. 'But that's just *it.* It's our perceptions that are faulty, the evidence is actually pretty clear. Our fundamental approach is, I believe, just plain *wrong*, one hundred and eighty degrees wrong, Dan. Think about it. Whenever we find a new Moche symbol or picture and it shows something ghastly or deviant we conveniently presume, time after time, that it is part of their mysterious mythology, part of a folklore, nightmares of an underworld, who knows? But we can't just keep this up. The paradigm is cracking: it can't support the accumulating and contrary evidence. The evidence that they *did* most of this stuff!'

'I see.'

'How many times have we found human and animal remains that *exactly* match what the Moche show us

137

on their pots? Think about it! How many pots show amputees? We now have endless skeletons with amputations. We also have hundreds of murals showing ritual dismemberment, arms and hands and feet – chopped away from the living, then scattered. And that's what we are finding in the tombs, right? Dismembered bodies, people pulled apart as they struggled, literally chopped up alive.' She was almost breathless now. 'And what about the people thrown off the mountain, as a sacrifice?'

'The sacrificed victims discovered at the bottom of the Huaca de La Luna? Yes, I suppose that's true. There may be something here. But it's very ambitious and somewhat unsupported, I think we still need Steve Venturi's verdict before we can go anywhere. We – you – need empirical data: we need the truth about the amputations. If you get *that*, then we can talk some more.' He gazed right back at her. 'Of course, if your theory is in any way correct it means virtually all the erotic practices on the ceramicas, the *ceramicas eroticas*, must depict sexual acts the Moche actually performed. Rather incredible, no?'

'Not incredible. That's my perception. They did it.'

'Sex with animals?' Dan was half laughing, yet his expression was sickened. 'Women masturbating dying men, men who had been half-flayed? Sex with skeletons, foreplay with mutilated corpses? Christ.'

'Bestiality and necrophilia, in fervent variety. Yep. I reckon that's what they did.'

'It's hard to take, Jess. Hard to believe any society could be that sick. Unless you get Venturi to back you up on the amputations I'm going to hang fire. And think some more.' His gaze was troubled. 'However, even if we eventually accept that the Moche did some of this stuff, we still need an explanation *why*.'

'Sorry?'

'Well. I'm wondering if it occurred, perhaps it was a reaction, to terrible societal pressure, possibly an El Niño event?' His eyes were alive now, as he calculated and theorized. 'That makes sense, Jess. Doesn't it? We know El Niño ruined cultures around here. A bad El Niño might have traumatized an ordinary civiliza-tion into performing . . . appalling acts. Yes.' He smiled. 'Anyway, darling! Get me Venturi to confirm you on the amputation, then we can talk some more.'

This time she ignored the *darling*. This time, in truth, she realized she quite liked it. Why not? They were going out, they *were* lovers. Maybe it was time to get over herself, and tell the world. This is me, and I'm with Dan. Jessica excused herself to go to the washroom. She felt a rising elation as she did. So long as Venturi came through she had a chance at proving her Big Theory. Once they understood the Moche rites, they would be close to understanding Moche beliefs.

And yet there was still so much more to be unravelled and explained. Was it really El Niño that had caused all this? It seemed hard to credit; the sacrifices and tortures had been going on for centuries. They had not sprung into being after just one drought or flood, however apocalyptic. And then there were the ulluchus, the blood of the unknown god. Why was the god bleeding?

Jess dried her hands, and walked quickly towards the door but the last washroom mirror caught her attention. She lingered, examining herself. Her pale European face. Her blonde hair. Her lips. Her face. What did that face say? Was she really OK?

Jess gazed over her hands. The fine tremor had gone. Hadn't it? That sudden thought about her father was paranoia, surely. He had died of cancer. That's what she knew. That's what she had been told.

No. Yes. *No.*

She chastened herself for her hypochondria. Pushing the door to the washroom, she walked back down the long corridor to the main lab. Concentrating on science, not silly fears.

But a noise made her pause. Ten metres from the lab door.

Shouting.

What was this?

Someone was shouting in the lab. And it wasn't Dan. The voice was harsh, Spanish, probably Peruvian – and the voice was angry, and brutally aggressive.

Where was Dan?

Jessica inched to the laboratory door, its tinted glass panel. If she got close, she could probably see through, without being seen herself.

There!

Stunned by what she had seen, Jessica flattened herself against the wall, her mind roiled by panic.

A strange dark tall man had Daniel Kossoy pinned by the window, next to the bone fridges. A gun was pressed so hard to Dan's throat it had visibly whitened the skin of his neck.

The man was going to shoot. The finger on the trigger was squeezed with slow, delicious subtlety. About to kill her boss. About to kill her lover.

18

Rosslyn Chapel, Midlothian

'Are you all right?'

Adam extended a hand to Nina, and as they crossed the snowy car park of Rosslyn Chapel.

'It's just a wee bit of snow! I grew up in the Borders, we're used to snow.'

He tried again. 'No, I meant, you know, coming back here to Rosslyn . . .'

'*I'm OK!* C'mon let's just get going.'

They reached her car, chucked their coats on the back seat, and climbed in. Nina turned the key and they took the main road out of town, past the site of the crash. Adam stared out of the window.

A casual passer-by would never have guessed that this chilly stretch of urban road was the scene of a recent suicide – or murder. Virtually all traces had been erased: just a few broken bricks in the snow-capped wall – where Archibald McLintock's car had impacted – told the story.

'So.' Her voice was firm, probably masking the emotion. 'What did that tell us?'

Adam didn't know what to say. What *had* this visit to Rosslyn told them?

They knew, from her father's receipts, which Nina had sorted into a time sequence, sealed in different noted envelopes, that her father had spent two days at Rosslyn. He had visited on two consecutive occasions before embarking on his long journey south to the Templar sites. But why?

Nina was swerving the car – a diminutive Volkswagen – on to the A1. The high road for the south.

'Ach,' she spat. 'Dammit.'

More snow flurries had slowed the traffic to a maudlin crawl, behind gritting lorries which were spitting their loads into the fresh white snow, soiling it brown.

'Take us six hours to get to Berwick, this rate.' She gazed across the gear well at him. 'Come on, Adam. Talk to me. Mr Australian Journalist. *Rosslyn.* Tell me we found something.'

Reaching in the damp pocket of his wax jacket, he took out his notebook. 'I did make some notes.'

'And?'

'Whatever he found in Rosslyn has to be *mysterious*. Your dad was an expert on the Templars and the Grail legends and medieval European history. In that light, what could Rosslyn have told him that he didn't know already? It must be something no one has solved . . .'

'With you so far, Sherlock. What did he find?'

'Well . . . What about under the floor of Rosslyn? The alleged vault?'

She tutted. 'Puh-lease. The vault almost certainly doesn't exist. *Da Vinci Code* nonsense. Next?'

Adam turned a page. 'OK, what about the Green Men? There are hundreds of Green Men – stylized images of pagan fertility. One of them in Rosslyn seems to be dead. Is that interesting?'

She shook her head as they overtook another gritting lorry, spewing its pebbledash into the settling snow. 'Green Men aren't unique to Rosslyn, they're a common motif in European architecture. Nope. Tell me another. There must be *something*. What did my father see in that chapel? He visited it two days running. He must've found something.'

The road was emptier after the final gritting lorry; the car was accelerating. Adam half-sighed, and flicked the pages. 'Er . . . An inverted Lucifer. Musical cubes. Corn on the cob. Adam and Eve?' The idiocy stifled his energies. 'Look, Nina. I reckon this is pretty *pointless.*'

'Why? Rosslyn is *key*. Dad said so.'

'That's what I mean. Rosslyn is the key. That's what he said: *it's all here.* So it's the *centre* of the puzzle, or at least something like that. So we're going about it the wrong way.'

'Don't understand.'

'Imagine this was a jigsaw puzzle. Do you start at the centre?'

She gave him another look. 'Ah.'

'Exactly. You'd start—'

'At the edges! Yes. Straight lines, the easy bits. The frame.' She tutted at her own stupidity and nodded. '*Yes.*'

'Therefore we start at the edges. The Templars. *That's the frame.* Then we work our way to the centre. Rosslyn.'

The car was now silent. Adam gazed out. The resonant place names sped past on either side: Athelstaneford, Luggate Burn, Longniddry.

'Yorkshire.'

He started from his reverie. 'Sorry?'

'I'm starting with the edges! The first place he went in England was Yorkshire. That's the second envelope. After Rosslyn. That's our destination. Look it up, Ad. In the bag?'

Adam reached into the back seat and grabbed the large duffel bag. Inside were the envelopes containing the assiduously sorted receipts.

He rummaged, and located a white envelope. Handwritten on the front was *Yorkshire, July 23–26.* 'I'm impressed with your bookkeeping.'

'Told you, I'm good at the boring stuff. But it bores me. Where did he go first?'

Adam found the first receipt. 'He stopped to get petrol at a garage in *Suffield-cum-Everley*. At 3.20 p.m., July twenty-third.'

'Suffield-cum what?'

Adam found the fat paperback roadmap in the glove box and scanned the page. 'It's here, near Whitby. In the North York Moors.'

'OK. Now check the book – I brought it along. *The Templars in Europe*. See what's near Whitby.'

Adam reached behind once more. And saw with a rush of poignancy the book on the scruffy backseat, under Nina's snow-damped anorak, a big impressive authoritative hardback: *A Guide to Templar Sites in Western Europe.*

By Archibald McLintock.

Inside there was a neat and beautiful handwritten inscription: *To my beloved daughter Nina. Dad.*

He saw Nina glance at it, quickly, then look away. A choking silence filled the car. Adam paged through the book. It was an exhaustive gazetteer of Templar sites. He swiftly found the entry.

'Westerdale Preceptory. "Every other preceptory in Yorkshire was built on the very highest ground. Westerdale Preceptory, uniquely, is not,"' he quoted. '"Scant traces remain of this once-extensive Templar possession, but we know that it stood at the base of a small green hill, behind the present-day Westerdale Hall."'

'So that's where we go. Westerdale.' She checked the car clock in the bleakening gloom. 'But we're never going to make it tonight.'

They chose a cheap roadside hotel: a Travelodge. Two non-smoking rooms on the same gloomy corridor. When it came to eating – a couple of steak sandwiches in a garish pub by the hotel, a pub which smelled entirely of vinegar – they had their first moment of awkwardness. The intimacy, a young man and a young woman eating dinner alone, and together, was too much, too soon.

Nina seemed very sad, and trying to hide it, talking bravely and pointlessly about football. So they hurried through the meal, and retired to their separate rooms, where Adam watched TV and fell asleep half-dressed, and dreamed of Alicia smiling in a chair in a room, quite naked and pale, watching a movie about astronauts, floating in space.

He opened the tatty curtains of the morning to another snowfall. They flung their bags in the boot. Breakfast was a brace of snatched coffees and Danish pastries bought from the Take a Break service station and consumed in the car. This time Adam drove. His driving was faster than hers; they talked about the past as he took the curves at speed.

'So. Banking?' He changed gear to come off the motorway. Listening to her story.

'I enjoyed it, at first. Moving south, living in London: it's a great city. And bankers and brokers are much maligned, I like them, they are honest. Authentic. They're just greedy. Like sharks. There's no agenda, nothing hidden.'

'What happened then? You left because . . . ?'

'Got bored. And . . . the lifestyle was . . . hard partying. Champagne and coke. I got . . . I had . . .' Her face was blank but pained. 'I had a wee bit of a breakdown. Year ago. Anyhow, that's when I came back to Scotland. Trying to think of what to do with my life. Something worthwhile. If there is such a thing.

That's my life. Nutshell! Tell me about you, Ad? Why the fuck would anyone leave sunny Oz to come to shivering Britain?'

He shrugged, overtaking a tractor in the slush. 'Because it's the mother ship, isn't it? For any writer, for any English speaker. London, England, home of the English language. Walk to work where Shakespeare worked! You don't get that in Sydney.'

She gazed at him. 'So there was no other reason, then?'

He drove in silence for a minute. Had Nina worked him out? Had he given some clue? He struggled with the dilemma; the urge to be honest was as great as his desire for reticence. And Nina had been straight with him, so maybe he should reciprocate.

'OK, there *was* something else. I was running away. Doing a geographical, as drug addicts say.'

They skidded through a junction; a melting snowman stared at them, sadly, from a farmhouse garden.

'Running away from what?'

'Death. My girlfriend—' The words were cold in his mouth, cold and tasteless. 'I was in love with a girl, Alicia Hagen, and – and – we were about to move in together . . .' He swerved, taking a sharp and icy left. 'And she was . . . she was run over, crushed, on a bicycle. She was just twenty-four, riding at night.'

'That's horrible.'

'It was worse than horrible. The police said she had been drinking, like it was *her* fault a fucking truck driver didn't see her. And . . . we'd had a row that night, she went off, she was . . . she was a little neurotic but I loved her, the only girl I've loved and then suddenly she was dead and . . . and I just couldn't stay there, not in Sydney, not in Oz. So I ran away from my guilt. From the sadness. Coward that I am. I think the last thing I ever said to her was angry. Angry words.'

Nina was staring ahead, and saying nothing. Adam switched the radio on. Then he switched it off.

'That's not cowardice,' she said. 'That's just human.'

'Maybe. Can we talk about something else?'

They talked about her lack of ambition; about the time he almost got scurvy working on a sheep ranch; about her sister's rich boyfriend. The conversation brought them the whole way, to the snowy, undulant hills of the North York Moors.

Wrapping themselves in jackets and scarves, they scrunched through the frost-hardened, overnight snow. The wooded path led to a bleak hillside, where rooks cawed in black alarm at their approach. Adam got the book out, and they looked around: at the snow and the grey-black dead leaves, and the crows, and the nothingness.

And then they headed back for the car. There was indeed nothing to see in Westerdale. Adam checked the book. Archibald McLintock was quite right. 'Scant traces remain . . .'

So why did he come here?

Adam drove them across Yorkshire. A revived sense of futility gripped him as they made their way cross country, over motorways, under bridges, through the winter landscapes of city and moorland. He resisted the darker thoughts, and watched the whitened bleak landscape, the crowbound trees.

Penhill Preceptory is located at the high point of a ridge in the Yorkshire Dales.

'This is it.'

The map in the book showed them where to go. Uphill a hundred yards.

'Here.'

'Is that all there is?'

There was almost as much *nothing* in Penhill Preceptory as in Westerdale. It was just a low ruin of stones, on a freezing cold slope, deep in high and bony Yorkshire countryside. Nina stood shivering in the cold by the scattered remnants as Adam read from her father's book, his hands numbed by the wind.

'"The main objects of interest are the curious graves."'

Nina pointed. 'He means those?'

They walked halfway along the largest ruin of wall, and looked down. The curious graves turned out to be odd slots of hollowed-out stone: like small stone coffins embedded in the frozen soil. The coffins were shaped like silhouettes of human corpses, with a narrowing at the neck and a larger space for the head. The effect was sinister.

Again Adam consulted the book. '"These bizarre coffins are almost unique in the British Isles; the only other place where something comparable can be found is in Heysham churchyard, Lancashire, which likewise boasts rock-cut graves, dating to the Dark Ages."' Adam paused, and thought, and then read on. '"Other than this, Penhill Preceptory is largely ruinous and lacking in great interest, though its spectacular position makes it a delightful place for an historical picnic."'

'Picnic?' Nina shook her head. 'This is just a few wee graves! Just a bunch of nothing. Let's go. Give me the keys.'

He handed her the keys and she marched off, stalking down the hill to the car. Adam followed, sensing her frustration, trying to think of some encouraging words. But he couldn't. Maybe this entire escapade *was* a silly idea. He felt sorry for her; yet he was mute.

They climbed a farm gate, and stepped onto the road. Nina pressed her car keys to unlock the doors. And then a voice pierced the cold.

'Nina McLintock?'

She swivelled. A middle-aged man in a flat cap was staring at them.

'I'm sorry, do I know you?'

'Do forgive me. William Surtees.' He extended a hand, Nina took it, warily. Adam watched, observant. *Always get the details.*

The man was well spoken, tweedy, a rich farmer maybe.

'Sorry, but I knew your father. I recognized the old VW as I was driving by. His car? And you, of course, he used to show me your picture. Such a terrible shame.'

'Dad knew you?'

'Absolutely, yes. I'm so terribly sorry. The way . . .'

The man looked at Nina, then at Adam. 'It's no ending for a man. Suicide. But he was so ill, perhaps . . .'

Nina raised a hand.

'My dad was *ill*?'

The man, William Surtees, gazed at her, perplexed. 'Yes of course, ah, yes, your father was dying.'

19

TUMP Lab, Zana, north Peru

The stranger's coarse, shouting voice was baffled by the fireproof glass in the panel. But his malign intentions were apparent.

The gun was now circling Dan's temple. Teasing. Sensual. Malevolent. Waiting. Hungry. The words came quick and angry. Building to a climax.

What could she do? She couldn't do nothing; she couldn't do *anything*. She was of course unarmed. She couldn't simply run in.

Dan was talking now. She strained to hear the muffled words, his fearful responses, but it was said in Spanish, and his voice was quiet, and meek – apologetic. And inaudible. Then the gunman came back, urgent and harsh.

Again Dan demurred, cowering, shaking his head. More fierce queries from the aggressor. The gun was pressed to Dan's throat once again. And now the intruder was smiling, eerily; maybe getting off on Dan's terror. Or smiling with satisfaction at a job nearly done.

She cringed, hidden behind the door. Waiting for the *bang*.

But there was no *bang*.

Jess crept up a few inches closer, and stared, again. The gunman was still there. Taunting. Teasing. Dan was now almost on his knees. Begging for his life.

She could make a phone call, but to whom? Seeking anxiously for her phone, she tried to remember the numbers she'd been told to keep, by Dan when she had first arrived: *North Peru is a pretty lawless place, take down these numbers. Police. Hospital. Me. The US embassy . . .*

What had she done with those numbers? Keyed them into her phone? *No*. She'd never got around to it. They were in her bag, in a notebook, and her notebook was in the lab.

In the lab with the man with the gun, who was about to kill Dan.

The shouts were louder. So loud she could hear them quite clearly.

'¡Dímelo! ¡Necesito la respuesta!'

Tell me! Give me the answer.

But I do not know

Tell me. Or you will die. Here. Like an old pig.

What can I say? I have never heard of him! Please do not kill me, please do not kill me . . .

The intruder scowled, and ceased talking. Jess pressed closer to the thick wire-grilled glass. She didn't care if she was spotted now. Dan's voice was supplicant, so

154

frightened, so pleading, she wanted to rush out and save him.

The man had the gun calmly aimed at Dan's head. As for a simple execution. Enough: she could bear it no longer. Summoning all her courage, Jess pushed at the door but even as she did, she heard voices from a different door. Jess paused to see. It was Larry and Jay casually walking into the lab. And then gazing in horror at the tall intruder.

The gunman didn't waste time. He levelled the gun first at Larry, and then at Jay, wordlessly telling them to back off. They backed off. Then the intruder poised the gun tenderly, this way and that, as if deciding who to shoot first.

Yet he didn't fire. Why? Halfway through the door, Jess saw what the gunman had already seen.

A crowd of villagers was pushing into the room. Jay and Larry had obviously been recruiting: hiring local men, for the dig, as they often did. They'd found a dozen farmers and fishmeal workers; big, dark-skinned Zana men who were staring right back at the gunman, utterly unafraid.

Now the intruder looked seriously confused. It was a stand-off. The locals gazed at the gunman, daring him, chins uptilted; three of them had drawn machetes, used for cane cutting: the challenge was obvious. *You can shoot one of us, maybe two, maybe three – but you can't kill us all, we will chop you down.*

The tension tautened. The fridges buzzed. The Moche pots stared in reproach across the laboratory.

The gunman swore. '*Que chingados! Yo matario tu!*'

But he was edging to the door, and the gun was slack in his hand.

The tallest villager lifted the machete. '*Tiratu a un poso!*'

The glinting machete was pointing at the exit, inviting the gunman to go.

And he was going. Barging through the dark villagers, the gunman pushed his way to the door, and then he slammed the door open and was away down the steps: sprinting. A few seconds later they heard the noise of his car, screeching away very fast, leaving a cloud of dust which was visible from the tall laboratory windows.

Gone.

Jay and Larry were already at Dan's side, helping him to his feet, and sitting him on the stool. He asked, limply, for water. Bewildered, and urgent, Jess fetched water from the fridge. As she took the small bottle of Evian from the refrigerated depths, the Moche skulls smiled at her from their yellow foam cushions.

'Thank you,' Dan said, gazing deep into Jessica's eyes. His hand was visibly trembling as he tried to open the little water bottle; but he was shivering so much he couldn't open the bottle. Jess did it for him; he guzzled the water.

Then someone pushed through the scientists, and poured a liberal measure of the local liquor from a small glass bottle into a plastic cup. Dan looked at it for a moment – and sank the booze.

'Aguardiente?' The villager with the bottle nodded, quite shyly.

'Gracias, amigo,' Dan said. '*Gracias.*'

The villager spoke in a deep Zana voice. *You pay us. You feed our children. You are our friends. We are not afraid of guns.*

Dan thanked the villagers again, and then some more. But the men just bowed, and turned solemnly; then they moved to the door, and disappeared.

Jessica watched as Dan took another gulp of the liquor; he saw her scrutinizing him.

'Jess. Guys. Thanks . . . I'm OK.'

Jay was the first to ask, 'How the hell did he get in?'

Dan shook his head. 'The front door. I guess. Just kicked it open?'

'Who *was* he? How long had he been here?'

'Five minutes. Jess was in the washroom, he just marched in and he pinned me to the wall and . . . started . . . asking *questions.*'

Jess had so many questions of her own. But her boss – her boyfriend – was maybe too shocked for an interrogation. She looked at Jay. 'Do we tell the police?'

Dan shook his head. 'The police? What can they do? I'll give them a description, but, eh, how many criminals are there in Peru? Who are they gonna ask? What are they gonna ask? Did you see a tall Peruvian?'

Larry persisted. 'So who *was* he? Race, accent?'

Dan shrugged.

'Peruvian, probably. Mestizo maybe. South American for sure. Maybe a local villain?'

'A *Haquero*, perhaps? A graverobber?'

'Could be.' Dan sighed, and held the cup in his hand

157

as if it was the Holy Grail, the Eucharist. 'I just don't know! He stank a little of this stuff, aguardiente. Not too much. Not a total lush. More professional than that.'

'The gun was a Glock,' said Jess. And three male faces turned her way. 'My uncle is a gun nut. In Utah, I used to vacation on his ranch. A Glock's a pricey gun for a local criminal. Glock 23, .45-mil, five hundred bucks minimum.'

Jay gestured in frustration. 'Which means?'

'I don't know either!' Jessica sighed. 'But this wasn't some average cane farmer with a grudge. Where would they get a smart gun like that? *How*?'

Larry suggested, 'A haquero, then, like I said?'

Dan answered. 'He wasn't interested in new finds, new tombs. He just kept asking, me the same f— the same damn questions. Endlessly. With that gun.'

'What questions?'

'What we were *doing* here. What we'd found, stuff like that . . .'

Jess walked around the lab, pacing, thinking, thinking hard; she paused by the first large jar, and turned. 'He was asking you about a man. Wasn't he? I overheard it.'

'Did he? Yes. Yes, maybe he did. I was so damn scared. But he did . . . yes, he did.'

'Did this guy have a name?'

'Something odd. Something strange. Yes. I remember: *Archibald McLintock*.'

'Who?'

'*McLintock.*' Dan repeated. 'Ar-chi-bald Mc-Lin-tock. He said it precisely. What did I know about . . . Archibald McLintock. Such an odd name – that's all.'

Jay looked at Jess and at Larry. 'So who the fuck is *that*?'

Larry snorted. 'Does it matter? Someone just tried to kill Dan.'

Jessica raised a hand. 'I think it matters, I think it matters a lot. It's gotta be *linked*.'

'To what?' Larry's voice was verging on angry. 'Jess, what the hell are you talking about?'

'The truck. In Trujillo. That slammed into the garage.'

'Eh?'

Her voice was almost as passionate his now. 'Think about it. First an explosion, then a gunman. Can it really be coincidence? All this violence.'

'Sorry, Jess, no idea.'

'*Maybe, in Trujillo, it wasn't the garage they were aiming for.* Maybe it was Pablo himself, Pablo *and the museum*. Maybe someone is hunting down people who are connected with the Moche.'

'Where's the evidence?'

Jessica insisted, 'I remember him saying, Pablo, the day it happened, that he'd had people in the museum – asking questions. He said they were . . . unpleasant people. Knowing Pablo, they could have had guns and he would call them "unpleasant" – isn't that just a bit strange? And now this. Here. A gunman.'

A silence. Dan looked at her long and hard. 'So you reckon that whoever they are, they are coming for anyone – *anyone who knows too much about the Moche?'*

'Yes. I do.'

The only sound in the room was the buzz of the fridges. Containing the smiling Moche skulls in their soft collars of yellow foam.

20

Mornington Terrace, Camden Town, London

DCI Mark Ibsen was standing in the scruffy beer garden of a large London pub near Regent's Park. It was a frigid afternoon in mid-December; the beer garden was deserted. But he wasn't here to drink, he was here to watch.

Larkham came into the garden with a couple of plastic coffee cups. He handed one over to his boss, then sipped from his own cappuccino.

Ibsen stayed silent, and staring. Larkham followed his superior officer's gaze: which was directed over the wall of the beer garden, to the curtained sash windows of 74B, Delancey Street, a first-floor flat in a long, early Victorian terrace, which diagonally faced this pub across the road, and also the deep railway tracks that led down to Euston Station.

Larkham frowned, and swallowed his coffee. 'What do you think, then, sir? We haven't got a warrant yet.'

'I know.'

'Not that always stopped you in the past.'

Ibsen chuckled; but his mood was as sour and cold as the day. They were tracking down all the people they had seen in the photo with the tattooed man. Most of them had been located: more rich kids, all with the same boring story. *I can't remember that guy. He was probably a friend of Patrick Klemmer. No, I don't know anything else.*

Only a couple of people in the photo were yet to be traced and interviewed. And one of them was Imogen Fitzsimmons, twenty-five years old, an aspiring TV researcher, who lived here in Delancey Street. She was known as a party girl; she was a purposeful socializer. Yet she hadn't been seen for two days. No one knew where she was; she hadn't called in sick to work; she did not have a holiday scheduled and she had missed several professional and social engagements. Her close friends said she was maybe out of town with a secret boyfriend – could *that* be the tattooed man?

Ibsen stamped his feet against the cold, staring at the closed and curtained windows of 74B. 'Larkham. Tell me again about the secret boyfriend. How secret? If he's secret how come her pals all know about him?'

Larkham opened his notebook. 'They don't know for sure. Could be they're just guessing. Her best friend is Lucinda Effingham, also in the photo. We interviewed her this afternoon. Effingham told me that in recent weeks,' Larkham tilted the notebook to read better, '"Imogen had been acting strangely. Going off in the evening, not telling me where. We all reckoned she might be having an affair, she seemed happy, but she was furtive, and evasive. We speculated that she maybe met a married man at work."'

Larkham closed the notebook. Ibsen tasted some of the rapidly cooling coffee, and put the cup down on the beer garden table. 'Neighbours not seen or heard *anything*?'

'Not in two days.'

'Her phones . . .?'

'Going unanswered. Landline and mobile. We *will* have a warrant by tomorrow. The landlord has keys and we can pick them up tomorrow morning.'

DCI Ibsen scowled. 'No. This is wrong. This is giving me the collywobbles, Larkham. I think it's the damn curtains.'

'Sir?'

'They are just too bloody *shut*. Look at them.'

'Too . . . shut . . . sir?'

'Yes, too bloody shut. When you go away for a weekend you don't close curtains with such emphatic exactitude, do you? I think someone is in there, someone who wants to be in the dark.'

'But—'

'Come on – sod the warrant. This is a life-threatening situation. Call for some back-up.'

For the third time that day they asked the downstairs neighbours at 74 to open the external door, profusely apologizing as they did.

Larkham and Ibsen ran up the communal stairs to

the flat on the first floor. 74B. They paused on the communal landing.

'Armed response will be here in a few minutes—'

'I don't think she's going to be armed, Larkham.'

Ibsen stepped back and vigorously kicked at the door; it nearly gave at the first attempt; Larkham kicked it a second time and the door swung open without protest, the lock cleanly snapped.

The flat was black as midnight, made very deliberately dark. And yes, Ibsen could sense a human presence: someone was either here or had been here, very recently. A slightly poisonous fragrance – of something ominous – hung in the stifled air.

Larkham punched the lights on and they gazed around.

The first thing they saw was the blood on the hallway floor, and on the opposite wall. Little seasonings of blood, like sprinkled cinnamon: blood spatter from a serious wound.

'Jesus,' said Larkham.

There was more blood in the living room: it was smeared on a white china mug, daubed in childish fingerprints on a magazine, and on a TV remote. Most bizarre was a mouth-shaped splodge of blood on a mirror at head height; as if someone wearing far too much scarlet lipstick had kissed the glass.

'So,' said Ibsen, 'where is she? The blood is contained. She's in the flat. She must be. She's still here—'

They searched the bathroom and found trailing smears of blood on the shower curtain and dark crimson blood drops in the toilet bowl. The bathroom floor was oddly clean.

The kitchen revealed something worse: a sink covered with blood, as if a small mammal had been crudely slaughtered over the plughole.

Larkham pointed with a pen. 'What is that?'

It was a sliver of flesh, lying on the bottom of the metal sink, surrounded by thick gobbets of blood. Was the flesh human? It was so mangled it was impossible to tell.

Ibsen didn't know whether to feel sick or scared. 'Larkham – the bedroom – she must be in there.'

The bedroom door was at the end of the landing. They pushed against it, but it seemed to be obstructed by a rucked carpet: a second, heavier shove got it open.

Ibsen didn't know what he had expected to find in the bedroom; he didn't care to imagine it. But he certainly didn't expect to find nothing.

Yet there was no one in the bedroom. No body, no suicide victim, nothing. The bedsheets were liberally marked with blood, a white cotton T-shirt was also rusted with drying blood. The room was in chaos: a mirror was smashed, a TV was lying on the carpet, drawers had been flung open and clothing scattered, as if a fetishist had been seeking underwear, but there was no one here, and no one in the bedroom. Lots of blood but no body?

The flat was empty.

'So what happened?' Ibsen gazed at his own crazed reflection in the shattered mirror. 'The guy came here and took her? Why did no one see this? Or hear anything?'

Larkham was opening the floor-to-ceiling wardrobes. The wardrobes were big; the whole flat was large and airy. This was a rich girl, yet another rich kid, with her own flat in a pricey part of town and lots of nice clothes, and she was very probably dead and yet her body had disappeared.

'Sir.'

'What?'

'Jesus . . .' Larkham's voice was uncharacteristically choked. 'She's here, sir.'

Ibsen stiffened his resolve, and came across the room. If Larkham was shocked by the sight of the body, it had to be pretty bad.

It was far worse than pretty bad.

Imogen Fitzsimmons's body was huddled in a corner of her own wardrobe, kneeling on the floor staring at the expensive coats.

In her stiff, blood-caked left hand the girl clutched an old-fashioned cut-throat razor, stained with blood.

The body was clothed: she was wearing tight skinny jeans and white socks. And a black T-shirt with a small Guinness logo. The blackness of the T-shirt made the body look almost normal – from the neck down. It had evidently absorbed a lot of blood but the redness didn't show. And before she died, this young woman had obviously used the razor to progressively mutilate her face.

Ibsen closed his eyes as he felt the vertigo of nausea

hit him. He calmed himself with two deep breaths, then looked again at poor Imogen Fitzsimmons's face.

It was difficult to work out quite what she had done to herself in her final hours, so elaborate was the cutting. She seemed to have sliced off her own lips, which gave the horrible impression that she was grinning fiendishly: like a skull. She had also cut open her nostrils, or at least tried to. The damage was too complex to see which parts of her nose remained intact. The earlobes were missing: drools of blood trailed down each side of her neck.

Most disturbing was the way she had diligently sliced out the flesh of her cheeks, as if she had been trying to skeletonize herself. The skin and flesh had been so drastically cut away that the teeth and the bone were partly visible through the holes in the side of her face. She was half pretty young woman, half bleeding, horrific skull.

Larkham was pale and perspiring. 'How could anyone do that? To themselves?'

It was too much. The two officers gazed at the corpse. Helpless, dwarfed, and mute.

Then, as they stared at the white face of Imogen Fitzsimmons, the girl's head tilted, and she blinked, and a trickle of blood ran from her lipless mouth, as she desperately tried to mumble a word.

She was still alive.

21

The Angel Inn,
Penhill, Yorkshire

It would have been an idyllic setting, Adam thought,
if they hadn't come here to discuss the terminal illness
of Archibald McLintock.

The pub was timbered and earthy; a huge log fire
roared at one end in a baronial hearth, a dog snoozing
before the flames. Two farm-workers sat in a corner,
nursing pints of Theakstons, conversing away the
gloomy winter afternoon. The bar even had a buxom
and giggling maid. She served the farmer, William
Surtees, who returned to their table with a tray.

'You didn't have to buy the drinks.'

Surtees returned his change to the watchpocket of
his mustard-coloured waistcoat. 'Nonsense. Least I
could do. I should learn not to be so – gah
– indiscreet.'

Nina took her pint of Guinness and Adam his half-
pint of orange juice. Surtees sipped at a scotch and

water, then said, 'Now, please, what can I tell you? How can I redress things?'

'Start at the start. How did you know my father?'

'He first came here ten years ago. Researching the Templars. The preceptory is on my land. Most people who come sightseeing just jump the gate and have a gander, but your father very graciously asked permission to visit the site, in person. Subsequently, we became acquainted. I saw him about once a year, sometimes more: he would stop over if he was driving down to London. We're just twenty miles from the A1, though you wouldn't know it. Darkest Yorkshire!'

'He never mentioned you.'

'We weren't boon companions! But definitely friends, in a distant way. I would look forward to seeing his old car pulling into the farm, that Volkswagen you were driving.'

'He gave it to me last year. Bought himself a big shiny new one.'

Surtees nodded. 'Well. That's why I stopped just now, when I saw that car. Hold on, I thought, that's old Archie's car. And of course I knew, from the terrible . . . from the . . . ah . . . from the ah . . . that he couldn't be driving it. Most perplexing. But here we are. The Angel Inn. You know there are often Angel Inns wherever there are Templar sites? Archie told me that.'

Adam interrupted. 'So when did you last see him?'

'July last year, I believe.'

'July 24th?'

'Yes, quite possibly.'

'Is this when . . . ?' Adam paused and looked at Nina; she urged him on with a fierce but subtle nod. 'Is this when he told you he was dying?'

'Yes. He stayed over, at the farm. My wife was away and he and I stayed up late and had a few jars. He liked a drink. And then it just— Well he just confessed. He said he had terminal cancer, had a year or two to live at most. Awful. But he was keeping it quiet. As many do.'

Silence. The dog was staring at Adam, for no reason. Baring its fangs. Surtees elaborated, 'The strange thing was he didn't seem that downcast. He was of course upset. But more for his children, for you, Nina, and . . . Hannah, is it? Working in London?'

'Yes, Hannah.'

'It was your future that concerned him most. The girls. He worried about you, your financial future and suchlike. But other than that he wasn't perhaps as depressed as one might have anticipated. Actually he was quite *enthused*. Gloomy yet enthused. An odd mix.'

'Enthused about what?'

'He said he had some startling new theory. Relating to the Templars. A radical new departure. Wouldn't tell me more. Probably would have gone whoosh right over my head anyway! But, yes, that's what he said, he was intellectually excited by it. Very sad, in retrospect. Did he ever publish anything?'

'Nothing,' said Adam. 'That's one of the reasons we're here. Following up clues: we're trying to find out what he was researching.'

Nina added, 'We're going to Temple Bruer next.'

Surtees grimaced. 'Temple Bruer. Ugh! Went once, can't stand the place. Too spooky, all those legends! Your father would chide me for this, for believing in ghosts!' He paused then asked, 'So, the other reasons?'

'What?'

'You said you had other reasons, to be here?'

Adam stayed quiet, waiting for Nina to answer. This was her call.

Nina said, 'It's the suicide. I still don't believe my dad committed suicide. Even if he was terminally ill. It just, ach, wasn't his style. And he didn't even leave a note! It doesn't make any bloody sense.' She glared at Surtees. 'And I want to prove it. Somehow. Just somehow.'

The waistcoated farmer looked at Nina with an expression of sincere sympathy, but also curiosity. 'I must say Archibald McLintock didn't strike me as the kind of man to take his own life. He was not a bolter, not a coward. He squared up to the world. But if not suicide then what? Perhaps the cancer spread to his brain? Sorry, awful to speculate.'

'Nope. He was lucid and fine at the end. Happy even. As Adam can vouch?'

Adam nodded, unsurely. Nina continued, 'I really do think he was murdered. Or at least intimidated in some way. Forced? Hmm. I don't know.'

Adam winced at the word murdered. It felt a little insane. But the farmer was looking at Nina, his expression anxious, yet knowing. 'Miss McLintock. It may be irrelevant but . . . there is . . . something . . . just possibly . . .'

'What?'

'Something rather peculiar.'

'What?'

'Three weeks ago, I spotted two men in the field by the old preceptory. They were staring at those little stone graves. These chaps seemed so out of place I went to talk to them.'

'Out of place?'

'Their clothes were . . . rather odd. This was November. In the Dales. But they were wearing thin leather jackets. And city shoes! I was walking the dog, but I saw them over the gate, and they struck me as conspicuous, abnormal. So I went to have a chat, say hello as it were.'

'What did they look like?'

'I'd say they were in their thirties, or so. And they were swarthy, if one is still allowed to say that! Italian or Spanish looking, I mean.'

He paused, staring gravely at his glass. 'And, they were hostile, positively menacing.'

'You spoke to them?'

'Just one. I only heard the one man talk. He had an American accent.'

A heartbeat of a silence. Adam leaned close. 'Did the American have tattoos?'

'I can't properly recall. Yes, perhaps. Why do you ask?'

'Doesn't matter.' Nina hurried on. 'What else did they say?'

'Well. This is the sinister bit, this is the element that perhaps you ought to, ah, be aware of. When I said they were on my land, they didn't bat an eye. Instead they asked about your father, very aggressively. Did I know him? Archibald McLintock? What did I know of him? What were his reasons for visiting Penhill?'

'What did you tell them?'

'Nothing! Of course I asked them to get off my land in short order. Lucky I had Alaric with me, big boxer, big three-year-old bitch. So they sauntered to the car, and that was that, really. I watched them drive away. Most peculiar. As I say. I called your father to tell him, naturally – but he seemed . . . rather unsurprised. Perhaps alarmed, but unsurprised.' Surtees sighed. 'That was the very last time we spoke. So. There it is. Not sure if it is relevant. I am afraid I have to go in a minute, it's already dark out there.'

Their drinks were finished. The conversation was finished. Surtees stood, solemnly shook them by the hand, gave his sympathies once more and exited into the dark and the cold.

All the other drinkers had left. It was just Nina and Adam in the bar, and a Christmas tree, fairylights frantically flickering, on and off.

A secret that will get you killed.

Nina was furiously texting something into her phone, her dark head bowed. A sudden, troubling notion unbalanced Adam. 'Nina, have you been updating the Facebook page? And tweeting?'

She looked up. 'Sorry?'

'Are you still updating? Telling everyone where we are and what we're doing?'

Her eyes expressed innocence, then anxiety.

'Yes. Of course. But—?'

'The whole world could be reading,' Adam hissed. 'Anyone at all. We need to get going. Right now.'

22

The American Christian Hospital, Trujillo, Peru

Dr Andrew Laraway, silver-haired, brisk and archly Bostonian, gazed sympathetically at Jessica.

'You have no evidence of mercury poisoning, Miss Silverton.'

Jessica knew this. She'd always known this. Before she even got here she'd known this. But she just wanted to be here. To have a reason, however feeble and phoney, to escape from Zana. But she could not escape her fears, even as she ignored them. She had been pestering Laraway to explain her symptoms, even as she wanted to deny them.

'I understand, Dr Laraway. I'm sorry for wasting your time. Asking all these questions.'

'You're not, Jessica, not at all . . .' He hesitated, for a moment. 'But I must ask – why did you come all the way here? I imagine you are aware that cinnabar is inert. After so long.'

'Yes. I am.'

'So what is it, Jessica? The mild diabetes we discussed when you were last here?'

'No. Yes. No.'

An awkward silence intervened. The doctor sighed, delicately, and looked at her. 'Can I ask you some personal questions, Jessica?'

'Yes . . .'

'You seem to suffer – and this is not meant to be insulting – a notable concern for your health, almost an obsession?' He sat back, tutted at himself. 'No, that's not the *mot juste*. My sincere apologies. You are not hypochondriac, you are clearly very intelligent, determined, hard-working, even bold. Quite admirable. And yet . . . there is a hypersensitivity and a gentle neuroticism. Therefore, and before we go on, I'd like to know more about you and your life.'

This was strange, and a little unnerving. She said, 'All right.'

'Let's start with your life now, your profession? How are things professionally? Is there anything in your career that has troubled you?'

Jessica knew she needed to talk about everything that was happening at Zana. But she didn't want to. So she diverted, as always. 'My last job was in Calcutta.' She tried to seek Laraway's eyes, like a truthful person. 'That was tough. The anthropology of poverty.'

'Please explain?'

'We had to work with . . . these children, infants even. We had to research these poor kids that actually live

176

under the platform at the railway station. This big British imperial railway station, you know. These street kids live there in utter poverty. They were attacked, molested, abused. I met one boy . . .' Jess shook her head. She was being candid now. This memory was brutal. 'He used to sleep under the platform, with a razor blade under his tongue. He showed me how to do it.'

'I don't understand.'

'The razor was to ward off attackers: men, abusers. He was eight years old.'

Laraway sighed. 'The world is too much with us. That's awful.'

'But, actually, you know, it wasn't entirely bleak. There were people helping them, charities. Some of the stories were inspiring. Kids coming from nothing, from this dire poverty, and remaking themselves. The human spirit is really there, everywhere, indomitable. In Calcutta. India. It's the best and the worst of places.'

The doctor leaned forward. 'But what about Peru, Jessica? You never talk about what you are doing here.'

Jess didn't really want to talk about Peru. But maybe, she thought, maybe she needed to talk about it. Maybe the perceptive Dr Laraway was just doing his job, and doing it well, and she needed to be honest.

'There is something.' Jessica inhaled, profoundly, as if she was on the stage of the Met and about to sing an aria: and maybe she was.

It took her ten minutes, fifteen, then twenty. But she told him everything. The Moche, the Muchika, the Museo Casinelli, the amputations, the intruder at Zana.

Slowly and eloquently she recited the entire and recent demonology of her work in Zana.

At the end, for perhaps the only time in their acquaintanceship, Dr Laraway was entirely silenced.

It took him a long time to respond. 'My God, that is quite a narrative. That is indubitably extreme. Anyone would be unsettled by such a sequence of events. Really. Astonishing. And very perturbing. I have never heard of the Moche. And this man McLintock. Goodness.'

'Yes.'

'And you believe the intrusion was linked to that awful explosion last month, here in Trujillo? The Texaco garage?'

'Possibly.'

'What do the police say?'

'Not much, they're looking into it. I reckon they think it is a bit far-fetched. Why should anyone be intent on destroying archaeological knowledge? It is bizarre.'

Another silent hiatus. The manioc trucks were hooting in the streets below. Now Laraway swivelled in his chair, and tried a new tack.

'Very well, then. Now let's talk about your background. I know some of it, but not all. Your father . . . ah . . . died of cancer.'

Jess felt her throat close against the words. This subject. This subject. 'When I was seven. Yes.'

'Your mother is still alive?'

'She lives in Redondo, LA.'

Laraway nodded. Then he picked up, and put down,

a pen. 'You were witness to your father's *decline*? I do not wish to sound glib or presumptuous. And I am not a psychologist. However, you must have been quite traumatized?'

Jess tried not to blink too fast. To give anything away. She wanted the Sechura sea fog to slide in through the windows and fill the room and wreath her, wrap her with phantasmic shrouds, hide her away from this.

'I guess I was . . . Yep. Yes, of course it did. I was very young. My brother was much older. He took it better. Losing a father that young, like I did, I must, it must always affect a child.'

'Especially a daughter, vis-à-vis the father.' Andrew Laraway smiled, distantly. 'I do understand. My own father lost his father when he was just nine. I believe it affected him all his life. When you lose a parent at an untimely age, it is fundamentally destabilizing, you forever have the sensation that even the world beneath your feet cannot be relied upon. My father used to compare it to living in an earthquake zone, the Pacific rim of the emotions. Like here in Peru!' He leaned forward, spoke more quietly. 'Could you describe your father's symptoms? As much as you remember them? I know it might be hard but it would be beneficial.'

Jessica felt the sick dread of something hideous approaching. Faltering, she gave her answer. For several minutes she recalled, as best she could, her father's trembling; perhaps a fit; his anger and fear; his terrible decline at the end.

179

'I was seven, like I say. Maybe I've blocked some of it out, maybe I am totally wrong.'

The next silence was the worst of all.

'No. I don't think you are wrong, Miss Silverton.' Suddenly Andrew Laraway's expression had gone from avuncular concern to something much, much darker. He cleared his throat. 'Jessica. This is very difficult to say. I want you to prepare yourself.'

The panic was rising in her throat.

Laraway spoke very softly, his words like a soothing prayer in a silent chapel. 'I wouldn't normally do this but you have been demanding answers, any answers—'

'Go on!'

'Well. Here it is. The symptoms you describe in your father don't sound like any cancer I know. They sound like Huntington's Disease. And that is . . .' He took a deep breath, and continued. 'That is a very evil way to die. It begins, innocently enough, with a slight loss of coordination, maybe an unsteady gait, and . . . fine trembling in the hands. As the disease advances, the body movements become repetitive and jerky: spasticated; this is accompanied by wasting of the muscles, heart decay, and many other symptoms. Violent episodes, terrible depressions. Then comes the terrible darkness of pure dementia.' Laraway's gaze was unblinking. 'There is, of course, no cure. Moreover, Huntington's Disease is genetic. Many people who might have inherited the disease actively refuse a genetic test to see whether they are carriers. Why? Because it is incurable – therefore they don't want to know. Likewise, some parents keep the knowledge of the disease from their children, so their lives won't be blighted by the fear. As the poet said, "Sufficient to the day is the evil thereof".'

The panic in Jessica's throat had been replaced by an icy cold. She was swallowing coldness. 'You think I am a carrier?'

His smile was bleak, yet empathetic. 'There are certain early indications. You have some symptoms which are otherwise rather contrary. The only way we can know for sure is if you have a genetic test. But that . . . well that is something many people resist.'

Her heart was pounding now.

'Do I have all the symptoms?'

'One of the crucial early presentations is epileptic fits, that's a clinching diagnostic sign. The beginning of the real decline. You've not had any of those?'

'No.'

'Well, then we do not know. As I say, only a genetic test can tell us.' He stood. 'I am so very sorry. One is never sure whether to impart a frightening and potentially false diagnosis like this . . . However, you seemed distressed and confused, and very much wanting to know. And now it is up to you to decide. You might also consider calling your mother, and asking for the truth.'

He was reaching out a hand. After delivering this possible death sentence, he was just reaching out a hand.

Jessica stood, and shook his hand.

'Jess, you must call me any time you like, you must feel free to come here whenever.'

'Thank you.'

She walked to the door, looking at her feet as she did so. Was she stumbling? She was not stumbling. She was dazed, that was all.

At the door she turned; she had to ask one more question. 'Dr Laraway, if you were me, would you have the test?'

His smile was sadly sincere. 'I really don't know, Jessica, I really don't know. And that's the truth.'

Closing the door behind her, she walked past the receptionist and took the elevator to the ground floor.

Outside, the thrumming, grimy, fervent and slummy city seemed the same as ever. Bewilderingly normal and scruffy; and yet everything had changed. Jessica stared at her cellphone. She could maybe call her mother right now and get the truth: did her father have that disease? Had she been lied to, to protect her from the fear? If they had lied to her, the lie was no longer working: she had the fear. She was too scared to even call.

Instead, and for a reason she could not fathom in herself, Jessica took a taxi from the centre of town to the Texaco garage, and the Museo Casinelli. Or where they used to be.

Climbing out of the taxi, she stared. She was glad she had come here. The charred and ruined buildings were a fittingly melancholy sight: a temporary wooden fence had been erected around the shell of the building, but it was rickety and already broken. She could see, through the gaps, the black spars of burned concrete, the spoil heaps of ash and dust.

At first she tried not to think of poor Pablo, down there, consumed in the fire. But she couldn't resist: maybe she wanted to think of him. Maybe that was a good way to go. Burned to death, a few minutes of pain. Better than months and years of decline and terror, then madness and agony.

Jessica felt sick, right down to her lungs, sick and somehow guilty. Maybe she had brought this on herself. Perhaps she had dug up something horrible, an ancient evil, the god of death and killing.

She had woken the sleeping gods of the Moche, and now they would not be dismissed.

23

Highgate, London

The angel was sleeping and quiet.

Ibsen gazed, perplexed, at the marble angel lying on the marble grave. It was an odd concept, even in a graveyard sculpture. Did Victorians actually believe that angels slept? Or maybe it was dead? Could angels die?

'Mark?'

'Sorry.' He wiped the last crumbs of all-day-breakfast sandwich from his lips, with a Prêt A Manger napkin. 'Just thinking, love. Sorry.'

His wife Jenny smoothed her nurse's uniform; she had a small tray of takeaway salad on her knees. 'You know I've only got thirty minutes.'

'For lunch?'

'We're busy, Mark! Short-staffed in Maternity, there are a couple of girls with flu . . .'

'The bloody Whittington Hospital is always bloody busy.' Ibsen tutted. 'They work you too bloody hard.

You're too bloody good for this job. You've got a bloody first-class degree. Bloody hell.'

'But I *enjoy* it.' She laughed. Dropping her plastic fork in her plastic tray, she stroked him under his chin and gently kissed his cheek, then murmured, slyly, yet shyly, 'Besides, Detective Chief Inspector. You always told me you liked the uniform.'

As ever, his younger wife's solicitations melted Ibsen, inside him, somewhere very important. For a second they sat together, staring silently across the mossed old statuary of the empty cemetery, at the stooped and wintry willows that loomed over eighteenth-century tombs, like tall but servile chamberlains admiring a royal baby in a crib.

Mark and Jenny occasionally came here to eat lunch, whenever Ibsen was free and in north London, near Jenny's workplace. It was more for her than for him. DCI Ibsen always found Highgate Cemetery unsettling even as his wife found it obscurely soothing.

Today, on a cold December afternoon, the ancient graveyard was at its most melancholy, but at least it suited their subject. Suicide.

'How come *you* suddenly have all day, anyway?'

'We're waiting on a lead, been waiting for two days. I thought I'd take a break and see my lovely, overworked wife.'

'A lead? You mean you got something from that poor, poor girl? Imogen . . . Fitzsomething?'

'Yes.'

'But Mark, I thought she died.'

'She did, Jen. The blood loss was horrific, stage 4 hypovolemia – a coma – she drifted in and out but the haemorrhaging was too profuse.'

'So?'

'She wrote an address, when she was lucid, she wrote down an address for us, just before she died. And a taxi driver has reported he took her there, three days before her suicide.'

'And you think it's where this guy lives, the bloke with the tattoos?'

Ibsen nodded, flourished his mobile phone. 'Larkham's checking it out now. I may have to go any moment.'

Jenny stood up. 'Well come on, then, let's be quick. I can explain *everything* you need to know about suicide clusters. In about twenty minutes.'

Ibsen grabbed her empty salad tray, and his voided sandwich packet, and dumped them in a bin. Then they walked the paths between the crumbled and mouldering graves. He sneaked a glance at his phone. Nothing yet.

'OK. Suicide clusters work by social contagion, often spread through the media, or the internet. Social networks. Sometimes there is a celebrity suicide, widely reported, which is then copied by young, impression-able people.'

'That doesn't sound like our situation. There's no rap artist who cut his own head off.'

'No. Which is why I reckon you are better looking at mass suicides. Which are different.'

She walked on and he followed, attentive.

186

'There have actually been quite a few large-scale suicides in history. Masada in ancient Israel is a famous example. Okinawa in Japan in World War Two's another. One of the worst was the suicide of the women of Souli, in Greece: they threw their children over the precipice, and then jumped themselves, to avoid capture by the Ottomans.'

They turned left, past the Egyptian Avenue, with its Luxorlike pillars, its pharaonically slanted arches. The silence here, at the centre of the cemetery, was extraordinary.

'But modern-day mass suicides are usually related to some kind of cult, or cultic religion. Led by a charismatic leader, some clever evil man with a hold over them. Think of Heaven's Gate. Or the Order of the Solar Temple. The most famous, naturally, was the People's Temple in the Jonestown incident.'

'I remember that one – the audiotape—'

'Yes. A whole community who willingly killed themselves, hundreds of them. They literally drank poisoned Kool-Aid, at the behest of some ghastly tyrant. And so they all died. Awful.'

Ibsen recalled the famous images: the bodies sprawled on the damp Guyanan grass afterwards, women and men and children, side by side by side, as if they were sleeping peacefully, as if they had just lain down in orderly rows to kip, and yet they were dead. So, yes, Jenny was right: suicide could be induced en masse. In an intense religious setting. But what did that actually mean to this particular case? With individuals? He shook his head. 'I dunno,

187

sweetheart. These victims in London – they're not teens copying some doomy, wrist-slitting guitarist, but they're not desperate god-botherers in the jungle, either. And they're not all in one place at one time. They are smart, rich, young, very well-educated Londoners, with everything to live for, and no reason to die.'

Jenny stepped over a snaking root of ivy. 'Well. Exactly. I think it's a cult with something else too, some other element.'

'What?'

'Hypnosis for a start. Some kind of sexualized hypnosis. This explains your victims' profiles. Psychologists know that the most easy people to hypnotize tend to be the most intelligent.'

The crows barked in the skeletonized trees.

'So you're saying you can hypnotize people into killing themselves?'

'Why not? If you combine hypnosis with sex and religion, some kind of death cult, a sophisticated sex-and-death cult, then you have the beginnings of an explanation, a sort of upper-class Jonestown – isn't that possible? You did say these people were all going to sex and swingers' clubs, right?'

'Yes.' He mused. 'Yes. That is true. So there maybe is a particular sex club where they got into some stranger, darker, ritualized stuff? Some cultic trance.'

The idea was good.

Jenny tugged him down the darker of two paths; Ibsen pondered as he walked.

This theory was certainly plausible. In which case they

needed to look for more links between the victims. They hadn't found a common denominator of this sort, yet – a specific sex club they all went to – but something like this had to exist. Somewhere, out there, was maybe a ghastly dungeon in a rich man's home, a drawing room decorated with skulls. It was absurd yet it made a ghoulish and awful sense.

A rotting angel stared at them from the enormous tomb of Julius Beer. A great monument to someone entirely forgotten.

Jenny said, 'I also think these suicides are, in some way, autoerotic. The pain itself is the pleasure. The pain is the cause of the pleasure.'

'How?'

'Think of it this way. We get lots of people in Casualty who are cutters, self-harmers. They cut themselves on the arm, they slice their fingers, gouge themselves. Usually women. Why do they do it? Because they are depressed, exhibitionist, self-haters, masochistic, blah-de-blah, but also because, on a purely mechanical level, they enjoy the pain. They are addicted to the pleasurable release from self-inflicted pain, the endorphins.'

Another crow heckled the dead from somewhere in the birches and oaks, then flapped further into the chaos of ivy green. The large portals of the dynastic tombs gawped at Ibsen. Like open mouths. Shocked.

She squeezed his hand. 'Moreover, some psychologists believe that we can actually be physically aroused by death itself. We find it erotically pleasurable to die. Relatedly, the French call an orgasm *le petit mort*, the little death. Shelley called the climax the death which lovers love.'

Ibsen murmured, 'Hanged men are said to orgasm. Hmm. At the moment of asphyxiation.' He shook his head, 'It's prison folklore. I've often wondered if there was any truth in it . . . but I don't know . . .'

They were right at the end of the path, heading back towards daylight: the trees and shrubs and menacing tombs were yielding to street noise. Ibsen felt an urgent need to jog, to get the heck out of here.

'This also fits with the idea that you are dealing with a cult, or a secret religion,' Jenny added. 'Because many religions in the past have played upon the eros–pain nexus.'

'Once more in English?'

'Think of the Catholics, think of Saint Theresa ecstatically pierced by arrows. Or some Shia Muslims, flaying themselves – that could be sexual. Or even the Nazis. The skulls of the SS. They certainly sexualized and fetishized pain and death, the smart black uniforms, the *totenkopf*.'

'Christ! You're saying we're dealing with some kinky Nazi-Catholic-Muslim sex cult. In central London?'

'I'm just giving you ideas!' She smiled, and looked at her watch. 'Anyway. Time's up. Emergency C-sections won't wait, not even for handsome detectives.'

'But—'

She was already kissing him, and already walking to the cemetery gate. He followed, still asking questions; she waved her hand impatiently.

190

'I'm just guessing, Mark! But I've got to go. Bye, sweetheart – don't forget to get some milk!'

She waved goodbye, and was gone. Running down Highgate Hill. Sweet and young and happy. His lovely and intelligent wife. Ibsen gazed at the dark blue of her anorak until she was entirely lost to view.

Then he made his slow way past the venerable redbrick Georgian houses to Highgate Tube, which was so confusingly far from Highgate Village.

His phone trilled. He took the call. Larkham.

'Antonio Ritter!'

'What?'

Detective Sergeant Larkham repeated, rushing his words in his excitement,

'Tony Ritter. The man with the tatts. S'his name, sir. He lives at the address, near the Barbican, we've seen him going in. American. Half Puerto Rican. In and out of prison. FBI record. Smart. Links to the Camorra.'

'I'm on my way. Text me the details. Meet you there. Now.'

'Sir.'

Ibsen snapped shut the call. Even as he felt the excitement rise, he felt the doubts. A simple career criminal? That didn't quite fit. What was a gangster doing in the middle of this? But his wife's ideas were all too chillingly believable. Some kind of suicide cult.

This meant there could be – there must be – many more victims out there. Waiting to die. At any moment.

24

Temple Bruer, Lincoln Heath

'"Temple Bruer grew up in the middle of the vast Lincoln Heath, which spread out south of the city. The heath would have always been sparsely populated, and in the Templars' time would have been especially desolate and forbidding."'

'Unlike now,' said Adam, 'when it is so amazingly inviting. Jesus, this road is useless.'

Nina put her father's book down and gazed across the flatness. Everything was flat, monotonous, and bleak. The morning snow had turned to heavy sleet – which thrashed the windscreen, almost defeating the wipers' effortful thump.

'Could that be it?'

Adam followed her gesturing hand. As far as he could tell, she was pointing at rain-smeared glass, blank grey sky, and endless fields of grey grass. And nothing else.

'What?'

'There. That building. Over there.'

Adam slowed the car, entirely blocking the narrow country lane. It didn't seem to matter. Theirs was probably the only vehicle for miles. He hoped it was the only vehicle for miles: therefore, no one was pursuing them. And now he saw.

'Ah . . . Yes.'

He could just make out the low darkness of some buildings, half-concealed behind a copse of stark trees. He drove on very, very slowly. The mud churned; pebbles rattled against the chassis; the wheels slid and groaned.

'A sign. Adam.'

He gazed up; she was right. A tiny and splintered wooden sign, virtually hidden by blackthorns, showed the way.

Temple Bruer. Ancient Monument. 1¾ miles.

Adam wrenched the car left and they patrolled the little side-lane. He could see patches of snow left in the ragged fields, and hazel and holly trees, sheared by the easterlies. 'So . . . We know your dad spent a whole day here . . . it must be important. Right?'

'He goes on about the loneliness.' Nina scanned the lines quickly. 'Apparently, in the eighteenth century this was the one part of the London-to-York route which stagecoach owners couldn't insure. Too many highwaymen. Too many legends of witches and ghosts.'

Her face was looking his way: white and uncertain in the gloom of the car. Then she turned, and scanned the rainy horizon. Adam could make out a tower now. Barns and a kind of farmhouse – and a squat grey tower.

'Listen to this. "The Reverend Dr G Oliver, vicar of the nearby village of Scopwick, undertook the first historical survey of the surviving tower of Temple Bruer preceptory."'

'And?'

'"Oliver reported finding charred bones and bodies encased in walls, evidence of murder and infanticide. He proposed that these remains had belonged to victims of severe Templar law enforcement."'

'Seriously?'

'Quite serious. My dad actually quotes Oliver's survey. Verbatim. "Some of these vaults were appropriated to uses that it is revolting to allude to. In one of them a niche or cell was discovered, which had been carefully walled up; and within it the skeleton of a man, who appears to have died in a sitting posture, for his head and arms were found hanging between the legs. Another skeleton of an aged man was found in these dungeons; his body seems to have been thrown down without order or decency, for he lay doubled up. And in the fore part of his skull were two holes which had evidently been produced by violence."'

'Christ.'

They were just a hundred yards away now; and the sense of remoteness was deepening. Just a few miles from a main road, yet they were lost in England's deep and darkening winter.

'Wait.' Nina turned a page. 'There's more. "In a second corner of these vaults, many indications of burning exist: cinders mixed with human skulls and bones. This horrible cavern has also been closed up with masonry."' She read on, silently, then half-closed the book, 'Look, you can park here. By the tree.'

She was right. The road, which was now little better than a mudded track, opened out into a kind of farmyard which surrounded the ancient Templar tower. A light was already on inside the farmhouse. They climbed warily from the car. The sleet had abated, yet the very air was soaked.

'Are we just allowed to park here? Is this private property?'

'I don't think so,' she said, shivering, and pulling up the hood of her anorak. 'Dad's guide always indicates when a site is private, doesn't say that here. I guess the farm must date from the Templar times, but the buildings have changed? Ach. Imagine living in a house with this . . . thing in your back garden. Staring at the vaults where they walled up people. Children entombed alive. Spookfest.'

The same thought had occurred to Adam. The cold surly horror of staring at this tower every morning, knowing what the vicar, back in 1841, had discovered. Horrible.

The tower was guarded by a pitiful little railing, barely a foot high. They walked up the stoop of grey and weathered stone steps, and pressed the only door. It swung open on smooth hinges.

The interior was incisively cold, but not as cold as the heath. The light was pitiful; sad winter light filtered by an arched, eight-hundred-year-old leaded window. The interior of the tower was just a single large, tall, cold and echoey stone room.

'No light switches?'

'Nope.' Nina consulted the book, using the torch from her mobile phone to read.

He recalled her using the same flashlight when they had broken into her father's apartment. He shuddered at the memory of the intruder: they needed to hurry. Someone could be driving down the lane right now, parking next to their car, walking to the tower.

'He says there are apotropaic signs everywhere. Apotropaic graffiti.'

'What the hell are they?'

'Ritual protection symbols, used since ancient times by all cultures to ward off evil. "Some of the apotropaic graffiti in the tower of Temple Bruer dates from the fourteenth century, indicating that the place had a sinister reputation from the time of the Templars' demise. The carvings were continuously inflicted on the fabric for many centuries thereafter. Clearly, the local peasantry must have felt a certain desperation to rid this place of its devilish connotations. Perhaps they knew of the tormented skeletons concealed within."' Nina paused, then concluded. 'This bit . . . is odd. This is not like my dad. To say this bit here.' She quoted, '"Even today the place retains a definite ambience, which might lead the most materialist of scholars to feel a frisson of doubt. Certainly, this is no place to linger."'

'Too true. Look. Down here.' Adam, using his own mobile phone light, picked out some scratched graffiti on a wall. *Suffer the child that comes unto me.*

Nina examined it. 'That's new, there's no weathering. Local teenagers probably. This stuff, over here, is the old stuff.'

Carved ferociously into the next slant of wall was a series of ancient symbols. Runic and bizarre; deeply cut triangles and inverted letters. Adam stared: the cuts in the stone were severe, yet weathered: chamfered by time.

'Here's the wee cat.' She had moved away in the murk. 'Dad said there was a cat, a gargoyle of a cat. It's just here. And this must be the tomb, the stone effigy, in the corner.'

He was hardly listening, transfixed by the graffiti. The backwards R? The inverted A? And now he realized he could hear . . . howling.

Fierce howling.

'Nina?'

The howling echoed around the stone chamber. It was unearthly, and bloodfreezing. A choir of suffering and lamenting, from somewhere just outside. Who – or what – was producing that direful noise? Adam felt a rush of juvenile, even infantile, dread: he didn't want to open the door.

He opened the door. They stared out. The deathly, late-afternoon light was just good enough for them to see.

Foxhounds.

A man was striding down the farmyard, a riding crop in his hand; he was repetitively slapping the whip against high leather boots; and before him was a river of canine tongues and ears and tails. It was a hunting pack, being exercised; the dogs were barking and yawling, raising that horrible, humanlike whimpering. The steam rose from the torrent of dogs as they lashed into the cold, snowmelty fields, yearning to kill.

The huntsman turned, for a second, as he reached the gate and looked directly at Nina and Adam. His face was an oval of blur in the winter gloom, his expression indiscernible, and odd. What did he want? Did he know something? Adam could feel the sordid clench of fear, a dragging attachment. The terror of going to Alicia's flat, after she died. Seeing all of her things; the stuff she left behind.

'London. Come on! There's no point hanging about in this horrible place. The next stop is the Temple Church in London. We can stay with my sister. You drive. You're quicker than me. Please.'

Once inside the car, Nina flung the book on the back seat. 'Let's just get out of here!'

The ignition kicked, Adam flicked on the lights and they reversed at speed, as if they were fleeing the darkness heading their way, trying to escape night itself.

They approached the whirring traffic of the main road, where car lights shone mistily through the fogs of rain. The desolation of the Heath seemed almost welcoming now, after the creeping dreads of Temple Bruer.

'Evil!' Nina said, with great emphasis. 'It's evil.'

'Sorry?'

'I think that's what Dad found, Adam. Evil. Something evil. That's what he discovered about the Templars, an evil secret, and someone paid him to do it. That's why he had all that money.'

Adam said nothing, because a further thought had just occurred to him. Whoever was the dark villain in this piece, the man with the tattoos, the murderer, the man guarding or seeking the secret that gets you killed – that same person might be the one who had stolen Archie McLintock's notebooks.

Which meant that even though Nina had stopped alerting the world via the internet, anyone who had the notebooks would still know their route: because they were following the exact same route Archie McLintock took and noted, eighteen months previously, through the Templar sites of Western Europe. Every move that he and Nina made was therefore pitifully predictable.

The cold rain angrily lashed the window. Adam changed gear, and accelerated past a vegetable lorry, speeding through the darkness on the A456 to London. Racing across the drizzly and dismal heathland road, with all its legends of witches, and highwaymen, and ghosts.

25

Outskirts of Chiclayo, north Peru

'So tell me more. Please.'

Steve Venturi was on the phone. Jessica was in the cab of the TUMP Chevy; Larry was driving them the last few miles into Chiclayo.

The signal dropped for a few moments, then Venturi's languidly intellectual, southern Californian drawl returned. 'Well, I've written it up – and emailed a PDF. Do you want to hear the summary?'

'Yes. Yes please.'

'OK. "Described below are three possible cases of foot amputation in skeletal remains associated with the Moche culture of north Peru. The three skeletons belonged to young male and female adults, and date from the eighth-century AD . . ."'

'But—'

'Wait, Jess. Here's the lox in the bagel. "Each case exhibits non-functional tibio-talar joints with proliferative bone occupying the normal joint space. The robusticity of the tibiae and fibulae suggest renewed weight-bearing and mobility following recovery. There is no evidence of pathology in any of the skeletons which might imply a surgical need for amputation. The osteological evidence is therefore consistent with details shown in Moche ceramic depictions of footless individuals."'

Jessica kept the phone pressed tightly to her ear. They were stuck in the seething and seedy traffic of peripheral Chiclayo. Blood-red graffiti, on a low white-washed wall behind Larry, shouted *Ni Democracia! Ni Dictadura!* 'Let me get this right, Steve. That means, in plain English, they cut off their own feet while they were alive, when they were perfectly healthy.'

'Yup.'

'Because they wanted to! They just wanted to? What's wrong with them? It's like Jay said, this is just the sickest society ever. Who the heck are we digging up?'

Steve Venturi laughed, long and laconic. 'The mad and terrible Moche. No?'

'Sure . . . I know, but . . . Jeez Denise.'

'OK, Jessica, I gotta go. Any more of these scientific coups and you'll be after my job!'

The call ended. Larry turned the steering wheel. 'So, tell me, what did he say? Give me the Full Venturi.'

Jess explained the confirmation of her suspicions: the amputations were done when the 'victim' was alive, some time before death, years before death

201

even. Voluntary amputations: perhaps as some kind of spiritual payment, some sacrifice, to the unknown Moche god.

The first, virulent suburbs of Chiclayo loomed on either side of the scruffy road – battered adobe shacks, hovels of concrete, a sullen lavanderia.

'So they really . . .' He scanned the busy road ahead, and swerved past a motokar with a dead black goat strapped to the back. 'They really did it! Just like you predicted, uh-huh?'

'Yep.'

'I can't believe it. It's just incredible.' Larry smoothed a worried hand over his jaw.

'He's emailing a PDF. You can see it if you like.'

'No, no. I believe you.'

They passed a row of uninhabited concrete houses, one of them used as a garbage depot: a great green pile of plastic Sprite bottles was heaped within. The next corner revealed a dirt road that dwindled into a cloud of grimy haze; open concrete sewers full of trash divided the busted hovels from the road.

It was a scene of apocalyptic dereliction, a scene from Iraq just after the war: shattered suburbs of desolate beige, with helpless brown wide-eyed kids staring in mystification at a world so totally destroyed by the grown-ups. The only difference was here there had been no war.

The traffic slowed and surged, and slowed; she thought of her father, being tested. In hospital. The blood test. Jessica had already accepted her own denial, she knew she wasn't going to get the test, she wasn't even going to call her mother. She was going to live her life until she couldn't live it any more, whatever was really wrong with her. Anything else was intolerable: the knowledge of certain and appalling death was worse than the fear of her ignorance. Her conscious decision not to know actually gave her an odd elation, a kind of liberation. Self-acceptance.

Larry grabbed a slug of Inca Kola from a big yellow plastic bottle in the gear well. 'You hear about Jay?'

'No?'

'Says he has been having nightmares. Nightmares about the Moche god, coming to cut off his head!'

'Except of course technically, the Moche cut off their hands, as well, and their feet. As we now know.'

Larry's sigh was derisive, yet resigned. 'That's the damn crux, isn't it? They did it to themselves, voluntarily. I have no conceptual way of understanding this—'

'The Aztecs self-mutilated.'

Larry accelerated into a traffic gap, between two green and red motokars. 'OK, yeah sure, they spiked their penises with cactus thorns. They drew blood from their ear lobes. They scarred themselves. And lots of cultures scarify, Jessica. But this crazy-ass Moche shit is on a whole new level – cutting off your own healthy hands? To impress? To please the gods? Why? And then there's the sex, the kinky stuff. Sex with skeletons? Sodomizing each other during horrible ritual murder?

It's like – like they must have been getting off on it. All the torture.'

'Clearly. But the eroticism is a leitmotif throughout the culture, Larry – victims and perpetrators are all involved, all sexualized. We have the evidence of the murals. The aroused naked prisoners, brothers and sons, brothers and . . . and fathers . . .'

'So they flay them and torture them and tie them up, their own sons and brothers, and then they slowly bleed them to death, and then someone drinks the blood from a special cup, and as all this is going on someone else thinks, hey, I know, let's have anal sex in the same room at the same time just in case it gets a bit goddamn boring.'

'And all this while the rest of the people are singing and dancing and watching, yep, it is incredibly bizarre.'

'And then they bring in the pumas. They have sex with pumas.'

'We don't know the puma sex was consensual.'

'Ah, no. Muy stupido.' Larry's laugh was wild and bitter. 'Might have been puma rape, right? Now they've really crossed the line. Sodomizing old corpses, cool; drinking your brother's blood, that's fine and dandy; but puma rape? Heck. Someone call PETA!'

The pick-up took a turning, at speed. They were closer to the centre of the city now. The buildings fled past. A red Nova Scotia bank, a white concrete evangelical church, then a statue to a fat, forgotten general in an anonymous and dusty plaza jammed with imprisoned traffic.

Larry sighed. 'It's just beyond – beyond anything . . . It's just . . . way out there.'

'Yep. And Dan still doesn't quite buy it, he's still resistant. Emotionally. He doesn't believe it really happened, and if it happened – well then he wants to blame it on El Niño. He can't actually come out and say the obvious: that that this is just what the Moche did. Stuff they liked to do. Chop off their own hands, or feet, or noses. Mutilate themselves.'

A pink San German bus was passing them on the right, stuffed to the broken windows with poor tired people: weary fish-workers and bag-clutching house-wives staring soulfully at the gringos in the Chevrolet.

'So you fault him for this?'

'Actually, yes, I do.'

'Why? I thought you two were in love.'

There was a long silence. Jessica blushed, fiercely. 'Is it that obvious?'

Larry laughed. 'Yes. It's that obvious. Everyone in Zana knows about you and the boss, babe. You're not very good at sneaking around, you two. But don't worry!' He laughed again. 'We're all happy for you. You make a nice couple! And Dan is a very decent man and he was kinda lonely before you came along . . . So it's a good thing. Don't fret.'

She shrugged, half-embarrassed, and yet half-pleased. 'Don't know what to say. But I want you to know it doesn't affect the science, for either of us. That's separate, we're still professionals. And Dan and I disagree on the Moche.'

'How?'

'I think he is hampered by political correctness. Like so many academics of his generation. Take cannibalism.'

'If you insist.'

'These days, if you believed most senior anthropologists and archaeologists, cannibalism never happened. Never ever, or hardly ever, and certainly not when poor brown people are being discussed.'

'Right.'

'Yet we know for sure that cannibalism has been, through history, a pretty widespread phenomenon. Dozens of cultures have recorded it, from the Anasazi to the Sumatrans to the Maori. Fiji. New Guinea. The Amazon. Scientists have even found bones, with saw marks on them, next to human middens with evidence of human flesh digested by human alimentary canals. And yet the *bien pensant* ethnologists still say – oh no, it's racist, how can you accuse these poor people of such horrible things, perhaps a bear came in and used a knife?'

They were much closer now. The streets were definitely older and narrower, low-slung Spanish colonial buildings painted dirty orange or red, flickered past.

'OK, Jess. But look at it the other way. Accusations of cannibalism were also, like, used as a neat way to disparage non-Europeans, right? So the questioning of cannibalism is a justified reaction to that, to the racist jokes about boiled missionaries, decades of horrible eugenics, fuzzy-wuzzies with bones through the noses.'

'But it's bad science. Science should be science. Uninfluenced by politics.'

'I agree. But maybe not everyone is as ruthlessly clear-headed and ambitious as you.' Larry was half-smiling, obviously teasing. 'And Jessica, you gotta recall the emotional context.'

'How?'

'Dan has been studying the Moche for a decade. It's like they are his family. The Moche are his people. Now someone comes along . . .'

'Me?'

'Yes. His smart and ambitious young girlfriend. And you say uh-oh sorry, Dad was a sex-killer and Mom liked threesomes with goats. He's offended on behalf of his family. The Moche. So just . . . go easy, Jess. You're vindicated. Be magnanimous.'

'All right.' Jess permitted herself a nervous laugh.

'You had any thoughts about the gunman?' Larry asked quietly. 'Dan won't even talk about it.'

'Been trying to not think about myself, if I'm honest.'

'Sure. But, didn't you say you got some scuttle on this dude? This . . . McLintock guy?'

'He's a Scottish historian. Or he was.'

'Killed himself recently?'

'Yes.'

'Coincidence? The suicide?'

Jess shook her head. 'I've no idea. Perhaps. There's a cached Facebook page about it. Deleted but still readable. It's strange. But the thing is . . . He was a historian of medieval Europe. It's difficult to see a connection between him and the Moche in eighth-century Peru. Fifteen thousand miles away.' She was one kilometre away from her destination. 'Yet that is definitely who the gunman named. Archie McLintock. A dead Scottish medievalist. Who recently drove into a wall. About the same time someone killed Pablo.'

A silence in the cabin. The squeal of brakes. Larry was pulling over. 'All very sinister. I might ask for a raise if there are gonna be evil assassins. Anyway. We're here, babe. The *supermercado*.'

Jess alighted from the Chevy pick-up, smiling. 'Thanks for the lift, Larry.'

Larry lifted a dismissive hand. 'Hey, the company was good. We all need to stick together. Buzz me on the cell when you've finished shopping and I'll pick you up later. Stay safe.'

The Chevy pulled out. Jessica watched it depart into the dust and mêlée. Then she turned and waited; then glanced at the burbling noise of the shadowy market across the square from the modern supermercardo.

That's where she was really headed; she didn't want the Roski supermarket: that was a ruse. Jess felt a need to keep her investigations to herself right now. She wanted the witches' market, inside the town market. She wanted to ask about ulluchu, and she reckoned that maybe, just maybe, some of the people here, descendants of the Moche themselves, might know something about it. The blood of the unknown Moche god.

Immediately she crossed into the darkness, she was lost in the bustle and the shouting and the odours. Boiling tripes in cauldrons. Piles of yams and dirty potatoes and lurid red peppers and secondhand mannequins with gouged-out eyes wearing terrible nylon clothes. Headless, goosepimpled chickens sprawled on blood-smeared counters. Women in bowler hats sat at rough wooden benches eating skewered beef hearts, *anticuchos*, under a saccharine portrait of Jesus in a luminous toga. Here was the corner which led to the witches' market proper. She paused.

A baby was lying on the floor of the market. Just lying there, face up, in nylon swaddling. Staring quietly at the ceiling, all alone, with damp concrete beneath him. Peruvians often did this, especially native women – just left babies on the ground to go off to do their shopping. Probably the baby was fine. Yet the sight was reflexively painful for a Westerner: it broke every taboo, abandoning a child on the dirty floor of a crowded market, where it could be crushed or run over or kicked.

The least she could do was put something under the baby, protect it somehow. She had to do something. Hurrying across the dirty concrete, she rushed up to the blank-faced child and as she did she wondered if something was wrong. The baby's face, the way it wasn't doing anything, it was just a doll, was it just a doll? And then she saw blackness.

She was grabbed and hooded, roughly. Musty sweat and horror flared her nostrils, she kicked out and screamed; heard a suppressed curse, voices raised. The hood tightened like a noose around her neck, her arms were lashed. Jess was being kidnapped.

26

Barbican, City of London

'Everything is in position? Everyone?'

Ibsen was sitting nervously in the front seat of his Met car, listening to his police radio, hanging from a hook on the dash.

A radioed voice came over, loud and distinct: DS Larkham sitting in another car two hundred metres down Whitecross Street.

'Yes, sir. We have his flat on surveillance. Kilo 1 and Kilo 2 are right outside.'

'Armed response at the ready?'

'Yes.'

'And the door, you're sure it's the only one?'

'Yes, sir. Checked a dozen times. If he comes out we will see him.'

Ibsen sat back, half-satisfied, and watched some noisy London schoolkids swinging satchels at each other, ambling in that loud, sweary, litter-chucking,

211

end-of-school way that was so typical and so persist-
ently annoying to anyone over eighteen. The air was
freezing outside, bitterly icy, and the sky was that
pure, expectant whiteness that precedes a heavy
snowfall.

He regarded these lanky, lairy teenagers, thinking
about his own children: ten and eleven years old. Would
they soon end up like this, surly teenagers, scattering
swear words and empty crisp packets?

The radio crackled.

'Sir!'

'Yes?'

'He's coming now, he's coming out right now.'

'On his own?'

'Yes.'

'OK, so, you know what we discussed. Send me
shots *and* a video, immediately. Follow him, but don't
do anything else, until I've given the go-ahead.'

Ibsen estimated his own pulse rate had reached the
115 mark. Extremely alert, but nothing dangerous. Not
the 175 where you make a terrible decision. With an
armed response team.

He listened to nothing, saw a single flake of snow settle
on the windscreen. Just one, then two. And then his
computer pinged and he found the communication.

It was the video, shot by surveillance officer Kilo 1
two minutes ago. The quality was excellent, the zoom
precise, the face clearly pictured – the same face as in
all the photos Ibsen had seen over the last few urgent
hours. This was their man: Tony Ritter.

212

'Team K,' he said firmly and clearly, into his radio. 'You are good to go. Surveil and pursue. Follow but do not apprehend.'

The DCI motioned to his driver: go that way, very slowly.

Their car was a good three hundred yards behind the surveillance officers, who were on foot. Their duet of reports buzzed over Ibsen's radio.

'Suspect X walking quickly up Goswell Road.'

'Turning right, into Clerkenwell.'

'Walking fast, very fast.'

'I can see him stopping, looking at something in his hand—'

Ibsen intervened. 'What? What's in his hand?'

A defiant pause. What was going on? Ibsen cursed the lack of time to get a proper surveillance team, to call in more officers, to put a GPS on Ritter's person, somehow; this was fly-by-your-seat police work, with a potentially very dangerous suspect, involved in some brutal 'suicides' that might not turn out to be suicides at all.

'Samsung Zaf.'

'What?'

'He's looking into a mobile, sir. Think he's reading a map. He's just standing by a bus stop on Clerkenwell Road.'

The pause returned. A third and fourth flake of snow settled on the windscreen; then more. Ibsen churned, mentally, what little else they knew of Antonio Ritter. He was a serious Californian villain, father Texan, mother Puerto Rican. He was linked to organized crime in Europe and elsewhere, people trafficking in particular. He had several convictions for violence. And he'd gone to ground recently after a stint in an LA jail.

What about those prison terms? Ritter had done some hard time in some nasty Californian clinks. Is this where he had got the tattoos? Did this suicide sex cult originate in some gruesome Californian jail? Full of Latinos and Yardies and Koreans, each with their lethal gang? And their own special tattoo?

The snow was whirling, thickening, settling.

Ibsen mused. The tatts could be gang colours of some kind.

'He's moving again – fast. Walking briskly. Like he suddenly remembered where he's going.'

'North up Clerkenwell.'

'He's almost running, sir.'

'Yes, he's running'

'Jesus, the snow!'

It was now coming thick and hard, almost horizontal, turning into a blizzard. A man could barely see more than five yards. A man could easily get lost.

Urgently, Ibsen pressed the speak button on his radio. 'Team K. Can you see him? Kilo 1, do you have visual contact?

'Yes, sir.'

'Kilo 2?

Silence.

'Kilo 2?

'I think so sir . . . Yes, I can see him now. I think he's doubling back, he's changed his mind—'

'Maybe he's going for his motor, because of the weather. Larkham, get ready to follow in your car.'

Kilo 2 interrupted. 'No. He's heading down Goswell Road, not turning left—' The signal crackled into lifelessness for a moment then, 'Sir, I reckon he's taking the Tube. Barbican Underground.'

'Get on it! Christ. Kilo 1 and 2! Don't let him get on that Tube without you!'

Ibsen slapped the dashboard in anger, his frustration intense. But for now, Ibsen just had to sit it out. They were down in the Tube, so he had radio silence, and no information. What was going on down there? Had they arrested him, lost him; had he spotted them on the Tube train; had he turned on the officers, shooting a gun, spraying a carriage, killing a kid with a ricocheted bullet? The silence was like waiting for a returning space mission to go through the atmosphere. Would anyone be alive at the end?

Ten minutes. Fifteen. Eighteen.

They had an armed response team ready, down the Pentonville Road. But that was a bit late if the guy was already culling infants on the Northern Line.

An efficient little crackle, like a throat clearing, brought the radio to life. 'He's up. We're out. On the surface.' It was Kilo 1. 'We're at the Angel, sir. Angel Tube.'

Just four stops away. Ibsen signalled to his driver. 'OK, Kilo 1, Kilo 2, keep following him. We're here for the whole ride.'

'Sir. Walking up Upper Street.'

Kilo 2 kicked in, 'He's stopped, sir. By that weird low building . . .'

'Antique arcade.' A more authoritative voice, crackled through. I'm just parked across Upper Street, sir. He's stepping inside—'

Ibsen shot back, 'Larkham? You're there? How did you know?'

'Took a guess, sir, followed the Northern Line overground north.'

'Good man! But I know that place.'

'Yes?'

'If he goes in there we can lose him, a warren of old gaffs, all those lanes outside!'

'He's gone in.'

Ibsen barked, 'Kilo 1 follow.'

'I'm inside, can't see him – wait . . .' His pulse rate was now 125, 130.

'Kilo 1? Can you see him?'

Silence.

'Kilo 2? Can you see him?

Silence.

'Kilo 1? Fuck sake, Kilo 2?

A breathless voice. 'He's running, sir.'

Running?'

'He's sort of running, and – and these little alleys are filled with shoppers – all the snow – it's chaos. Maybe he knows we're here . . .' The policeman was panting. 'I can just see him, the snow is so heavy, Sir . . . is that . . . wait . . . I can't . . .'

216

They were going to lose him.

Ibsen waited for half a second. He waited for another half a second, Pulse maybe 140, 145, 150.

Kilo 1: 'I've lost him. No visual contact. Repeat, no visual contact.'

'Kilo 2?'

'Me too. Lost him. Sorry, sir. The bloody snow . . .'

'Fuck fuck fuck fuck fuck.'

Ibsen slapped the dash again. He had one last hope. His brilliant junior, the one man he could rely on, his go-to guy for not utterly fucking things up all the fucking time.

'Larkham?'

'Same here, sir. I got a glimpse. Then he just— You should see the snow, you can hardly see your own . . .'

Ibsen let the bitterness seep into his conscience for another half a second, then switched into a more professional gear. 'So he's gone to ground. But he's somewhere around. Who saw him last, and where, precisely?'

Kilo 1 answered: the antique parade; Kilo 2 agreed. Then Larkham said, 'Think it was me who saw him last. He was jogging up Islington Green. Just a glimpse, through the snow. I could see his head, then nothing.'

Ibsen closed his eyes for a second. Repressing his anger and guilt. 'Just stay there, patrol discreetly, and keep your eyes open, we might just get lucky again.'

Ibsen knew they weren't going to get lucky. The suspect's last movements were all too indicative of a professional criminal who was aware he was being followed. He watched the delicate star-clusters of

217

snow fall and melt on his windscreen, in prolificity and profusion; like lemmings, killing themselves on his glass, and melting into nothing. Suicidal snow.

The driver pierced the silence, jolting Ibsen from his reverie.

'Are you all right, sir?'

'I'm fine. Bloody furious, but otherwise fine. So we lost him. We still have a lead. He must have had a reason to come here in the first place What is it? Why has he come to Islington?

27

Temple, London

From Temple Station they walked briskly up a steep narrow street lined with venerable buildings, made somehow more scholarly – and picturesque – by their new, white, lawyerly wigs of snow.

They were at the Temple Church, an eight-hundred-year-old survivor. It looked impossibly beautiful and quaint, the arched windows and golden buttresses surrounded by Christmas Carolly scenes of snowbound gardens, and liveried beadles, and eighteenth-century doors decorated with green wreaths of berried holly.

Nina opened her rucksack with shivering hands and recited: '"The London Temple was one of the three administrative centres of the entire Order, along with the Paris Temple and their headquarters in Jerusalem. All the Templars' British wealth was held here, in the London Preceptory, in a treasury so renowned for security that the English king stored the Crown Jewels herein."'

Adam said nothing. A face was peering at him from behind a large sash window. The curtain fell.

Nina went on. '"At the time of the Templars' fall from power, this reputation for hidden wealth gave rise to the rumour that the London Temple was the storehouse for the Templars' "secret treasure". Over the years this notorious treasure has been variously reckoned as the Ark of the Covenant, the True Cross, the Turin Shroud and the Holy Grail. In truth, there was no such secret treasure; these absurd rumours of secret wealth rose arose simply because the Templars were the first bankers of Europe, and their vaults were filled with noble loot, held as surety, or deposited for safekeeping."' She finished, and shrugged.

Adam sighed. 'Your father was a sceptic. We know. The question is: how did he go from all that to believing that there really was a deep Templar secret?'

A secret that gets you killed? Adam baulked at saying it. Instead he looked at the exterior of the church. He had no need of a guidebook to tell him about this. From research on earlier articles, from simple sightseeing as a young Aussie in London, he knew that most of the exterior of the famous church was twentieth-century work, cleverly restored following the dreadful damage of the Blitz. Only the west porch remained from Templar days. So they could be pretty sure Archie McLintock didn't come here to admire the exterior.

Which left one choice.

They entered the church, through the low side door. The building was empty and hushed. Slender candles

220

twinkled; the blonde wooden pews were empty; winter daylight striated the floor. The old church was beautiful and sad, and vacuous. There was no sense of mystery here, no sepulchral clue, no air of intrigue that might imply what Professor McLintock had found. It was an echoey cenotaph, laid with effigies.

Frustrated, he strode around the circular nave with its grotesque gargoyles. Here was a man screaming, with his ear being bitten by a creature. Why?

Nina was crouching beside a gravestone, reading quietly from her father's book. Adam took some photos: of the delicate black marble pillars, then the elegant circular colonnading, then the effigy of William Marshall, Earl of Pembroke, laid out in full battle-kit, chainmailed, a sword in his hand. Ready to fight violently for Christ, even now.

'This bit dates right back to 1200,' said Nina, standing and gesturing at the clean golden arches, the chevrons of wood in the ceiling.

'Still looks new,' said Adam.

It did look new. Too new. As if it had been recently restored. Adam thought about the evil ambience of Temple Bruer. What linked these two places? Somewhere very old and dirty and pungent with atmosphere, and somewhere cleaned and spruce and empty.

Adam stepped to the side where there was a table stacked with helpful pamphlets, advertising opportunities for charity work in West Africa, and schedules of festive carols in the Wren Churches. He heard voices. Nina was talking to someone a gowned man, the verger, or the vicar maybe. Adam knew nothing about church hierarchies. The man had a fusty, middle-aged, churchly air and a black gown over his shoulders. Walking across, Adam extended a hand, just as Nina's conversation with the man dwindled to silence.

'Adam Blackwood. The *Guardian*.' It was a lie, he'd been sacked; but he didn't care. He wanted information, and saying you were a professional seeker of information just sped things up.

The man had strange eyes, as if he was wearing tinted contact lenses. A hint of livid blue. The word *restored* was a continuous bass organ note in Adam's mind, waiting for the treble, the tune, the harmony, as the man swivelled.

'Name's Baldwin. I'm the churchwarden. I was explaining to your friend that I never met her father. The name doesn't even ring a bell. Sorry.' His accent was northern. Perhaps Yorkshire.

Restored?

'She tells me he were a great expert on the Templars! But that he recently . . . passed beyond?'

Nina was trying again. 'You're sure you never met him ever? He came here last year, two days in a row.' They knew this because of receipts from Caffe Nero, on Holborn.

The churchwarden gazed at Nina as if she was mad.

'Miss McLintock, I don't meet every tourist, even famous ones! We have so many visitors. Anyhow, I wasn't here last summer: no one was. We were restoring.'

The lock yielded at last; Adam turned the mental key. 'Do you mean the whole church was closed?'

'Yes. Exactly.' The man's smile was sincere and bored. 'The whole church were locked for, ooh, eighteen months. We allowed no visitors. Not a soul. It were the biggest restoration we'd had since the Blitz. Cost millions, but the Corporation were very generous, the large legal companies, and so forth . . .'

'All visitors?'

'Yes! We had an iron rule. Anyway, I must be getting on . . . Tempus bloody fugit. If you want to make donation, the offertory box is near t'exit.'

The gown swished and the churchwarden departed through an interior door. Nina looked with mystification at Adam.

'I don't understand. So Dad didn't come here. Why come here, twice, if you can't get inside? Did he go somewhere else?'

'The exterior!' Adam grabbed her hand. 'It must be. We know he came to the Temple, but if he couldn't get in – that means he must have been looking at the exterior. And there is only one bit of the exterior left—'

The excitement was mutual. Not pausing, they rushed outside to the West Porch: a large, dark door, filigreed with ironwork and iron studs; and surrounding it an intricate stone jamb, with a semicircular arch, semicircles within semicircles, like ripples of stone. Decorated with peculiar and significant sculptures.

The sculptures were all of Green Men. Dozens and dozens of Green Men, faces of the pagan past, wreathed in stone ivy and tendrils, grinning at him. Adam yelled with excitement. 'This is it. Must be it. This is it! This is what he came to see. This. It's our first real clue, Nina, this is it: Green Men, just like those at Rosslyn. So we know he was on to something, and we know it definitely is linked to Rosslyn. He wasn't mad, he wasn't joking; he really was unlocking a puzzle.'

She smiled – anxiously and worriedly – but she smiled. 'Well done. Come on, let's go see my sister. She's been doing her own research; we need to compare.'

They ran through the alleys out on to High Holborn and Nina hailed a taxi. 'Thank you,' she nodded at the taxi driver, as they climbed in. 'Thornhill Crescent. In Islington.'

28

Mercado de las Brujas, Chiclayo, north Peru

The condor stared at her. It was dead, and hanging upside down. Next to it was the dried foetus of a llama, its eyeball poached and screaming in the skinless carcase.

Jess spat the taste of the rough nylon hood from her mouth. The hood now lay crumpled on the dirty floor; it had been whipped away by a lustrously dark, luridly tattooed man, with a necklace of shark's teeth and an Abercrombie & Fitch sweatshirt. The man was barefoot and muttering and smoking a spliff of dark jungle tobacco, and tightening the bonds that strapped Jess to the chair on which she had been forced to sit.

She knew immediately where she had been taken: because they hadn't gone far, and the environs were distinctive. Evidently, she had been dragged into the witches' market, a corner of the town market where shamans and *curanderos* and *brujas* came from many miles around, to trade potions and spells and malevolent juju. Ironically, the Mercado de las Brujas was where she had been headed. But now she was here as a hostage.

Jess struggled. *'¿Qué estoy haciendo aquí?'* What am I doing here?

The man ignored her, and just kept muttering. *'Ñqupaykunaq yuyay champi . . .'*

These words were Quechua. The man in the little stall, shielded from the rest of the market by plastic sheets and curtains, was speaking Quechua. Probably he didn't even understand Spanish. Nonetheless she tried again. *'¿Por qué? ¿Por qué me has secuestrado?'* Why have you kidnapped me?

It was pointless. She heard a small voice behind her, in the gloom. Jess caught a glimpse of other dark faces in the background; staring at her and whispering.

The man in the sweatshirt smelled of condor. And dung. And rainforest. And sex. As if he hadn't washed in several weeks. It was a primal smell of jungle and mountain, Quechua and Inca. He was obviously a curandero, one of the mountain shamans, down from his Andean village to do his weekend business, hawking talismans and voodoo dolls to the local wizards.

Jess tried to pacify her terrors, to rationalize them. She knew these people: the real Peruvians, the country-folk and mountain-dwellers, the descendants of the Moche and the Chavin and the Cham Cham who believed and practised the ancient magic. They were not usually killers. If anything, they were all too inert and passive, ruefully resigned to the terrible forces of nature – drought and El Niño, white men and dictatorships.

But her rationalizations only got her so far. And then they gave out entirely. Jess was terrified.

And now something was happening. The curandero in the Abercrombie sweats had reached into a smelly plastic tank – to pull out a large wriggling lizard, almost a foot long.

The lizard writhed and yawned in his hand. With the air of someone who had done this many times before, the man took a lazy puff on his foul-smelling cigarette, shifted the butt in his mouth, exhaled pungent smoke through clenched yellow teeth, then stuck a knife in the animal. A pitiful, wheezing cry emanated from it. The curandero lifted up the lizard, which was now bleeding copiously from the half-gutted belly.

Hamuy kayman llank anaykita ruway!

The tone was abrupt: it sounded as if he was ordering someone into action. A boy stepped nervously from the shadows, and reached around Jess. She flinched at his touch. The feel of his grimy infant fingers on her tee shirt, under her denim jacket, was chillingly unpleasant. The boy lifted up her T-shirt, exposing her naked stomach.

The curandero hoisted the thrashing lizard over her stomach and dribbled copious warm blood from its riven gut so that the blood fell on her bare skin, like drops of melting red wax from a candle. The urge to clean it off *immediately* was unbearable.

227

'*Para, por favor. ¿Qué estás haciendo?*' Stop. Stop. What are you doing?

No reply. The shaman had his eyes closed. He circled the dying, writhing lizard, sprinkling its hot reptilian blood on Jess's arms and thighs now. Then he vigorously squeezed and twisted the creature as if he was squeezing the last drops from a wet rag, flicking tiny drops of darker blood all over her breasts and her belly. At last he flung the dead reptile to the dirty floor.

'Stop . . .'

Her voice was weak with fear. The curandero bent down and blew cigarette smoke over her chest and face, talking and muttering as he did, blowing more smoke on the lizard-blood pooled in her navel; then more hot smoke in her face, chanting and smoking, and blowing, his breath soiled with the smell of green soup.

Her attention was diverted to her own legs: Jess gazed down in horror.

The little boy was doing something *down there*. Rolling up her jeans, to expose her ankles. She gazed in urgent terror as he reached up and dipped his fingers in the blood on her stomach; then used it to draw lines around her ankles, like a surgeon marking the lines of incision.

Were they going to cut off her feet at the ankles?

Jessica screamed as loud as she was able.

The curandero sighed, took a fetid cloth and rammed it in her mouth. Jessica screamed, but silently now, muffled and helpless. The curandero's boy had finished drawing blood circles on both her ankles. Straining against her bonds, Jess tried to cough out the cloth, but it was no good. They really were going to do it: they were going to cut off her feet, like the mad and terrible Moche.

Lifting a tobacco-stained finger, the curandero ordered the boy back into the shadows. Then he took up the long vicious knife he had used to gut the lizard.

Jessica rocked violently back on the chair, trying to fling herself away, without success. She was stuck here, in this terrible shack, stuck with the painted caiman skulls, the meek little statues of Jesus, the bowls of raw coca paste.

She felt the first touch of the blade on her ankles. A shy and tentative gesture, explorational. Jessica closed her eyes and waited for the driving pain as the metal cut into her skin.

And then her bones.

29

Thornhill Crescent, Islington, London

Hannah McLintock scrolled through the page on her laptop. The room was getting dark, as afternoon declined into twilight; her blonde Celtic hair was illuminated by the glow of the screen. Adam sat back and watched as the two sisters leaned nearer to the computer on the kitchen table.

The older sister spoke. 'So the porch at the church was covered with these Green Men? Like tiny gargoyles?'

Adam nodded. 'Yes, and there were about fifty of them. And it's the only chunk of the ancient Temple left, on the exterior. We know your father went there to look at the church. But he couldn't get inside. So *that's what he must have come to see.* The Green Men in the porch. There are, of course, Green Men at Rosslyn too.'

Hannah nodded, distracted. And scrolled down her screen a little more. Then she sat back, with an air of *et voilà!* 'Here it is, in *Wikipedia*. The Green Man.'

'Read it out,' suggested Adam.

Hannah obliged. As she did Adam glanced around the dimly-lit kitchen. The fridge was large and brushed and steel. Fashionable cookbooks filled a shelf, next to tall glass vessels full of obscure pasta. The selection of olive oils was intense. A glamorous party invitation was stuck by magnets to the fridge door.

It was all very eloquent, and it said: this is a nice prosperous house. The home of a young, attractive, privileged metropolitan London couple, a couple doing well, a couple maybe thinking of having children.

And where did Nina fit into all this? The unmarried unattached younger daughter, with her drinking and her dark, dark hair.

Adam could discern the dynamic between the sisters. There was a strong bond there, but also perhaps a tiny bit of resentment. Nina was the prettier one: she was certainly the more damaged and neurotic, the more fragile.

Hannah was attractive but more stolid, more sensible perhaps; yet she had already made a slight and apparently jesting remark about Nina being 'Dad's favourite'. Adam had also noticed a definite bickering underlying their mutual sadness at their father's death, Hannah apparently feeling that their father's final illness, the cancer he had kept quiet, entirely explained his suicide.

The older sister finished her recitative from *Wikipedia*. 'So we know the Green Man is a common architectural motif. Originally pagan. We know that they represent, probably, a wild man of the woods, a fertility figure,

231

or even a pre-Christian heathen god like Woden. Commonly they have leaves for hair and beards, and sometimes shoots growing from their mouths, eyes, and noses. They are found—' she checked the screen, '—across Europe. They date from the eleventh century to the twentieth. Some of the earliest can be seen in Templar sites in the Holy Land.'

Nina sat back on the kitchen stool. 'What does that tell us? Cube root of fuck all.'

Adam gazed at the dark black rectangle of kitchen window, smeared with snowmelt. Who was out there, pursuing them? The serious anxiety was actually a flavour in his mouth: as if he was sucking a key. Sour and metallic. And the winter night was so dark.

'Can we have a light on?'

'Sorry,' Hannah said. 'I got carried away, I didn't realize, yes of course.' Her accent was almost perfectly English, the Scottishness long since departed. There was a stark contrast with Nina: blonde and brunette, English and Scottish. But he could also sense the sincere love between the sisters *as well*: their hugs and kisses on meeting had been unabashed.

Soft bright light flooded the kitchen; Adam gazed at a photo perched on top of a breadmaker: a recent holiday photo of Hannah and her boyfriend with palm trees behind them. He was as blonde as her.

'Where is . . . ah . . .'

Hannah followed his gaze to the photo. 'My fiancé? Nick? In Paris working, but he's back tomorrow.'

Adam felt the barometer of risk twitching further

232

towards danger. The fiancé was away. So he was the only man in the house. If anything *happened* he would have to defend them. *Follow the notebooks to the daughter.*

But this was absurd; he chided himself; what was really going to 'happen'? They were in an agreeable house in an agreeable Georgian suburb of north London, a fashionable district with delis and restaurants and gastropubs serving Portuguese custard tarts. The idea of brutal violence erupting into this nice kitchen with its different kinds of balsamic vinegar was purely surreal.

Yet so was the notion of an academic being killed because of what he discovered about the Templars.

Nina was using Hannah's laptop now, pointing at the screen, and going through it all again. 'So. The Templars were obsessed with Green Men. And Dad was aware of this. But what did the Green Man mean to the Templars?'

Adam gave the obvious answer. 'That they worshipped something pagan, pre-Christian? Or at least elements of this? Maybe *that* is the big secret?'

'Something like that,' Nina agreed.

Hannah was making coffee. She voiced her thoughts with her back to them as she filled the cafetière with grounds. 'The Templars were accused, of course, of worshipping the devil, in their trials, weren't they?'

'Yes. Baphomet,' Nina said. 'Baphomet. That was the name of the god they were meant to idolize. A head. A grotesque wee head. Wasn't it? I'll have mine black, Han.'

'Wait,' said Adam. He took out his notebook. 'Let's write down *everything* that links the Templars to pagan worship, in a proper list.' He clicked his pen. As he did so, a shadow passed across the window. Adam stared – alarmed. But it was just people coming home from work, momentarily blocking the streetlight.

The cafetière filled, Hannah turned back. 'Wasn't there something about weird rituals in their initiations?'

Adam wrote a sentence in his notebook. 'We know the Templar rites were deeply secret. They were held at midnight, or before dawn, which got people intrigued. And your dad mentioned the initiation rites at Rosslyn.'

Nina looked at Adam. 'So. What did happen? At these rites?'

'We don't know for certain. People have been that asking since the Templars emerged. The King of France was so obsessed with finding out that he actually installed a sleeper agent in the Templars, who was meant to report back. But the man went native and refused to tell the King. Which was one reason the French King was so enraged by the Order he finally took vengeance on them. That's the legend anyway. Could be garbage.'

Hannah plunged the cafetière. The dark grounds roiled and agitated in the coffee liquor, like tiny trapped living creatures. 'What about . . . the gay sex thing?'

Adam answered again. 'Yes. That's also . . . curious. We know the Templars were accused of committing strange homosexual acts during their rituals. Novice knights supposedly had to kiss the "base of the spine" of the superior knight. They were accused of conducting sexually perverse rituals, almost a Black Mass, drinking wine to get drunk, then . . . well, fellating each other. Anal sex. Gay orgies basically.'

'So they were gay, so what?' Nina accepted her coffee from her sister. 'Lots of these monastic orders were gay – young men sworn to chastity, living in dormitories in a desert, it would be amazing if they weren't a bit that way.'

Adam agreed. 'The sexual angle is interesting, but it's not necessarily or even remotely *pagan*. And, besides, many other heretical sects were accused of homosexuality and blasphemy, quite unjustly. It was a standard way of demonizing unwanted communities. What else?'

'Cats.' Nina said. 'The Templars were alleged to worship a cat. There is a cat gargoyle at Temple Bruer.'

Adam wrote. 'What else?'

'What about all the blasphemy? Go back to the blasphemy.' Nina sipped her coffee. Adam wrote down the word *blasphemy*. 'You say it's crap but they confessed, didn't they? The violent gay knights? At the trials? To spitting on the cross, urinating on it, stamping on it.'

Hannah interrupted. 'But those confessions were extracted under torture. They are wholly unreliable, Nina. They had their feet roasted over fires; one poor Templar came to the courts with the bones of his feet in a bag, the bones had fallen out, he was tortured so horribly. You would confess to anything in that situation, wouldn't you?'

'Dad used to talk about the tortures. The pity and the horror.' Nina screwed her mouth up in that peculiar way which Adam had come to understand meant she was repressing some deep, conflicted emotion.

A stagey and anxious silence stifled the kitchen. The sisters were staring into their Met Museum coffee mugs, Thinking About Dad. Adam looked around, prickling with nerves. The windows were so *dark*. Was that someone staring into the house? He yearned for curtains. Why did upper-middle-class English people have an aversion to curtains on the ground floor?

'What about your father?' said Adam, just to break the awkward moment. 'Did he ever talk about anything pagan connected with the Templars?'

'Not much,' Hannah answered. She revolved her mug clockwise, then anticlockwise, staring into the black, black coffee. 'Maybe the head worship. The adoration of this Baphomet idea. He found that intriguing.'

A jarring thought occurred, Adam voiced it. 'And what about that horrible piece of pottery we saw, in your dad's study? The one he brought back from South America?'

It was Hannah who responded. 'I looked into that. It's from Peru, from a culture called the Moche.'

'And they were?'

She hesitated. 'Some kind of strange pre-Inca civilization, a very bloodthirsty people. Sixth century, I think . . . But we know Dad went to Peru from his receipts, so there might be a link.'

'It fits with the Green Men,' Nina said. 'Yes. A pagan

head? A pagan deity? Then that explains the evil skeletons in Temple Bruer! No? Sacrificial victims? Adam, this must be it – the Templars worshipped a pagan deity: they were involved with some violent, evil, pagan religion, for real. It must be this. But what is so terrible about this revelation, that even today . . .' She stopped.

It is so terrible that it gets you killed was written in chilling silver letters in the very air between them.

'It seems an awful long way. From medieval Europe to Peru in the sixth century,' Adam said dubiously.

'Sure,' Nina answered, 'but if my dad saw a link there must be a link. Otherwise why did all these people steal his notebooks, then come back and burgle his flat afterwards? They wanted what he found!'

'And they still want it,' Adam said. 'They still want it now.'

The atmosphere was as dark as the windows outside. Hannah spoke, over-brightly. 'Does anyone want supper? I think I've got some sea bass. No pud I'm afraid . . .'

Nina smiled, sadly. 'I'd love some, Han.'

The doorbell rang.

Hannah got up. 'That'll be the delivery guy, Ocado to the rescue. Thought they'd never make it through the snow.'

Adam watched Hannah walk to the door. He drank some more coffee. Hannah opened the front door to the darkness outside.

30

Canonbury Square, Islington, London

He was thwarted. For almost the first time in his police career, DCI Mark Ibsen felt utterly defeated, and also at fault. Why had he even agreed to this tail, when he'd known the risks? There was always the likelihood that the suspect would limbo neatly under the radar – slip their feeble knot. And so it had turned out.

Morosely, he gazed out of the Met Police Lexus at the snowbound Georgian terraces of Canonbury Square. They were parked in a part of old London made more beautiful by the flurries and eider feathers of snow, now settling contentedly on every lateral surface.

'Maybe we'll get a visual, sir,' said Larkham from behind the wheel, sounding entirely unconvinced. Their suspect had absconded with disdainful ease.

'Yes,' said Ibsen. 'We'll get a visual when we find the next body, with its fucking head hacked off, pretending to be a suicide.'

This was harsh and overdone. Ibsen didn't care. A freezing cold December night had fallen on his hopes. He picked up his iPad. He'd been doing this on and off for the last hour as they sat here, helpless, waiting for Kilo team to pick up the scent of Antonio Ritter, who was somewhere out there, in Islington, doing whatever it was he did. *Persuading people to cut their own limbs off.*

The image of the girl in the wardrobe returned to him, uninvited. The pure horror. He needed to work. Deftly, Ibsen Googled the words 'death cult'. A number of rock bands topped the screen. Southern Death Cult. Monolith Death Cult. Horizon Death Cult. Lots and lots of death cult metal bands. This was useless. He turned and asked his junior a question.

'Larkham. Do you ever think of jumping under a train?'

The answering silence was amplified by the muffling snow. Eventually Larkham shrugged and said, 'Not really, no. Except when I am changing my ninety-eighth nappy of the day. Why d'you ask?'

'I'm just thinking about suicide – as a concept. I wonder if we are all capable of it at some time or other.'

A solitary pedestrian scrunched past the parked police car. The man was dressed as for an Arctic walk to a remote Inuit village.

Larkham spoke up again: 'Actually, sir, there was this one . . .' He scratched his nose: the universal body language of uncertainty.

'Go on?'

'I remember, when I was a kid, my grandfather

239

had this old well in his back garden. It was very deep and mysterious, and kind of scary. We used to drop stones and coins down it when we were kids, me and my sisters, listening for the plop when it hit the water. Took ages. And I used to have nightmares about that scary old well. About falling down it and not being able to get back up. And yet . . . sometimes I think a bit of me *wanted* to fall down the well. Just to know what it was like, how horrible it would be, never able to get back up. I guess that may be the same thing? Some kind of internal death wish? Bit ghoulish!'

Ibsen gazed at his driver. 'Yes,' His voice was low. 'Yes, it is. A bit ghoulish. But interesting.'

The car was quiet. London was quiet. Quietened by the ward sister of snow, hushing everyone, tucking them all up in stiff white quilts, then turning off the lights.

He glanced at his radio, as if looking at it would make it crackle into life. Nothing. Kilo team were drawing a blank. Larkham was lost out there, in the icy wastes of failed police work, trudging towards the North Pole of pointlessness.

He switched on his iPad again. But Larkham was sighing impatiently. Ibsen glanced across.

'Everything OK?'

'I could slaughter a coffee.'

'So why not go and get a coffee?'

'You always get to the heart of the matter, sir. That's why I respect you so much.'

'Ditto your sarcasm, Larkham. I'll have an espresso.'

Larkham laughed, and climbed out; the car door slammed shut behind him. Ibsen bent to his iPad and typed 'Islington cult'. Of course he drew a zero. 'Islington murders' was equally unfruitful, not least because Detective Chief Inspector Ibsen already knew all the murders in Islington.

'Islington suicides' seemed just as unproductive. But Ibsen read the citations anyway. There were a lot of suicides. An old lady in a care home. A kid with some pills. Not rich, just a kid. Then a Scottish academic with Islington relatives, who drove into a wall.

This Scottish guy even had a Facebook page, cached; the page itself had been deleted. Ibsen scanned the contents and one of the photos struck him, but he wasn't sure why. It was just a photo. And so he moved on, and glanced at some more examples. And then he stopped.

The sudden, retroactive realization *impaled* Ibsen.

There was something about that photo. Something he had seen, subliminally maybe. What was it? Quickly he paged back through his history to the cached Facebook page and read the text carefully.

Archibald McLintock had driven himself into a wall. The daughters thought it was not suicide. They had set up the Facebook page. They were appealing for information. Their father was an elderly but distinguished historian who had no cause to *blah blah*.

Now Ibsen went to the Contacts. One daughter was called Hannah McLintock. She was an 'economist, living in Islington'. The Facebook page gave no other info, and no phone numbers, just an email address. So what *was* it about this photo that had so struck him?

With a flick of two fingers he enlarged the photo. It showed the suicide victim, the late Archibald McLintock, sitting in some kind of study. It was a portrait of a scholar in his work room: behind him were shelves and cases full of old books, in front of him was a big, handsome desk. It was a very posed photo, presumably a publicity shot, for the jacket cover of the guy's own history book, maybe.

Ibsen looked closer. What was that? On the desk?

Another protraction of two fingers enlarged the photo further.

There. Sitting on the desk, was a very strange pot. The strange, old-looking pot showed a man in a loin-cloth kneeling at an altar.

Both of his feet had been cut off.

Ibsen swore out loud, cursing himself for allowing Larkham to wander off. This was it; *this was it.* They needed to get going now, right this minute, not wait around as they did with Imogen Fitzsimmons. And they needed to go in hard, mob-handed, and with armed response: Ritter was very dangerous.

But finding Hannah McLintock could take hours.

31

Thornhill Crescent, Islington, London

Adam sensed the danger immediately. He leapt from his stool and ran to the door; just as the dark, leather-coated man kicked it with a boot-heel.

Adam's fist connected with a chin, satisfyingly; the man reeled back; Adam punched again – but this time his fist missed, and instead the hard butt of a pistol cracked Adam's head, sending him spinning. And then, with great speed, the intruder twirled the gun and pressed it hard into Adam's stomach. Ready to shoot. Adam froze.

'Good move, *mate*, very sensible. Back off.' The man spoke, in an American accent. He eyed Nina in the semi-dark. 'Same goes for you. *Back the fuck off, bitch.*' His gaze switched between them. 'So we're all here. Very good. Both of the girls, both of the McLintocks. And you, the brawling Aussie. Adam Blackwood, right? My name's Ritter. Not that it's going to help you now, *mate*. Get over there, join the girls. And put all your fucking cellphones on the counter. Right now. Or,' he angled the muzzle of the gun at Hannah, 'I will put my gun in her cunt. And shoot.'

The phones clattered on to the counter.

Ritter briskly filled a sink with water, and chucked the phones in the liquid. Then he commanded, 'Upstairs. Let's have ourselves a little downtime. A meeting. So we can share. Condemned Fuckers Anonymous. Hi, I'm Adam and I'm about to die. *Hello, Adam. Hello, Tony.*'

His pistol pursued them up the stairs into a green painted sitting room. Leather couches, some not-too-abstract art.

'Typical. No proper fucking chairs. The fucking English bourgeoisie.' Ritter sighed.

Adam watched, waiting for a moment to fight, it could be the last chance. Ritter's thirty-something face was darkish. And he was big. A fleck of foam silvered at the corner of his mouth as if he had the lips of a rambling coke addict. But he did not seem high; eager, alert and bright-eyed, but not high. He seemed wary, wised up, lean, ruthless.

Ritter produced three sets of handcuffs from a pocket of his capacious leather coat. Hannah, Adam and Nina backed into the corner. Adam edged further, as discreetly as he could, to the window.

'Don't scream out of the window. Or I will hurt your friends. Very, very badly.'

Hannah was close to crying, her face a crumpling mask of failing courage. Folding on itself, into tears.

Nina was impressively blank. Adam admired her display of courage, even as he realized what appalling danger they were in: this man wouldn't have let his name slip unless he aimed to kill them all, tonight. Indeed, Ritter was *taunting* them: evidently enjoying the horror.

Ritter spat: 'Right. All of you, sit there. In front of the radiator. Now. In a nice row like dogs at a show.'

They did as they were told. Adam squirmed, and furiously calculated the chances. A desperate rugby tackle might just unbalance the man. Ritter was big, at least six foot, but not as big as Adam. He looked fit, but not real Aussie Rules fit, like Adam. It could be done. Adam could take him, if only he could get near. One more time. He'd got that first punch in, he could do it again. Better this time.

But Ritter was blithe and clever in his long leather coat, he kept his distance, and his gun cocked, and his eyes on his captives, as he went from window to window, locking them and closing the curtains.

Ritter kicked out the landline phone sockets and stamped on them, trashing the phonelines. With the mobiles drowned, they were now entirely incommunicado.

Now he turned to them. 'I need to keep you safe. And quiet. So we can *talk*.' He tossed the handcuffs in Adam's direction. 'Put these on the girls. Chain them to the heater. Now.'

Adam did as he was instructed. The radiator was uncomfortably hot: he was already sweating. His moist hands slipped as he snapped the cuffs first over Nina, on one side, and then over Hannah, on the other side. Perhaps he would get a chance – one last opportunity to tackle this guy – before he himself was secured.

He got no chance. Ritter came over fast and locked Adam, likewise, to the firm ironwork of the radiator pipes. Now they were all shackled. Ritter extracted a cylindrical black silencer from an inside pocket and screwed it on to the muzzle of his pistol. 'The Tundra Gemtech Suppressor,' he said, almost murmuring. 'As they say, it does not render the shooter inaudible, so much as invisible.' A flash of a grin. 'Reckon we're ready.'

Traffic passed outside, oblivious to the hideous drama herein.

'Did you kill my father?' Nina asked.

Ritter laughed. Tall in his long leather jacket. Looking like a renegade Nazi, a Spanish Nazi with a Texan accent. 'You still think that shit? Your dad killed himself. He was dying.' Another laugh. 'Or do you really think he had found something amazing?' Ritter stopped closer to Nina. 'Mmm? Would he do all that and then just top himself? Without even a note to say thanks for the motherfucking haggis?'

He slapped her gently across the face, twice, like a cat cuffing a ball of wool. 'Tell me, Nina McLintock. I researched you. You're the fucked-up little sister, right? You tried to kill yourself didn't you? Last year? So why are you so fucking surprised that your dear old dad had the same gene?' The gun stroked Nina's white cheek. Then the muzzle edged to her neck, her pale sweating neck. Pointing down to the incipient curve of her white breasts under her sweat-dampened shirt.

'I've got a knife. Cut you up a bit. Shall we have some fun? Think Adam likes you.'

'Leave her alone,' said Adam, involuntarily. 'I'll fucking . . . I'll fucking . . .'

Ritter scoffed. 'What? Pull the radiator outta the wall, Aussie hero? If you raise your voice I will chop off Nina's ear. And feed it to the roaches under the fridge.'

He stood, looking at Nina, then at Hannah. 'Need to put the damn heat on. In the meantime I will gag you.'

Three gags were swiftly produced. Ball gags with steel links.

'Sex toys. From Soho. Amazing what you hoity-toity English like to use in bed.' The chains were tight around the neck. The fat plastic balls, rammed in their mouths, stifled any words. They could only mumble, softly, desperately. Ritter chuckled. 'Interesting, though. And relevant, no? Amazing how close sex is to violence. Orgasm to murder. Talking of which . . .'

Ritter disappeared to the corner of the room and adjusted something on a wall. With a shudder of apprehension Adam realized it was the thermostat. He was turning up the thermostat. They were chained to a large new radiator and he had evidently put the heat on full.

Within moments Adam felt the boiling water percolate into the metal radiator. It was burning the sweat from his shirt, burning his back, burning burning

247

burning. The oversized plastic ball filled his mouth so he could barely swallow.

The gunman returned. 'Now, to work. I want to know what you know. Before you die. *What have you been looking for and what have you found?'*

First he unchained Nina's gag. She spat out the plastic ball and then spat in his face, 'Nothing!'

Ritter sleeved the spittle from his cheek.

The radiator was scorching into Adam's back. His heartbeat was erratic. Could you burn to death from a radiator? He had to Do Something.

Ritter tried again. 'You've been following your stupid fucking dead dad around Britain. Have you found what he found? You may as well tell me because I'm going to cut out your clitoris with a razor if you don't. And even if I don't, someone else will. You are very, very . . . hot properties. Hot hot hot. All three of you. You don't know how many people want to torture you and kill you. You have no idea. I think I can smell burning.'

He took Nina's head and pressed it back hard, with a clanging thud, pushing it against the almost red-hot radiator.

'Is that too fucking hot? Pretty bitch? Is it too hot? Tell me what you found!'

He unchained her gag and she spoke.

'Nothing. We found nothing. Nothing! We've been searching but we found nothing. A few sculptures. Green Men. Nothing else.'

There was an obvious truth in her desperate response. The leather coat creaked as Ritter sighed, dropped Nina's head, and regagged her, shoving the vile plastic ball in her mouth, chaining it round her neck. Her defiant shouts became moans of pain.

He moved on to Hannah, repeating the process, asking her the same questions. 'We don't know anything. We think he may have found some truth about the Templars. The initiation rites.' Half-crying.

'The Babylon rite?'

'What is that? Yes. No. Yes, that. And and and . . .'

'And what else?'

'Nothing! That's as far as we got.'

Like a disappointed university tutor, Ritter dropped his head and sighed. And then he moved and knelt – and licked Nina's face. Licked her from chin to eye.

'Sweet. Very sweet.'

Next to her sister, Hannah gave a muffled scream.

Ritter licked again. 'Mmm. Cherry Garcia.'

Ritter moved along, to Adam. He had produced a knife from somewhere. He angled it towards Adam's groin, as he unloosed the gag with his other hand. Grotesquely nauseated, Adam spat out the plastic.

'Tell me, you Aussie cocksucker. What were you after? You're a journalist, aren't you? You must have been following a story.'

Adam shook his head. 'There is no story. I think he committed suicide. Maybe he found something about the Templars but we've got nowhere.'

For once Ritter's mildly handsome, faintly unshaven face flashed a look of disappointed belief. Angry acceptance. 'You know what, I believe you.' He stared at

Adam, then at the girls, and smiled. 'But the night is young, and you are still alive, so I think it's time for fun. I think I'll leave the pretty one for pudding. A nice sugary dessert. Yes. You first, plain Jane. Gotta eat your greens.'

With the gun at Hannah's head, he unchained her from the radiator, cuffed her hands behind her back, and lifted her to her unsteady feet.

'Let's leave these people to cook. Leave them on the *backburner*.'

He dragged her through the door to the bedroom. Adam strained to see, and watched as Hannah was pushed on to the bed. Then Adam could see very little but, grotesquely, he could hear. Struggling. Writhing. Bed slats. He stretched as far as he could against the chains and glimpsed bare legs, Hannah's bare feet. Desperately fending him off. Ritter kept his boots on. All he could see was his boots. Ritter was on top of her.

Nina sobbed. Ritter was evidently raping her sister.

'Quit your sobbing, bitch.'

The sound of a hard slap echoed. Then Hannah's muffled sobs. Then there was just silence apart from the rhythmic creaking of the bed. He was raping her again. All Adam could see were bare ankles, kicking, listlessly, at Ritter's leather boots. Then the kicking stopped. Hannah's feet were stroking the boots.

Stroking?

'Rapingggg her.' Nina somehow choked the words around her gag. '*Hhheehmm*.'

Adam's anger and confusion boiled with the blood in his back. It was self-evidently true: Ritter *was* raping her. Now he heard a stifled scream. Then a coarse laugh; and the muzzled groan of someone, doing something. Was he cutting her as well?

The bed slats creaked obscenely, again and again and again. Through the crack in the door Adam saw that Ritter apparently had her upside-down. Taking her from behind. The radiator burned. The creaking went on and on and on and still the rapist blurted his disgusting hoarse grunts. Hannah moaned as if she was dying.

The moans were followed by ardent breathing, and then whispered noises and sighing; and then quietness. Liquid noises. Gurgling. Then again nothing.

Gurgling?

Adam yearned and burned against the scorching radiator. Hannah's legs were no longer visible. What had Ritter done to her? Killed her? Suddenly he was sure Ritter had killed her. Raped her, then killed her.

Nina was crying again; Adam felt like crying himself. But he didn't. He found he was just waiting for the next scene in this grotesque yet inexorable melodrama. When Ritter would come out and unchain Nina, and take her into the bedroom. And do the same to her: rape her and kill her so Adam could hear. So he could *imagine*.

A brutal noise shattered his terminal reverie.

The door had crashed open. The noise was . . . *downstairs*.

Brutal shouts and noises.

251

Two seconds later police in blue steel helmets and flak jackets were swarming into the sitting room. Half a dozen of them, staring at Nina and Adam. Adam struggled in his shackles and motioned at the door – the bedroom – but even as he did so Ritter emerged, half naked, gun in hand. A dazzling and deafening helicopter light pierced the window shutters; and then the room filled with gas, or smoke – a smoke grenade – then there was a massive crash of glass; Adam strained to see – it was Ritter – he had run into the bedroom and hurled himself, bodily, through the window, which was just visible. The window was shattered; he'd jumped from the first floor.

The police ran into the bedroom. Adam heard shouts outside, and more gunshots: they must be pursuing Ritter, through the back gardens. Two other cops snapped the shackles that chained Nina and Adam to the burning radiator, then the metal links of their vile gags.

Nina hurled the plastic from her mouth, shoved herself to her feet and ran to the bedroom door.

But a large policeman stopped her. Stout and strong in his blue flak jacket.

'But it's my sister. My sister!'

The cop held her by her trembling shoulders. 'You don't want to see what's in there.'

32

Witches' Market, Chiclayo

'*Qasiy chay ruwasqaykita osqhayman!*'

This wasn't the curandero. Jessica opened her eyes. She looked up and left. It was Larry Fielding. And he was shouting at the wizard.

'*Mana ruwanki chayqa qanmantacha yachakunki!*'

Behind him was a policeman. A policeman? The Peruvian officer had a gleaming peaked cap, and a hand poised on the butt of a gun, ready to draw.

The wizard shrivelled away: cowering and protesting. Larry reached and pulled the rank cloth from Jessica's mouth; she phlegmed the horrible taste into the dust and coughed up her questions.

'What the – what the? Jesus – Larry – how did you find me?'

He shrugged: a bashful saviour. 'I was watching you, and you seemed evasive. We gotta watch out for each other! Didn't quite believe your supermarket shtick.'

'But . . .'

'The market traders told me someone had grabbed you so I went to get the cops to help.'

As the boy unfastened Jessica's bonds, Larry snapped questions at the shaman, who grovelled his replies.

'*Kay warmika milloymi apamun nunakunata.*'

Larry nodded, grimly and disdainfully.

Jess stood up. There was still lizard blood on her stomach. The policeman handed her a handkerchief; she did her best to rub the gore from her skin. The Quechua conversation rattled around the shack, coarse and staccato, like dried beans in a gourd. Larry was the only one in the TUMP team who could speak the ancient Incan tongue.

'What?' she said. 'What were they doing?'

He put a firm hand on her shoulder. 'It was just an exorcism. They weren't going to kill you, or even harm you. They just think you need exorcising.' He glanced around the sun-lanced shack, at the witchy little dolls, the sprigs of dried monkey paws.

'Exorcising! Why?'

Larry shook his head. 'You know why. They think TUMP is hexed! They reckon we have cursed the area, stirring all these ancient Moche demons – like the *pishtacas*.' He gestured at her rolled-up jeans. 'They weren't actually going to cut off your feet, it was just symbolic. They were trying to placate the Moche god by performing, I guess, a phoney Moche ceremony.'

The policeman spoke, impatiently, and in very fast

254

Spanish. But Jess could clearly discern the meaning: he wanted them to leave the market.

'We'd better go,' said Larry. 'This is their world. The Quechua speakers. We'd better go now.'

Jess was unlikely to disagree. Unsteadily she walked out of the shack. In the darkened aisles of traders she breathed the reeking air of the main market with abject relief; it was just as it always was. People were sitting at dirty counters drinking from steel mugs of coca tea, eating rancid plates of brown octopus, and buying eels in bottles. And monkey paws.

Behind them, in the shack, Jess could hear the policeman yapping angrily at the bruja. 'What will happen to them?'

'Slap on the wrist, maybe. The police sympathize with the locals. They don't want us here either, Jess.' He grabbed her by the elbow and they stepped into the grubby sunshine of Chiclayo. Black turkey vultures circled, inevitably, in the dusty blue sky over the dusty orange cathedral. As if the whole city was carrion.

'The cop told me something.' He gazed at her. 'That gunman who came for Dan has been here too, with friends, asking questions, terrorizing people, asking about us in Zana. And asking about McLintock.'

'*Here*?' Jess shook her head. 'They came here?' She was still trying to shake off the memory of the little boy with his dirty, wet finger circling her ankle with warm blood. 'And this guy, McLintock. How does he fit into this?'

Larry ignored her question. 'There's something else you need to know.'

'What?'

'They've made a discovery. At Huaca D.'

'I know, I was there. I—'

'No. A new discovery. This morning. A major, major discovery. Dan phoned me an hour back. And it changes everything. Apparently.' Larry sighed. 'That's all I damn well know! That's all Dan said. It changes everything.'

They sprinted to the car.

Two hours later she was back in Huaca D. The same dust, the same sleeping bones; yet this time it was all different.

'*All* children?'

Dan nodded, making the beam from his headtorch jiggle forlornly. 'All of them children.' He stepped into the antechamber. 'We broke in by accident, this morning. One of the villagers put a shovel through the wall; we found a little passageway, and then this. We hadn't geosurveyed this section, we had no idea; this is so unusual.'

Jess stared. Her hands were shaking with the tension. This discovery was a revelation: it altered everything – as Larry had said. The large, low antechamber, concealed beyond the main tombs of Huaca D, contained more skeletons than any other Moche tomb to date. Here they were, laid out in little sleeping rows.

All of them children.

Dan stooped to the nearest line of small and silent bones. 'We're guessing they were first sedated, at least

I hope they were sedated, maybe with nectandra, then their throats were slit and their chests cut open. Here, look, you can see the breastbone. This one here.'

Jessica leaned. The breastbone was crudely severed. 'A heart extrusion?'

Dan sighed and nodded and rubbed a dusty hand over his dusty face. He looked wearied: even in the quarter-light of this dismal adobe hall she could see he was beyond tired. He was vanquished. But his voice retained some professional lucidity.

'Probably they used a tumi blade. To hack the children open. Alive. Some of these fibrous remains imply . . . look—' He pointed. 'The children were tied by the hands and feet before the ritual began.'

Jess felt sick. First the horrors of the witches' market, now this. She gazed at her shaking hand, and wrestled away the terror.

Dan was intoning now, like a priest who had lost his faith, who nonetheless had to deliver a sermon for Easter, 'The remains are, we think, the earliest evidence of ritualized blood sacrifice and of the severe mutilation of children, the earliest evidence that has so far been seen in South America. It may even be the biggest mass sacrifice of children . . . anywhere in the ancient world.'

Picking up a flashlight, Jess played it along the dormitory of bones. The quiet little children were all present and correct, all tied and hacked and dismembered, and left here. In neat little rows. She remembered her own nursery school, in sunny LA, when they would sleep in the afternoon. This was like that, but satanically upended. Here was a kindergarten of evil. Like the children of the Goebbels family, in the Berlin bunker, *schlaft gut, schlaft gut, meine kindern.*

'It's ghastly,' was all she could say. 'Ghastly. Just . . . just ghastly.' Her flashlight played across the hideous space and picked out a different bone, a larger, cruder, horsier skull. Just visible in the morbid shadows at the far corner of the antechamber. 'What's that?'

'A llama head.' Dan's voice expressed a shrug. 'There are other llama remains all around. Jay thinks they probably had a feast. As they did it. Eating llama as they killed the children.'

'Horrible.'

'Possibly they played music as they did it. Feasting and music, and killing their children.'

'How many corpses?'

'Eighty.'

Jess swayed in the darkness. The orphanage of sleeping bones stared back at her, reproachfully. A gassed Montessori; a tiny Holocaust school for infants. It was worse than Jessica's experience of Calcutta. It reminded her of her father in the hospice. The absolute tyranny of death: the oncoming darkness.

One small skull was tilted to the side, as if the child had tried to sleep as they cut open his chest. Tears sprang to Jessica's eyes.

'Are you OK?' Dan touched her gently on the arm.

'Yes.'

'I heard what happened in Chiclayo, eh, Larry told me on the cell – sweetheart, are you sure?'

Her headtorch caught his face. She muttered, 'Really, I'm fine. It was just a ritual, imitative magic, apotropaic theatre.'

'Getting rid of the evil we bring? Ah, yes.'

The adobe dust hung in the ancient air. She said, 'They think we are the vampire gringos, Dan. Like in the Inca legends of the conquistadors, the white men who eat the fat of the Peruvians: the pishtacas. And they also think we are digging up demons. Digging up the God Who Mustn't Be Named, the terrible god we cannot identify. That's what Larry said.'

'Who knows, they might be right? Eh?' He gestured across the pitifully neat little remains, the speechless silenced rows of infant skulls and infant femurs, stretching into the darkness of the antechamber. 'You know, this really is different. Unique. What are we digging up? Mm? What kind of people? Maybe it should be closed down.'

'You should be pleased.' She tried to sound sincere, even encouraging. 'This is a tremendous find. As you say, Dan, there probably isn't anything like it in the literature.'

'Oh, of course. But . . .'

'But what?'

He seemed to shiver. 'Do you mind if we step outside?'

Stepping outside meant a short, muddy crawl through the zigzagging adobe corridors into the wider tomb which had contained the insect corpses and the coral headdresses, only some of which had been removed. The ground was now carefully latticed with strings, marking out square-metre grids. A low wooden bench had been brought into the tomb, where the archaeologists could have lunch and talk. They both sat down. The great mud tomb was otherwise empty.

'The child sacrifices make nonsense of it all,' Dan said at last.

'Sorry?'

'The pottery in the antechamber with the children is precisely datable. By style.'

Jessica was perplexed. 'And?'

'*It is not coincident with any El Niño event.* There were no El Niño events which might have, eh, triggered these sacrifices.'

With his hard hat taken off, Dan's hair hung lank and lifeless. Jess stared away, embarrassed somehow. She looked along the lamplit tomb, where the princess had been laid out. The princess who cut off her own feet during her life, for no reason at all.

Dan remained quiet, so Jess reached out a hand and squeezed his hand. 'Which means your theory is wrong.'

'Yep. Which means that my damn theory is *wrong*. I've been wrong all along. And you were right, Jessica, the Moche were just . . . they were just . . .'

'Evil?'

'Perverse. Deviant. Wicked. Psychotic. Maybe downright evil. I don't know. Whatever you like.' He ran tired fingers through his hair. 'I'm not sure I want to do this any more.'

'But you've made a major discovery!' Jess could feel her lover's anguish. It was unjustified. He was beating himself up too much. 'Dan, come on. Don't say this. So you found something that changes the paradigm, but you still found it. You! You *did* it.'

'And the guy with the gun?' Dan looked at her. 'And Casinelli? And now you in Chiclayo? This may embarrass you, Jessica but I don't care. You know that I have strong feelings for you. Heck, you know I love you. Don't you? And I know you don't love me but there it is. And I cannot put you in any more danger.' He talked over her protests, and continued, 'Whatever this is we've somehow strolled into, we've stirred up something we don't understand. I'm not risking lives any more. And I'm not telling lies any more.'

Jess caught the word. And examined it. And asked, '*Lies?*'

He rubbed some dust off his shirt, another hockey team T-shirt now stained red with adobe mud, like unwashable old blood from a horrible fight.

'What lies, Dan?'

'McLintock. When that . . . the gunman asked me about him, I knew exactly who he meant. I knew very well.'

'Sorry?'

Daniel Kossoy could barely bring himself to look her in the face. But he tried. 'Archibald McLintock was a Scottish historian. He visited me, very discreetly, in Zana about a year and a half ago. Long before you came. No. Wait.' He lifted a hand to halt her questions.

'Wait, Jess. Let me finish. He wanted, eh, to know about the Moche, everything. Especially the ulluchu: he was fascinated by the mythos of the ulluchu, the blood of the gods.'

'Why?'

'He had a theory. That there isn't just an unknown Moche god: he thought there was an unknown, ultimate god, underlying *all* pre-Columbian American cultures. A god that unites the Aztecs and the Hopi and the Moche, the Anasazi, the Chavin, the Nazca and Apache and Cahokians, all of them, which explains why they were all so obsessed with cruelty, and ritualized violence, and sacrifice.'

'So he had a theory, so what, why did you lie?'

'Because he paid me money.' Dan's eyes were shining with guilt. 'At first I said to him I was busy and didn't have time to talk, which was true, but then he offered me money, and TUMP needed money, and the money was . . . eh . . . very good, ten thousand US, enough for a few months' digging, but I knew it was probably illegal, not going through the proper channels, and anyway McLintock swore me to secrecy, so that was the deal. So I took the cash, and said nothing. And I gave McLintock a secret tour of the site, and told him everything, even the stuff we haven't published. And then he disappeared, went to Lima, I think. I don't know.'

'And you never told anyone?'

An agonized shrug. 'I never told a soul, Jess. But now you know. You. The person who means more to me than anything. But it's over now. There's too much violence. Even this McLintock guy is dead. I have no idea what is happening but I'm gonna hand in my notice, if TUMP want to continue – and they probably will, now we've found all these poor kids – then they can appoint someone else. That's if the police don't close us down, which they might, because we are disturbing the locals.' He spat out the words. 'Damn it all, Jess. Just damn it to hell. I'll be glad to get out of here, out of this disgusting place.'

Jessica couldn't find the words. What to say?

'The irony is,' Dan went on, 'I believe McLintock may have been on to something. A proto-god. A uniting mythology, underneath it all. It makes a kind of sense. There are too many sinister similarities between all these American cultures. Something unites them. A god, a hidden god, a terrible god, the god of death and of blood.' He laid a gentle hand on her arm, lifted her wrist, and kissed her chastely on the hand. 'There. Jessica Silverton, sweetheart. If you want to be famous, pursue that, make that your thesis. You are young and bold. I am not. I am done. But be careful. Beware the demons of the Moche.'

He didn't even say goodbye. He just switched off the tomb lights, turned and crouched, and began the long crawl back to the huaca entrance, through the dark adobe tunnels.

Jessica followed him, churning with emotion. Suddenly, and to her own surprise, she wanted to tell Dan about her father, and about the doctor: she had to tell someone, she had to share and divide her anxieties, and he was the only man she could really trust. Maybe she even loved him back; her sudden feelings were stronger than she had suspected. She didn't want to lose him.

Strapping her hard hat on her head, and turning on her headtorch, Jess crawled urgently through the narrow, claustrophobic, zigzagging tunnels. Dan was so eager to get out he was twenty metres ahead, a barely glimpsed glow of receding light.

The final corner turned: and now Dan was gone, he'd stepped out into the fresh air.

Jessica urged herself on, to confess and to share, but then she halted, her heart straining with fear, in the last yards of darkness, looking towards the grey light outside.

She could hear voices. Curt, laconic, contemptuous voices. And it wasn't Larry or Jay. *It sounded like the intruder in the lab*, the same man, the same accent. The same violent sneering voice.

This time there was no argument, no preamble, no chance for Dan to escape his fate. The sullen gunshot echoed down the adobe passageway. Another shot confirmed the horror: they had shot Dan! Jess could actually see his body, fallen at the entrance, blood trickling into the dust.

She gazed, paralysed by terror.

Then a torchbeam pierced the dark of the passage. Jessica pressed herself flat against the mud walls, trying to hide. A figure was kneeling at the adobe entrance, peering in, pointing the torch up the tunnel.

'Marco! *Creo que hay alguien aquí.*' I think someone is in there.

They were going to search the huaca.

Jessica began to back up the passage. Crawling with infinite and painful slowness, away from the light.

But the torchbeam followed her.

33

Clapham, south London

DCI Mark Ibsen gazed around the clean white flat. It was decorated with framed photographs. Some foreign locations, some sombre, monochrome photo portraits.

'It's been a week now. How is she? *Where* is she?'

The young journalist, Adam Blackwood, nodded at a closed door to the left. 'Sleeping, she sleeps in the day and she doesn't sleep at night. She cries at night.'

'You?'

Blackwood waved a hand across a weary face. 'I'm OK. I sleep on the sofa.'

'Ah.'

'It's not like that, Detective. Not me and Nina. Not that this really bloody matters.'

'I understand. And please, call me Mark.'

Blackwood stood and walked to a bookshelf that was dedicated mainly to bottles of whisky rather than books. He took a bottle of Macallan, unscrewed the top, poured a good measure into a tumbler and glugged down the amber-dark Scotch.

'You?'

'I'm on duty. Your friend is generous.'

'You mean lending me the flat? Or letting me drink his good Scotch?'

'Both.'

Adam Blackwood shrugged. He poured himself another, and drank some more of that with a faintly trembling hand. 'Jason's a photographer, he works with me a lot, very good mate. Ironically, he was working with me the day this all started, in Rosslyn, when all this lunacy began. Now he's on assignment in Spain at the moment, some story. He said we could stay here as long as we wanted. Obviously we can't stay at my place in case they . . . whoever they are . . . are still looking for us.'

'I'm glad you took my advice. We'll have cars outside, twenty-four/seven. There's one on the corner by the Common, another at the junction with Nansen Road.'

'You got the guy, didn't you? You shot him . . .'

'We cornered him in Barnsbury Square. An hour later. He went down fighting, refused to surrender. A marksman took him down.'

'But who was he? Why did he want to kill us all?'

Ibsen looked at Adam's brave but frightened face. 'Cammorista.'

'Italian gangs? But he was American, he had an American accent.'

'He's half-Puerto Rican, brought up in California. But he's been in Europe a long time, and he had strong links with southern Italian gangs, especially the Camorra, in Calabria, in Italy.'

'And—'

'They are known for people-trafficking: Moldovan girls, Romanian girls, sex slaves, high-class hookers.'

'He was a pimp?'

'Sometimes, yes. Sometimes drugs. High-level crime. He was a definite pro, with psychopathic tendencies. As we have seen.'

Adam whirled the whisky, his journalistic mind churning through the facts. Computing the puzzle. 'So that explains the sex. The girls, I mean. Ritter imported whores, poor girls . . . so that's how he hooked up with the sex party crowd, the rich kids?'

Ibsen nodded. 'Yes. We believe so. Probably he supplied girls for the sex parties, for the millionaire swingers, or what you might call them. That's how he got an *in*. To those elite circles.'

'You know, if I wasn't the bloody target of mad Puerto Rican sex-murderers this would be a bloody great story. Christ, why are they trying to kill *us*, Mark? Why did he kill Hannah McLintock? Like that?'

'You stumbled on a trail first trodden by Archibald McLintock. He must have discovered something that the gangsters really want. Someone suspects you and Hannah and . . . sorry, you and Nina. They suspect that you know something. But you don't. But they don't know that. It is confusing, taken at face value.'

'Confusing, and terrifying.' Adam closed his eyes. 'It

was *truly* terrifying. I pissed myself. I did. I was sitting by that radiator chained to that radiator and I actually wet myself. Isn't that pathetic?' He opened his blue eyes and stared, intently, at the wall. 'He was going to rape and kill Nina, after he raped and killed Hannah. And then he was going to kill me. And there was nothing I could do about it and so I wet myself like a baby. Jesus.'

Ibsen shook his head, feeling real pity. 'It's a reflex. Don't be ashamed. They say the landing craft at D-Day were like open sewers because of men voiding themselves with fear. It's only human. You tried to tackle him straightaway, which was brave. Remember that.'

Ibsen glanced at the window. The December afternoon was falling into darkness outside. Larkham was waiting for him around the corner, parked inconspicuously. They had some more leads to attend to. He had been here two hours and he needed to shift things along. 'I have to broach a painful topic, Adam. I'm going to tell you something crucial and difficult because . . .' He glanced at the door, behind which Nina McLintock was sleeping. 'Because you are probably closest to Miss McLintock right now.'

Adam looked at the policeman, thoughtfully, as if he was digesting this: he was the person closest to Nina McLintock. 'Tell me.'

'Hannah McLintock *wasn't* raped.'

Adam stared at him. He shook his head. 'No way. I can't believe that . . . I saw . . . I heard—'

'I'm afraid it's true. We have had the report from Pathology.'

'But I watched, Mark. I saw! He dragged her in there at gunpoint. It's crazy.'

'I know, I know.' Ibsen raised two pacifying hands. 'I know. It seems impossible, but the evidence is clear. When a woman is raped, especially if it is a very violent rape, there is nearly always bruising around the perineum, and there are usually other marks of similar trauma in the area. We have found none on Miss McLintock's body. None. It seems she was aroused. And maybe quite receptive. I am sorry.'

'But . . .'

'We also have evidence that she possibly orgasmed. Forensics have analysed the bedsheets.'

Adam Blackwood said nothing; then he said, in a slow, bewildered voice, 'This is horrible. Just . . . totally . . . horrible. And yet . . . some of the noises. It did sound, a little like . . .'

'A bit like sexual climax?'

'I don't know. Christ. Yes. No. Maybe . . .'

'I understand your perplexity. But the facts, horrific as they are, are the facts. We also believe – again you must prepare yourself – that she had anal sex. And, even more astonishing, she slashed her own throat. Ritter didn't do it. She reached around with a cutthroat razor, that he gave her, and she slashed her *own* throat. The fingerprints and the bloodspatter and the angles of incision all point this way.'

Adam Blackwood looked down at the ground as if

he was going to vomit. 'But she was plainly terrified. I saw her face, when he dragged her in there. It doesn't remotely add up.'

Ibsen sat forward. 'I have a theory. It's only, ah, the faintest theory at the moment.'

'Tell me. Tell me something. *Anything.*'

'We are thinking along these lines: that there is some kind of *hypnosis* in play, maybe involving a cult. And we think this hypnosis or autosuggestion stimulates the libido.'

'A cult? Hannah McLintock?'

Ibsen ignored this. 'It is likely that the hypnosis or trance state leads to autoerotic, or perhaps hypersexual, arousal. But this also leads to a desire for self-mutilation, and the consequent sadomasochistic rush that comes with the pain.'

'You're talking about those horrible suicides?'

'Yes, the horrible *brutality* of the suicides. Self-mutilation that generates a rush. A suicide that gives an orgasmic rush, perhaps the ultimate buzz.'

'So this guy Ritter hypnotized her! And she cut herself.'

Ibsen paused, and shook his head. 'It's not as simple as that. Experts say you can't just hypnotize people into killing themselves in a few minutes. That's just nonsense, stage hypnosis, rubbish.'

'So . . .'

'What you *can* do is inculcate a kind of hypnosis over weeks and months, sessions of it, perhaps in a sacred or ritualized setting, so that this hypnosuggestion can be turned on by a trigger word, some time later, even years later. That is possible. It seems.'

Adam downed the last of his whisky. 'I don't believe it.'

'Nor did I. At first. But all other explanations are coming up short, and in the right setting, of slowly and steadily ritualized hysteria or hypnosis, we think you can induce people to kill themselves. Like Jonestown. Guyana.'

Adam Blackwood shook his head. 'But that means Hannah McLintock must have had . . . must have been . . .'

'Connected with the other suicides. Yes. Perhaps in some sex club with strange rituals, and initiation ceremonies. Hannah and her fiancé, they are – they were – a rich young London couple. Correct? Not entirely unlike our other victims. So we need to know more about her. Which is why I want you to ask her sister . . .'

'No!'

'Adam. We will question her ourselves. But you are close to her.'

A very long silence ensued. The muffled sound of traffic was restive, stirred in its dreams. Ibsen filled the silence. 'I also think that this cult stuff, this sexual hypnosuggestion, might be linked to Archibald McLintock's researches – his discoveries.'

'Why?'

'He committed suicide himself. In a fairly unusual way. Serenely. As if he was mesmerized. I have spoken to the Scottish police, read your own interview notes,

Adam – you said he had a certain air of serenity that morning in Rosslyn.'

'Archibald McLintock? A sex cult? Absurd. It's surreal. He was seventy years old!'

Ibsen began to speak, but suddenly Adam interrupted.

'Except . . . there was . . . something . . .'

'What?'

'The pots. The strange ceramics. He went to Peru. And brought them back. They are macabre, from the Moche culture. And some of the Moche shit, in the archives, is weird and bloodthirsty. I got a book and read up. See—' He crossed the room and returned with a hardback book bristling with bookmarks.

Ibsen read the title. *Sex, Death and Sacrifice in Moche Religion*.

'I got it off Amazon.' Adam stared down at the book. 'I've been reading it all week. It's all in here. The Moche were very strange. Obsessed with bestiality. And sex with the dead. They were possibly into self-mutilation. I don't know what the link is, but there must be a link.'

Ibsen was already scribbling in his own notebook. Noting the title of the volume. 'Yes. The pots! I saw them in the photo. Thank you. We will look into this too.' He put down his notebook and glanced at his watch. 'OK. Adam, as I say we need to get cracking. I appreciate your help, and I understand your scepticism. But before I go I should say I also have one more hunch, which is a little more substantial, and relevant, which you should know.'

'Yes?'

'I believe there might be rival gangs after the McLintock discovery.'

'How come?'

'Differing descriptions. Remember the man you saw in McLintock's flat, the intruder?'

'Of course.'

'That wasn't Ritter. Was it?'

'I guess not . . . I only got a glimpse.'

'The man you saw in the flat had tattoos on his hands, right?'

Adam nodded.

'But Ritter had tatts on his arm. So that means we probably have two *different* burglars in the flat in the space of a few weeks. The first intruder, the American who confronted McLintock, that was probably Ritter. It makes sense. The second – the one you saw – was someone else. We don't know who yet.'

Adam leaned over. 'I need another drink.' Reaching for the whisky bottle, he unscrewed it and poured another inch and a half.

Ibsen waited, then gave his explanation. 'Here's the logic. Let's say McLintock discovered this erotic hypnosis, this ancient or forgotten ritualistic trance, or whatever it is. In Peru maybe. God knows. Ritter, it seems, certainly had access to it. And he or his gang presumably got it from McLintock, or stole it from him. Ritter used it on Hannah, the hypnosug-gestion, and it's been *tested* on these rich kids. And it works. It is extremely powerful. I guess they want to make sure no one else gets it . . . Like a rival mafia.'

Adam swallowed then said, quietly, 'I suppose that does make some sort of sense.' He was frowning. 'Because . . . They would want this great and precious bloody secret, this trick, this whatever it is, they would want it to *remain* a secret, to remain *their* secret. Right? Which means they'd want to snuff us out more than anyone, because we are on the same trail.'

'Yes.'

'Which means we are really in danger. Horrible danger.' Adam offered the policeman a fearful smile. 'Thanks. Thanks a whole bunch.'

'I am truly sorry. But yes, that's how I see it.' He offered Adam his hand. 'We'll be in touch. And you must call whenever you want, day or night.'

Adam shook the policeman's hand. Ibsen noted how tall the Australian was. Tall and muscular, yet deeply frightened, and who could blame him?

The evening was cold outside, a wind was skirting off the Common. Ibsen walked quickly to the car where Larkham had been patiently waiting. They had parked several streets away, down a dark and unused side road, just in case anyone had been observing and following them. He quickened his pace, thinking hard about the interview. The Moche pottery: how had he forgotten that? The sheer velocity of the case was knocking him off his stride.

He passed the open door of a brightly-lit newsagent, dispersing a tinny Christmas carol into the freezing air.

The last corner turned, he saw the car at the end. Dark and waiting. Larkham was just a silhouette in the car in the gloom.

A strange silhouette. Ibsen walked quicker.

A very strange silhouette.

He stopped. Larkham was stiffened with early rigor mortis. Larkham was dead.

34

Huaca D, Zana, Peru

The beam of the killer's flashlights probed deeper into the passage, illuminating the floating dust. Jessica flattened herself, in animal panic, against the mud wall. Her heart galloped in her chest, so loud she reckoned it must be audible, booming down the adobe corridor.

Again the torchbeam flicked this way and that, investigating, while the male voices at the passage entrance debated. Evidently they knew she was in here, or they suspected *someone* was in the huaca. Jessica listened, intent. Sure enough she heard the word *matar*: to kill. They were discussing whether to kill whoever was inside.

She had to hide.

Stealthily, she inched up the passage, sidling into the darkness, turning off her own headtorch as she went.

The blackness absorbed her at once: an intense and devouring darkness. And Jessica hated the dark. The fear of what she had to do, where she had to go – crawl into the huaca, towards the tombs, in the terrible darkness – would have been insurmountable if the alternative hadn't been worse: a callous death in the dust outside.

But the blackness was hateful. It grasped at her: it took the air from her mouth. Putting one palm in front of the other, patting her way along, Jessica negotiated the zigzagging passageway, crawling like a blind mammal in the darkness. Like a human mole.

Here the passage turned, she turned with it, smelling the warm earth all around her, scraping her hard hat on the mud ceiling, knocking her knees against pebbles and rocks. Or maybe these were bones, not rocks. The huaca was riddled with tombs and corpses.

Breathing quickly in the warm, humid, constricted air, Jessica looked back. The darkness extended as far behind her as in front of her. The blackness was so intense it felt viscous, as if she was drowning in a sump of crude oil.

What was that?

Maybe a noise, a whispered voice carried along the passage. She heard voices. They must have made their decision, and now they were coming after her in the dark, following the same confusing and circuitous passageways, hunting her down.

Urgently she continued her eyeless crawl, chafing soil from the ceiling with her hard hat, soil that fell in hissy little whispers on to her body; one especially vigorous mudfall made her stop, and wait, tense, until the drizzle of soil concluded. Then she pushed on, into the black heart of the tombs.

She'd made it to the antechamber of Tomb 1. She could tell because she was kneeling on bones. Under her hands and her knees were the disarticulated skeletons of the servants, with their willing amputations. And now she had to crawl straight through them – straight through the middle of the skeletal remains – so that she could get to the senior tomb.

The bones crumbled under her scrabbling sneakers. She couldn't see the skulls, she couldn't see anything, but she could sense their sad, immortal grins. Jessica kicked the last metre and climbed the low mud shelf and as she did she heard the voices, very near.

They really were coming after her. And they were very close behind.

She had to hide, quickly, somewhere in the tomb. Racing on her scratched and bleeding knees Jessica forced herself through the stone portals. At once she tripped on the square-metre strings that gridded the floor; with a loud crack she fell into the piles of corpse beetles, the trashy, gaudy crunch of thoraxes. She had fallen face first into the pile and now they were in her mouth: she was eating the beetles who ate human corpses; it was disgusting.

Spitting the vileness from her mouth, Jessica moved on, slithering through the crackling insect shells, and then at last she half-stood, and ran and threw herself blindly at the wall.

A light.

The torch beam of her pursuers was now visible in the antechamber beyond: a dim and troglodytic light, sinister and subterranean. And coming her way. Fevered with desperation and terror, Jessica groped her way to the corner of the room where the secret entrance to the second antechamber was concealed.

The passage was virtually a hole in the ground, hidden behind a mud wall. Would the killers see it? This was her only chance. Jessica squeezed herself into the tight and grimy final passage. It was so narrow it seemed to her that she was now being *swallowed* by the mud, swallowed by the Moche pyramid, eaten up by their unknown gods.

A minute later she was in the antechamber. She could sense the higher space around her, even if she could not see it. And she could stand up. She could also sense the little skeletons of the children, sleeping in their kindergarten, their hearts removed.

There was nothing Jess could do now but wait. She squatted in the far darkness of the chamber, her eyes closed to the terror; but the terror was the same with her eyes open or shut. She wiped the mud from her blinded eyes and just stared into the blackness.

Subdued murmurs, echoing down the long huaca passages. The word *ulluchu* . . . they were talking about ulluchu, and the way they said it was strange, not quite right, spoken in a different accent. Not Peruvian? The pronunciation chimed in Jessica's mind. But she didn't know why, and she didn't care, because now the voices were dwindling, they weren't getting any nearer, they seemed to be moving away.

Time passed. With no sign of the killers. Maybe she was going to make it?

But then despair grasped at her, in the darkness. Even if she did survive, what was the point? If she lived longer, that maybe just meant she would die soon, but more slowly. From Huntington's. And that would be worse. Much, much worse.

Maybe it would be better if she was shot now: simple and painless.

Yet even as she thought this, her soul stirred with rebellion. Clinging to life.

Jessica stared into the blackness, where the Muchika children lay sleeping. Devoid of visual stimuli, her mind conjured up pictures of its own: she was seeing her father again. Thrashing in his bed, angry, then crying, then angry, then very silent again: the longest silence of all. And now Jessica could see herself in the hospice: she was a child, looking at the body on the bed, looking at the body where her father had been, and she was wondering where he had gone.

Jessica remembered her own reactions. Staring at the dead body, outraged, tearful, and wondering where the life had gone. Her mother's soothing stories of Jesus and angels and heaven had not consoled her. With a seven-year-old's basic sense of morality, she felt she'd been *robbed*. Someone or something had stolen her father away, and he would surely be returned.

But he never returned.

There. Now.

A voice. In the tomb.

She returned to alertness with a startle and suppressed a cry of fear.

The voices were getting louder. They were coming down the passageway into the hidden antechamber.

So this was it. They'd found the concealed passage. Death had not relinquished her, after all.

The killers emerged into the chamber; they had dazzling headtorches. They were tall silhouettes flashing beams of light right into her eyes. She held up her hands in supplication, visoring her eyes in the glare. But she could see one thing well enough: the men had raised their guns, and they were pointed her way.

35

Clapham Common, London

The carol singers were gathered under the bare-boned plane trees, by Holy Trinity Church, warbling of merriment and figgy pudding. The hardiest joggers sprinted past, white earphones in place, oblivious and sweating despite the chill.

Nina sat between Adam and Jason, on the cold park bench. She pulled the sleeves of her blue jumper over her small white hands. 'Poor bastard.' She shook her head. 'And he had kids, didn't he? A baby?'

Adam nodded. Fighting off the fear and despair. This was the first time he and Nina had really discussed what the detective had told him: that Ibsen had returned to his car to find DS Larkham dead. Garrotted, while he sat in his car; his face contorted into a smile.

'And there was a note, right?' Jason said.

'Yes. *"One of ours, one of yours."* That's what it said, that's *all* it said.'

Nina interrupted, 'So they must have been looking for us, failed, but found the poor cop. But we're next.'

Adam quickly replied. 'We don't know that.' Though he knew it to be true. Ibsen had said as much to him, sounding shaken.

Jason sighed. Adam's best friend had been back from a hard assignment in Spain for just a few hours, and the tiredness showed in his face. Now Adam felt a deep shiver of guilt, dragging his old friend into all this terror.

'So what the hell do we do now?' Nina asked.

Adam looked into her eyes, seeking her real feelings. Ever since the discovery of Larkham's death, she had appeared to strengthen, paradoxically. The sobbing had stopped, the rheumed eyes had disappeared. She had slept. Probably, Adam guessed, she was faking the strength, but the fakery was good, and necessary. He answered as best he could. 'Ibsen suggested we could go into protective custody.'

'You mean put us under bloody house arrest? Yeah, great.'

Jason gestured at the police car parked at the edge of the Common. Two officers sat patiently inside: their protection. A pair of officers didn't seem quite so impressive, not any more.

'You're already pretty restricted. But living with the cops in some dismal safe house, that could be even worse.'

'Exactly. It's pish. I'm not doing it!' Her voice was decisive. 'Who knows when we'd ever emerge? These guys, the Camorra, are famously patient: they will wait years if necessary, didn't you say that, Jason?'

Jason agreed. 'I did a story once on them once, they will cross the world to take out enemies and rivals.'

'Well they're not doing it to me.' Nina swore. 'My sister is already dead. My dad is dead. They've killed two-thirds of my family. I don't care any fucking more. I'm not hiding in some stupid hole.' Her voice was impassioned, maybe a little broken, but it was undefeated. 'I'm not going to hide for the rest of my life.'

Adam stared at her: she was like Alicia, yet she was also much, much stronger. 'What do you suggest we do, then?'

'We get moving. We find the answer.'

'We continue searching? The trail your father laid?'

'Of course.'

'But they will just hunt us across Europe.' Adam gazed at the police car, dwarfed by daunting London traffic.

Jason interrupted. 'You could set a decoy? Pretend that you're still in Britain, get a mate in the press to leak a story saying you've been taken into protective custody. That would buy you some time.'

'Yes,' Nina said. Her eyes were fiercely bright. 'Yes. Adam? Yes? Would Ibsen buy that?'

'I don't know. I guess. Quite possibly. Yes . . .' The idea began to quicken in Adam's mind. Fight back: do something. Stop the terrible waiting. It was tempting, but there was a problem. 'But what about you, Jason, what would you do? They might—'

Jason shook his head. 'I'm flying to the States Tuesday. A three-month assignment on the West Coast, Canada, Oregon. I'll be just fine, dude. Will that cop agree to this?'

'Yes, I think so. In the end it's up to us. Of course we'd have to come back as witnesses at some point. But that could be months.'

'So,' said Nina, 'that's what we do. We do it fast, and we keep moving. We don't give them a chance to catch us. Here.' She reached for her jeans pocket, and brought out an envelope.

Adam recognized her writing. *France, August 4th-9th.* 'Your father's receipts. You brought them?'

'I had the feeling we would make this decision.' Her smile was fixed. 'This is where he went next.' She opened the envelope. 'Southwest France. Near Bergerac.'

'Where?'

'It's a castle. The Templars were imprisoned there. It's called Domme. He spent three days there. It must be crucial.' She murmured the words like a prayer for the dead. 'Domme Castle, Sarlat-le-Canéda. In the Dordogne.'

36

Huaca D, Zana, Peru

'*Mio Dios.*' The torchbeams played across the little skeletons, illuminating one tiny skull, then another. '*Esto
es terrible.*'

The voice was unexpected: not the same as before.
Jessica squinted to see who was in the tomb, then
she glimpsed the shine of a cap badge. Police. It was
the police.

The Peruvian officers lifted her to her feet. The police?
She felt a sudden urge to fight back, to protest: they
had frightened her so much, sent her into the darkest
terror. Vainly she slapped a hand away, pushed at one
of the officers. Almost flailing.

They looked at her in the semi-dark, perplexing,
questioning, bewildered. 'Señorita . . .'

This was foolish, and Jessica knew it. She was chiding
them for what? Saving her life? They were doing their
job and they had done it well.

'Señorita?'

She calmed, a little. 'I . . . *soy* . . . *Lo Siento*. I am sorry – I was scared . . .'

They dismissed her words with a wave: they wanted her out of the huaca straightaway.

Stumbling over the bones, she obeyed: following them slowly out of the antechamber, and down the passageways, making the long retreat out of the huaca. No one spoke: the only sound was the scrape of boots in mud, the whisper of dust disturbed.

She steeled herself for what she was about to see as she approached the quadrangle of light that was the pyramidal exit: Dan's body, prone in the Zana dust. But as she reached the fresher air, her apprehension was replaced by confusion. The body was already gone: only the bloodstains remained.

The tallest policemen, a handsome English-speaking man with a gentle smile, touched her mud-dusted shoulder. 'Your friend is already in an ambulance.'

'He is alive?'

'No. I am sorry, no. He was killed, but we must examine the body.'

Jessica resisted the surging sadness, the tears she hadn't cried. 'What about the killers?'

'They escaped. Someone from the village, from Zana, called us, they heard the shooting. Please—' He gestured at one of three police cars, their red lights flashing absurdly, in the desert air. 'We would like you to come to Chiclayo, and make a full statement. Is that permissible?'

288

'Yes.' Jessica shrugged. She was exhausted to the point of indifference; numbed by it all. 'Of course.'

The questioning, in Chiclayo police headquarters, lasted four hours. It was polite, efficient, depressing, and repetitive. Towards the end Jessica found her mind wandering, gazing at the maps and mug-shots on the wall of the grubby office. What was she going to do now? TUMP was obviously finished. Her life was probably in danger. She didn't especially care. Her lover, Dan, was dead: at the moment when he'd told her he loved her, almost exactly as she'd realized she probably reciprocated his feelings, he had been taken from her.

Death had a cruel sense of humour.

The police drove her back to Zana to collect her stuff. They expected her to move out of town for her own safety, she had to pack at once.

The police car stopped near the town plaza. Jessica alighted, reassuring the police that she could drive back to Chiclayo on her own. But they insisted on escorting her. She yielded to their protection, and agreed she would meet them at the lab in three hours. Then they could follow her Hilux to Chiclayo.

Jessica began her walk to the lab, and her little apartment next door. But as she walked, another enormous wave of melancholia almost knocked her legs away. The sadness was like a sack of rocks, as if she was hauling eighty kilos of grief on her back.

She needed to pause and think. Finding a broken bench in the town square, Jessica sat down, under fraying palm trees with gangrenous trunks.

Taking a can of cherry cola from her bag, she cracked it open, and drank. She was also hungry, but she had no food. Drinking the cola, she stared up the road. It terminated after two blocks with a rubbish-filled maize field, and then came the huacas. With the little children. And the bloodstains. The sadness was unbearable.

She stood and tossed the can in a bin, and began her walk to the lab. But a small black child was in the way, kicking a football against a wall of the grimy Panateria Tu Casa. A peeling wall poster for Inca Kola, *El Sabor de Peru!*, flaked a little more paper onto the dirty street each time the ball thumped.

'*Ola*, Eduardo.'

The kid stopped, and turned, and grinned at Jessica. He was the son of the cleaner at the archaeology lab, at the other end of town. Jess often saw him running late to school, in shoes so battered he might as well have gone barefoot. She would never see him again. Eduardo answered, eagerly, '*Buenas dias*, Senorita Silverton!' Another kick of the ball, '*¿Quieras jugar?*'

Do you want to play?

Jess smiled, sadly, and turned down the offer. '*No, gracias. Los estadounidenses somos muy malos jugando al fútbol.*'

I am an American, we are useless at soccer.

The boy grinned, and Jessica said goodbye, feeling herself stumble on the finality of the word – *adios, adios* – then she walked quickly to the lab.

She found Larry inside hastily packing away equipment.

They looked at each other. And Jessica knew that anything they said would feel pointless and wrong.

'What are you going to do, Jess? Go home to California?'

Jessica sat on a stool. 'Christmas in Redondo, with my mom?' She sighed. 'Maybe. You? What about you? And Jay?'

'Still thinking. Jay's already bought his ticket to Chicago. But I'm not sure.' He picked up a Moche pot, then set it down. 'The police say they might want us as witnesses pretty soon. So we'd just have to come back.'

'They told me the same. I might go to Lima till the New Year. Lie low.'

Larry pulled up a stool and sat beside her. 'What a freaking mess! Poor Dan.'

'I know.'

'You must . . .' His embarrassed eyes barely met her gaze. 'I mean, Dan and you, it must be horrible . . .'

She shook her head. She didn't want to talk about Dan.

Larry seemed to understand. He stared at the window. 'Just who the fuck are these people, Jess? Who is doing this?'

Jessica did not reply; there was no reply. No one had any idea. The fridges hummed in the silence; she wondered idly what would happen to their contents. The Moche bones and skulls. The notion of these things made her faintly nauseous.

Larry swivelled, and leaned closer, his voice lowered.

'Jess . . . Did you, did you find the police kinda . . . odd?'

'What do you mean?'

Her colleague shrugged, his concerned face was darkened by a puzzled frown. 'I thought they seemed . . . scared. Like they knew something, or sensed something, and it frightened them. Gut feeling, is all. But I definitely got the sensation they were trying to close this all down: close down the lab, get us out of the way, get shot of the whole business. They don't seem keen to follow up leads. Like, Archibald McLintock, he must be crucial to this case, yet they weren't interested when I told them. They were more interested in asking me when I was going to leave Zana, and go to Lima, or America. They just wanted me gone.'

Jessica stared at him, absorbing the information. He was right: the cops hadn't even asked her about McLintock. Why not? What were they avoiding? 'But, Larry,' she had to ask the obvious question, 'what could be so bad it frightens the *police*?'

37

Domme Castle, France

'*Et ici, le graffiti du diable . . .*'

The guide was brisk to the point of rudeness, evidently keen to get the job done. And Adam could see why.

A howlingly cold wind was scouring down the Dordogne Valley, surrounding the walls of ancient Domme, besieging the town on the rock. There were very few tourists in all Domme, as they had already discovered: the Hotel de Golf was shut, the famous 'grotte' was shut. The Café de Dordogne was so shut it looked as if it would never reopen. The only tourists for many kilometres were huddled here, in the castle. Doing the rudimentary tour.

Adam tried to understand the fat female guide as she talked in relentlessly fast French. But he didn't have enough of the language to even begin to understand.

It wasn't much of a castle anyway. More of a glorified medieval gatehouse with bulging walls and plain stone rooms These were the two large notoriously severe cells, in which dozens of Templars had been incarcerated for several years after the arrest of the entire Order in 1307.

The squalor and stench would have been indescribable, Adam decided. Dozens and dozens of men locked in here *for years*.

'Et voici un dessin, satirique, du Pape, et ici Saint Michel, á droit.'

The terrors of the knights would have been intense. Waiting in here, ragged and half-starved, half-crazed even, fearful of the jingle of the gaoler's key, wondering if their turn had come to be taken for the torturing. To have their feet burned with hot irons, to be put to the rack.

To be persuaded to slash your own face into ribbons.

He glanced anxiously behind him at the big old wooden door where Nina was gazing closely at some of the medieval graffiti. Like a botanist inspecting an orchid. Then she turned and asked the guide a question, in French. Adam didn't understand any of it, though he tried to overhear. He heard the name *McLintock*.

The corpulent guide nodded, and answered. Nina frowned and nodded and then she looked at the graffiti. There was something in this conversation, something significant, maybe something worrying.

Frustrated, he turned to scrutinize the graffiti. All

the interior walls of Domme castle were covered with it. His reading of McLintock's book had told him the graffiti had been carved into the stone by the Templars – with their teeth: their own rotten, fallen-out teeth. Because they had no knives, no metal tools. To carve symbols in stone with your teeth meant real, determined purpose. The graffiti assuredly, therefore, meant *something*.

But what? To Adam the graffiti just looked like random scribblings, inane doodles, squares and runes, grail bearers and cartoon popes, all of them surprisingly coarse, but then maybe that was to be expected.

Etched with human teeth.

His mind drifted back to Temple Bruer. More brutal and strange graffiti, in another cold and threatening place. The fear lurked, and stirred. He wanted to get going. *Always keep moving*, that was their mutual agreement. Their pursuers still had the notebooks. Once they realized that his and Nina's protective custody in Britain was a sham, just a paragraph in the press – and that could happen at any time – they would come after them. Fast and ruthless.

Gesturing vividly, he gained Nina's attention, made a car-steering motion with two hands. She acknowledged, and swivelled, and raised a finger: one more minute.

Nina used the minute to converse with the guide. The fat Frenchwoman tutted and sighed, she was evidently keen to escort them all out of the chilly dungeon that was Domme castle, probably so she could hurry home to a nice hot lunch. But she dawdled at Nina's insistence, answering her questions.

The dialogue was quick, and intense. Nina's white face seemed paler than ever. Shocked? Then the guide shrugged as if to say, *I know nothing else*. And they were led from the building.

As they walked quickly to the car, parked beyond the town walls, he gave in to his frustrations. 'So, what was all that about? What did she say? The guide?'

'She recognized me.'

'You? Jesus!'

'Not in that way. She recognized my accent, and my name. And she remembered Dad's visit.'

Adam opened the car door and slid inside. She did the same. He buckled his belt. Trying to calm the jitters. 'How could she remember your dad, out of thousands of tourists?'

'Because my Dad spent three whole days examining the graffiti. And he was obviously a scholar and he asked the guide lots of questions.'

The diesel engine rumbled as Adam urgently turned the key, and they drove fast, away from Domme. The D783. East.

'OK. What did he want to see?'

'The guide recalled him asking about certain images.' Nina was writing in Adam's notebook as she spoke. Adam notched up another gear, driving even faster, and listening to her words. 'He was particularly interested in all the images of the Grail. And that odd one with the woman carrying the long cup or the yard arm thing.'

Adam had seen that. 'An alembic? Yes. Isn't that what they call it? Kind of a long-necked vase?'

'We know the Templars had associations with the Grail,' she said, 'but I don't understand.'

Adam braked, abruptly, at a junction. 'Nina? The map. Which way? I've no idea where I am.'

She reached for the atlas. 'Drulhe. Drulhe . . . it's barely visible. Totally remote.' Her finger rested on a page. 'Take the D801 to Gourgatel, we have to cross the autoroute, the A20.'

'How far? How long?'

She pouted, pensively, held the atlas up, to get the best of the frail winter light. 'Two hours. Three, maybe?'

He scrutinized the sky. They had just enough time to get to Drulhe today and see it in daylight. But only if they drove very fast.

As they drove, in tense and mordant silence, he thought of the sense of remoteness he'd felt at Temple Bruer, lost on blasted Lincoln Heath. So many Templar preceptories were hidden away, Penhill too. Why? What were they hiding? What did they do there, in their Babylon rites? Something to do with sex? Something brutal and pagan, related to the Green Men? Something with a Grail? But why the buried skeletons?

The answer was out there, in the ether. Adam felt like he was dialling an old shortwave radio. Picking up stray voices, snatches of foreign tongues, a jaunt of hissing music, and then glimpses of English: a phrase or two, glimpses of something that made some kind of sense.

And then it was gone and the message fuzzed out like a radio station lost on the motorway, and Nina said, 'No, Adam. South at Foissac, the D45. Adam!'

He squealed the car right, noisily. He was driving way too fast now, making locals scowl and gesticulate, as their rented diesel Renault raced through each pretty stone village with its little boucheries and stooped old women, scowling on street corners by La Maison de la Presse, all those yellow signs with a scarlet quill.

It began to drizzle as they reached Drulhe, which was utterly and defeatingly lost in the undulating green hills of Aveyron. They parked by the church. Nina fetched her father's book from the back seat.

There was virtually nothing in Drulhe. A sign at the church door, in four languages, admitted as much: *Once part of extensive Templar properties in Aveyron, Drulhe church was very significantly rebuilt in the nineteenth century, and almost no traces remain of the knightly presence. Today the church is part of the Route of Milk . . .*

The Route of Milk? Some desperate and failing tourist gimmick. This place was so devoid of interest they'd had to invent some useless ruse to get people to come here and save depopulating rural southern France from terminal decline. But, then, why did Nina's father come here, when there were so many more important Templar properties a few hours down the autoroute, like Saint Eulalie and Couvertoirade?

Yet Archie McLintock had brusquely ignored them

on his long odyssey across Europe, and he came to drear little Drulhe.

That was it. Adam turned to Nina. 'He came here.'

'Aye. I know—'

'No, Nina, *he came here*. He didn't go to Chinon, or to Saint Eulalie, or to any of the really notable Templar sites. La Rochelle. Sergeac.' He didn't care if he was getting the pronunciation wrong. He grabbed the book rudely from Nina's hands. 'What does your father say about Drulhe in the book? Look! Nothing at all. It's so insignificant he doesn't even mention it. Whatever traces of the Templar there are here, he must, at first, have decided they were so unimportant that when he wrote the book, he didn't mention the place. But then when he was putting together his theory – he came back *here*, not anywhere else.'

She took the book back, clutched it to her chest.

Adam pointed at the glass-fronted sign by the church door, spattered by the hesitant rain. 'Look at what the sign says. "There are virtually no signs of the knightly presence". What does that mean, Nina? That there is something here, some scant trace. And therefore whatever it is must be totally crucial. Because your dad drove through the endless bloody hills of Aveyron to get here, not anywhere else. Come on!'

They went inside the church.

And it was *empty of the knightly presence*.

The entire church was devoid of signs. It was yet another typically disappointing French church interior, almost rebuilt during the nineteenth century, scoured of accumulated meaning by the Revolution and French secularism.

'Outside, then,' she said.

She was right. Whatever they sought had to be an exterior feature: like the door of Temple Church in London.

The winter daylight was almost gone; the drizzle had hardened into solid rain. Everything was telling them to give up, there is nothing here, the knightly presence is undetectable. Drenched by the wet, they crept around the dull grey church. A man watched them from a parked car.

Panic and fear were irrepressible but Adam repressed them, convincing himself: why shouldn't this man watch them, out of sheer curiosity? What they were doing was bizarre, inching around an Aveyronnais church in the pouring rain, in frigid December, in a deserted village, looking at Victorian guttering as if it was the Ark of the fucking Covenant—

'Adam!' She reached for his hand, pointed. 'Up there.'

It was the tiniest slab of medieval stonework. Just a metre long, yellow and old, and inset into the nineteenth-century bricks. And into the stone the Templars or their masons had carved several symbols.

The stone was so high up that Adam could barely see what was inscribed on it. He swore at his lack of binoculars. He looked again. It took him a few seconds to visually compute. On the right was some complex symbol. Squares in circles? He had no idea what that was. The middle symbol could have been a Grail, or maybe not. But the symbol on the far left was much more easily interpreted.

It was a pentagram. An angular, five-pointed star.

Nina was writing in the book, trying to shield its pages from the rain with her arm as she did so. Adam was thinking as hard as he had ever thought, and furiously searching the net on his phone.

A pentagram, a pentacle, a pentagram. What did that symbolize?

The wounds of Christ.

The five senses, the symbol of health. The key of Solomon. Maybe the elements.

And the devil. The pentagram symbolized the devil.

38

Rodez, France

They slept in an Ibis hotel off the autoroute in Rodez. And then it became a kind of blur as they raced the freeways of France, careering down the Autoroutes du Sud. Sometimes it rained, sometimes it didn't – sometimes there were sudden gashes of vivid blue in the steely winter sky. Then they stopped for diesel. Twitching. Nervous. There were Garfield cartoons plastered on the petrol dispensers.

And onwards. *Etape de trucks. Piquenique spot. Toilettes.* Two hundred kilometres whirred past. Nina asked him about his childhood to pass the hours and kill the tension. He gave her the précis: boozy brawling father, fragile intelligent mother, a decent school. Then journalism school. Then fistfights with his drunken father, which had left them estranged. Then Sydney. University. Parties. Alicia. And then Alicia dead. The only woman he had ever loved.

Nina was silent, Adam asked, 'Have you ever been in love?'

The question was intrusive, but it didn't seem to matter any more; they were so deep into this, together, there was no need for concealment.

'Maybe,' she said. 'Yes, when I was twenty. For a year or two. It scared me.'

'How?'

'Because it's a kind of death, isn't it?'

'Sorry?'

'Love.' Her voice was soft, and resigned. 'You lose a bit of yourself, in the other, so it's a kind of dying. It's frightening.'

'But that's the point,' said Adam. 'Without it, we are atomized, whole but alone . . .'

He paused. The word alone was too much, Adam immediately realized. Nina was alone. She had lost her father, and now her sister. At once he wanted to say sorry, but that, he thought, might compound his error, so he said nothing. Nina was quiet: lost in her grief, probably. He glanced along the autoroute.

The sign said *L'Espagne*. Spain.

The afternoon was already dwindling, the dark clouds over the Pyrenees were a grey blanket threatening to drench. Suddenly, she said, 'Do you want to hear about my suicide?'

Adam shrugged his awkwardness. Antonio Ritter had mentioned this: her suicide attempt a year ago. Obviously Ritter had been researching them. Adam had not mentioned it since. 'Well – uh – Nina – only if you want to.'

Nina stared ahead. 'I want to. I want to talk. Stops me thinking. About Hannah.'

'OK.'

'It was just the once, it was . . . I'm not sure how serious it was. I took some pills – it was right at the edge of my breakdown. In the worst part, the blackest place. I was drinking and drugging and . . . y'know. Despair. So I popped some wee helpers and someone found me and my stomach was pumped. And there it fucking is and I will never ever do anything like that again. Because it is so incredibly selfish, now I see what the possibility of my father's killing himself has done to me. It's the most selfish act. You have to fight on, even if you can't. The best way out is always through. Robert Frost.'

Her speech concluded, she sat back and looked at the atlas.

Adam wondered if he should take the chance, and talk about Hannah's 'suicide'. Nina had refused to believe this when the police had told her. Maybe he could approach it obliquely, now she had truly opened up. It might be cruel, but maybe he had no choice.

'Nina. Do you believe what the police say, about . . . Hannah being in some kind of cult?'

Her reply was unfazed, but unbelieving. 'Ach, no.'

'You sure? How can you be sure?'

'Just am. She was not that kind of girl. Just not. A swinger? Sex parties? No, not Hannah. She was pure vanilla. A sweetheart.'

Adam glanced across the gear well. Her eyes were wet and shining, staring at the dark mountains ahead.

'So what connects her to the other suicides? You know what, um, what Mark Ibsen said?'

'I don't know. I do know the police are not infallible!' Her voice was cracked. 'A sex-and-death cult? In London? Including my dad? Linked to Peru? How much sense does that make, Ad?'

'It makes sense given that it is the only explanation that covers all the bases . . . all the many . . .' He swallowed the awkwardness like a tiny fishbone. 'Like the . . . you know . . .'

'The fact my sister wanted to be raped? Aye. By a psycho. Thank you. Thank you so very fucking much.'

Her bitterness and anger filled the entire car. Perhaps, Adam felt, this was necessary. Let it all out.

It was dark now, and silent, and so he could hear her quiet, half-suppressed sobs and so he said nothing. He turned on the radio as they ascended the Pyrenees; the cold air of the mountains surrounded them, even colder than the frigid Aveyron hills.

The tense and waiting silence lasted an hour. Adam was just beginning to think about places to stop, another little hotel, a pension in the hills, somewhere near the frontier, discreet, when she spoke. 'Let's just drive through the night.'

'What?'

'Let's just get into fucking Spain. The next place my dad visited was Sierra de Gata. That's almost two days away, right across Spain, in Extremadura near Portugal. A thousand miles. We need to keep going.'

They were up in the high mountains now, off the motorway, and driving through some large but grimy Pyrenean town. His headlights picked out posters and adverts, a sign for Monsieur Bricolage. Christmas decorations swung dangerously back and forth, above the roads, in the wind. *Joyeux Noël.*

'But . . .'

'Wasn't that the agreement – keep moving?'

He saw the logic; he nodded and yawned as he drove. The sky was high and black. Stars glittered down, the moon shone placidly on the concrete warehouses of Carrefour. The countryside returned. And with it the scent of a hard, cold, tangy mountain night. Adam inhaled, deeply, trying to keep himself awake, and not entirely succeeding.

'Let me drive Adam, you must be knacked.'

He was grateful for the offer; on a little meander of the mountain road he pulled up, and they swapped seats. She drove on, not as fast as him but he didn't mind. He wanted to sleep. He was exhausted and glad they were leaving France.

The border was barely there; a few flags fluttered in the ski centres and villages, on either side. The blue and red and white of France, then the red and gold of Spain, with its royal crest. The red and gold of blood and sand.

They were soon descending through long steep cold moonlit valleys. At last Adam slept, properly and for several hours.

When he woke up it had all changed. The mountains had gone, the green valleys had disappeared. The scenery was brown and flat and ugly: the lower Navarre, the sere and sullen Spanish interior. They drank *cafes con leche* in a noisy Spanish motorway service station with fatted hams hanging from the ceiling and truck drivers in thick coats watching a recorded Real Madrid football match on a crap TV and downing tiny glasses of alcohol with their morning *cortados*.

The immensity of inland Spain devoured them. This time Nina slept as he drove the dusty windswept regions. Navarre, Rioja, Castile – they were heading south into wilder, truer Spain. The first glimpse of mountains, far away, broke the horizon; a welcome sight after the brown and endless Castilian plateau. But still far away.

As evening fell they arrived in a town which was only half built, surrounded by white, hollow, unfinished concrete apartment blocks stretching into the cold semi-desert where no one lived, the abortions of a property bust.

They drove a couple of kilometres and found a turning to a motorway hotel, another Ibis: same soap, same unsatisfactory narrow pillows in their rooms. Supper was a few average tapas and cheap Rioja in an almost deserted hotel bar where they talked about the Templars, not just because it was central to their pursuit but because it allowed them not to talk directly about what had happened.

Nina finished one saucer of *patatas bravas*, and

napkinned the hot tomato sauce from her lips. 'So we know the Templars allegedly had a Babylon rite. Some of the medieval chroniclers actually called it this – "a Babylonian rite or ritual". Referring to the, y'know, whole gay sex thing. The initiation ritual.'

'Yes. The phrase was pejorative, hinting at the homosexual acts. So, what we need to know is, where did this initiation ritual come from, and what did it comprise? Possibly some pagan gods; that seems likely. And they must have got it from Peru, the Moche. There *must* be a link. Otherwise your dad would not have gone there.'

'And this pagan ritual must have hypnotized them, or put them in a trance . . .'

Adam looked at her. 'And of course this Templar rite must have been the same ritual, or very similar, to that enacted by the kids in London. The suicides?'

'Yep.' She drank half of her glass of wine. The barman was staring at them with definite interest as he counted the day's meagre takings. There was just one other customer, playing the fruit machine, fruitlessly. The pings and electronic whistles filled the bar.

'By the way the ritual also explains the—' she stabbed at the last chunk of fried chorizo, glistening with oil, '—the violence and courage of the Templars.'

'Sorry?'

'We know they were famously brave, right? A few of them on the battlefield could turn a whole battle in favour of the Christians, even if they were *totally* outnumbered.' She reached for her bag and brought out Archibald McLintock's *Guide*. 'Listen, my dad says in the intro, "In the early years of the Latin East, the Templars quickly developed a fearsome reputation as the best-trained soldiers the Franks possessed, showing an almost suicidal bravery at times. This reached an apogee under the Mastership of Gerard de Ridefort, who died during a reckless attack at Acre."' Her eyes met his.

'An almost suicidal bravery . . .?' He swallowed the very last of his Rioja. 'Yes. If they were aroused to a homoerotic frenzy by these rituals, then they would have yearned for pain and violence, even to the point of death.'

'So the only question is what the actual ritual was, what they believed, what exactly they worshipped. And of course how this hypnosis worked. Still quite a big list.' She sighed.

Adam was writing, and nodding. Then he closed his notebook. Nina stood up. They kissed formally, even chastely, like brother and sister. The kiss was somehow too chaste: a new awkwardness. And then they went to their separate rooms. Adam took with him another bottle of Leclerc Rioja, and drank half of it in his room, watching a Spanish lottery show on the cheap Korean TV, as he waited for sleep. For the inevitable dreams about Alicia, wandering around a school, looking for him, naked. He'd been having this dream for a week. Every single night.

The dream was cruel because sometimes the school turned into a white pristine spaceship and still he

309

couldn't talk to her, and then he realized why he couldn't talk to her: because she was outside the spaceship, beyond the thick glass, she was outside and floating, against the stars, floating away and smiling. And he was inside, trapped.

And then at 4 a.m. he woke, startled, horrified, panting. Horrified by what? A frightening noise: a rat? Something scratching at the door? Someone trying to break in? The man with the gun going to slice out his heart? Adam's pulse was frenzied and erratic. He reached for the light, then went to the door. Outside, an Ibis corridor carpeted with Ibis carpets stretched down to the Ibis fire door. He heard a door slamming downstairs. He sat on the bed for an hour, staring at nothing. And then realized what the dream meant. It was something Alicia had said once: that we are all, all mortal humans, like astronauts, heading on a mission into deep space, heading for the stars: every day we live, we are all on a journey to a place we do not know, on a mission from which we can never return. Sailing for the edge of the world. Goodbye.

Adam felt like crying. *Alicia.* But instead he slept again.

In the morning a scratchy sun was cold, trapped behind the glazing of thin wintry clouds. The tawny Spanish plains stretched to a horizon of pylons. Then those far, tempting mountains.

Adam's mind was more focussed. Perhaps interpreting the dream had helped. He said, firmly, 'America.'

Nina frowned. 'What?

'America! That's still the other big mystery. How did the Templars get all this stuff from South America, from the Moche, from Peru? Columbus didn't reach Hispaniola till, what, 1489? The Templars were long defunct before by then. How did this ritual, this sacred trance, get from Peru to Europe, before Columbus?'

Nina shrugged, inertly. She looked as if she had been crying again, in the night. Adam pursued his own thoughts.

By the afternoon the sulking, ugly plains had at last given way to those prettier, if chilly, hills, and to murmurous wind-bitten pine forests. Here was their destination, a village called Trevejo. They parked and disembarked.

The wind was cutting as they walked through the humble streets, staring in perplexity at the low stone hovels, made from field boulders. These incredibly mean, almost Neolithic thoroughfares apparently led to the Templar church and castle.

The Templars built here in hilly Trevejo, Adam knew from his research, because it was the frontier of the Reconquista, when Spain and Portugal were wrested back from the Moor. The castle was built during another violent Templar crusade against the heathen.

As they walked, he thought of that effigy in Templar church: the knight still clutching his sword, eight hundred years later. Ready to fight for Christ, entranced by the violence of his trade.

He already knew about Extremadura: he'd been here on holiday years before. This land was notably poor

311

today, just as it had always been. This was Extremadura, literally the Land of Extremity, a place of impoverishment and drought and burning sun, yet rich in men and valour.

Extremadura, the lost realm of Spain, was the womb of warriors. This was where Habsburg eagles soared over bleak little villages, which somehow bred men who conquered entire empires. Pizarro. Valdivia. Alvarado. Cortés. All of them came from here. Together, these men had defeated the mighty Aztec and the imperial Inca, together these men from poor, provincial sun-lashed Extremadura had vanquished two continents, discovered new deserts and jungles, and sailed the entire Amazon for the very first time.

Adam mused. He thought very, very hard as they walked to the castle.

Extremadura was *also* the last refuge of the *Spanish Templars*. A small town south of here – Jerez de los Caballeros – Jerez of the Knights – was a town once owned by the Templars, and it was the place the Templars had made their final stand against the kings of Spain: one tower of the Templar castle was still known as the Bloody Tower, because this was where the cornered Templars threw themselves off the battlements, hurling themselves to their deaths, rather than be captured.

And tiny little Jerez de los Cabelleros *also* produced two great conquistadors all by itself: Hernando de Soto, who travelled with Pizarro to Peru, and who became governor of Cuba, and who died near the Mississippi searching for some legendary gold in Florida; and Vasco Núñez de Balboa, the first European to cross the Americas, the first European to see the Pacific from the American coast, another man obsessed with gold.

Two great conquistadors, from just one tiny Templar town?

Was that really mere coincidence?

'There it is, the castle,' said Nina.

The ruined Templar castle of Trevejo was perched on the loftiest outcrop high above the village, which itself stared down from the Sierra de Gata on the roads into Portugal. It was a good site to build a castle if you wanted to watch the passes, or check any Muslim attacks.

For a few moments they stood on the silent precipice, just outside the castle, gazing down at the roads which snaked through the green, hilly pinewoods. There was a Templar flag flying from the keep of the castle: the red cross pattee on a field of white. The silence all around was imperious. Just the wistful flicking of the flag in the wind, and an eagle mewing in the distance, as it circled above the wintered emptiness.

Then they descended, picking their way through the perilous rocks, until they reached the Templar church, a few hundred metres beneath the castle on a ledge.

'My God.'

Adam didn't have to ask what had surprised her. Graves. Tiny little slots of graves, human-shaped slots in hard stone. *Just like the graves at Penhill.*

Adam took some brisk and anxious photos. Then

they retreated quickly down the stone road, past the raddled houses, to the stoneflagged plaza of Trevejo, and they climbed in the car and Nina drove down the winding road, as Adam furiously searched the net on his phone.

At last he sat back and said, 'This is it. The connection. With America. *This is how it all links.*'

39

The Museo Larco, Lima, Peru

Hairless dogs.

That was one thing that united ancient Mexican culture with ancient Peruvian culture. What else?

Jess was sitting in the sunlit courtyards of the Museo Larco, enjoying some rare Limeno sunshine, taking a few minutes to relax herself, as best she could, after all the violence and grotesqueries of the last week. She'd been in Lima for three days, and this was the first day she had summoned the courage to leave her hotel room.

So here she was. The Museo Larco, the greatest collection of ancient north Peruvian art in the world; if she hadn't been terrified for her life this might have been a nice afternoon jaunt, a chance to chill out in this pretty colonial palazzo, with its orange trees and fountains, and the gardens haunted by the strange, black, friendly, stray dogs, *descendants* of the hairless dogs once eaten by Aztecs and Inca and Moche alike.

A thought nagged at her. But what was it? Not the possibility of her illness; *something different, very different.* But the thought eluded her. She closed her eyes and breathed deeply, trying to meditate away the stress and tension.

When she opened her eyes again the little dog was just a few metres distant, gazing right at her, his sad head cocked imploringly, his hairless tail whipping. A Museo Larco security guard lazily clapped his hand, chasing the dog out of the courtyard, and into the street.

Jess rose and walked into the dark twinkling rooms of the museum. Her stride was purposive: she ignored the magnificent imperial Chimu goldwork, the warrior priest's diadems from the Apogee Epoch, the sacred spondylus shell bottles, and went straight to the Moche collection.

Her eyes ran along the shelves, assessing the pottery of screaming bats, hunched demons, Moche with their limbs removed, Moche women having sex with the dead, or sex with animals. Nina moved down the aisle, examining the pottery of Moche people who deliberately skeletonized their faces.

The questions thronged. How did these last pots relate to the pottery showing sex with corpses and skeletons? More importantly: how did these pots relate to the death of her boss from Toronto, *of her lover*? How and why was the horror of Moche culture being re-enacted in the grubby streets of modern Peru? And maybe even in Scotland?

Jess sat down on a bench in the darkened chambers of the Moche rooms of the Museo Larco and went over what she knew.

She didn't doubt that necrophilia actually took place in Moche society, there was too much ceramic and textile evidence for this. People had sex with the dead, and probably quite frequently, judging by the abundance of art dedicated to the theme. But equally some of the pots that showed people with skull-like faces raping women were probably representations of men who had slashed their own faces to look like skulls, cutting off their own lips and noses and slicing off the flesh from the cheeks, men who were maybe allowed to take women at will.

Imagine a society like that. People with no lips and noses and faces, wandering around, like living screaming skulls. Smiling, eating, having brutal and coercive sex. How did these skull-men avoid infection? How long did they live with these terrible wounds exposed? Weeks, months, years?

A tourist was gazing at one of the sex pots. A backpacker. Twenty-one or twenty-two. American maybe. And giggling. The backpacker turned to his friend. 'Jesus, sweetheart, look at this – the guy is getting an enema. Gross!'

The girlfriend was apparently around the corner, behind a glass pottery cabinet. Jess heard her young voice. 'Can we go, Todd? This stuff is just . . . *ewww*.'

They drifted away. Jess felt the helplessness weighing her down. She walked out into the patio once more.

317

What a waste it all was, what a terrible waste. All that digging, all that thinking, all those horrific yet exciting discoveries, all those moments of terror or exultation: it had all been for nothing. The TUMP site was closed. Dan was dead. The police were scared, and shutting all the doors. And still the killers were out there. Were they coming after Jess?

She sighed and looked at the dog. The hairless dog with the sad, sad eyes, so similar to Aztec dogs. As she gazed, she remembered the men in the pyramid. Their accents.

The way they said the word *ulluchu*.

Accent. Aztecs. The Aztecs. Ulluchu. Accent.

Ulluchu was a pretty strange word. *Oo-ll-oo-choo*.

And yet there was one other word which was just like it, from a different culture a thousand years later, four thousand miles away. In Pre-Columbian Mexico.

The Aztec word.

Ololiúqiu. And *ulluchu*.

They were one and the same.

40

Tomar, Portugal

The grandiose castle and church of medieval Tomar loomed above the small, surrounding town, like the great wooden effigy of a saint held aloft by humble peasant hands.

Nina and Adam sat sipping bad Portuguese coffee in an inconspicuous corner of the cobbled main square. The palm trees rustled in the December wind, a few shops were already selling lurid, clownish costumes for Carnival alongside Christmas treats: festive pumpkin fritters, *broas de mel*. Adam startled himself with the realization: it was Christmas Eve. He had lost track of time, like a lonely child at a fairground, bewildered by the fleeing colours. Was he going to ring his dad for Christmas? No, he hadn't spoken to him in three years, not since they had last come to blows, when Adam was defending his mother.

He wondered how his mother put up with it all, now he wasn't there to protect her. His father had never actually *hit* his mother; but he certainly bullied her, and in the end Adam had found it too much. The urge to protect had made him eventually intervene in one of his parents' rows, and so he and his father had fought. And yet, now he considered it, maybe his mother was at fault as well: she tolerated it, passive-aggressively. Maybe they both liked it.

You can't choose your parents, but you can choose not to be like them.

What effect had this all had on Adam? He often wondered. Maybe he was drawn to vulnerable women, women he really could protect. Like Alicia. Except he hadn't protected her, not in the end.

And what about Nina? She was different to Alicia, much stronger, much more defiant; yet she also had that protectable quality that he found so desirable. And so troubling. He looked her way. She was anxiously scrutinizing an old woman, at the next table.

'I don't think the Camorra recruit elderly widows,' Adam said, sipping his scorched black coffee.

'Ach. Who *knows* who they recruit? There's something wrong here. I don't like it. Everyone is staring at us.'

'Everyone is drunk. It's lunchtime on Christmas Eve.'

She stared at him. 'Jesus. Is it really?'

He could see the hollowness in her eyes, the void where her family should be: yet *all killed at their own hands.* And now it was Christmas.

Quickly he tried to fill the gap. 'Shall we go over it again? The American link. You said you had questions.'

320

'Did I?' Her moist gaze was vastly regretful. 'OK, then, Ad. Tell me.' The pigeons warbled on their churchly sill: beneath the rose window of São João Baptista.

'I remembered what your, uh, dad said. At Rosslyn. He referred to the Norse serpents carved on the Prentice Pillar. We know there is a strong link between the early Templars and the Scottish court.' Adam opened his notebook. 'In 1128 the cousin of St Bernard of Clairvaux, and Hugues de Payens, the founder of the Templar Order, met King David in Scotland, and established one of Europe's first Templar preceptories, in Scotland. Payens had been on the First Crusade with Henri St Clair, Second Baron of Roslin.'

'Are you going to rehearse all that Holy Blood Da Vinci stuff? Sinclairs sailing to Los Angeles in a coracle—'

He doodled viciously in his notebook. 'The St Clairs *did* have Norse links. The Sinclair lineage dates back to a Viking raider called Hrolf the Ganger, who invaded Normandy in the tenth century. This is all recorded in the Norse sagas. But even without the Sinclairs we know the medieval Scots court had strong Norse connections. The Scots royals intermarried with Viking aristocracy, with the kings of Orkney, and with the Lord of the Isles . . .'

'Adam. We are on the run from people *who killed my family*. Hurry up.'

'The graves are also crucial. Those strange little slots. We have seen them in two Templar preceptories

– Penhill in Yorkshire, now Trevejo in Spain. As your father says in the book, there are scarcely any others known in Western Europe. Apart from Heysham in Lancashire, England, in the graveyard of Saint Patrick's church. And I've *checked this place*. Historians know those graves at Saint Patrick in Heysham are *Viking* – used for interring skeletons, temporarily. So that's it, Nina: we now see unusual Norse cultural practices were adopted by the Templars.'

Nina tucked a stray lock of black hair behind a small white ear. Somehow nervous and beautiful at the same time. 'That doesn't prove much.'

'Why did the Templars go to Scotland so early in the Order's history? For what? The Scottish court was hardly rich, and it was at the ends of the earth, as far away from the Holy Land as you can get. What were those first Templars after?'

'The big dark secret?'

'Exactly: this secret technique, this warlike trance, that would make the knights brave and fearless. We know the Templars' first forays into battle were faltering, and uncertain: they were just a tiny band of men. Two guys on a donkey, the icon of the Templars, the icon we see in Rosslyn. But some Scottish knight with Viking forebears, perhaps a Sinclair, must have told Hugues Payens a secret, on the First Crusade: a way to bind his brethren together, to attract new recruits, something attractively occult and mysterious, the Babylon rite, the group hypnosis, a way to inculcate sexualized blood lust. And this something was itself a technique the

Scots had learned from the Vikings. The Vikings were wild fighters, madly bloodthirsty, like the Templars. And so the Vikings knew the trance, and they got it—'

'From America.' Nina nodded, unhappily. 'I do get it, Adam. The Vikings were in America in . . .'

'In the tenth and eleventh centuries they had several settlements in Newfoundland *where they met the natives.*'

'That's still a fucking long way from seventh-century Peru. Tenth-century Newfoundland?' Nina finished her tiny cup of coffee, and stared at the silt at the bottom. Her expression was morbid.

The pigeons chattered. Adam sighed. *Christmas Eve*, and here they were, a long way from anywhere, many miles from home. But maybe there *was* no home any more. Maybe they were exiled from everything, for ever. So they had to focus on the present because the past was too horrific and the future too frightening.

Adam sprinted through the rest of his argument. 'Some cultural practices were shared across pre-Columbian South and North America: human sacrifice, pyramid building, styles of mural painting, for a start. This is a fact. It happens. Look at Indo-European languages, sharing similarities from the Punjab to Portugal. So it's quite possible the Babylon rite made its way from Peru, where it began, then into Mexico, then further north, even to the east coast of Canada.'

'Come on,' said Nina, standing, abruptly. 'The castle will shut soon and I want to get out of here tomorrow.'

He dropped a few euros in the saucer and hastened after her. Small, determined, fierce and vulnerable, she was striding up the medieval stone steps of glorious Tomar. The path led through the cypresses and pines of the wooded rise, and led to a car park and a scratchy kiosk, where a woman with a faint moustache took their money, and gazed at them with a curious squint.

A little gate opened. They stepped through. The contrast with the humdrum car park and ticket booth, with the citadel itself was quite stunning.

The Templar church and castle of Tomar were as 'monumentally stupendous' as Archibald McLintock promised in his gazetteer. It was also eerily empty: they were the only tourists, because everyone else was already preparing for Christmas. The vastness of the churches and gardens and battlements and cloisters obliged them to whisper; Adam didn't know why.

Together and quickly they explored the dormitories and ambulatories, the monastic kitchens and Renaissance chapterhouse. Then they climbed high steps to the mighty and battlemented walls.

The views of the town below were contemptuously lofty. Another Templar flag rippled, arrogant and proud, in the stiff, chilly breeze. Nina said, 'It's so bloody big.'

'This is where the Templars survived longest in Europe; in fact they never went away,' Adam said, quoting his own research. 'They survived because the Portuguese king protected them, and refused to reduce them. Eventually the Portuguese Templars evolved into the Order of Christ. So this Templar citadel became the global headquarters – of the Order of Christ.'

'But what was my *dad* looking for here? He spent a day here, or at least an afternoon.'

'Pretty sure he didn't come for the view. Quick. Let's go down.'

A claustrophobic stone staircase led them down to the third cloister. The cloister of the washing. The *claustro de lavagem*. Again they were the only people here. A few Templar gravestones were propped against the delicate marble pillars; in the central patio a crudely carved fountain fluted water into the Christmas air.

The old knightly graves had pentagrams on them.

Nina said, very quietly. '*The Order of Christ*, I did them in history, at S Level. The Age of the Explorers. The Order bred all the great Portuguese explorers, right? Like Henry the Navigator. The guys who went to Africa and South America. It's another link with the Americas. But the wrong way round. I don't . . . Wait.' The whisper was loud. 'Someone's following us.'

Adam looked behind. It was a man in a blue uniform. Emerging from behind a door, and staring in their direction. He relaxed, slightly. 'Nina, they are about to close early, it's Christmas Eve. That's just a *guard*, waiting for us to go.'

She shrugged, impatient and frustrated, and walked into the next cloister, the *claustro de cimeterio*. There were more odd, propped gravestones here, with more silent yet eloquent pentagrams carved on them.

Pentagrams, thought Adam, buttoning his coat tighter against the cold. How did pentagrams fit in? And the Grail? Those mysteries were still unsolved. And did he really believe his own Viking theory? It was possible, but it was also very tenuous, and it needed more evidence. There was still so much missing.

They had one more place to visit. Nina rejoined him and they paced to a stone staircase, and quickly climbed the helix of weathered cream marble into a spectacularly vivid and perfectly circular chapel, with a gilded ceiling raised on delicate pillars – a ceiling almost impossibly high above their heads.

'Why's it so tall?'

Adam consulted the little guidebook. 'The Templars used to take communion here on horseback.'

'What?'

'Yes. Apparently. The knights would ride straight in and take mass on their stallions. And it's round because it is modelled on the Holy Sepulchre in Jerusalem, and maybe Solomon's temple.'

Nina gazed up at the smoky distant colours of the ceiling. The whole chapel was ornately painted and silvered. Gold and sombre scarlets framed her black, black hair. 'They really were nuts, weren't they? Militant ravers. Murderous hippies. Taking communion on horseback. No wonder people suspected they were odd. This and the Babylon rite. Jesus.' She paused. Then said, quite calmly, 'Adam, I don't buy our own theory. I don't.'

'Why?'

'Because. Look at this. Look at *this place*.' She gestured at the spectacular ceiling of the circular chapel. 'This is stunning: this isn't fake.'

'What do you mean?'

'I don't believe the Templars were pagan. There is no real evidence for it, yet there is enormous evidence that they were sincerely, even militantly *Christian*. They built churches everywhere. They were famously *devout*. They kissed the cross before going into battle. Yet we're trying to claim they were secret Satanists with a sexy cat fetish? Pfft. It doesn't pan out. It doesn't make sense. Just disnae make any sense *at all*.'

Her words died away with a faint echo. Adam sighed, deeply. If she was right, they were nowhere closer to solving the problem.

A secret that gets you killed. The Babylon rite. They'd come halfway across Europe and they were still lost in the ominous dark.

Nina was sitting on a bench, disconsolate. Adam turned and looked at the exquisite decoration of the pilasters, feeling as if he had nothing else to do. Vegetal motifs adorned every square centimetre: stone vines and painted garlands wove around stone men, snaking into their mouths, and out of their eyes. Just as with the Green Men in the Temple in London. Here were figures and faces intoxicated with the vines of life, spewing the tendrils, eating the greenery.

A memory returned, unwarranted. *You've got to eat your greens.* A man raping Hannah. Or, even worse, not raping her.

'*Bom dia.*'

Adam jumped, the adrenalin thumped. But it was just the guard, again; the official was keen to usher

327

them out and go home for a Portuguese Christmas, for the *consoada*, the reunion of the family.

Hastily, they retreated to a bar in the old town by the ancient Tomar synagogue, a bar of drunks, of people on their own, people with no *consoada*, people like Nina and Adam.

Nina drank too much and talked about memories of her family. Playing chess with her dad when she was a little girl, playing footie with Hannah by the river in the little Borders town where they grew up. And as she drank more of the cheap *vinho tinto*, the night got darker and the bar noisier, and the lonely men stared at Nina, and ogled her white skin and her low top and short denim skirt with black tights, and her lips and teeth got more and more stained from the dark Douro wine, and her words became more and more slurred and Scottish. *Brae. Birl. Skitie. Drookit.*

And Adam sat there thinking how much she reminded him of Alicia, beautiful and drinking and funny and risky, and how much he couldn't go there, not again, not ever again.

She stopped talking and gazed distantly at Adam in the blur of the fuzzy night and the tawdry skirl of Brazilian pop music. 'Aren't you *ever* going to try and fuck me?'

He stared her way. Embarrassed. And aroused. She was drunk and he could understand why she was drunk: the total horror of her recent experiences, the loss of her father and sister. He would be drunk every day in that situation. But this, here and now, was wrong.

'I mean. Am I doing something wrong? Giving out the wrong signals? Don't ya even want to kiss me *at all*?'

He said nothing because he was at a total loss. What should he say?

'Fuck this, then, I'll find someone else.'

She stood, quite swayingly drunk. Then she went to the door of the bar and pushed it. And she was gone.

For a few minutes he remained, riven by indecision. He should go after her. But he didn't trust himself not to take advantage. He *did* want her. He'd been captured by her beauty that first time he saw her: the ravenly hair, the slender elusiveness. He wanted her more than he had wanted any woman since Alicia, maybe even more than Alicia. But if he touched her once he would never stop touching her. And if she tried to kiss him he would be unable to resist her red lips and her white skin, the colours of Christmas itself, of berries in the snow—

But what if she was in trouble? She was drunk, and he had to look after her. They had to look out for each other, they were still being hunted. She could be in trouble *now*.

As soon as he stepped outside the bar into the freezing old alley, by the ancient old synagogue, he saw her in the shadows. And the man holding her against a wall.

41

Rua Pablo Dias, Tomar, Portugal

Whether it was attempted rape or just a fumbled kiss
Adam had no idea: in the dim lamplight, which he ran
towards, he just saw a very big man, one of the thugs
from the bar, in a dirty leather jacket. With his left
hand the man was wrenching up Nina's skirt.

She yelled, 'Let go, *leave me alone*!' Adam's shout
froze the chilly air. *'Leave her alone*!'

The Portuguese man, tall, and thickset, turned and
gazed at Adam. 'You talking big?' The man grinned.
'Stupid English fuck, I open you up. Stick you in the
ribs.'

He flourished something: Adam saw it was a knife,
flashed from his inside pocket. *That* was why he was
so confident, so brazen.

'Adam, let's go! Let's just go!' Nina cried.

But something in Adam said *No*. He'd been running
away for weeks; maybe he'd been running away for

years, ever since Alicia. Running from feelings, running from situations. And this nasty bastard, this boozed-up pig, reminded Adam of Ritter. Leather jacket, leather coat, creepy smile. Another arrogant bully. He gazed from the knife to the man; from the man to the knife. 'Come on, then. Try me.'

The man waited half a second, then lunged.

The blow was wayward: Adam swerved the blade easily, then brought a forearm smashing down on the guy's wrist. The knife twirled into the gutter. Then Adam leaned back a fraction and *punched*.

His fist connected so hard with the side of the man's head it felt as if he was thumping steel, a literally stunning blow: his knuckles rang with the pain.

The reaction was instant: the man wheeled away, spinning on the spot, like an enormous toy. Eyes rolling.

Adam remembered his dad's instructions. *Never let them recover.* His next punch was immediate, to the stomach, hard and perfect and kidney-level, making the guy double up and groan. In the dark Adam grabbed the man's hair, and pulled his head down on to his upthrust knee, crunching his nose in a disturbing explosion of blood and of cartilage. The man reeled back, and fell to the pavement.

'Adam—'

All he could hear was his own anger. *You think you're so tough, menacing a girl half your size? How about THIS?*

Adam drew back a boot and then laid into the man's stomach, and a groaning bellow of pain made it all better; a third violent kick produced a whimper. He knew he was going too far now, but all the horrors and frustrations of the last weeks were concentrated in the shining toecap of his boot as he kicked this man twice more. This was for Antonio Ritter; and this kick was for everyone: for the truck driver who hit Alicia, for the man his father became, for the guy who killed the cop. All Adam's challenged masculinity was disappearing with each richly satisfying thump of his boot into dull human flesh—

'Adam!'

Nina had him by the shoulders, pulling him away. His face stung – suddenly. She had slapped him, hard.

'Stop! You're going to kill him. *Stop.*'

She was crying.

It was a bucketful of cold common sense, poured over his head. It made him shiver. What the fuck was he doing? She was right. The man was utterly beaten, lying on the floor clutching his balls, and groaning. He was a boozed-up fool who thought he could grope some drunken girl in an alley; but then he had drawn a knife on the wrong guy at the wrong moment.

'Let's get out of here.' Nina grabbed his hand and pulled him. 'The police will be after us. Come on, now – come on!'

Detaching himself from her grasp, Adam stooped, and lifted the guy's copiously bleeding head. Yes, he'd live. He'd surely suffer some cracked ribs. Maybe a ruptured organ. But he'd live.

Glancing up, he realized that a CCTV camera was patiently observing him. *Fuck.*

332

The man moaned in his pain. Adam's conscience roiled.

'Call an ambulance,' he told Nina as they fled down the road to their hotel. As they made it to the river he heard her fumbling through the Portuguese, *emergencia, sinagoga, obrigado*. She was swiftly sobering up.

At a fountain he stopped and washed the blood from his hands. In the moonlight the blood looked black. His knuckles were scraped raw from the initial enormous blow to the man's skull.

Despite the guilt and revulsion at his own violence, a tiny ripple of prideful pleasure ran through him. The victim was a big ugly yob, a stupid bully with a knife, so he got what he deserved: a thoroughgoing beating. And Adam had delivered it. *Righteous justice*.

'Get your bags,' he told Nina. 'We should check out right now.'

For all the lateness of the hour, the hotel was humming with old people eating, and drinking. Christmas Eve. Some elderly ladies were in the bar, drunk, carolling songs. The barmen looked bored yet busy. It was perfect cover.

Seven and a half minutes later they were in the car, speeding away from Tomar. The streets were utterly deserted: only the churches were doing business, as people trooped out of the rooster's mass, excited children in anoraks laughing and holding balloons.

The auto-estrada was like a racetrack out of season. Not a car in sight. Adam realized he was drunk-driving, and he didn't care. The police would be after him now, anyway, as soon as they saw the CCTV footage.

Nina was silent. Finally she spoke, and her words were unslurred. 'He came out and followed me, wanted to kiss me, I just shrugged I didn't care, God knows why—'

'You were drunk.'

'But then the kiss got nasty. Ach. I tried to push him off. If you hadn't got there he'd—'

'He'd have raped you.'

'Maybe . . . He was drunk.'

'But he had a knife.'

'Yes. He did. And it's my stupid fault.'

'No, it wasn't your fault, he was just a thug. Anyway, he won't be troubling anyone now.' Adam steered them off the motorway. *The Algarve 15km.* 'My temper overtakes me, sometimes, I get it from my dad . . .'

Reaching across the gear well, she went to touch him, then seemed to think better of it. She pulled back her hand, and asked, 'D'you think there were any witnesses?'

'I've no idea. But the ambulance will find him, the police will ask questions – and I saw a CCTV camera in that alley. We're in trouble.'

'So what do we—'

'Let's just finish this: there are just two more places to go, right?'

Nina turned on the car lights and scrutinized the final European receipts. 'Nosse Senhora de Guadalupe, in the Algarve. He went there on August nineteenth. The morning. Then that afternoon he went to Sagres, had a beer. And that's it. After that, Peru.'

'We'll do exactly what he did, today. That church, then Sagres; then we get out of Portugal. We have to hide somewhere else, anywhere else. And we need to solve this puzzle fast.'

'One last chance then.' Her voice was melancholy.

The moonlit Atlantic silvered in the distance. A glow of towns and cities, and nocturnal sea. They had reached the southwest extremity of Europe, where the continent ended, where the Templars lived out their final years, and became the Order of Christ, the sect of journeyers – medieval knights becoming Renaissance explorers, like dinosaurs evolving into birds. And then those knights lit out for the oceans, carrying the Templarite cross on their white-sailed caravels, heading west, always west, to the distant empty shores of a bold New World.

There was a beauty to it.

It was Christmas Day and they were on the Algarve. The church was just twelve kilometres short of Sagres, the most southwesterly point of all.

Empty roads led to the darkness of the ocean. Behind them the rosy-green caress of dawn was now visible, above the orange lights of distant Faro. The first light of Christmas Day.

He parked. The little church was tucked down a lane off a side-road. The church was so humble it had no gate, no car park, no nothing: just a tiny chapel in the middle of a field, off a farm lane.

She flicked the light again and read the book.

'"The secret chapel of Henry the Navigator, and built

to his precise instructions, the chapel of Senhora de Guadalupe is drenched with Templar associations. Local legends attest that French knights, fleeing the suppression of the Order in France, took to their boats at La Rochelle, then sailed south, bringing their notorious secret treasure with them. Supposedly they landed here, on this safely remote part of the Algarve coast, and built the first church on this site."'

'Go on,' said Adam.

'"These fanciful speculations aside, it remains an object of puzzlement as to why Henry the Navigator, a leading figure of the Order of Christ, the direct descendants of the Templars in Portugal, ordered this tiny chapel to be built, in secret, in this immensely lonely part of his vast estates. It is said he came here to worship in private, whenever he was able."'

She closed the book and they stepped out of the car into the hushed pink light of Christmas dawn. It was cold but the sky was clear. The endless west wind was slicing along the coast.

The church was disappointingly small and empty. A timorous light shone through the unstained windows on to empty pews and bare walls. The only point of interest was a curious gargoyle, or boss, in the ceiling: it showed a human face licking a leaf. Another Green Man image, yet different, less stylized, more direct. A man licking a leaf, or a plant.

Licking?

Nina stared for a long time at the gargoyle, her face drawn into a deep frown.

Back in the car, Adam rubbed his tired eyes, then looked at his hands. Now the sun was coming up he could see the torn knuckles, and he still had a peppering of dried red blood on his shirt. He felt properly sickened now at what he had done. Where had the violence come from? All that terrible aggression. Locked inside him. Was he as bad as Ritter, in his own way? It was a close call between righteous anger and pure sadistic pleasure. He shuddered at the memory of his own glee, swinging a boot, aiming for the face.

In the silence of the car, Nina said, 'Vikings.'

'What?'

'You fought like a Viking. Mad. Crazy.'

He shook his head. Embarrassed. 'Did I?'

'Don't you remember, when we were talking about America, you said the Vikings were famous – for fighting like madmen?'

'Guess I did . . .'

'Adam.' Her voice had taken on a strange, portentous quality. 'Tell me. Wasn't there a particular kind of Viking who fought with special ferocity?'

He mused. 'You mean – the berserkers?'

'Yes. Them. I remember studying Vikings in school, Eric the Red and all that. The berserkers would get so crazy before battle that they would bite their own shields in bloodlust. Waiting to kill. *Yearning to kill.*'

She toyed with the glove box, opening and closing it. Carefully yet pointlessly. The movement of the world seemed to slow to a stop, here in the car, in the

337

rose-amber dawn, on the most southwesterly point of Europe – till she spoke again.

'And they took drugs, didn't they? The berserkers, they were rumoured to take drugs. I remember that too. They took drugs, but no one knows what drug it was . . .' Slowly she turned and gave him the brightness of her eyes, fierce and gazing. 'Adam it's a fucking drug. It's drugs. It's always been a drug.'

He didn't understand. But she looked triumphant. 'The Babylon rite wasn't ritual hypnosis, it wasn't a sexual trance: *they took a drug*. Yes? *The Templars had a drug, some secret drug.* That was their secret treasure! That's why people thought they buried it: they *planted* it. A seed, that made a golden flower. A flower that made a drug. A drug that made them stronger, more violent. Increased aggression, increased testosterone. Hence the gay sex. It's a drug! Hence the gargoyle in the church, the man licking a leaf.'

His pulse raced at the idea; yet he calmed himself. Slowly, quickly, slowly, Adam ran the numbers. Did the maths. She was possibly right. She was *probably* right. 'That explains the Grail!' he said at last. 'They must have taken it as a liquid, in a ritual, like holy sacrament, late at night.'

'Yep. Drinking the Babylon drug.'

'From a Grail, in liquid form: hence the Templar worship of the Grail; hence the woman with the alembic, in Domme. That's a vessel used in medieval alchemy, or chemistry, as we discussed, and that was for preparing the drink . . . But what about the pentagram?'

She shook her head. 'Dunno! But *this* is why we keep seeing the Green Men. Eating foliage, with vines in their mouths, Adam. Likewise the vines in Tomar, and that gargoyle in the church. That's exactly what they did: prepared a drug from a plant and ate it. Drank its liquor. Secretly at night, in the Babylon rite. The Templars weren't pagan, Ad: they were just addicted to the high of this substance, which made them brave but also violent, sexually violent to the point of self-destruction. Adam it's the case. We found it—'

He was shivering. The idea was deliciously good. But there was a problem. A deep flaw. Adam voiced it.

'DCI Ibsen told us he'd tested *everyone* for drugs. That's one of the first things he did, and he got no results.'

'But what if it was a *new* drug? Or at least one not seen in a thousand years? What if it produced a . . . an alkaloid, that no one had seen since medieval times? Then you couldn't test for it, could you? They'd have no idea *what* to test for!'

She was right. She was so right it was rhapsodic.

He started the car and began the last drive. They talked urgently as he motored the last few kilometres to Sagres. Thoroughly and diligently they worked through the scenarios. Someone had elucidated the existence of the drug and its links to Templar history. Someone, the Camorra maybe, had paid her father to trace or rediscover the drug, using his Templar knowledge.

Nina was so excited she rushed her words. 'Dad

must have found the drug in Peru. Then he brought it back.'

'However, most of the drug he sold to the Mafia gangs, who paid for it handsomely—'

'My dad? Gangsters?' She shook her head. 'But it's gotta be true. Though he kept some of the drug for himself. It probably helped with his cancer: made him happier? Able to face death. Like a berserker. Like a Templar knight. Facing death. That's why his moods were so weird.'

Adam added, 'But the drug he kept – a small amount no doubt – was wanted by a rival gang, and they came looking for it, stole the remaining drug, or most of it, and asked him where they could get more. That must've been the argument Sophie Walker heard. But he refused to hand his theories over. So they stole his notebooks and attempted to find out where he'd got the drug for themselves.'

'But why the kids?' Nina interrupted. 'Why did they have to die, Nikolai Kerensky and Klemmer?'

Adam already had the answer. 'Don't you see, Nina? The drug that the second gang obtained, they needed to test it, so it was tried on willing victims. *They tested the drug.* We know that Ritter got an in with the rich kids, the experimental set, the swingers. These people were into new thrills, new drugs, so he must have said: *here try this, it's great, a real turn-on.'* He swerved the car, then continued, the story playing out in his mind. 'The rich young Londoners loved the drug. But the drug worked too well, if anything. They killed

340

themselves, they became too aroused, too fatally sexualized. And then Ritter gave some to . . .'

'Hannah.'

'I'm sorry, but yes. He must have. Ritter was also on
the drug himself, of course. Hence his sexualized
sadism.'

Nina sighed, bitterly. 'So it wasn't rape.'

'It *was* rape: she was drugged, Nina. It wasn't her
fault. No more than if she'd been unconscious. He raped
her.'

'Then it must work incredibly fast, Adam. He must
have given it to her there and then. In the bedroom:
is that even possible?'

'DMT.'

'What?'

'Businessman's acid, I used to do it in Oz, with Alicia,
we tried everything. DMT. Dimethyltryptamine. It's a
kind of short-acting, very strong hallucinogen. It's found
naturally in plants in the Amazon jungle, ironically
enough.' He searched the wide coastal horizon: nearly
there. 'Anyway, you inhale it, and it works in micro-
seconds. They call it businessman's acid 'cause you get
extremely high instantly, then hallucinate wildly for
ten minutes, then you come down at once. You can
do it in a lunch break if you like: you can go to the
moon and back, instead of having a sandwich. There's
no reason our drug couldn't do the same. Act
instantaneously.'

At last, he pulled up at the cliff edge of Sagres. They
climbed out of the car and stood, and stared,

momentarily rapt by the view. The sun was shining on the vast, cold Atlantic. They were parked at the ends of the earth, on the flatness of Cabo de São Vincente, jutting out into the churning seas. This was the great embarkation point for the Portuguese explorers, who lifted anchor in the coves below, and set white sail for the treasures of the Unknown.

'That's it,' said Adam. 'That also explains why there are so many conquistadors from here, from Portugal and Extremadura.'

Nina frowned.

'The Templars' last redoubt in Spain was Extremadura, right?' Adam went on. 'Their last redoubt in all Europe was Portugal. And this is the same place, Extremadura, that bred the *Spanish* explorers. It was from towns like Trujillo and Cáceres and Badajoz and Jerez de los Caballeros, that Balboa and Cortés and Pizarro and the rest of them emerged, determined to go west, to find a city of gold, buried treasure; their El Dorado.'

Her thoughts followed his. 'They were looking for the Templar drug? So . . . maybe it was lost over time, that's why the Templars declined. But the legends remained. Of a great golden drug. From a land far away. That made men superbly warlike, yes, peerlessly brave. These men were warriors. They wanted it again – the golden drug—'

The seagulls wheeled, white and crying in the Christmas light.

'It must have motivated them, motivated them all, including Henry the Navigator, to find it again. Because the drug must have disappeared: maybe they couldn't grow it any more, maybe medieval climate change affected them? It was lost but the legends lived on, the myth of Templar treasure.'

The two of them stared out to sea, watching the mighty waves. The fortress of the Order of Christ sat on the very furthest promontory, urging the bravest to go and find, to explore.

Nina said, 'We have to get away.'

They both knew where 'away' would be. They were going to find it again. To find the Templar drug.

He nodded, and said, 'Peru.'

42

The Radisson Hotel, Lima, Peru

Deck the halls with boughs of holly . . .

Jessica Silverton sat in the lobby of her hotel. It was Christmas Day: the PA was playing endless carols on a loop. She'd rung her mother. She'd rung her brother. She'd told them very little of her predicament; she couldn't bring herself to regurgitate all the misery. For a second she felt like asking about Dad – *how did he really die?* – but of course she didn't: the fear of hearing the wrong truth was too great.

Now she was pounding her laptop, oblivious to the warbling voices of the festive muzak. Here. She scrolled up the page once more and read it for the third time this afternoon.

Ololiúqui. '*Turbina corymbosa* (syn. *Rivea corymbosa*), also known as the Christmas vine, is a species of morning glory native throughout Latin America from

Mexico in the north to Peru in the south and widely naturalized elsewhere.'

Tra la la la la la la la la . . .

'It is a perennial climbing vine with white flowers, often with five petals, shaped as a star. It secretes copious amounts of nectar, and the honey the bees make from it is very clear and aromatic.'

Don we now our gay apparel . . .

'*Turbina corymbosa* is also known to natives of north and central Mexico by a Nahuatl name *ololiúqui* and by the south-eastern natives as *xtabentún* (in Mayan). Its seeds were perhaps the most common hallucinogenic drug used by the natives of pre-Columbian Mexico, and elsewhere in Mesoamerica.'

Tra la la la la la la la la . . .

'In 1941, Richard Evans Schultes of Harvard University first identified ololiúqui as *Turbina corymbosa* and the chemical composition was first described on August 18 1960, in a paper by Dr Albert Hofmann. The seeds contain ergine (LSA), an ergoline alkaloid similar in structure to LSD. The psychedelic properties of *Turbina corymbosa* and comparison of the potency of different varieties were studied in the CIA's MKULTRA Subproject 22 in 1956.'

Follow me in merry measure
Fa la la la la . . .

'The plant is called *coaxihuitl*, "snake-plant", in Nahuatl, and *hiedra* or *bejuco* in the Spanish language. The seeds, in Spanish, are sometimes called *semilla de la Virgen* (seeds of the Virgin Mary).'

While I tell of Yuletide treasure
Fa la la la la la la . . .

She'd had enough. Taken at face value, this sounded as if she had solved the problem in one go. And yet maybe she hadn't. An hour ago she'd telephoned her old tutor, in Iquitos: Boris Valentine. He was, after all, an ethnobotanist, working in the Amazonian capital of ethnobotany: he had the expertise. And he had sent his reply by email, and it provided a very different perspective.

'It's a moot point, Jessica. The story is famous of course, how, after several weeks Schultes found *Turbina corymbosa* growing around the porch of a witch doctor's house in Santo Domingo Latani, south Mexico. But in recent years, yes, some have questioned his identification: various other forms of morning glory (*convolvulae*) have been suggested as alternative candidates, or other plants entirely.

'To my mind it is actually unlikely that *ololiúqui* was *Turbina corymbosa:* the descriptions of Aztec intoxication by *ololiúqui* do not match the effects of *Turbina corymbosa*. So it is quite possible that you are looking for a different plant. If your theory is correct, you could disprove the mighty Schultes! Find the real ulluchu and the real ololiúqui! That would be a remarkable achievement. Indeed I'd love to help you out. It's likely this entheogen comes from the jungle out here: that's where the ancient Peruvians sourced all their drugs. We have the best pizza these days, as well. Bx'

The holly and the ivy, / When they are both full grown /

Of all the trees that are in the wood, / The holly bears the crown . . .

She sipped her iced coffee, and wrote some notes in her pad. The coffee was decaff; the caffeine of excitement inside her was quite sufficient. Jessica sensed she was in danger of running away with herself. So she slowed down and reviewed what they already knew for sure.

To start with, it was generally accepted that the Moche – like most pre-Columbian societies – took mind-altering drugs. They had found cocaine-taking implements in most Moche tombs: bird bones for tooting, elaborate snuff-boxes. The sacrificed children were probably given *nectandra* before they were killed: an analgesic and mild psychedelic derived from the laurel. So there was no doubt the Moche experimented with intoxicants.

Now there was tantalizing evidence of a different intoxicant, an underlying drug, the ur-drug; the secret drug, so sacred it could only be symbolized iconically, in the shape of its seeds.

Her thoughts halted at the obstruction, which was yet a way through. Like a car at a locked gate.

The seeds!

Of course. Why hadn't she done this before?

Speedily, she Googled 'morning glory seeds'. Then stared at the screen of images, her eyes quite wide.

The seeds of morning glory, in almost all species, looked like little drops of blood. Like ovals or commas. Just like the iconic blood drops, in all the Moche murals and pottery.

347

The holly bears a blossom, / As white as lily flower, / And Mary bore sweet Jesus Christ, / To be our sweet Saviour . . .

Ulluchu was therefore, very possibly a *kind* of morning glory, like ololiúqui, but perhaps not the precise one identified by Schultes. It was likely to be a more powerful and maybe volatile drug, a drug that stimulated the sex drive and induced violent cruelty. It was probably given to prisoners before the sacrifice ritual. Which was why the men had erections in the murals of El Brujo.

Who else gave drugs to people before executions?

She found another web-page. 'The Sacrificial Customs of the Aztecs': 'Many Aztec sacrificial ceremonies were small, with the sacrifice of a single slave or captive to a minor god. Others were savagely spectacular, involving hundreds or even thousands of doomed and shuffling captives. Aztec history claims that Ahuitzotl (1468–1502), the ruler before Moctezuma II, sacrificed twenty thousand people after a battle in Oaxaca.

'Whatever the size of the rite, the sacrificial ceremony was nearly always conducted with the same brutal ceremonies. Four priests held the victim on an altar at the top of a pyramid or temple while the presiding official made a cut below the rib cage with a blade of obsidian – a black volcanic stone – and pulled out the living heart. Commonly the victim was given a drug, before the ritual, which meant he went more willingly to the altar.'

The victims were given a drug.

Surely *this* was ulluchu. The drug that made you

want to cut off your own hands and lips; the drug that made you accept being led up a pyramid to have your pumping heart torn out by Aztec priests. The drug of sex and violence, the drug that led people in a state of erotic and psychotic bliss to kill others or mutilate themselves, to drink their brother's blood, to permit their own destruction.

Jessica's fingers were trembling. Entheogenic and psychedelic drugs united *all* the cultures of pre-Columbian America. The Aztec and the Inca, the Maya and Mazatec, the Zapatec and the Mixtec, the Chan Chan and Zuni, and Hopi and Chimu, and Nazca and Navajo and beyond. The practice stretched far north: the Kiowa of Oklahoma took peyote cactus buttons; it reached west into the deserts, where the Tarahumara ate mescal; it reached deep into the jungle, where Amazonian tribes took *ayahuasca*; it reached unto the Olmec, who delighted in datura; it reached long into the Great Plains, where Apache imbibed nicotine, and down the Andes, where virtually all cultures sniffed and chewed cocaine. It reached into the Sonora wilderness, where ancient men licked the cane toad, and into the pampas, where Argentine tribes endured psychedelic enemas of liquid-ized snuff made from the ground seeds of *Anadenanthera peregrina*.

The Aztecs even gave hallucinogens to their *jaguars*.

The holly bears a berry
As red as any blood
And Mary bore sweet Jesus Christ
To do poor sinners good

349

Jess sat back. She had her proof; or, at least, an excellent theory. Drug use was *the* unifying factor that underlay all pre-Colombian cultures from Patagonia to Canada, and therefore perhaps all their rituals and religions. And maybe their iconography, too: perhaps they all hallucinated in the same way, because of this unknown plant, explaining the similarity of pre-Colombian art from the Maya to the Aztec to the Inca and Muchika.

A universal proto-drug that eroticized sadism or masochism would also explain the terrible cruelty of all these religions and cultures: the obsession with sacrifice and blood letting, with blood drinking and decapitation.

The words of the carol were still spinning in her mind, though the PA had been switched off, long ago.

The holly bears a prickle
As sharp as any thorn
And Mary bore sweet Jesus Christ
On Christmas Day in the morn.

So what happened to this precious and terrible drug? It must have gone north, from Peru to Mexico, and then gone to ground. But now, it seemed, ulluchu had re-emerged. Someone had found it, taken it, used it. Others were looking for it.

Jess felt a tiny frisson of exultation, but then her epiphany passed, and the fear returned. Who would be the most likely people to want such a powerful and dangerous drug? Who would be prepared to kill to get it? To murder indiscriminately?

They were all in much more danger than they had

ever realized. She reached for her phone. This time she wasn't going to be fobbed off with cached Facebook pages and unanswered emails.

Getting put through to the right person took an hour, and it probably cost her two hundred dollars. But she didn't care.

Finally a warm but wary British voice answered her query. 'Yes, I am Detective Chief Inspector Mark Ibsen. I'm in charge of the McLintock case. But who are you?'

43

The Embassy of the United States, Lima, Peru

'Carlos "El Santo" Chicomeca Monroy.'

Jessica looked at the besuited man in front of her. He was young: about thirty; his head was close-shaved, his eyes were piercingly blue, the shirt was the whitest shirt she had ever seen. Clearly he was CIA or FBI, or Drug Enforcement Agency. DEA. She asked, 'El Santo?'

'The Saint.' The man smiled. Very briefly. 'It's a joke, Mexican black humour. Carlos Monroy is about as far from a saint as you can imagine. Even by the sick standards of the Mexican drug wars, he is a sicko. Pathologically violent. We think he drinks blood.'

Jessica had phoned the embassy with her theory just after she had spoken with the British police, and made several other connections to cover her bases. The embassy had immediately asked her in for an interview the following day. But now it was their turn to talk.

The official pulled out a sheet of paper from a file on

the desk and swivelled it so that Jessica could see. 'This is the best image we have of Monroy.'

She leaned to look. 'He's handsome. Very young?'

'It was taken a few years ago, when he was at Harvard.'

'I don't understand.'

The DEA guy leaned back, steepling his fingers, as if in prayer. 'How much do you know about the Mexican drug wars? The drug cartels? You told us that you suspect the drug gangs are somehow involved in the events in Zana, and Europe. But what else do you know?'

'Well.' She shifted in her seat. The room was airless. Windowless. Featureless. Buried deep inside the embassy, like a safe room. 'Not that much. I've been abroad the last three years. India, then Peru.' She shrugged, awkwardly. 'I mean – I hear about the awful murders of police. I know it is seriously violent across the border. I know that if the Mexican drug gangs are involved in all this, then it's important. And dangerous.'

'Indeed. *Seriously violent* is something of an *understatement*. Since 2003 at least *fifty thousand people* have died in the conflict between the various drug cartels of Mexico, who are competing to supply cocaine, marijuana, methamphetamine and heroin, primarily to the USA. Moreover, in recent years the death rate in this drug war has actively *worsened*. The death toll is far higher than, say, the Troubles in Northern Ireland. The rate of killing is actually higher than the Afghan war. One city alone, Ciudad Juárez, on the Texan border, sees thousands of murders a year: it is the most dangerous city on earth.' A terse pause. 'And the violence is unbelievably brutal. People are tortured to death on YouTube. Victims are beheaded and mutilated and stripped naked and strung up from bridges in Juárez, with obscene notices slung around their necks. Women are mercilessly raped and tortured, then killed. In 2009 a series of victims were dissolved in acid by the "stewmaker" – so called because that's what he did, he made human stew. A stew of dissolved humans.'

The young man frowned, stood up, and walked to the side of the room. 'One reason for the violence is the vast amounts of money provided by the narcotics industry. We estimate the drug trade in Mexico generates at least forty *billion* dollars in profits a year. One cartel leader, Chapo "Shorty" Guzman, was listed amongst the world's richest men by *Forbes* magazine. The income these guys make is phenomenal, and they will fight to the death to own the "plaza" – the place of trade. They will kill indiscriminately. They will walk into a wedding and spray the place with machine guns just to show they can. Just to terrorize.' He gazed at a wall, as if it were a window. 'The drug lords, of course, become famous. Even glamorous. Songs are sung about them – about the narcos, the enviable billionaire drug bosses, these songs are so popular have their own genre, *narcocorridas*. There is a whole culture of narco this and narco that. When the drug lords die they are buried in elaborate *narcotumbas*. Their beautiful teenage mistresses are called *narcoesposas* – narco-wives. There is a

354

narco-architecture: the vast lurid villas they build. You get the idea. It is an entire civilization of cruelty and killing, based on the misery of addiction.'

He turned. Talking directly at her.

'A couple of years ago, straight into this maelstrom of horror, walked Carlos Monroy. His family is aristocratic: they can trace their descent from the Aztec royal family, and from the conquistadors. This is not uncommon, of course. There are many descendants of the Aztec Emperor Montezuma living today; some went to Spain, to Europe. President Chávez of Venezuela was descended from Montezuma. Similarly, the conquistadors had many children, when they interbred with the Aztec and Inca royal families. But it is unusual for the leader of a drug cartel.'

Jessica felt a need to speak now, to interrupt this ceaseless flow of knowledge. To show she existed. 'I don't understand. Why is his lineage so important?'

'Because it meant he got a very good education. Most cartel bosses are from the slums, the barrios. They fight and kill their way to the top. But Monroy went to Harvard, where he studied history and science. He is extremely intelligent, cultivated and educated, and his family is already wealthy. Why then did he become a cartel boss? He seems to be motivated by some hatred of the West. Of the gringos. A resentment which makes him particularly vicious. His Harvard education has also given him a business acumen and, we believe, a skill at drug synthesis. His meth, for instance, is some of the best on the market. He is ruthlessly superb at his

355

chosen career. When he returned to Mexico, he took over a small cartel, the Catrina cartel. And since then, by utilizing a brutality that is shocking even by Mexico's appalling standards, he has turned Catrina into one of the most powerful cartels of all, such that they are challenging the supremacy of the Zetas.'

'Who are?'

'*Los Zetas* are the dominant cartel in Mexico, founded by a small team of Mexican special forces deserters, which has since expanded to take in corrupt local police, state police, federal officers, prostitute informers, teenage assassins, and so on. They employ thousands across Mexico and beyond. This is why the Peruvian police were maybe less than eager in their investigation of your situation. If they suspect the drug cartels are involved, especially the Zetas, then they are quite right to be scared. The Zetas are fearsomely well equipped – their arsenal includes assault rifles and submachine guns, grenade launchers, surface-to-air missiles, helicopters. Even submarines.'

'Submarines?'

'Submarines. Until recently it was feared that the Zetas were threat to the Mexican state itself. Until recently, the US authorities regarded them as the most potent paramilitary drug gang in Mexico. That is . . . until the rise of Carlos El Santo Monroy. Until the Saint arrived on the scene.'

Jessica stared at the picture of the US president on the wall. She didn't particularly want to look at it. This was just the only thing to look at, apart from the man opposite her telling her all this frightening, frightening stuff. 'How does this fit with my information?'

The man lifted a single finger. 'One more thing. El Santo is, as I say, a student of history. One of the reasons for his rise is, we think, his astute use of psychology. He has turned his cartel into a kind of military religious order. What is special about El Santo's brand of faith is that he has deliberately utilized the imagery and culture of Santa Muerte. Holy Death.'

'I've heard about this. About Santa Muerte.'

'He uses it as a bonding mechanism, and also as a kind of branding. It is not unlike the way Hitler built Nazism – the impressive iconography, the sense of religious purpose in the adherents. Holy Death is a criminal and working-class cult religion in Mexico, which combines Roman Catholic elements with ancient Mesoamerican and Aztec motifs. It may even be a direct and living descendant of Aztec religions, which survived in poor areas of Mexico City and then re-emerged in the last few years. Practitioners of Santa Muerte worship death herself, in the image of a white lady, also known as "the skinny one". They venerate her presence as a skull or a skeleton in a dress or robe or veil, sometimes she is called Catrina, hence the cartel's name.'

'But why is Santa Muerte so powerful? For Monroy?'

'Because Santa Muerte idolizes death. Therefore the practitioners are especially murderous, they want to kill. El Santo's lethal emissaries see killing as an *ideal*, an end *in itself*. A way of worshipping the white lady. They are tattooed with skulls and may regard these tattoos as magical protection. The use of such magical tattoos has now spread to other gangs. You know about the deaths in England, of course—'

'The McLintocks, those poor young people, yes.'

'Some of the suspects in this case have Santa Muerte tattoos on their *hands*: that certainly indicates the Catrina cartel. But the man Ritter, who was killed in London, he was tattooed on the *arm*, which is more a Zeta trait. And he was firmly linked with the Camorra, in Italy, who we know are allied with the Zetas.'

Jess gazed at the bare white walls, then at the officer. 'You've spoken to people in London?'

'Yep. We have already been in touch with the British authorities. Indeed we spoke to London this morning, to further our investigation, and to help them if we can. And this is where you come in . . . We were fascinated by your information. We know El Santo took an interest in ethnobotany at Harvard. He is obviously after new drugs. Or, should I say, old drugs. Please tell us *everything* you know about the history.'

Jessica did as she was instructed. The DEA officer took copious notes. The president of the United States of America smiled down from the wall.

An hour later the officer put down his embassy pen, stood up, shook her hand, and thanked her, solemnly. Jessica felt a sudden terror: at leaving the safe, guarded confines of the embassy, with its body scanners, and smartly saluting Marines. She had to go back out there, where the soldiers of El Santo were prowling, with the skull tattoos, yearning to kill for the sake of killing.

The man evidently sensed her unhappiness. 'Miss Silverton, let me repeat the advice I gave you on the phone.' His eyes met hers. 'Yes, you are in serious danger, there is no point in denying it. But it is arguable that California could be just as dangerous for you, for anyone, as Peru. The US cannot guarantee safety even for its own officials – we have lost many good men in Mexico and elsewhere, diplomats and businessmen, families with children, not just soldiers and DEA operatives. In your case, my hope is that they regard you as subsidiary. They will have no idea that you have this . . . special information. I would advise you again, however, to change your cellphone pretty quickly. Just in case. And don't go back to Zana of course: the Peruvian police were quite correct in that advice. Moreover, if you do feel threatened in any way, *please* come here, we can guard you, you can certainly be safe here, if nowhere else. But of course on the streets – well, that it is more difficult. The choice, naturally, is yours.' Another handshake. 'Goodbye Miss Silverton, and, once again, thank you. You have assisted your government in a very serious situation. Happy Christmas. Please be careful.'

By the time she had emerged through the various security levels of the embassy, which was like ascending from the dark blue depths of the sea to the gasping surface, Jessica's hands were shaking. She definitely needed a coffee. And when she reached the coffee shop she asked for a mug because she didn't trust her trembling hands to hold a delicate cup.

Her trembling hands? She ignored the symptom. Strenuously, and as best she could. She was frightened. That's why her hands were trembling. Frightened, or diabetic. Frightened.

Halfway through the mug, her cellphone rang. For a moment she considered blocking the call, hurling the phone in the trashcan. Then she realized it was a British number. Prefix +44.

She picked it up. 'Hello.'

'We're just outside.'

She looked up. Standing at the door was a pretty, dark-haired girl and a much taller man. They were here. Nina McLintock and Adam Blackwood.

44

Radisson Hotel, Lima

They talked in her room for two hours: Jessica, Nina and Adam. Though they had only spoken twice on the phone, and sent a few urgent emails, though they had been brought together by a the most circuitous of routes – a call from Ibsen to Nina's secret cellphone, the number only DCI Ibsen knew – by the end of these two hours, Jess felt as if she had been reunited with lost siblings. As if they were united by some high and benign agency because they shared the extraordinary DNA of this story.

It took an hour for Adam and Nina to share all their crucial information. As Nina passionately explained the role of her father, and the police, and the terrible scenes in London, and the way they had followed the trail of the receipts – from Temple Bruer to Tomar, from Rosslyn to Sagres and finally to Peru – Jessica sensed the dynamic between this fiercely determined girl and the tall, brooding Australian. The tragedies that bonded them.

Once more, Jessica felt the pang of her own loneliness. Her dyingness? No. That was stupid. She chided herself for her self-pity, and urged Nina to continue.

Finishing her third black room-service coffee, Nina mentioned their discovery in Portugal, the sculptures in the church, the pentagram in old Tomar—

Jessica leaned close. 'Pentagram?'

'Yes.' Nina looked at Adam, who shrugged. She turned back. 'That's the only bit we couldn't work out.'

'But I can – I *know* how it fits!' Jessica pulled her little laptop from her bag, opened it, and tapped a few words. 'See. The pentagram is not a symbol of the devil or Christ's wounds – at least, not in this case. It is also symbol of a *flower*. The five-pointed flower of the morning glory. That's the final proof: with the seeds, and the uncanny similarity to ololiúqui, and now this, that's enough proof. We now know ulluchu is definitely a morning glory, we just don't know *which one*.'

Adam was gazing at the laptop screen and its row of pentagrams, juxtaposed with morning glories. He nodded. 'So, please. Now tell us what else you know.'

This took less time: Jessica skipped the more gruesome episodes; she couldn't bear to reveal them. At the end Adam nonetheless looked shocked; she waved away his sympathies and said, 'Show me the last receipts again.'

Pulling out an envelope saying *Peru September 2nd – 13th*, Nina handed them over.

362

Jessica opened the envelope. 'So your father went to Iquitos? For a week – that makes sense.'

'Why?'

'Because Iquitos is the capital of the Amazon rainforests and the Amazon is where *everyone* goes to look for new drugs. Amazonia is just seething with undiscovered plants and trees and fungi, with all kinds of medicinal and psychotropic potential, a five-thousand-mile-wide pharmacopoeia. I have an ethnobotanist friend researching there now who is willing to help you, if you want. He is good. Very good. And this is the kind of stuff he loves.'

Adam gave her a sardonic expression. 'We've made it all the way here. Another thousand miles: so what?'

'Of course.' Jessica was focused on the receipts; she had picked out the final chit, a small piece of paper bearing the handwritten word *Toloriu* and the figure 5; and the date: September 18th.

'It's a taxi receipt, we think.' Nina said. 'Ach. His last movements are opaque: his plane tickets are missing. But we found this, five days after all the others: it's a town in the northern Andes?'

'Yes, I know it. Near Huancabamba. Quite famous for its curanderos. So maybe he got the ulluchu in Iquitos, then had it prepared by a healer. It's possible.'

Jessica stared once more at the chit, then returned it to the envelope.

'OK. We need to be straight. You know the danger. The Mexican drug cartels are the most powerful criminal syndicates in the history of—'

Nina smiled bleakly. 'The visible universe. Aye. We know. We've been through a few wee scrapes ourselves.'

'Sorry. Sorry, yes, of course.' Jess handed back he envelope of receipts. 'So we go to Iquitos tomorrow?'

'We go to Iquitos tomorrow.'

For a moment they sat in silence. Nina and Adam seemed pensive; but Jessica was more animated, she was positively distracted. She had just this moment grasped another shining fragment of the puzzle.

The Aztec legend. The great Aztec legend.

45

Iquitos, Amazonia, Peru

Boris Valentine was about forty-five and tending to fat. He was adorned in a lurid Hawaiian shirt almost open to the navel, he had a silver medallion dangling way down this chest and his eyes were vigorously blue, yet he looked like he hadn't had a proper night's sleep since the 1970s. Indeed he looked, to Adam, as if he belonged in the seventies or eighties. A sleazy entrepreneur running a celebrity disco in New York, with a tiny coke spoon at the ready, and three anorexic girlfriends.

Yet this was the renowned ethnobotanist from UCLA, according to Jessica Silverton, this was the man who could track down ulluchu, out there in the jungle. And the man was evidently *keen* to do it: to get out there in the bush and make his name in the jungle: he already exuded ambition like an over-musky aftershave.

'So you're the drug-hunting gringos. That's just what

we need here in Iquitos. More kids after a headrush. We only have three thousand of them.' Boris laughed and shook hands with Adam, and then he kissed Nina's hand and then he just kissed Jessica. Turning, smartly, he marched them off the airstrip in his incongruous and finely-tooled cowboy boots, talking the while. 'Welcome to Iquitos my friends, the largest city in the world that you cannot reach by road. Welcome to the capital of the Amazon. Shall we hurry the fuck up before the Zetas come and start a Facebook appreciation page in honour of your arrival?' He laughed at Nina's expression. 'Sorry, be of good cheer! We are going somewhere even the biggest cartels in Mexico won't find us: out there—' he waved at the trees, prowling the airport perimeter. 'And we're going upriver. There are places two hundred miles from here no white man has ever seen, at least not on the ground, or not without getting himself killed by the poison at the end of a dart, made from the venom of killer bees and the extruded toxin of the curare vine. Here's the Valentinemobile, hop in. Chuck your luggage in there. On the seat. Let me get rid of the ten-inch millipede. We have a great number of very large insects here. A lot of them *extremely* venomous.'

It was a rusted, stripped-down VW minibus with all the windows punched out and the roof torn off. Like the shell of a vehicle hit by a mortar.

'Air conditioning, Iquitos style. Boy, you are going to like this city. Well, like it I, most of the time; but I'm in a good mood because I haven't had half my family killed.'

They all climbed on the minibus. Boris Valentine belched robustly, turned the key, and the rattling old vehicle sped out of the airport precincts into the whirl of Iquitos traffic: languid and barefoot kids on motorbikes, motokars with *Lenin Es Ma Vida* on the transparent covers, more VW Beetles and buses with the roofs shaved off, as if there was a tax on automobile roofs.

Boris and Jess talked animatedly at the front of the minibus. Every so often one of them would glance behind at Nina and Adam, as they sweated like gringo tourists in the back of the bus: the breeze through the punched out windows was indeed welcome. The humidity was profound, a wet suffocation; Adam felt he could almost rub it between his fingers, the air, it had a viscosity, even a greasiness: the exhalations of the jungle – the jungle that entirely surrounded them, like a besieging army.

Jess turned, and talked loudly, above the traffic noise, to Adam and Nina; lecturing from the front seat as if she was a tour guide introducing them to Hell. 'Boris says we're going to Belen market. If anyone knows of ulluchu it will be there, he reckons. All the river people go there, he says: the river pirates, the river gypsies, the river tribes. It's the trading centre of all Amazonia.'

'How long, exactly, have you known Boris Valentine?'

Jess looked at Nina. 'Quite a few years. I took a couple of his lectures at USC. As I said, he really is the go-to guy for the plant life of the Amazon. Entheogens and psychedelics, medicinal plants. All of it. He's been working upriver for years.'

Adam scrutinized Jessica Silverton as she and Nina talked, a little awkwardly, as they wove through the madding traffic. Behind the self-conscious self-confidence he could see fear and anxiety in the American woman's brown eyes: and a definite wariness, too. She was scared about something, haunted even. But of course she had recently seen friends and lovers killed, and that was probably enough reason for mistrusting anyone and everything.

Jess had shared her theory about the Aztecs with them on the flight from Lima. It was a fine insight. So fine, Adam wanted to hear it again: this time he was going to write it down. Like a proper journalist. He tapped her on the shoulder, and requested a reprise. She smiled, uncertainly. 'OK. This is how I see it, after the Moche, the cruellest and most drug-addled of all these American civilizations were surely the Aztecs. They must have possessed ulluchu in almost as strong a form, perhaps stronger. A distillation maybe, or a new preparation.'

Adam raised a hand. 'Wait, please.' The Valentinemobile was swerving wildly, avoiding potholes. Adam steadied his pen. 'OK. Sorry. Go on.'

'However, the Aztecs were also the last great civilization in North and Central America: the last of the ulluchu users. So what happened when the white men came? The Aztecs hid it from the conquistadors. They hid the drug! That explains the legends of the famous buried treasure of Montezuma: the gold the Spanish could never quite find. It wasn't gold: it was a golden flower, a *golden morning glory flower*, the flower of evil, which disappeared.'

A page of his notebook was filled. Adam thanked her and pocketed his pen, and felt the pungent Iquitos breeze on his face, scented with sewage and spice and squalor. The idea was good, the theories were good; the reality was still very dangerous. He gazed about, nervously.

The streetscape was ageing and narrowing as they approached the centre: older Spanish colonial buildings, decaying in the decades of jungle storms and wetness, were lined up on either side of the narrow boulevards.

Nina was just gazing: wordless now, as she had too often been of late. It was a growing contrast to the chatterbox girl he had met in that pub in Edinburgh just a few weeks ago. Then he could feel her extroversion, her effervescence. But the tragedies and the violence and the grief had ground her down; they were corroding her, diminishing her: she had got quieter and quieter. Maybe he hadn't helped, with his stupid violence in Portugal, but he had done it because he was defending her. He wanted to kiss her. He was never going to kiss her. He was never going to allow himself to do this, not after Alicia. Not again. A girl who would occupy his heart and soul and then fuck him up with grief or heartbreak or loss: never again. But if he couldn't allow himself to love her, he could win this, solve this, defeat this: *for her.*

He wondered what she was thinking, right now. He wanted to squeeze her hand and ask, but he couldn't. Probably she was thinking of her dad, who came here eighteen months ago. They knew from his receipts that he had taken a ferry upriver, and stayed six days – somewhere – and then came back. They had no idea where he stopped, and disembarked, *but they knew his direction.*

But if this trip was recorded in the notebooks it also meant the Zetas were probably out here too, in the riverine slums, hunting them down. And they weren't just hunting him and Nina, they were hunting for more ulluchu, of course.

The ripples of the puzzle suddenly froze into a pattern.

'They're looking for ulluchu. They want more ulluchu,' he said, to the whole vehicle, to no one.

Nina said, 'We know that.'

'No, I mean *both of them*. The Zetas, and Catrina, they *both* have limited supplies, and they are *both* trying to find more.'

'But my dad must've sold the Catrina a lot, we discussed this—'

'Yes.' Adam nodded. He noticed that Jessica was staring at him, intently. He went on. 'But consider the actions of the Zetas, all this killing, the explosions, murders. Of course they are desperate to find more ulluchu, to source it, that is why they stole the notebooks, as we know – to find out what your father knew, where he went, where he got the drug – but at the same time they want to prevent the other gang, Catrina, from following the same trail. Because maybe Catrina are running out of ulluchu too.'

The minibus rattled over a pothole.

'It makes a load of sense,' Jessica said. 'Horrible sense. That's why the Zetas blew up Casinelli, and killed Dan, and tried to kill you: they want to extract all the information they can, and then silence their sources, prevent El Santo from getting the same information.'

They all fell silent, in the hubbub of Iquitos. Adam stared around: if he was right – and he knew he was right – this meant the Zetas were *surely* here. And not just the Zetas. The soldiers of the skulls, the soldiers of Catrina, if they had guessed that Iquitos was the key, they would *also* be here: waiting on the next corner in the next mosquitoey café, their Glock revolvers hidden under the dirty table. Hands tattooed with Santa Muerte skulls. Yearning to kill for killing's sake.

He stilled his nerves, as best he could – and listened. Boris, who seemed oblivious to their anxieties, was now talking, loudly, as he crashed the gears up and down, joining the squealing and discordant symphony of the wild Iquitos traffic. 'Look at this place. Look at it! I just *love* this city. It's just so damn absurd. Frankly speaking, it shouldn't even *be* here any more, the only reason they built it was the rubber boom in the nineteenth-century. Back in the day, when this place, along with Manaus, were the capitals of rubber, you could get anything, any luxury imaginable. Four hundred bucks would buy you a fourteen-year-old

Polish virgin: they had whores from everywhere, Cairo, Tangier, Paris, Baghdad, Budapest, New York, fricking Tashkent. They watered their horses with iced Taittinger champagne. The donkeys got Veuve Clicquot. They had banquets costing a hundred thousand dollars. Caviar by the scoopful, cured meats from Paris, top hats from England, Danish butter imported on barges filled with ice. Cuban cigars they lit with their hundred-buck notes. The rubber barons lived in these mansions here—' He was gesturing at the mouldering, decrepit, colonnaded buildings, collaged with posters for ARPU the Peruvian socialist party. 'Anyway, all this talk of caviar – I'm famished. Shall we eat? We can we get some arepas – rounds of milk cheese wrapped in banana leaves, best drunk with small thimbles of tinto coffee. Delicious. You know the Peruvians believe Christ ate guinea pig at the Last Supper? *Aqui!*'

He parked the minibus. They climbed out and bought some food from a stall. Adam gawped. Rats ran under their feet, next to a new luxury hotel already mouldy from the heat and the wet, the air which pretended to be air.

The arepa-seller handed over the banana leaf wraps of cheese, which were delicious and disgusting at the same time. They climbed back in the minibus. Boris continued talking. He never stopped talking, it seemed. 'Now poor old beautiful mad Iquitos is having a second boom. It's the trade in lumber, in hardwoods, and oil of course, and all the good stuff of the jungle, and it's also *pesos turisticas* from the mad gringo and Jap kids who come here to take drugs. Because the Amazon jungle contains the vast majority of the globe's naturally occurring recreational substances. You know what indole is?

'No,' said Adam.

'Indole-containing plant hallucinogens are concentrated, overwhelmingly, in the New World, and in Amazonia especially. Hell, you could probably eat the rats around here and have a decent little trip, if you don't get leptospirosis first.' The car raced past a tall woman loitering on a corner wearing a dizzying blonde wig; Adam looked again: 'she' was a transvestite. 'What I was saying, yeah, the Amazon is the most amazing place of all for discovering new mind-altering drugs. It all started in the 1850s. Two Brits, Alfred Russell Wallace and Richard Spruce, they travelled around here and on the upper reaches of the Rio Negro, Spruce saw a buncha Indians preparing a strange foodstuff, then he noticed that the main ingredient was a liana, a climbing vine – he called it *Banisteria caapi*. Finally he realized this plant was the main ingredient for ayahuasca, the vine of the gods, the great hallucinogen of the jungle, and that's why we get kids coming here from all over: backpackers, British students. You Brits like to get high, don't you? Is it the rain that depresses you? Damn it anyway, look, there's one: I'll try and run him over – stoned as a lizard – look at him, god-damn hippies.' Boris swerved the battered windowless minibus and scared the bedraggled Western youth onto the sidewalk. 'They come here in their fricking pyjamas and sandals hoping to meet a shaman and take some ayahuasca in a stupid clearing in the jungle and they pay two hundred bucks to take some crappy old *yage* mixed with dope and diesel and lord knows, and they puke their guts up for eight hours and claim they've had visions of monkeys with dentures and then they come back to Iquitos and get off their gourds on coke and heroin, and then they wander around like zombies and get run over. Sometimes by me. We're here. Belen river market. Prepare yourselves. You ain't seen nothing like this.'

The minibus pulled over. The heat and humidity was now joined by the intense noise of a pullulating market. Boris gave some kid a few pesos to watch the bags and the gutted bus and he dived straight into the mêlée, expecting them to follow.

Jess turned to them. 'I know he seems crazy. I know. But he really knows this stuff: he's the best ethno-botanist around. Come on before we lose him.'

It was all too easy to lose someone in Belen market. The place was teeming with tribespeople from up and down the Amazon. Little boys and girls ran naked between stalls selling potatoes and cheap Valium and huge catfish and sad-looking sloths in cages and dead turtles on their backs with slimy, yellow intestines tugged out and displayed. Ingots of raw sugar were stacked like building bricks in huge piles next to plastic sacks of cornflour. The rats were everywhere: big, sleek and smug.

A man sang the blues with a three-stringed guitar. Women wearing three hats at once cackled and shouted, '*Hay chambira, hay uvas, hay jugo de cocona a cinquenta centimos*' as they stood over trestle tables piled high with crude cigarettes made from mapacho jungle tobacco, and arrays of reeking salt fishes, and piles of large gourds and camu-camu fruit; selections of parrots, bell peppers, and fat manzanillas; chunks of wild black jungle pig; hooves of tapirs still bloody and frazzled with flies; tiny coconuts the size of ping-pong balls; strips from the ten-metre-long great river fish called *paiche*; plates of platano mush being hungrily eaten by off-duty river captains; plantains, chambira, copaiba wood, spices in supersaturated colour; dead buzzards which might have been on sale or might just have died and fallen from the sky.

'Here,' said Boris, 'try this.' It was a bottle of white liquid, in a clear plastic bottle, like runny yoghurt. 'Go on, try it.'

Adam was thirsty, and sweating, in the intense humidity; he grabbed the bottle gratefully, and swigged. It was sweet and drinkable. He glugged some more, wiping his mouth with his wrist.

'It's good. What is it?'

'Chicha beer. Made from manioc. They ferment it by chewing it up and spitting it out. It's basically a beer made from old woman's drool. This way.' He turned and dived back into the mêlée.

Adam knew he was being tested. He refused to flinch; but the gorge rose inside him as they walked on.

Finally they reached the floating market, where the just-after-the-rainy-season Amazon reached up to the waist of the city. Boris, of course, was first in the little boat; the rest of them climbed in, unsteadily, sweating, dirty, energized, frightened.

The motorboat puttered between stilt houses and houses floating on balsa platforms. This part of the market was mercifully quieter: Adam got the idea that they were in a different emotional zone of Belen market.

Jess said quietly, 'It reminds me of the Witches' Market in Chiclayo.' She paused. 'These people are curanderos, I think. Shamans.'

There were men and women in tribal costume hawking their goods from the floating houses and tethered balsa rafts. Men in loincloths with parrot feathers in their hair. Women in nylon ra-ra skirts with tattoos on their faces. They sold strange-coloured fungi, withered vines, tiny seeds in little calabash pouches, dried birds' heads, and litres of ayahuasca in old Johnnie Walker whisky bottles. At several spots Boris stopped and chatted discreetly with the shamans and the shawomen, mostly in Quechua or some rare Amazon language.

Occasionally Adam caught the odd snatch of Spanish, and what he could interpret was not encouraging. '*Se los lleva el sol.*'

They are being taken by the sun.

'*¿Que es eso?*' '*Eso es el polvo de yohimbina.*'

What is that? It is just yohimbe.

The sun was beginning to set, to thankfully sink into the Amazon beyond the floating market. Adam's anxiety rose. The cartels could be following them anywhere. They were all-powerful. They could arrange for a London policeman to be silently garrotted, just as a kind of lurid *joke*. The cartels were richer than some *countries*. They had the weaponry of modern armies. They carved words into your skin with knives and filmed it, and then they dissolved you in vats of acid.

Even Boris was looking defeated and anxious. He muttered something about trying again tomorrow. Glancing nervously at the setting sun. 'You don't want to be in this part of Belen after dark. Specially with Catrina on your case, *mes amigos*. Let's try this one last house.'

The last floating house had the most flamboyant shaman of all, a Kofan shaman with a coloured mantle that fell to his knees. Festoons of multicoloured beads hung around his neck, alongside necklaces of shells and seeds and curving white jaguar teeth. His eyebrows had been vigorously plucked and painted, his lips were dyed a sombre purple-blue, his wrist was braceleted with iguana skins, his flat brown nose had a singular emerald macaw feather pierced through the septum, and his long earlobes were studded with caiman fangs. Surmounting it all was a resplendent headdress of violet hummingbird feathers, scarlet macaw feathers and wild sapphire parrot tail feathers, like the halo of an archangel.

'What does he say?' whispered Adam, in awe.

'He says we should talk to his wife.'

There was an awkward pause. Then the shaman's

wife came out from the floating shack wearing denim shorts, flip-flops and a dirty T-shirt with a picture of Justin Bieber on the front. She listened to Boris's question. Then she nodded, casually. '*Ulluchu si.*' She talked quickly in her own language.

The excitement quickened with the dying of the day. 'Where?' Adam asked. 'What is she saying? Where?'

Boris turned. His face was uncharacteristically grave. 'She says we will find it two hundred miles upriver. That makes sense. It tallies with what we know of Archibald McLintock's movements.'

'Two hundred miles?' Nina interjected, her forehead slightly streaked with river mud, and the inevitable thick Iquitos sweat.

'Two hundred miles up the Ucayali. With the Pankarama. Protected tribal wilderness.' Boris looked perturbed, for the first time that day.

'So?'

'*Amigos.* The Pankarama are headhunters. They kill gringos. They kill everyone. And then they shrink their heads.'

46

The Amazon, Peru

They left at dawn the next day, bribing their way on to a small cargo ferry, the *MV Myona*, transporting mahogany and ebonywood and camu-camu and jungle spices to Pucallpa, via 'a certain number' of jungle villages and settlements.

The captain was half shaven, evasive, a clichéd drunk at 3 a.m.; a quarter Colombian, he wore flip-flops and long Billabong surf shorts, and a Brazilian flag T-shirt that was stained with diesel. Two of his bare-chested crew members bore bizarre scars on their backs.

Adam stood on the roofed, open passenger deck of this hired apology for a boat, with their gently swaying hammocks behind him, watching Iquitos disappear in the early mist. If he'd still been a simple journalist he'd have been sad to leave this city so soon, this place of apparently endless stories; but they were being hunted. The Zetas were out there, right now; and probably

Catrina too. So he was very glad to leave, before they could be taken, or killed, or brutally chopped up with machetes like the forest hogs in Belen market.

He leaned over the taffrail and stared down as the last cargo was longshored aboard; then the good ship *Myona* belched dirty water into the muddy riversurf and they moved out, treading the sludgy waves. The mist was still covering the mighty expanse of river all around them, rising like an army of wraiths.

Nina joined him at the taffrail, gazing at the river slums of Iquitos where the backwash curtseyed on the grey beaches of litter, and naked children with white teeth laughed and bathed in the citrusy sewage that guttered into the dawnlit water. She asked, 'Do you trust him?'

'Boris?'

'Aye. Boris! He blethers. One minute he wants to scare us to death about visiting this place, this place with the headshrinkers, then the next it's all, och, it's fine we'll be fine, let's get goin'. Mm?'

'Well. He says the captain knows the Pankarama well. That makes sense if he trades with them. He says we'll be safe.'

'What if Catrina are there already? Looking for the same drug, like you said? They'll be expecting us. Them and the headshrinkers. What chance do we fucking have then?' She paused. 'Sorry. Must be brave. I know. But it's just hard, sometimes.'

He wanted to hug her, comfort her, but he couldn't. Instead, he turned and surveyed. Jess was in her hammock, sleeping; her face was pallid, sweaty. Boris Valentine was talking, animatedly, with the captain in the cabin, eating from a small paper bag of barbecued maggots. He'd been doing this since they embarked. Adam wondered if he did it just to provoke.

The endless Amazon stretched before the boat, a three-mile-wide road of river. The mist had now fled, scorched away by the tropical sun. Mighty ceiba trees, with flocks of green parrots flying between, lined the river like lofty guardsmen on a processional mall, with smaller lemon and moriche palms in between; every so often a clearing fed on to long steep wooden stairs, which led to ramshackle river piers and little riverine beer shacks. Kids stood on the piers selling mangos, guanabana fruit, and flat rounds of bread. Pineapples for a cent. Fried piranhas two cents.

The immensity of the river induced a kind of false serenity. It was as if nothing was happening, nothing was going to happen, nothing could ever happen. Not here, in the severity of the sun that silenced the birdlife, where the jungle stretched for a thousand miles in almost every direction. And yet somehow the jungle also seemed menacing in its silence. Watchful. And steadily drawing them in to the final revelation, the terrible drug. *Ulluchu.*

By noon it was hot and Adam was scared. The boat was doing ten knots: they wouldn't reach the next town for six years at this rate. If anyone came after them in a fast boat, and it wasn't hard to find a faster boat than this, they would be trapped. They could hardly swim for the shore: crossing miles of river, infested with watersnakes and piranha.

Out of nowhere, Nina asked, 'Adam, do you believe in life after death?'

He didn't have a clue what to say. He lay in the hammock in embarrassed silence for a few moments, then decided to be truthful. 'My mum used to say when we die we are . . . snuffed out like a candle. And that's it. I guess that's what I think. It'd be nice to think we go to heaven, or just a different place, with better food. But no. I can't. I think death is it. What do you believe?'

Her smile was the saddest smile he had ever seen. 'Ach, I never know. Sometimes I think . . . yes death is the end, the flick of the switch, like you say. But other times I think that it can't be the end. That consciousness is like light, it just goes on, the star that produces it may die but light is inextinguishable, it just goes on, it is the essence of the universe itself. Fundamental.'

'OK.'

She sighed. 'As you get older, life becomes more dreamlike, don't you think? It gets stranger. Sometimes ominous, yet, somehow, more beautiful.' Her eyes were abrim with the potential of tears. 'Not sure how to put it. I mean I always thought life would make more sense as I aged. It doesn't. It gets mistier. Scarier. But lovelier, even in its sadness . . .' A single tear slid down her face.

'You shouldn't think about it, about your dad and . . . Nina. Just don't.'

She reached out a hand from her hammock, and took

his hand, and this time he didn't resist or reject – and she stared at him with her green eyes, as green as the jungle *out there*, and she said nothing. Nothing at all. The only sound was the baritone churn of the boat's knackered engine.

Then she dropped his hand and turned over and slept almost at once. And he watched her sleeping: her white face, white arms, she looked like a marble angel on a Victorian tomb. For ever sleeping. Not dead, just sleeping. And beautiful.

He shook the foolishness from his head. Jumping from the hammock, he walked across the deck. Boris and Jess were conversing, hurriedly; they turned and looked at him. Adam sat down on an upturned and empty metal keg of propane 'Tell me about ulluchu. About all of it. This guy Schultes.'

Boris finished his bag of barbecued maggots, looked quickly at Jess, and nodded. 'Richard Evans Schultes, Harvard professor, born 1915, died 2001, *el príncipe de la selva*! He was the greatest ethnobotanist of the century. He dedicated his life to discovering new plants in the Americas, especially in Mexico, and Amazonia. He was the first person to identify and collect specimens of teonanácatl, the sacred mushrooms of Mexico, the so-called flesh of the gods.'

'How?'

'By deduction, *mi amigo*, by deduction. All the scholars who had examined Aztec records believed teonanácatl was, well, a psychoactive snuff, or perhaps datura, maybe a nice chocolate McFlurry. No one even believed there *were* psychedelic shrooms in America! Yet Schultes as a very young man had researched the Kiowa of North America, and he knew they used peyote mushrooms in their ghost dances. So then he went back to the records.' Boris sat forward, engaged, his silver medallion swinging gently like a pendulum against his chest hair. 'There are several documents like *Codex Vindobonensis* in the Spanish colonial archives, which refer to sacred mushrooms. Lots of other Aztec codices make similar references, if you know what to look for. One of them describes a mushroom teonanácatl – as being served up at the coronation of the Aztec emperor Ahuitzotl in 1486.'

A macaw swept past the boat, red feathers vivid in the pointless blue sky. Boris smiled, and continued, 'Indeed the Spanish were obsessed with discovering the identity of this mushroom, a mushroom so *muy import-ante* it was dished up for an emperor. What could it be? What purpose did it serve? During and after the conquest, they tried to torture the truth out of the Aztecs.' Boris's small eyes sparkled with glee; then he reached for his apparently bottomless bag of snacks and pulled out an egg. 'Iguana egg. Very nutritious. And *muy sabroso.*' Carefully he peeled the egg, then munched the white softness.

'So. Here we see the crucial obsession of the Spanish seeking out the truth of the entheogenic substances of the New World: they wanted to get high, like any gringo – like the ayahuasca-addled backpackers in old Iquitos.'

He swallowed some egg. 'But the Spaniards, of

course, never did discover the true identity of teonaná-catl. It remained a riddle. But there was enough in the archives to guide the gifted and determined *modern* explorer. And Harvard scholar Schultes was just such a man: he had *cojones* of tungsten and a steel-tipped mind. He spent months in the summer of 1938 searching the wild Mazatec hills and valleys near Oaxaca, where he had heard that a mushroom cult, which sounded very much like the old teonanácatl cult, had survived. By talking with curanderos in Mazatec country, he narrowed down the options. He went to little towns like Huautla, where the sacred use of fungi was still quite intense, and then, finally, in July Schultes was invited to witness a ceremony in which the cunning men took a psychedelic mushroom.'

The *MV Myona* tooted as it passed another Amazon river ferry. The larger ferry tooted back, and burped a friendly puff of exhaust smoke. It was heaving with passengers, leaning over the rails, sleeping on the roof; screaming babies in slings and old women in rags.

'Except it wasn't teonanácatl. The way the priest reacted did not match the accounts. Ten days after the ceremony, back in Oaxaca, Schultes was preparing to leave. He had failed. So he went for a final resigned and defeated walk in the city streets – and there, at the last moment, a native shyly approached him. The Mazatec man pulled out a tiny package wrapped in newspaper and offered it gently to him. Inside the newspaper were three species of mushroom. The first was a kind of *panaeolus*, which Schultes immediately recognized; the second was smaller, brown-and-white, and unknown; but it was certainly not black. But then the Mazatec man pointed to the third *black* mushroom and said "Colores". He meant he had taken the mushroom and seen colours, visions! Schultes, of course questioned the old guy a lot more – and the hallucinations matched, exactly, the ancient descriptions of teonanácatl intoxication. Richard Evans Schultes of Harvard University had finally identified and discovered the sacred mushroom of the imperial Aztec, the very flesh of the gods.' Boris paused, as if on stage. 'That afternoon he went for a walk in a nearby meadow and found hundreds of 'em. They'd been there all the damn time.'

Adam gazed at Boris Valentine. 'OK. Fascinating. But how the hell does that help *us*? We're looking for *ulluchu*, which we presume is the same as ololiúqui. If Schultes identified ulluchu and he's so good, what are we doing here?'

For the first time Jess spoke; her voice was weak, scratchy. 'Adam, it shows that ancient and very important drugs can disappear over the centuries, then be rediscovered. Second, Schultes was undeniably a great botanist, but that doesn't mean he couldn't make a mistake. Quite the opposite.'

'So he fucked up?'

It was Nina. She'd approached and sat down on another empty propane keg.

Jess nodded. And her voice was almost a whisper. 'Schultes is such an authority everyone was, and is, scared to dispute him. But the fact is . . .' She coughed. 'The descriptions of ololiúqui intoxication extracted, with torture, by the Spaniards, from the Aztecs, just *do not* match the inebriation produced by . . . *Turbina corymbosa*.'

Boris interjected, 'Friar Clavigero said that Aztec priests went to make sacrifices on the tops of the mountains, or in dark caverns. They took a large quantity of ololiúqui, and the burned corpses of poisonous insects, and beat them together with ashes and tobacco, rubbed the resultant mixture on their bodies, and became *fearless to every danger.*' He waved exuberantly at the entire passenger deck. '*Fearless to every danger? Like berserkers?* That doesn't sound like our humdrum and quotidian morning glory, like *Turbina corymbosa*. Does it? It sounds like ulluchu. And that's the effect it gives you when simply rubbed it *as an ointment*! Imagine what it would do if ingested as a snuff, or consumed as a distillation, a decoction, a liquid drunk from a Grail, like the Templars of Tomar!' Boris's medallion glittered in the hot slanting sun. 'Meanwhile, other colonial sources talk of terrifying hallucinations induced by the plant: it was also known to deprive one of judgment and make one "act crazy and possessed". Again this is *not* the effect of *Turbina corymbosa. Not at all.*'

'Also,' Jess said, her white face shining with sweat, 'the Aztecs revered ololiúqui above all others, even more than teonanácatl. And they were even keener to protect its identity from the Spaniards.'

'Very true,' Boris confirmed. 'Hernando de Alarcón

wrote in 1629 that they venerate ololiúqui so much they do all in their power to prevent the plant coming to the attention of the church authorities. See the evasion? Desperate not to tell a damn word. And they never did. So we are definitely looking for something different, guys. A different morning glory. And if we find it, everything, all this, everything you have been through – will be worth it. Alternatively, and at the very least, I'll get a Nobel.'

It was late afternoon now, there was a heaviness to the air: the exhaled air of a billion trees. The world was reduced to mile after mile of green, and mile after mile of grey river-water. A silence possessed the boat as they all suffered in the furnace. That was all there was to do on this damn boat. Stare at the endless river, or think about death, or lie in your hammock and get bitten by mosquitoes the size of ravens, or look at the horizon and imagine a speedboat accelerating near, with men, with guns, and tattoos.

He thought of Alicia's death. And Hannah, and Archibald McLintock. Is that really all it was? Death? Just like a candle, snuffing out?

Jess joined him, leaning on her thin pale arms, gazing at the turbidity, the flash of a tern in the dying light of the Amazonian day. 'It's incredible isn't it?'

'The immensity.'

She nodded. 'You know, there's a story, that when Francisco de Orellana sailed down the Napo in 1541, and became the first white man to reach the Amazon, he went temporarily insane – he was unable to conceive that God's earth could be so fertile and so vast.' She stopped, and stiffened, and turned, oddly, on one foot.

Then, like a tree hacked with one swoop, she fell to the decking of the boat, convulsing. Her legs thrashed, her arms flailed. Spittle frothed at the corners of her mouth and then her eyes rolled white and then whiter.

47

MV Myona cargo ferry, Amazon River, Peru

Jessica's fit subsided within minutes; half an hour later she was sitting in her hammock, pale but conscious and apparently unharmed, as the captain gave her water from an old whisky bottle and the deckhands muttered.

'*Un poco de fiebre, señor?*'

'*Borracho y sucio.*'

'*No no, señor, Solamente un fiebre de dios . . .*'

Jessica insisted she was fine, that she had very occasional 'epileptiform' fits, and that she had pills to take for the problem. But Boris looked at her sceptically and insisted, in turn, that they stop at a jungle research station, the UNESCO Biodiversity Research Centre, UBRC, an outpost of First World science in this New World wilderness; there would be a doctor there, and mobile phone masts.

'Guys, we have to turn there anyway,' he said, 'that's where the Amazon meets the Ucayali, and the captain wants to navigate in daylight, it's a very tricky operation, *muy peligroso,* and look,' he gestured at the lowering glow of the sun. 'It's nearly dusk so we can sleep at the Centre then head on tomorrow. Yes?'

By the time they docked at the little steel pier of the UNESCO Centre the sun had drowned itself in the sea of green and the twilight was purple and gauzy. Adam walked down the gangplank on to the pier and he paused, rapt: he could feel the welcome, indeed blissful, change, as the day swooned into evening. The cooled and sweetened air was filled with swifts and flycatchers, skimming the river with cavalier swoops, the trees yielded twinkles of colour and movement after the stasis of the day: jacanas and nunbirds, toucans and kingfishers.

A pair of squirrel monkeys leapt between the palms, a sloth clung, like a baby, to the bough of a cecropia. Jessica and Nina walked quickly past him and climbed the stairs up the steep bank of the Amazon.

The scientists were bespectacled, distracted, intense, moderately welcoming and busy erecting huge silvery nets to catch jungle moths. Elegant laptops were scattered incongruously on coarse wooden tables in rough and prefab metal rooms with no glass in the insect-screened windows. Radar dishes provided TV and phone access. A kitchen stood next to a generator: detailed maps of faunal and floral data adorned the walls.

Jessica was guided to the Centre's doctor, who turned out to be a vet, but it didn't seem to matter. For an hour Nina and Adam and Boris sat in tense silence on a wooden terrace in the soft and humming and dim and insect-buzzed electric light, which petered out a few feet from the Centre perimeter. They were like a pitiful oasis of civilization in the Dark Ages, with guards on the battlements watching for Vikings, or dragons.

Now the sun had entirely gone the insects were calling from the blackness of the jungle: rasping and chirruping, clicking and buzzing, a great musical melodrama of angry insect calls. Nina was in shorts and T-shirt and flip-flops; she slapped an insect. She gazed at the large squashed mosquito on her hand. The deadness weighed heavy. Boris broke the terrible silence. 'You ever wondered how much this drug could be worth if we sold it to armies?' He grinned, mischievously. 'Imagine if someone could get hold of ulluchu, and isolated the alkaloid, and gave it to soldiers. No wonder the drug cartels are keen. This is a seller's market, guys, a seller's market!'

No one said anything.

'Personally, I think we should try and sell it to the Germans. Because they are the masters at this caper. You ever thought how weird it is: just how many serious recreational drugs were invented or refined by German scientists, often as part of their general war effort? Take heroin. Heroin was named by a German scientist in 1897, who synthesized it for use by soldiers, so they could be more heroic! That's *why* it's called heroin. And ecstasy? That was invented to help soldiers in the German trenches. True story. And cocaine was perfected specifically to serve as a stimulant for German troops in WW2. My God, even methadone, the heroin substitute, is German. They called it dolophine after one of its users: Adolf Hitler. Because they were running out of morphine to give the Führer so they invented a substitute. Incredible. Ergo, I suggest we should ring the Germans when we're done, ask for a few million euros for the *Bundeswehr* and the *Luftwaffe*, for just a few little seeds – why not make a few bucks to go with the fame?'

Boris gazed at the listening faces. 'Guys, I'm kidding. This is too depressing, lighten the hell up.'

Adam said nothing; he wondered how he had ended up trusting his fate to this strange and mercurial man. A noise from the rear of the terrace disturbed the insecty silence. They all turned: Jessica was back, with the vet who was also a doctor, a laconic Australian. The vet allayed their questions: 'Your friend is fine . . .'

Jessica stepped down on to the terrace, and gazed at them with a slightly faked triumphalism. 'I told you I'm OK. Really.'

Boris squinted. 'You are sure, *bonita*?'

The exchange was pointless. Jess was evidently determined to continue. Besides, as she said, what else could she do? Go back on her own?

Boris nodded. 'OK, guys, I suggest we call it a very early night. Bob says we can sleep in the dorm, and then we leave first light.'

'Wait.' Nina lifted a hand. 'I've been thinking. Something we gotta do.'

'What?'

'We should *burn the receipts*. We know everything now. We know exactly where my dad went, we have no need for them: if we burn them now no one could ever follow our path?'

Jessica nodded. 'Yes. Very good idea.'

'Because,' Nina said, 'the Zetas and Catrina are still out there. Who knows what details were in my dad's notebook, and who knows what was missing? They could be riding the river right now. Burn the evidence so no one else can *ever* follow our trail.'

No one disagreed. Nina found her rucksack and she pulled out the receipts; Adam sourced a metal trashcan, Nina threw the chits and slips into the can, Boris flicked a Zippo, ignited one large invoice, and threw it in with the others.

The flames licked and thrived, and then they died. Then Nina made a glove with a T-shirt, and carried the hot metal pail of charred papers to the top of the stairs that led down to the river. She seemed so alone, standing there, silhouetted by her sadness and her grief, that Adam joined her. Together they shook the bucket and the ashes scattered in the evening breeze, fluttering tiny scraps of blackness scattering into deeper starlit blackness.

Nina murmured, 'All life death doth end and each day dies with sleep.' She put a hand to her saddening face. 'Ach . . . I'm exhausted.'

They found the dorm, with its sextuplet of little beds. The instant he slipped twixt the clean scratchy sheets Adam slept, he was so tired.

When he woke he was so groggy he couldn't work out why he had woken. It was still dark: why was he awake? Then he heard the horrible screeching. Everyone else was asleep in the little soldierly cots. Couldn't they hear this? What was this horrible noise?

A noise rustled on his right; he saw in profile a figure, sitting up. It was Jessica. He could only see her eyes, wet and shining in the light. The rest of her was a phantom blur.

'God, Adam what was that?'

'I don't know. *I don't know.*'

The screeching repeated. Human but alien. Horrifying.

It was as if he was a kid again, with his sister; two kids afraid of the dark, scaring each other with ghost stories. Except that this was real: there really *were* monsters out there.

'Christ!'

A flash of scarlet in the dark afforded a second of relief. It was just macaws, squabbling in the trees. They sat there, saying nothing. The dark minutes dragged themselves along, and nothing else happened, and at last they slept once more.

The next time Adam awoke he realized at once what he was hearing: *silence*. The incessant rasping jungle insects had stopped, because it was dawn. The morning was already embroidering, with tints of blue, the pantherine blackness of the sky. Mist rose from the damp, chilly earth.

'*Buenas dias.*' It was Boris. 'Wake the others. Let's get going right away!'

This didn't give them time to wash, let alone shower. But Boris was adamant. He wanted to get out of here *right away*. Nina and Jessica and Adam thanked the yawning scientists; then they shinned down the ladder and climbed on the boat and the stubbled captain turned the engine even as he drank a plastic cup of Jim Beam, and they chugged away, knifing through the dull brown silk of the waters.

The Ucayali jungle was, if anything, even thicker than the Amazon forests. The sun burned down on occasional and abandoned plantings of manioc; all else was seamless wilderness. Only the animal life enlivened the numbing monotony. Hoatzin birds in the trees; the odd pod of pink dolphins. Otherwise the jungle, for all its supposed life and biodiversity, evinced a paralysing and menacing sameness. There weren't even any flowers. Just an intensity of green and repetitive trees, like the bars of an endless cage.

After six hours the captain pulled up at another pier. They apparently now had to walk. No one spoke. The anxiety and tension was making everyone silent. They were in headhunter territory.

The captain sent one of his noticeably unwilling deckhands along, to help. He was called Jose. He was so scared his teeth actually chattered; or maybe he was ill.

They trekked. The jungle here was pristine, and purely hostile. Every tree concealed something that stung, or pricked, or hissed, or bit. Lianas snagged the path. Adam grasped one liana to vault a fallen bough and immediately he felt the screaming pain of his error.

'Jesus, Jesus fucking Christ!' The liana carried a stream of army ants who attacked him, as one, racing on to his body, making him yell, and writhe, as they bit. 'Get them off me! Please!' It was a miraculous agony. He'd only touched the liana for a mere second and there were hundreds of them all over him, stinging and biting: he ripped off his T-shirt and flailed at them helplessly. 'Shit!'

Boris took one big ant between thumb and forefinger and ripped the torso away from the head, which remained pincered to the flesh. Slowly and capably, he pulled several fiercely biting ants from Adam's arm. Nina and Jessica helped.

'Natives use the ants for sewing up wounds,' Boris told them as they worked. 'They get the ants to bite and the ant heads stay attached, closing the wound, very clever, very clever. Nature's suture. Hurts like all hell though, doesn't it?'

It took twenty minutes for all the ants to be plucked from Adam's bleeding skin. He put his T-shirt back on; his back stung ferociously. Then the hike continued: endless and hot and painful. A sloth glared at them, half-dead, in the trees. Sweat-bees hovered, seeking the moistness of the human eye. Tarantulas reared up, absurdly demonic. Daring them to go further.

Nina said what they were all thinking. 'This place is a nightmare.'

Boris chuckled. 'Imagine what it was like for the

conquistadors, eh? Hacking through here in full body armour, for months, for years, over thousands of miles. Those damn bastards were crazy. Some of them went *real* crazy, there was one totally *loco* conquistador called Perez Quesada: he was a real nice guy; he would slice breasts off the women, and chop off the noses and ears of children, for amusement. He killed babies so their moms could walk faster. As the expedition went on he started impaling the men – mainly because they weren't scared of being hanged. He went further and further into the unknown, going crazier with every mile, him and his psycho friends, Juan Pedro de Grau – he went on to Mexico, married some wild queen – and Rodrigo de Cuellar: he was even more brutal . . . You know sometimes I wonder if the conquistadors *found* ulluchu? Mn? That might explain their extreme cruelty, no? Maybe – hey, look, look!' He was pointing. 'See that? It's *flor de quinde*, the hummingbird's flower. Bright red tubular flowers – *Bastante bonita* – probably psychedelic, but everyone's too scared to try, and there: that's the tree of the evil eagle. Borrachero, *Brugmansia sanguinea*, subspecies *vulcanicola.'*

They all stopped to look. Adam was glad to hear Boris talk, to have him pointing out the trees and flowers, because it distracted him from the strange noises behind them. He was sure they were being followed. But the noises could be anything. A tapir. A monkey. A fallen sloth. A drug-running gangster with a big machete. The jungle was oddly dark, the canopy above thick. You couldn't see far, even by day.

'Borrachero contains scopolamine, y'know that? That's a goddamn tropane alkaloid, same as belladonna. Take a big whack, you get total delirium, they used to give it to women in very painful labour; they called it "twilight sleep". And there, that one there, that's *chibcha*, that was the one psychedelic plant you turn to when all else fails, except of course for our sacred ulluchu.'

'Boris. Shut up.' Jess sounded tense.

Everyone turned. In the middle of the clearing ahead stood at least a dozen native warriors. They were bare-chested, and exuberantly tattooed, and carrying knives and spears. Several of them wore Adidas sneakers. Three had noses pierced by macaw feathers; and two had small, leathery, grapefruit-sized objects dangling from their belts.

Shrunken human heads.

48

Pankarama Settlement, Ucayali River, Peru

Jessica knew she was dying, now; or rather she knew that she had turned the final curve in the river, that led to the inevitable and unavoidable waterfall. Huntington's. The fit had been the clinching diagnostic symptom. She had her father's disease. But when she searched inside herself for tears, or rage, or anger, or grief, they were not there.

Instead, she felt oddly calm, unexpectedly at peace: saddened yet soothed. There was no disputing what she had to do now. She was glad she had made those phone call and emails in Lima: she had prepared the ground well.

But something was wrong. She could sense it. The headhunters were too friendly. They recognized the captain's mate, Jose, and eagerly embraced him. The Adidas sneakers were all-too-new. And the shrunken heads were old: they had the prognathous quality – the protruding lips and tongue, the wildly bulging eyes – of heads severed and shrunken many years ago.

Jess had encountered authentic hunter-gatherer tribes before: communities almost sealed from the outside world. They had been self-sufficient and therefore hostile; or at the very least indifferent. These guys were far too amiable, and needy, and supplicant.

The Pankarama warriors led them through the forest to their settlement. As Jessica had anticipated, it was not a pristine Neolithic forest hamlet: the scruffy huts and shacks were built from metal sheets and Toyota car parts as much as from palm fronds and river-mud bricks. There was new garbage strewn in old pools that looked suspiciously rainbowed and oily. Fuel oil?

Which meant these rather degraded people had cars or motorbikes or trucks. Maybe even a generator for a television hidden behind some shack . . .

On an instinct she checked her cellphone. And there it was. *A signal.* She actually had a reasonable signal in the depths of the supposedly pristine Peruvian Amazon!

Quietly she showed her phone to Adam, as the others walked on. He gazed at it, then at her, perplexed.

They rejoined Boris and Nina. The Pankarama man led them to the chief's hut. Jessica flashed a dark, urgent glance at Boris. He shrugged. '*Believe me.* It's all changed,' he said very quietly. 'Came here four years ago and they were the real McCoy. Untouched. Someone's got to them in the meantime. Drug-dealers? But the climate's really no good for growing cocaine . . .'

'I got a signal on the cell.'

'Then it's definitely loggers. Illegal loggers. *Fuckers.* Putting up a mast. Don't know which is worse. *Gilipolas!* I hate this, Jess, it's tragic. Bet they've killed all the caimans too, shot all the tapirs.'

She looked at him, and the suspicions flared. 'I know how it works, Boris. They pay off the tribesmen. Here, have a plasma TV in return for us raping and plundering all your ancestral lands. Question is: what are *we* doing here now? What's the point?'

He hushed her with a finger, and whispered, as they ducked inside the chief's hovel, 'They may still have ulluchu!'

Jessica doubted their chances of success. The loggers – armed, violent, Peruvians or Brazilians no doubt – would have pressed the Pankarama to reveal all the natural resources hereabouts. An incredible wonder drug? The Pankarama would have offered it up immediately. In return for some liquor, and maybe a two-stroke Suzuki motorcycle.

Jess wondered whether it was time to make a call, to use this precious signal. How long did she have left? It was a fine judgment. She looked at her colleagues. Had Boris deliberately led them down a cul-de-sac? Why would he do that? Did she really trust him? Perhaps it had been a mistake to involve this famously greedy and ambitious man.

One by one they ducked under a wooden lintel. The chief's shack was dark and aromatic, and it was decorated with caiman skulls and orchids. The skin of a jaguarundi hung from one wall. Several tiny, mouldering human heads hung from an elaborate bone hook on the opposite wall, obscene and sinister, yet speaking honestly of the culture. But the Sony TV in the corner detracted from this impression.

Pleasantries were exchanged. The chief was a tired-looking, bare-chested man in his fifties, with stingray spines through his ears and a piranha-tooth necklace. Jess wondered if he had quickly taken off his Chinese shorts and Barcelona soccer shirt when he heard they were coming.

'Buenas . . .'

'Ola, gran jefe . . .'

He spoke good Spanish. Another sign of inauthenticity.

One by one they bowed before the chief, seated on his throne of bones and wood and clumsy nails.

Boris asked straight out, 'Do you have ulluchu, the drug of the flower, the drug of the ancients, the drug of the dead?'

That was what the woman at Belen market had called it. *The drug of the dead.*

The chief smiled a weary smile, and said nothing, prolonging the moment. Despite her doubts, Jessica felt a helpless surge of excitement. *Say yes. Please say yes.* Maybe they did have it, maybe it would be here, why not? Would the loggers care about a strange and dangerous hallucinogen?

'Sí, tenemos la droga. Ulluchu.'

They had it. She experienced a foolish but giddy relief.

The chief clapped his hands – ceremoniously – and a

403

younger man rushed in. The two Pankarama men talked quickly in their own language. Then the man stepped out and moments later returned with a small, hollowed-out gourd. Jessica recognized the type: a lime gourd called *yoburu* – or in Spanish a *mujercita.* The little vagina.

That was definitely the real deal. The locals certainly honoured this drug, whatever it was.

The chief bade them squat on the floor. The younger Pankarama warrior also had a snorting pipe, made apparently from the windpipe of a toucan, and an elegant, ancient, intricately carved walnut snuffing dish. The man poured some fine powder on to the rectangular dish – the powdered seeds of the ulluchu?

Jess hissed at Boris. 'Tell them we want to see the flower, and the seeds, before they are ground up.'

Boris gravely nodded, and turned to the chief.

'Gran jefe . . .'

Two minutes later the young Pankarama warrior was back in the chief's shack with a plastic shopping bag. He opened it and several golden-yellow petals fell on to the floor. Jessica eyed them, excitedly. They were morning glories, without question; they were a beautiful pale sun-gold – the gold of the Aztecs? Next, the young man took a leather pouch, and poured the seeds on to the matting. The seeds were shaped like commas. But then nearly all morning glory seeds looked like commas. They were so very close; but were they close enough? Was this it? Was this, finally, the terrible drug of the Moche? The ur-drug of all ancient America?

'Boris?'

'Could be, Jessica, could be – right colour, a species I cannot identify, I believe them, I certainly believe they *believe* this is ulluchu – but the ulluchu we want – ahh . . .'

They were all crouched around the petals, and the seeds, and the toucan-bone tooting pipe.

Adam said, 'So . . . we take it back to a lab, or what?'

Nina spoke up. 'Boris? We need confirmation. Ask him. Do they remember my father? If this is where he came surely they would remember. I have a photo on my phone.'

Boris, his Hawaiian shirt dark with sweat, turned again to the chief. He spoke quickly, gesturing at Nina, then at the photo on the phone. The chief examined the image, and answered, in very fast and very accented Spanish. Boris nodded and made a slight bow.

'Yes they remember him: a tall old white man. A year and a half ago. He came looking for the same drug, and they gave him this. Heck. Therefore this *must* be ulluchu.'

Was this final confirmation? Jess pondered and decided. No, it wasn't. They still needed a test. They couldn't know for sure. There was only one way to find out *right now*. What did it matter any more? Exhilaratingly, it didn't matter at all.

She reached out and took a pair of the seeds. And swallowed them.

'Jessica! Are you mad?' Boris had his hands on her shoulders, remonstrating. Fiercely. 'What the fuck are you doing?'

She smiled back at him; she felt quite in control. Perhaps more in command of her destiny than she had ever felt before. She didn't care, not any more. No way was she going to die like her father. Thrashing and flailing. 'Are we really going to go all the way back to Iquitos, do loads of tests? It'll take days, weeks . . . This is the only way. The drug is meant to work quickly: just watch over me!' She smiled sadly at Boris. 'If I try to cut my own feet off, intervene. Swiftly.'

No one laughed. Jessica reached in her jeans pocket and handed over her pocket knife. 'Seriously. Just in case.' Then she stood and exited the shack, the others followed, shocked and gaping.

A short stroll brought Jess through a copse of enormous ceiba trees to the banks of the mighty Ucayali, almost as broad as the Amazon. She sat on a log and gazed at the river. Waiting for the drug to work. She sat for an hour. Colours drifted through her mind; she thought of her father and her mother and Dan Kossoy; she thought of the dead, smiling and waiting for her. The sky was green and the earth was blue.

She wondered if she could live here. In the jungle. For the rest of her shortened life. Eating melastom fruits, drinking medicinal teas brewed from *sacha ajo*, and chicha beer from the fruit of the miriti, and all the other regal palms. At night she would drink *chuchuhuasi* and rum, and stare at the electric eels in the river, glowing like slenderly curved neon lights.

A noise. A colour. Noises and colours. The *caw caw* of bamboo rats.

What was it? Death? It was just the immense, Amazonian delta of life. Nothing more. So many had already died out here, after the Spanish came: she remembered the terrible statistics. Three million Arawakans died between 1494 and 1508. Within a hundred and fifty years of Columbus the aboriginal population had been reduced from seventy million to three and a half million. In the Andes of Bolivia seventy-five Indians died every day for three hundred years; and yet – and yet the jungle survived. The world went on. The forest ate the sunlight.

And what was death anyway? Death was the emancipator, the good king, the liberator, the Abraham Lincoln who frees us all from the slavery of life, and without death life was nothing, pointless, lustreless, endless. Death was the blackness between the stars that made them shine.

Two hours had passed in a kind of trance. Jessica gazed over the wide sombre river where a patch of ochre clay glistened, where the grasses and sedges were shaved and flattened by recent downpours. An old canoe rose and fell on the languid surge of the river waves.

She knew now. This *wasn't* the ulluchu of the Moche. Or, if it was, it was a very very weak variant; perhaps the Moche took this wild ulluchu, this special morning glory, and cultivated it elsewhere, in a different climate at a different altitude, in the mountains. They were expert horticulturalists; maybe they had turned a feeble jungle specimen into the mighty drug over many generations, by breeding and selecting and grafting. Whatever the case, *this wasn't it*.

This meant Jessica had no choice.

A few minutes later, Boris came over. 'So, what was—'

A loud noise interrupted him. Big black-and-white speedboats were zipping up the Ucayali, braking noisily, sending big surf-waves of water crashing against the Pankaramas' modest wooden pier. A dozen men, at least, were standing in the boats. All of them were heavily armed. Some were shaven-headed, others were tattooed. One had a Z tattooed on his cheek.

Boris stepped back, his voice numb. 'Jesus. It's the Zetas. We're dead.'

Jessica reached desperately for her cellphone. This was her last chance. She dialled. They had a signal and she had to get help.

49

Ucayali River, Peru

The Zetas were grimly efficient: like proper soldiers. With barely a word they plucked the cellphone from Jessica's hand and barked a few questions into it.

The cartel officer turned and sneered. 'You call a doctor? In Peru? How can he help? You are going to need more than Tylenol.'

The cellphone was thrown in the river. All their phones were thrown in the river. Then Jessica, Adam, Nina, Boris and Jose were separated from the Pankarama and led at gunpoint through the weeds and red squelchy mud of the Ucayali riverbank.

The military efficiency was no coincidence, of course, as Adam realized: they were still an army, at their core. Jess had told them the entire cartel was founded by deserters from the Mexican special forces. This fact might have given Adam some frail hope, of a military logic that could be somehow appealed to, if it weren't for the captain, the obvious commander, who'd told them his name was 'Marco' – as he bluntly separated them out from the tribesmen. He was a stout, vigorous, muscular guy in his thirties, with skulls and wild roses and elaborate zeds for Zeta tattooed up his tanned, sinewy arms. And he had exactly the same gleam of strange, smart, sadistic eagerness in his eyes as Tony Ritter.

No doubt Marco too was on ulluchu, the real drug. What was he going to do to them? Were they going to be shot in a clearing in the forest? Away from witnesses? Or something else?

It was an effort not to show his fear. He wondered if Nina had noticed Marco's demeanour, and was therefore remembering what happened to her sister in the Islington house. Blood and terror and violation.

A slight bend in the riverbank brought them to a large metal barge, lashed by a thick rope to a ceiba tree, and sagging with age. It was an old cargo boat rusting in a lost meander of this vast river system. Marco tilted his expensive European pistol and ordered them on to the boat.

'The stairs. Go down those stairs. Now.'

Adam could see the fine jaw muscles moving in Marco's face, from the grinding of his teeth. He clearly wanted to hurt them as soon as possible, he was restraining himself.

They stepped down the metal ladder into a metal room: a sealed storage container. The Amazonian sun had heated the entire boat so that the metal was painful to the touch. And it was in this steel cell, this steel oven, that they were going to be kept.

One of Marco's men handcuffed them, again with soldierly swiftness and obedience, to the rigid metal pipes that ran along the side of the metal chamber. Just like the radiator in London, Adam realized: they were shackled in a line, like dogs in a row at a show.

The subordinate disappeared up the metal steps. Marco followed, then paused at the top, a dark figure silhouetted by the sun. He gazed at his prisoners in the bowels of the boat and his prisoners all stared up, at this last square of hope, this glimpse of tropic sky.

'Your friends,' Marco said, abruptly, taking some objects from a sack. He threw two footballs into the metal cell, which bounced along the steel floor. Then he slammed the trapdoor shut.

With the only opening to the outside world quite sealed, it was profoundly dark in the stinking, broiling metal chamber. Yet there was just enough sunlight, lancing through small rusty holes in the metal roof, to make out that the footballs were not balls at all, but two human heads: the captain of the *MV Myona*, and the other deckhand.

Jose wailed like a child and then made a retching sound. Adam stared, riveted and appalled, at the heads. They were lying sideways and staring wet-eyed at each other, like lovers talking on a shared pillow. The expressions on the heads were incomprehensible, terror and serenity. A tiny dewdrop of blood fell from the dead captain's hair on to the metal floor.

'We are finished.' Boris's voice was quavering. 'They are going to kill us all, but they will torture us first. The Zetas' cruelty is *famous.*'

'We know.' Adam said, flatly. 'We fucking know.' He yanked at the handcuffs looping him to the metal pipes. This was beyond useless. Yet he tried uselessly, for ten minutes, twenty, tugging at the cuffs until his wrists were scraped and raw and bloody.

Jess spoke, for the first time. 'We could bargain with them.'

Nina replied, fierce in the shadows. 'With what? We have nothing. Fuck all of them anyway. Let them kill us – even if we had something to give they would still kill us.'

Boris's once-macho voice was reduced to a low whimper. 'This is quite right, whatever we do, whatever we say, they will kill us – but first they will try and get any information: they will torture us.'

A shock of light silenced his lamenting.

The trapdoor had been opened. Marco came down the stairs, followed by two of his lieutenants. He reached the bottom of the ladder and surveyed them. Contemptuously.

'There is no ulluchu here. We came here a week ago. We asked all the tribes, we tried it. We have been following you. We spoke to the shaman in Belen. Boris Valentine is celebrated in Iquitos.'

His voice was surprisingly neutral. He spoke exceedingly good English: he was evidently very educated. This man could have been a rising young major in the

412

Mexican army, Adam thought. But the Zetas paid so much *more*.

Marco paced across the rusty metal floor, kicking a severed head out of the way as if he was practising football. Then he knelt by Nina. Adam strained in his shackles to see what was happening, there, at the other side of the chamber, in the shadows.

'What do you know, Nina? Your father's notebooks end at Iquitos. What did your father know? Where did he go after this? We think he went into the Andes. The mountains. Where the ulluchu grows better?'

She said nothing. Marco's sigh was ominous and heavy. He leaned closer, and Adam was reminded of Ritter, trying to kiss her, or lick her: like a predatory rapist.

'I could hit you, Miss McLintock. I could electrocute you, or cut you up. Maybe I could cut off one of your fingers. Or your lips. I could cut your lips off. Tell me.'

Nina said nothing.

He stood, with a slight jerkiness in his movements. The ulluchu maybe? Then he signalled to one of his men, who was carrying a plastic box, a kind of Tupperware container, quite ludicrously domestic.

Inside the translucent box were small creatures moving in dirty water: the wriggling shadows were visible through the plastic, they looked like long, dark tadpoles.

Boris, lying next to Adam, was already writhing and whimpering. What did he know?

The whimpering was evidently a mistake. Marco

swivelled, alerted by the noise. He scrutinized the fat man in the bright Hawaiian shirt and khaki trousers. The little fishes wriggled in the box in the dark chamber light.

'And you are Boris Valentine. Famous scientist. So you know what these are, don't you?' A slight, unpitying smile. 'For the benefit of your friends, who probably do not know, I will explain.'

Marco took the box and put it on the floor. He opened the lid. The little fishes jiggled, as if enlivened, exposed to the beam of sunlight from the open trapdoor.

Marco was putting on a very thick rubber glove. 'These fish are *candiru*. The toothpick fish. Or, more often, the vampire fish. Of the family Trichomycteridae. A type of parasitic freshwater catfish. Unique to Amazonia.'

He flexed his fingers in the glove. 'The vampire fish was once thought to be the matter of legend. Or, at least, their less pleasant habits were considered much exaggerated. But then the first case of true human parasitism was scientifically recorded. In 1997.'

He dipped a finger in the box, stirring the silty water. All the little black fish wriggled and jiggled, excitedly.

'The candiru has a *voracious* appetite for blood. Given the chance it will eagerly parasitize fish and mammals, including humans. Some believe they are attracted by the smell of urine. They commonly enter the human system through the penis, anus or vagina. Once there, they lodge themselves in the urinary tract, or maybe the fallopian tubes or ovaries. Or the

414

seminal vesicles? Is that the English word? Yes. Vesicles. And the ureter.'

Boris was backing away, kicking at the metal floor in his urge to retreat from the shallow box of dancing vampire fish. Marco's smile was brief. He reached in and picked out a fish with his gloved hand.

'Once it is safely within the human body, the fish grows, gorging itself on human blood and flesh. They can easily triple in size. Quadruple even. They eat away at your flesh *from the inside*. Their vicious spikes prevent them being removed without lethal damage to internal organs, once they are in *they are in*. The pain as they eat their way through the sexual organs and lower intestines is said to be indescribable. For a man, the only possible way they can be removed is by complete emasculation. That is to say, by cutting off the penis and testicles. Even then the possibility of death from blood loss, trauma and sepsis is extremely high. But first the little fish has to enter the body.'

He held the wriggling black fish in his palm and moved closer to Boris.

'Tell me what you know.'

Boris was wetting himself. Adam could see the stain on his khaki trousers. He sympathized fiercely. And he turned away. Helpless.

Boris yelped, 'He went to the mountains! He went to the Andes! The Andes!'

Marco tutted. 'Where in the Andes?'

'Huancabamba. He want to a place, near Huancabamba! It's true. I saw the receipts.'

415

Marco shook his head. 'Huancabamba? Why there? And where exactly?'

'A mountain, uh ah uh ah – a village called Toloriu.'

Marco shook his head, and dropped the little fish in the box. Then he pulled a knife from his pocket and quickly and brutally slashed open Boris's khaki trousers, exposing the professor's chubby white thigh. Then he diligently made a short but deep cut in Boris's skin.

Boris yelped like a dog being whipped.

With his gloved hand, Marco dipped once more in the box and retrieved one of the fishes. It wriggled in his palm. Then he carefully tipped the little fish towards the bleeding red gash in Boris's pale thigh. Adam stared, even though he didn't want to stare. The vampire fish in Marco's palm seemed to lift its tiny head, sniffing the blood. Then it slid gratefully into the open wound. Repulsively, quite repulsively, Adam could see the fish *under the skin*, intent and wriggling *inside* the flesh. Then it burrowed deeper and was gone.

Boris was screaming.

Marco gripped Boris's shaking head with his rubber-gloved hand. 'I can maybe cut it out now, before it reaches your groin, before it begins to eat your intestines. And your genitals. From the inside out. You have just a few seconds.'

Boris's voice was so thick with fear and pain it was barely comprehensible. 'Toloriu . . . Toloriu.'

Marco spat on the floor. 'Not enough.'

He turned to his men. '*He terminado con él. No sabe nada. Mátalo. Y también a su amigo.*'

Boris Valentine was unshackled from the pipes, the blood spattering from the wound in his torn-open leg, a sagging, dying figure, groaning with pain. The Zetas dragged him up the metal steps, and pushed him into the light. Then they did the same with Jose.

Marco departed, with a final blank yet thoughtful glance; and a keen little smile. It was the smile of ulluchu. Of pensive cruelty. Just like Ritter. The Zetas must have worked out a precise dose of the drug: enough to arouse the violent sexualized instincts of sadism, but not enough to self-mutilate. Something like that. Then they gave some to their top lieutenants.

The trapdoor slammed. The loud noise was followed by two more loud noises: gunshots. Then another. And another. The Zetas were executing Boris and Jose. A few seconds later, two loud splashes confirmed it: the bodies had been thrown in the river. For Boris it was probably a mercy, Adam reckoned. The piranhas eating his dead body was better than than the vampire fish slowly eating you inside out, as you screamed, fully conscious.

No one spoke. There was nothing to say. Apart from goodbye. Nina asked Jessica why she had called her doctor. Jessica looked at her helpless and pathetic. 'I don't know anyone else. He said he will call the police.'

The police? The idea of the police rescuing them from the Zetas was comically absurd. The police were *scared* of the Zetas. Everyone was scared of the Zetas. Except perhaps the rising force of Catrina.

An hour passed, maybe less, maybe much less: the

fear was so intense it made time illegible. Then Adam heard noises, loud voices. He shunted himself back to the side of the metal chamber. Pressed his ear to the steel. The voices reverberated through the metal barge. *He could hear.*

'Jessica. Listen – you speak Spanish – what are they saying?'

She pressed her ear to the steel wall. Then she shook her head in the pungent darkness. 'No good. Worse.'

'What are they saying?'

'Most of the men want to kill us now. Just shoot us. And move on. The guy, Marco, wants to . . . torture us some more. He reckons we might still know something – and he says he wants some more *fun*. That is the word he used. *Quiero divertirme un poco más.*' She closed her eyes. 'He wants to play with us a little more. That's the ulluchu talking.'

The trapdoor opened; Marco came down. He was carrying the same plastic box. Full of hungry little fishes.

'We were talking . . .' He was wearing rubber gloves on both hands now. He looked Nina's way and snapped: 'You. You rather desire your friend Adam, do you not? Would you still desire him if he had no penis, no *cojones*, if he just had a bleeding socket?'

Nina shook her head. 'Stop it.'

Marco ignored her. He crouched by Adam. The lid was off the box, the fish were wriggling. Grunting as he worked, he cut open Adam's jeans at the groin. A few crude slashes of the knife and it was done: Adam's thigh was exposed. Then Marco casually stuck the knife

418

in Adam's thigh, and made a sudden five-centimetre-long downwards cut. Adam refused to scream. He refused. The sweat of fear and agony made him faint, but he refused to scream.

'Very brave. *Muy bravo*. I do not think you will be so silent in a minute. Mmm? *Vale*. Say hello to the fishes?' Marco's smile was quite sincere. He put down the knife, reached for the box and pulled out a jiving little fish. 'This one, I think, is especially hungry.'

Then he paused. Because there was a noise outside. A big loud noise – people were shouting on the deck. Then gunshots echoed cacophonously around the metal hulk: an enormous and rattling hail of gunshots.

Male screams of anger followed the shots. *Men were fighting on the deck*. At once, Marco dropped the fish and dashed for the stairs, but even as he reached the foot of the ladder he fell back. Someone had calmly shot him several times from the trapdoor; Marco's body slumped, blood gushing from his stomach. The sound of the bullets echoed deafeningly around the metal cell; everyone shrank from the ricochet.

Except Adam. He was staring in terror at the fish. It had fallen from Marco's hand *on to his leg*. And now it lay there, wriggling, on his bared thigh. Right beside the open wound. It was sucking at his skin, urgently seeking the way in, trying to find the entrance into his body, where it could feed, and live, and grow.

Men were clattering down the ladder, he could hear them. They were in the room, snapping the shackles on the others; but Adam just stared, transfixed, at the fish: it had found the edge of the wound, and now it slipped inside. *It was burrowing into his skin*. He could see the shape of it. Adam screamed.

A knife flashed down, into the wound, and speared the fish, scooping it out of his thigh with a deft and practised movement. Like a gourmet skewering some buttery crabmeat. The fish wriggled at the end of the knife, then the fish was crushed under a military boot.

Adam looked up, faint with shock. He had been saved. But who were these men? The shackles on his wrists were cut by huge pliers; some wadding was applied to the wound in his leg, and it was wordlessly and hastily bandaged. He stood, unsteadily, then ran for the stairs and ran up and out, following Nina and Jessica on to the deck of the barge.

On the metal deck, in the hot sun, five more of these strange men gazed back at them. Implacable. Quite unsmiling. And very disciplined. It was the police. It had worked: Jessica's phone call had worked. Adam turned in elation to Jessica but he saw she was staring in horror at something. The men. And their hands, clutching their guns.

All the men had dark black T-shirts and toned muscles and pressed jeans, like off-duty soldiers or elite police.

And they all had skulls tattooed on their hands.

Catrina.

50

Riverplane, Ucayali, Peru

They were given just five minutes to pack a few items from their rucksacks, then they were loaded, at gunpoint, on to a speedboat. The Catrina *cartelistas* remained silent. The boat curved the river for several minutes, until it reached a broader stretch.

Adam stared. On the water ahead was a riverplane. Dirty and white and impressively large. They were forced on board the plane and most of the *cartelistas* followed, wordless. Proficient. Tattooed. Muscled.

The propellers of the plane turned, shivering the wavelets beneath, then they sped across the grey-brown waters and ascended over the infinity of green forest. Strapped in his seat, Adam could just see the first rise of the blue Andes, so distant they looked like clouds. His mind drifted in despair. A little boat unanchored, heading for the terrible sea.

Is that where the true ulluchu was, then? The Andes?

421

Is that where Archibald McLintock ended up, in some little mountain village, with shepherds in scarlet ponchos and trousers?

Or maybe it was in the high *puna*, the arid, bitter moorlands of Peru. He'd read about these windswept desolations, where the cold and mist and blowing rain was constant, where espeletia daisies grew tall and sad with bright yellow flowers. Like the ulluchu?

They were never going to find out. Who had betrayed them to Catrina? Nina? No, of course not. Jessica . . . ? She was ill, she was sad, she was ambitious, but she was not a traitor. Boris? Possibly. He wanted to sell ulluchu on, if they found it; and maybe word had reached Catrina or the Zetas or both. Then of course, there was the captain, the drunken captain, was someone paying him? If so he'd paid the final price in return, along with his deckhands.

But then again, maybe *no one* had betrayed them: perhaps Catrina had simply followed the logic and traced them. Quite possibly Catrina had been watching the whole show, waiting for their moment.

But why had they been kidnapped? Did Catrina hope they had information? Would they try to torture it out of them? But they had no information to give, they had nothing to offer, even if they were allowed to bargain. Which wouldn't happen. *Catrina were known to be even crueller than the Zetas.*

Nina reached out and held his hand. He squeezed it tight. The air was turbulent as they headed for the mountains. Maybe they would crash. Maybe they wouldn't. Did it matter? He squeezed her hand again and said nothing. No words were needed.

A man came down the aisle of the buffeted plane, armed and blank-faced. He opened up his palm, revealing a dozen green capsules.

Adam recognized the pills from his days in Sydney, with Alicia. These were Roofies. Rohypnol; the date-rape drug. Two of these would knock out a grown man for ten hours.

The Catrina man grunted. 'Four. Each.'

They obeyed – with a certain bleak eagerness. Oblivion seemed welcome, certainly preferable to thinking about what lay ahead, because nothing lay ahead but more suffering and pain. Adam swallowed his pills with water. Then he watched as Jessica took her pills, too, across the aisle.

She turned and looked him and shook her head, as if to say, It is Over. And of course it was. Everything was over.

Jessica swallowed. Adam turned. She looked at him, and smiled a strange smile; and then she swallowed. *Gute nacht, meine kindern.*

He gazed instead at Nina. *She* seemed almost happy as she put her head back. Happy?

Confusion surged through him, but there was nothing he could do about it. The Rohypnol hit him like a hammer thirty-seven minutes later.

When he woke they were on a different plane. A jet. Flying in the darkness. He groped to remember a vague dream about airports, hoods, or blindfolds, half-dream/half-reality. Everyone else was asleep on the plane, even some of the Catrina men. Nina and Jessica were sitting together. Strapped tightly in, and handcuffed.

Adam looked down: a handcuff jangled on his wrist. He motioned to the man guarding them. Jerking his head to the back of the plane. 'Toilet?'

The man nodded. He unlocked the shackle and Adam stepped unsteadily down the aisle. He stared in the mirror of the tiny washroom as he zipped up. His face was dirty with river mud, and a patch of red rust. Red rust? Of course, from where he had pressed his cheek to the rusting steel of the barge, to listen to the Zetas.

A vague groping of an idea entered his head. Los Zetas. The bitter rivals.

Back in his seat he was given a sandwich and some water. He ate and drank, trying not to think. Then he was reshackled and the cartelista opened his palm. 'Four. Each.'

Soon, the blackness of Rohypnol enveloped him again.

The second time he woke he was being unloaded from a vehicle. He was hooded; but he could hear sounds. The distinct sounds of a very busy city, Hispanic music, people, but echoey, and distanced, as if they were down a side street.

This was his chance. He yelled, desperately, into the blackness of his hood. 'Zetas! This is Catrina! Help us! Catrina have got us, police, anyone, *policia!*'

The thud of a rifle butt or a pistol butt on the side of his head felt like a hammer blow. He slumped to his knees. But he yelled again, more weakly. 'Catrina, the Catrina cartel have got us! Policia! Los Zet—'

Someone lifted the hood for a moment and shoved something in his mouth, a rubber ball maybe; he almost choked. Another vicious blow to his head sent him semi-conscious. They were being moved into the back of another vehicle, and forced to lie down. Adam gagged on the rubber ball. Would his desperate plan work? He had little hope, but it was their only hope. The two gangs were fighting over the drug, neither of them had enough of it, they were still trying to find the source. They were at war. And that war was the only leverage he and Nina and Jessica had.

Yet it seemed a ludicrous hope as he lay here on the floor of a van, bound and gagged and pathetic. Adam could sense Nina and Jessica, hear their desperate panting.

For a few kilometres, the traffic noise was intense. This was a big big city. Lima? Rio? Bogotá? Mexico City? Adam's eyes burned to see but all he could see was blackness. Then the van stopped. The hood was whipped away. They were in a courtyard: a large, pleasant, green and marble Spanish colonial patio. Tall armed men stood between palm trees. The noise of the city was still audible; but large and closed steel gates muffled the drone. Adam's hands were shackled behind him. He gazed around for Nina and Jessica.

He saw them being led in through a door. A gun in the back nudged Adam inside after them.

The house was big and airy, with majolica tiles and modern art in delicate juxtaposition. It was elegant and unboastful. A very rich man lived here, quietly and discreetly. Adam could guess who.

Carlos Chicomeca Monroy. *El Santo*.

And here he was: standing in the middle of a large room painted a pale straw yellow. His lean face was older than his years but still handsome. Thirty-three maybe, but toughened by ambition or ruthlessness. He wore a pale suit. Everything about him was slightly pale. To Adam, he looked like a silvery saint in a dark Spanish Baroque painting. A saint preparing to ascend to heaven, to evanesce. To float on water, to beckon the birds to his hands. Even his dark hair was pale. His eyes were pale. His smile was pale, but gleaming.

Ulluchu.

The ulluchu smile. He was on the drug. He was going to torture them to death. Adam looked forlornly around the room, seeking an escape route, knowing it was pointless. There was no escaping this.

On the opposite wall he saw what looked like a Rothko, a real Rothko painting. They were told to sit down. Adam recognized the design: Barcelona chairs, exquisitely *moderniste;* ten thousand dollars each, screwed to the floor. They were shackled to the iconic steel chairs.

Carlos Monroy smiled at them. A gesture to the guards and some of them walked out, leaving two alert, and silent, sentries. He spoke: 'The beating of our hearts is the only sound . . .'

He walked up to Nina, who was staring, rapt, at the drug lord, from her chair. Staring down at her white, mud-smeared face he said, 'Your father was quite a man, quite a man. The only man to outwit me in many years.'

His accent was pure East Coast going on British. Quite flawless. His pale and austere eyes were very slightly bloodshot. The tiny fleck of foam at the corner of his mouth again spoke of ulluchu.

'You've taken the drug,' said Nina. 'We can tell.'

'The dose can be carefully calibrated so you achieve the exquisite *high* of sadism, but not the horror of suicide. You are not unintelligent. You have worked out a lot, Jessica has told me.'

Jessica?

'But what you haven't worked out is what the drug ultimately *does*.' Monroy reached behind him, to a fine marble mantelpiece. He took down a small silver box. And showed it to Nina, then Adam. The small elegant box glittered in the sunlight through tall French windows that gave on to a balcony overlooking the patio. Adam wondered if he would survive a jump from that balcony.

Monroy turned the box in one hand. 'Made by Francis Harrache, in London. Joyous, isn't it? 1750. Solid silver. For tobacco, of course. Just one of the many drugs you Europeans took from the New World. And still you take our drugs . . .' He snapped open the lid. 'But we have less time to talk than I had hoped.' His shining eyes regarded Adam. 'Your outburst on the street was a sensible move. It is what I would have done in such reduced circumstances. And now the Zetas are indeed alerted: the street is a network of gossip and treachery. Just like the closest friendships. So. Here. This is ulluchu. This is what Archibald McLintock found. Look—'

The lid was open. Adam couldn't help his curiosity. If he was going to die he wanted to see what he was going to die *for.*

He peered. The powder inside the box looked not unlike tobacco snuff, only greyer and finer.

Monroy carefully placed the open box on a side table. He took out a tiny silver spoon from a pocket in his pale jacket. His eyes flickered across them, from face to face. 'Your theories as to the functioning of ulluchu were audacious. Creditable. But you missed the crucial factor, you failed to grasp what makes this plant so utterly unique even amidst the bounteous entheogenic richness of Amazonia.' He picked up the box again. 'Yes, the drug induces hypersexuality. Yes, it arouses violence and sadistic urges. Yes, the alkaloids therein work with extraordinary speed, just like dimethyl-tryptamine. Yes, the ulluchu commonly has gruesome or precise side-effects: the urge to drink blood is common, likewise a desire for sex *per ano*. Especially in a zoophiliac or necrophiliac context.' He gazed at them, 'And yes, the seeds, when powdered very, very finely, also have the happy character of being completely absorbed into the blood stream with great efficiency. The powder, we have elucidated, is best absorbed

428

through the nasal or oral membranes. That way the powder is dissolved in seconds; if it is taken orally it is undetectable a few minutes later; you would have to analyse the molecules of the glottis to discern what had happened, even if you knew *what* you were looking for.'

He turned. 'I deviate. You need to know what this drug *does*. You need to know because I am about to give it to you, approximately 0.5 grams, in a fine powder form, about five times what I take every day from my little Georgian snuffbox. When taken at that very concentrated level, in one single dose, the drug not only powers the libido and the aggressive and libidinous instincts, it arouses what Freud called the death instinct, thanatos, so closely entwined to eros, the sex drive, the life instinct. You see, the drug,' his smile was pallid and moist, *'makes you want to die.* It makes the user *yearn* for death, so that he . . .' He paused. 'Or she, will self-mutilate, tear at their own flesh, or hurl themselves into danger with urgent fearlessness. Hoping for a fatal wound. Like the brave Templars of the Crusader Levant, foolishly throwing themselves into battle, believing they died for Christ, believing they died *like* Christ. Sacrificing themselves, quite intoxicated with the death instinct. Quite, quite inebriated on ulluchu. So this really is the secret that gets you killed. The late Archibald McLintock so loved that phrase.'

He scooped a tiny amount of powder from the box with the delicate silver spoon.

'Half a gram. I am going to give each of you half a

gram of ulluchu. At first you will feel nothing. Then you will experience intense pleasure, and you will become aroused, and probably violent, possibly at the same time. This will be interesting for us all. Consequently the very high dosage will . . . *kick in*. You will feel an unconquerable urge to seek the end, to slough off this weary mantle of worldliness, perhaps to hack off your own lips, to gouge out your eyes, in short: to die. You will want to die: this is the death drug, the ultimate drug, the suicide drug. Then you will kill yourselves. I have no idea in what way. It seems to affect different people in different ways: how they actually perform the Babylon rite of self-murder. The entertainment will be potentially quite profound, even, it is arguable, desolately beautiful. A kind of artwork. A *gesamtkunstwerk*, a living theatre of sex and death, like the rituals of the Moche in the Pyramid of the Sorcerer, like the overdosed Templars torturing men and children in Temple Bruer and hiding the evidence.'

Abruptly, he stepped close and grabbed Nina's white cheeks, so hard that her mouth was forced open. He poised the heaped little spoon in front of her mouth, and blew the powder between her soft red open lips.

Then he let go. She coughed and hacked brown spittle on to the floor. Monroy shook his head. 'The powder is on the very back of your throat, already being absorbed. You cannot spit it out. And now for the gentleman.'

Adam tried to avert his face but Monroy's grip was very strong. He felt the powder hit the back of the

430

throat. Felt the bitter taste, extraordinarily tart, almost like a powdered acid. A tang of some heavenly dark citrus. The taste disappeared, and a surge of pleasure overtook him.

Monroy stiffened, and walked to the last chair. 'I don't have to force you, do I, Jessica Silverton? You want the drug, don't you? You want to die? That is, after all, why we are all here?'

She mumbled her reply, her eyes wet with tears. 'Yes.'

51

Le Casa de Carlos Chicomeca Monroy

'Why?' said Nina, softly, gazing at Jessica. 'Why did you betray us? Because you are ill?'

Jessica Silverton said nothing: she stared at the chevrons of the parquet floor. Handcuffed and miserable.

Carlos Monroy set the silver spoon on the marble mantel. 'I can explain for Miss Silverton. You have to understand. She is an expert in her field, one of the brightest. She guessed some time ago the possible true nature of ulluchu. That it contained a unique alkaloid. Let us call it *thanatine*. An alkaloid which induces the desire to die. An alkaloid we have tried, and failed, so far, to isolate, extract and synthesize. Despite all our valiant attempts.'

Adam looked at Jessica for confirmation. But her blonde hair curtained her downcast face.

Monroy continued, 'The second thing you need to know is that Jessica's father *died* when she was young,

432

of Huntington's Disease. And that is a very evil way to die. Progressive and degenerative and appalling. The kind of disease which makes you question the goodness of God.' He walked closer to Adam. 'There is, of course, no cure. Huntington's is genetic. Many people with the disease refuse a genetic test to see whether they are carriers. Why? Because a positive diagnosis induces many to commit suicide even before they fall ill, so great is their terror of the eventual affliction.' He paused. 'Jessica is, we now know, a carrier. What is more, she has the worst kind: a speedy and juvenile variety of the chorea. The clinching symptom is epileptiform seizure.'

Adam spoke, his voice hoarse. 'How do you know all this?'

'For many months Jessica admits she has been in denial of various symptoms – the initial signs that she had Huntington's. And who can blame her for denying such a terrible fate for herself? Then, when her situation became incontrovertible, in the last weeks, days even, the intense horror took hold: and she knew she wanted to kill herself rather than go through what her father endured. And she wanted to face this death with yearning rather than dread, face it with contemptuous courage even, face it like the noble Templars, or the gallant Moche, the fearsome berserkers. Rather understandable, wouldn't you say?'

'Jess.' Nina whispered. But still Jessica said nothing. Adam could feel the first rush of his own heart. The drug kicking in. They were *all* spiralling into oblivion, into the pure darkness of dementia. The sensation was blissful and terrifying.

Monroy paced the gilded room, like a gifted young lecturer, like the Harvard scholar he once was.

'Jessica guessed, a while ago, what ulluchu really did. That it was a drug that made you want to die, thus obviating the terrors of death and of suicide. She felt that you, in turn, were unlikely to achieve success in finding the real ulluchu. Certainly she could not rely on this, and she was ever more desperate. Yet she knew I was most likely to be in possession of the *echt* drug, and she could not be sure anyone else had any of the dwindling supplies – and she could not be sure anyone else would understand her side of the bargain. Therefore she kept her options rather cleverly *open* by initiating contact with me, from Lima, the day you met. She gave me a few clues as to her situation and your whereabouts. Following her seizure on your boat, when her genetic fate was confirmed, when she felt the cold kiss of death on her pale American neck, she called me once more from the UNESCO site. She said if you failed in the jungle she would do a deal. Cut a sweet little deal. She would, if she could, make a phone call from the jungle: we were monitoring her phone, we were able to triangulate her location. She took a risk, but she is not without courage. And we knew you were near Iquitos: Peru is a cheap place to buy friends. So we located you, and thus we were able to come and . . . rescue you. As it were.'

'What deal?' Adam's forehead was prickling with

sweat. His pulse was up. 'What deal could she do? What is her side of the bargain?'

'Jessica told me she probably knew where Nina's father had sourced the drug. She said she had seen the receipts and she had worked it out for herself, but told no one. The drug, she thought, had been removed from the jungle and cultivated elsewhere, by the Moche, probably in the mountains. They must have developed a much stronger variety, at certain distinct altitudes, with the perfect levels of rainfall and sunshine and frost – through centuries of horticulture. The Muchika were a very clever people. They were quite excellent irrigators.'

'So, where?'

Carlos Monroy raised a hand, his smile princely in the sun slanting in through the long tall windows. 'Let us ask her. She has yet to tell me. I do not know. Let us hear what she says.'

Colours menaced through Adam's mind. The drug was really in his blood stream now. Gorgeous sexual images. Nina. Jessica. Blood-red swirls of purple. He forced himself to concentrate.

Monroy walked to Jessica's chair. And crouched before her. 'Tell me.'

A short painful pause ensued. Then Jessica lifted her head. She had been weeping silently, judging by her red-rimmed eyes. But her voice was quite distinct and articulate. 'I saw the last receipt. Archibald McLintock went to Toloriu. After the jungle.'

Monroy frowned. 'A little town near Huancabamba. In the Andes, what good is that? Which mountain?

435

'No.' Jessica shook her head. 'Not Toloriu in Peru. The receipt was handwritten. A taxi. They—' she glanced at Adam and Nina, 'They didn't realize. He went to a different Toloriu. A tiny hamlet, in the Pyrenees. *Catalunya*. He went back to *Spain*.'

Monroy stood up. His frown slowly became a gratified smile, then a triumphant laugh. 'Toloriu. Casa Bima! The legend! The most obscure of legends!' His laughter died, but the gleaming smile remained. Happy and aggressive.

Leaning against the mantelpiece, he picked up his silver spoon. And then the glinting silver snuff box. '*Casa Bima*. What an ornate yet apposite denouement: the fulfilment of a very ancient story. Jessica, you were right: there are few people in the world who could have pieced that together . . . you, and me. And Archibald McLintock. Superb. You have earned your reward.' He shook his head. 'Of course I promised to save your friends and of course you knew I was lying and you didn't care. Correct? But I will not torment them unduly. Let them kill themselves. And now it is your turn for the sweet release. Please, open your mouth. You can have an entire gram, a large proportion of my dwindling supplies. As a token of my generosity. It will work that much quicker, and your death will be sweeter. It will be exquisite. A sensuous climax.'

Jessica opened her mouth. Monroy had scooped his tiny glittering spoon in the powder, now heaped with half a gram of ulluchu. He positioned it carefully, then blew it – a puff of snuff between Jessica's trembling

436

lips. He did it again – another half a gram. She swallowed, and looked at the floor.

Monroy stood. He gazed, hard, at Nina and Adam. 'Your cheeks are quite flushed. I see it is taking effect. I'd say you all have twenty minutes of consciousness and lucidity. I can tell you the rest of the story to fill these dull moments! Yes? Yes, I think so. But I'll be brief. When you are dead, in about an hour or two, at your own hands, I will have to leave here. Los Zetas are surely seeking me out right now, searching for this house, I took enough risks flying you into the country. They have spies throughout the system, they are the shadow state, at airports, everywhere . . . And your clever outburst in the street will have alarmed and alerted the entire city.' His face began to smear in Adam's vision.

Adam wanted to kill this man, to tear him open. Drink the blood. He thought of Nina naked. Deliciously naked. Then Alicia.

The red mouth of the pale man opened and closed.

'It was Harvard that changed me. All that wealth, all that *incredible* American wealth. The arrogant rowers on the Charles River, the egregiously regal Bostonians. When I got there, I compared it with my own country, impoverished, and ridiculed, and risible and – far, far worse – torn apart by the drug wars. How could I not? The drug wars are caused by America, by their ridiculous and bogus Puritanism, their absurd, adolescent prohibition on the purely human urge for intoxication, for altered states. Men have been taking drugs for ten thousand years: it is a human universal; mankind cannot bear too much reality. And the Americans are no different. And yet their same grunting American hunger for drugs, for cocaine and marijuana, for heroin and methamphetamine, for anything to enliven their absurdly dull materialist lives of gorging, shopping and corpulent waddling – this greed and desperation was killing *my* people, not harming *them*. Quite *invidious*.' Monroy snapped the snuff box shut, angrily. Adam closed his eyes and just listened to the voice.

'The hypocrisy sickened me. America imported the drugs, yet religiously banned them. This same American prohibition therefore made the drug-trade all too appealing and profitable, accelerating the deathly wars in my country. My country. Mexico. Indeed all Latin America. Thousands are dying, tens of thousands are slaughtered yearly, just across the Rio Grande from peaceful El Paso. To salt the wound of irony, America makes and sells us the guns with which to kill each other! They actually *profit* from our massacres, massacres caused by their canting hypocrisies. And *still* they didn't care, as long as they kept the death and destruction on the *other* side of the frontier, over the river, beyond the great big fence, that keeps the spics and wetbacks out, the fence that nonetheless lets all the dope and the meth and the cocaine in, for the kids in Harvard Yaaaard to get so pleasantly *zoned*.'

Sex and murder, sex and bloody murder. Alicia naked and dying. Adam felt his own arousal at the death of nude Alicia. He was aroused by the nearness of his own death. The sensation was tremendous and irresistible: he was being ravished by crueller desires.

'So I began to plot some revenge on America, on the gringo who was destroying my country. And what sweeter, more deliciously ironic revenge could there be, I realized, than finding a terrible drug which Puritan America simply could not resist? The ultimate drug, the terminal high. A drug that was initially blissful, and quite sublime, combining the languid rapture of heroin with the euphoriant buzz of pure cocaine, as you are now experiencing; and then something much much *better*. And then something very much *worse*.' He licked his lips, gazing at Jessica. She had her head thrown back, swallowing compulsively. He walked over and stroked her hair. She sighed. He stroked, and talked, 'And then one day I visited the Schultes Archives in Harvard, and I had my intimation. Maybe it wasn't just a daydream, a wild and foolish ambition, maybe there was such a drug; maybe in the great vivid pageant of pre-Columbian entheogens I could find something: what was it the Aztecs took, the Moche, the Maya, the denizens of mighty Teotihuacan? Maybe they had a drug they gave to men before they were sacrificed that made them all willing victims, victims of the reeking priests with the obsidian knives.'

He leaned to kiss Jessica on the neck, and then to caress her breasts. Adam yearned to join them. The three of them. The four of them. Dissolving into each other's bodies. Monroy drew back from Jessica, and continued, 'So I began my research. I discovered ulluchu. I deduced that it had disappeared, yet I also discerned that the drug had maybe once reached Europe, perhaps reached the Templars: hence the lust of the conquistadors, the warriors from the last lands of the Templars, the very inheritors of the Templar legends, to find it once again.' He flashed a smile, a brief, proud, exultant smile. 'Once you realize the Templars were drugged, it all coheres. But what was this drug? I had to know. So I contacted the one man who could help, the great Templar expert, Archibald McLintock. Happily, he wanted the money I offered, and he was intrigued by my description of this putative narcotic. I later discovered why, of course: he was dying. He wanted the money as a legacy for his daughters; he wanted ulluchu for himself.'

Monroy kissed Jessica's neck once more; his hand was inside her shirt. She sighed voluptuously.

Adam closed his eyes to the burning images, the image of a white naked body opened and bloody. He wanted to kill something. Drink the blood. Drink it all up. He was glad he was shackled to the chair. Monroy's voice was a mellifluous bass tone.

'McLintock fooled me. He unearthed the drug, said he'd found it somewhere in the Andes. He gave me a considerable supply which I in turn gave to my men – as an incitement. We planted seeds to grow bushes, but they all failed: this is a very delicate plant. Of course Archibald promised more in time, and I believed him. I planned my exportation to America, I planned how I would market this marvellous drug to all the fat greedy stoner American *kids*. I would get them hooked first, then introduce stronger supplies.' His hand stroked Jessica's cheek, tenderly. 'You see, as I say, at the right subdued dose, ulluchu merely induces extreme and blissful *sadism*, and of course intense addiction. Perfect for creating junkies – and perfect for creating loyal cartelistas, loyally violent foot-soldiers. I tried it on my men first. It worked. My cartel flourished; we began to threaten the Zetas, because with the ulluchu we were even *crueller* than them, and so the Zetas grew scared. But then, one of my closest men betrayed me, for money: he told the Zetas of McLintock, the man in Scotland, they went after him – stole his notebooks, and, I presume, most of the ulluchu he had kept for his own purposes. Since then they have been trying to prevent me retracing the McLintock trail, following the death of Archibald himself. Though clever old Archibald must have hidden a truly secret stash, to smooth the path of his own death, at Rosslyn Chapel . . .'

Nina was moaning, writhing. Monroy smiled.

'But then again, we all want to die, don't we? Isn't this the beauty of what you are feeling, Adam, Nina? To give in at last, to succumb to that dark, voluptuous urge, to throw yourself under the subway train, to drive into the oncoming truck.'

He was groping Jessica, she opened her legs, letting him touch her, her eyes were shut and she was sighing heavily, her throat pulsing, and then she spoke:

'—me—'

'Of course.'

'Untie me.'

He knelt and unshackled her. She reached for him. Monroy motioned to the guards: leave. The sentries nodded and quit the room.

Nina said, 'Me too.'

Monroy laughed. 'Please. You can drown in each other's blood when I am done. Here. Jessica. Beautiful, dying American blonde, Jessica Silverton, strip.'

She was pulling off her clothes.

'And show me.'

She pulled down her jeans. She was naked. Desperate. Shivering. He laughed. 'You are so very blonde – even here.' He pulled her to the sofa, 'Let them watch. I can cut you up as we fuck, like the Moche. Do you want that? Do you want me to cut you up, Jessie? It will make you come, you will have no face, it will be ribbons, it will be good, you will be beautiful, you are dying, it doesn't matter, you want to die, don't you? You want me to cut you, to shred your pale American skin, to—'

He was smiling. His neck was smiling. Adam stared. The blur of images in his mind was bewildering. *El Santo* was smiling twice.

Then he *saw*. Adam realized what had happened through the leering and erotic desolation in his mind. Jessica had produced a razor *from her mouth* and she had cut Carlos Chicomeca Monroy clean across the throat.

52

Tepito

Monroy was dying. The blood erupted from the vivid grin in his neck, spurting, joyous and plentiful. He barely had time to moan, to whisper; he clutched his fingers to the gaping wound but the blood kept spraying between them in merry little fountains: quite irrepressible.

Seconds later he slumped forward, like a post-coital lover, on to Jessica, she was naked and drenched in his blood. She stared at him with a languish of affection or desire; then she pushed his twitching, trembling body on to the floor.

Adam fought his own arousal; he couldn't work out whether it was Monroy's death or Jessica's nudity that made him so desirous; it was both, they were blurring. He needed an end to this: his own end.

An enormous crashing noise came from *beyond* the room. Jessica was standing, and rifling Monroy's pockets, taking the gun from his holster; but Adam was looking through the noble windows at the large courtyard: the noise came from the steel gates – they appeared to have been crushed by *an armoured car*.

Men were vaulting from the vehicle, crouching, firing rifles and revolvers in all directions. Military yet criminal: the Zetas, for sure. Again Adam swooned at the eroticism of the idea: he could walk into those bullets, he could just do it, pirouetting like a dancer as the bullets impacted his body, spinning him . . .

'Adam – wake up! Adam!'

Blooded, wearing Monroy's jacket, and nothing else, Jessica was standing over him, holding his handcuffs in her hand, and the keys in the other. 'I unlocked you. Get up, get up.'

He looked at the soft hair at the top of her legs, the red blood that had caught in her pubic hair, tiny red berries in a golden bramble. He wanted to lick the hair, lick her flesh where the blood was, taste it—

Nina pulled him to his feet. Jessica handed him a gun, Monroy's gun, and slapped him twice on the face. Very hard. 'You have about five hours to last, then I believe the ulluchu will wear off, you just need to get through the next *five hours*—'

Nina seemed more self-possessed than Adam. Why? Because she had attempted suicide a year ago? Was her thanatos, her death wish, already exhausted? His mind spun into turmoil once more.

Nina grabbed Jessica. 'Tell us!'

Jessica smiled and frowned. White-skinned and

almost nude and smeared with blood, her eyes were resigned and bright, obscurely serene. A marble statue scrawled with red graffiti, in the misty dawn. Still standing.

'I am dying. I thought if I could kill Monroy I would do one single good thing, something very good at the end of my life. That's why I didn't bargain with the Zetas: I wanted access to *Monroy*. El Santo. Something that would make my death worthwhile. He was too clever, he was going to use this drug to destroy my country, he had to be stopped. Your lives are just two lives . . . I am sorry, he was going to kill so many, if I could kill him first then my short life would mean something – I wouldn't die flailing, and futile, like my father; but the time is coming anyway, I am dying, it is good, not sad, not sad at all, it is good . . .' She was laughing. Yet not hysterical. But laughing.

'But—'

'I condemned you both! Your deaths were inevitable, no? Yet now here you are alive! So what are you waiting for? Run – *go now* – you have a chance, remember the Moche, they took this drug all their lives, at enormous doses, yet they lived on.'

'How?'

The noise of shooting in the courtyard was intense. The unnerving jangle of shattered glass, and the cackling rattle of automatic gunfire, men shouting, coming nearer.

'There is a chance. Eros and thanatos.' Jessica closed her eyes, and swayed, 'Eros and thanatos are entwined,

445

that's what Freud said. The libido and the death wish cannot exist without the other, even though they are in opposition. And maybe sometimes love *defeats* death, maybe God is death *plus love*. I do not know. Maybe. But why not try? Go now. Go now and make love . . .'

Adam watched: stunned and intoxicated. Jessica went to the sofa and lay down in the red puddles of Monroy's blood. A door slammed open: he swivelled. It was the guard, Monroy's bodyguard, saying 'Señor Monroy, capitano' – then the guard gazed in bewilderment at the scene.

The urge was orgasmic. And irresistible. Adam lifted the gun, and he fired, exultantly. He had never shot a gun in his life: but this was *so good*. The bullet slammed the man to the wall, silhouetting him with a corona of his own blood, another Jackson Pollock on the wall, the abstract expressionism of death.

He raised the gun again. But Nina pulled him away, saying *enough*. Yet the desire was so strong, he could shoot some more, or he could lie down here – touch the blood, lie down quietly . . .

'The stairs!'

A shard of lucidity entered his mind: Jessica. He turned. Jessica Silverton was naked again, on the sofa, and blood was draining from the deep wound across her throat. Her eyes were wide open. Staring at the ceiling, half rapt, ecstatic, saintly; the white arm dangled from the sofa, her gentle fingers lightly caressing the prone body of Carlos Chicomeca Monroy.

Nina pulled Adam out of the room and away. The

stairs were at the end of the wide landing; they ran down. Adam tightly clutched the gun in his hand, weighing the comforting metal hardness of its lethality; the stairs descended to the mayhem, the shooting, the Zetas and the Catrinas, kneeling, and firing, and dying.

'There must be a side door.'

They took the stairs in three leaps and then shrank back into the shadows of the courtyard. Adam could hear the bullets flying, a sizzle in the air, delicious, coming for him, he wanted to walk into the middle of it all, be devoured, in the wounding air.

'Here, look, this is a door, it must be!'

But Adam was not for using it. A Zeta man had spotted them. They were protected by a high-sided pick-up from the shooting in the wider yard, yet this Zeta had seen them, he was running over, gun raised, but not shooting, obviously he wanted them alive—

'Kill him!' screamed Nina. '*Shoot the fucking gun.* Kill him!'

Adam raised his arms, waiting to be shot by the Zeta cartelista, *wanting it, wanting to yield*. This is was it, the deliciousness of the end. He would die here, slip between the bedsheets and rejoin Alicia, kiss her cold lips once more.

Nina was firing. She had grabbed the gun from his hand and she was shooting the Zeta. The man gazed, perplexed, then doubled over, dead. Nina twisted on a heel and shot at the lock in the door in the external wall; Adam was too stoned to understand, he was a sexualized zombie, he couldn't move. The door opened,

Nina pushed him through and they stepped into the whirling streets of Mexico City. She hurled the pistol over the wall.

The lucidity again. He had a moment of clarity. Adam recognized these streets. He had been to Mexico City before: the green Volkswagen Beetles, the smell of tacos fried in rancid oil, the vibrant ugliness and the brown polluted air, the unmistakable thrum of the Distrito Federal: a truly vast city, a place they could hide in.

The shooting was still loud: Nina grabbed his hand and they ducked along the low streets – a left and a right, they sprinted another road, making a truck driver yell at them '*Hijos de putas!*' They crossed again, left and right, past a staring woman in a window, a cantina on the corner, a Superama supermarket, a beggar on the corner clutching a cross . . . a beggar with a cross?

He looked around. *Tepito*. He knew exactly where they were now: the infamous, Mexico City suburb of Tepito, the home of Santa Muerte, the home of the city's outlaws since Aztec times, perhaps the home of the Aztec worship of death, hidden here, underground, over the centuries.

Adam saw it all. Of course, this is where Monroy would live, in a big old house in the most dangerous old slum of the city, hidden in plain sight. Protected by the dangerous and villainous streets. He and Nina, were too conspicuous, sweating and scared and gringo-pale and flecked with blood.

But then the haziness took over his mind, once again, Adam felt the burning desire to *join in*. To join the strange Babylonian rites of Holy Death, to mingle with the street worship of Tepito.

People were crawling on their knees in the carless yet crowded boulevard. Mestizo and Indian alike, ex-prisoners and junkies, hookers in red pencil skirts, lowly criminals in cheap sneakers, youths in T-shirts with more tattoos than skin, were all crawling, slowly, along the street, towards a large platform on which was raised a grinning skeleton, adorned with a white wedding veil: Holy Death herself, the white lady, the skinny girl, the princess bride, with a reefer lodged between her shining teeth.

And when they reached the statue the crawling people prayed and bowed and sang little songs and made their offerings to Death. In the hot fresh pungent sunlight of the slum prostitutes were spraying perfume on the bones, or offering liquor to the skeletal mouth; and all around the White Lady other skulls sat smiling amidst the candles and tea-lights, skulls adorned with hats and football scarves, anointed with raw tequila. Adam felt the sweet delirium descending on him once again: he wanted be one of these people, to worship the skulls. Why not? Death was supreme: it was the democratizer. Death was the New World, waiting for the Old World to come, waiting for both the conquered and the conquerors.

But Nina was still quite alert.

'Think,' she said, turning him to face her. 'We just have to get through the next few hours and we will be OK. Jess said. We need somewhere to hide, it's not safe here, where – where can we go? You know this city, don't you? You told me. We need somewhere away from everything, somewhere with lots of tourists, where we shan't be spotted. Ach, Ad, fucking think, please *think*. We need to get as far away from Monroy. From all that.'

'Teotihuacan,' he said, surprised by the eloquence of his own words. *'Teotihuacan*. The temple complex. An hour from the city. Tourists there.'

Nina dragged him, as if he was an unwilling animal on a lead, to the corner of the street where the cars began. She hailed a taxi. It was green. They piled into the little car, with its ripped upholstery. 'Teotihuacan. *Por favor. Rapido!'*

The driver nodded without a word and the car pulled, rattling and old, into the hurling kinetic madness of Mexico City traffic. Adam closed his eyes and fought the lust: he wanted to push open the car door and jump out, into the racing traffic, but instead he held her hand, Nina's hand, her hot damp hand, squeezed it so hard he could see the pain on her face, but he liked that pain, he liked seeing her in pain . . . he could throw her on a floor and fuck her, rape her and hurt her, turn her over . . .

The struggle was obscene. His mind was filled with intense images, of love and destruction. His eyes tight shut, he focused on the noise, the honking, roaring drone of the traffic.

Then he woke up – somewhat. They were there: Teotihuacan. The great site of the pyramids, or at least

450

by the enormous car park next door. Tourist buses were parked in a row. Americans and Europeans were wandering around, in hats and sunglasses, buying presents, peering at souvenir stalls, haggling over Diet Pepsis sold from metal buckets. The incongruity of it all was stunning.

Nina showed him: she had their little bags – the stuff they had been allowed to take. Passports. Grabbed from Monroy's house. How come she was so lucid? How had she managed that? It must have been her recent suicide attempt. She had some resistance. For the moment.

They moved down a lane and found the first hotel, Los Pyramidos. In the lobby the tourists in shorts and new straw hats gazed at the two sweating young people in bemusement and alarm. The concierge looked at them likewise. Nina slammed their passports on the counter and the middle-aged receptionist shrugged, and sighed, and said *Vale* and handed over a key.

A corridor. Death. A hotel door. *To yield.* The door opened. Death. They fell into the room, and immediately Adam threw himself on the bed and curled into a ball, foetal, enclosed, fighting the persistent images, the insistent desires. He didn't care what Nina was doing. He wanted to relish and ignore and explore the thoughts that erupted inside him, the kaleidoscopic cascade of daydreams . . . Alicia talking and naked, blood running from her mouth, his hand between her legs, there, the softness, the redness, the surgical incision, the Moche amputation, the vampire fish under

451

the skin, in his heart, eating his heart. Why hadn't he drunk some of the blood, just a small cup, an espresso cup of blood, a tiny delicate china cup full of red blood? Delicious. Maybe he could throw himself from the hotel window: they were on the second floor, that would probably be enough, then it would be done, at last, then the whole fucking sadness, the pointless struggle, the bleak and godless agony, the grief over Alicia and his family and everything, the stupid getting and spending, then at last *it would be over*, all the suffering of human life would be finished, concluded, enacted, contracted. Stamped with a fat red royal seal of blood-red wax, and signed by the lady herself, her imperial whiteness, the Virgin Queen: his royal death warrant.

Adam stirred. How long had elapsed? An hour? Could have been two. It was still daylight. He could still hear the murmur of tourist business out there, in the car park, as Teotihuacan complex welcomed and disgorged its many thousands of visitors.

The hotel room was silent. Nina? He realized, with a painful start, that *Nina wasn't there*.

He had to use this moment of consciousness. He didn't know if this was the ulluchu wearing off or just another brief interlude before the madness began again. But he had to find and save Nina.

There. A noise. Panting? Someone was softly panting, gasping even, gulping fine breaths. The noise was muffled by a door: she was in the bathroom. He rushed across the room and pushed at the door and it was firmly locked: and he knew at once what was happening.

'Nina!' He thumped on the door. 'Nina!' He began to kick at the door.

She was locked inside the bathroom, probably dying. He was too late.

53

The City Complex of Teotihuacan, Mexico

He kicked at the door; it barely budged; he pulled back and kicked again, hard, and the entire thing buckled, and collapsed, half of it swinging on broken hinges, the rest a mess of angry splinters and shattered planking.

Adam stepped over the debris, and there she was. Lying in a bath full of water, nude. She had a broken safety razor in her hand – the blade exposed. And it was poised and trembling just over the arteries of her upper wrist.

The way she was holding the blade told him enough.

'Nina.'

She said nothing. Her head was bowed, she was staring at the razor blade in her white-knuckled hand.

'Nina.' His voice was gentle. 'Please.' He knelt. 'Don't. You're nearly through it. I feel different now, better, the drug really does wear off. Jessica was right.'

Slowly she lifted her head, her beautiful white face soiled with tears and grief, and she said, staring hard into him, and also beyond him, 'Why? It will never wear off. They are dead. Daddy. My sister. All dead. Why don't I just fucking join them?'

She was holding the broken razor blade so hard that blood was seeping between her knuckles. Her hand trembled and prepared: poised, ready to slash and to kill.

'Because you want to live,' said Adam. 'You told me, your father's suicide made you want to *live*, this is just the drug talking.'

'It's not. I've *always* wanted this. The fucking end of. End of story. End.'

'Nina—'

'The woman is perfected.'

She was panting, and gasping. As if she was being waterboarded by grief and despair, gulping for air for a moment, then slammed underwater again. Drowning in hopelessness.

The blade touched her skin. She was going to do it. Adam moved close and reached a hand for her wrist. She yelled, 'Don't fucking touch me, Adam!'

He looked at her angry, desolate, whitely beautiful face, the lovely face he was too scared to love, because of Alicia. Yet this *was* the face and the body he loved, or desired, or wanted, more than anything, *despite* Alicia. *Because of Alicia.* Love *defeats* death. God is death *and love.* He loved Nina purely and truly.

There was a terrible pause. Then he moved his hand,

455

and he touched her bare breast, he caressed the curve of her breast, soft and young and damp with bathwater.

Her eyes met his. Angry, yet yielding.

He reached for her, he reached into her and hauled her naked to her feet then he half-dragged and half-carried her over the broken door into the bedroom, and threw her on the mattress and tore off his clothes and opened her legs and it was as if she wanted it to be as violent as possible. She bit him and fought him and he scratched her, they scratched at each other, half-fighting, half-biting, scratching and coupling and fighting and kissing.

She bit him so hard on the shoulder he yelled; he reached out and grabbed at her slender white throat, and he realized he was killing her. She was staring up at him, choking, saying, 'Go on, do it, Adam, do it!'

He let go of her and plunged his mouth to hers and they kissed again, and he was deep inside her again; they were both riding the same terrible waves, and then the storm began to subside: the bites became less fierce, she was pulling him closer, she was touching him softly, and he was just kissing her, and making love to her, and then it was just tender, and they were through it, and then they just looked at each other for what seemed like an hour, and the next time he gazed at the window it was black and quite starry and night.

Nina lay there in the bed. She leaned and kissed his shoulder. She said that she loved him. He didn't need to reply. And then she cried for a few seconds and she shook her head and then she turned over and she closed her eyes.

Her breathing came slower, and longer. He watched her. A white marble angel, cold and warm at once, softly breathing, and sleeping deeply. Then he got up and dressed and went to buy some water from the machine in the lobby. It was the depths of the night. Four a.m. No one was around.

Something drew him outside. Into the night. He walked down the hotel path: and there he saw them, the great pyramids of Teotihuacan. Just over the fence. Ancient and moonlit and enormous and calm: purple ziggurats in the whispering darkness.

He went to a payphone at the hotel entrance. With his faltering Spanish he managed to get a call reversed: to London.

'DCI Ibsen?'

'Yes . . .'

He told the detective the story. The short version. Truncated to a few minutes. There would be time for longer explanations later.

'So that's it, Mark, we're out, but we're still stuck, we don't have any money.'

'Stay there. We'll sort it. We'll get this sorted: I'll call the embassy right now, we will get you out of Mexico tomorrow. Give me the hotel details.'

Adam did as he was told and offered his thanks.

Ibsen said, 'Incredible. Just incredible. You are one brave Aussie bastard. Or lucky. Or both.'

The call ended.

Replacing the receiver, Adam turned, shoving his water bottle in his back pocket, and he vaulted the little fence; and then he walked down between the great ancient pyramids of Teotihuacan, down the vast, silent, deserted Avenue of the Dead.

The Pyramid of the Moon was on his right, the even larger Pyramid of the Sun was ahead of him. He stopped at one smaller temple, with feathered serpent gods carved in stone, forming the balustrades: biting the soft Mexican air, angrily, and for all time. Unwatched in the dark.

There was a carving here, a frieze in relief on a side-wall, with the detailing sharpened by the slanted light of a nearly-full moon. Adam regarded the artwork. It showed people dancing, and stylized jaguars, and priests in feathered headdresses. Wreathing lyrically between these figures were seven flowers.

Unmistakably, they were morning glories. Five-petalled and beautiful. *Ulluchu*. As he gazed at the flower Adam thought of all the places they had sought this drug and yet never quite found it: Scotland and England and Spain and France and Peru. Then he thought of Portugal, and that extraordinary round chapel where the Templars of Tomar took mass on horseback, sipping from the Holy Grail, drinking the very drug of the Lord, the liquor of the gods that took them closer to death, or to Christ. Or to both.

Adam pulled the water bottle from his pocket and drank the delicious cold water. He wondered how exactly they would get home. Then he stopped wondering. The embassy would find a way. It didn't matter. What mattered was the mere fact they had survived. Everyone else was gone, everyone else was dead, but he and Nina: they were not. They had defied the drug. They had defied death. They were still alive.

54

Toloriu, the Catalunyan Pyrenees

What was he going to do with this place? Felip Portera gazed at the semi-ruined building: *Casa Bima*. He had been farming these steep green Pyrenean hillsides since he was a boy. The land itself had been in his family for countless generations, and in that time he'd seen the grand old house decay with increasing speed.

Now it was almost a ruin: his cows enjoyed it mostly, as a shelter from cold winter rain and hot Catalan sun, from the mountain winds and thunderstorms. The windows were all broken, the roof was worse than useless; snakes slept in the courtyard in June.

Yet it must have been magnificent once: the views across the valley to Felip's family house, in the handsome stone hamlet of Toloriu, perched on the opposing crag, were truly stirring. A suitable place for an emperor's daughter.

Felip whistled for Miro, his dog, who was intent on worrying a calf.

'Miro. *Parada*. Miro!'

The young dog perked his ears, and tilted his head; the old farmer tried to look serious and, frowning, he tutted and waved a finger; and then he abandoned the attempt at being stern, and he smiled at the puppyish animal, indulgently.

Leaning on his weary knees, Felip picked up a stick, and threw it; the happy dog galloped down the hill in the early spring sunshine.

Again Felip turned his attention to the house. One day very soon, as a family, they would have to decide: demolish it once and for all? Or rebuild it and refurbish, turn it into an attraction for tourists, by using the legends?

The story was indeed romantic. The daughter of the last Aztec emperor who married a bold Catalan conquistador, Juan Pedro de Grau, who then brought his imperial bride all the way across the seas, to this lonely mountain valley!

Amazing.

It must have been a bewildering experience, Felip mused, as he sat on a bare rock, and unwrapped his lunchtime bocadillo. She was the daughter of a living god, born into the court of an exotic empire, surrounded by priests and lords and bloody sacrifice on sunlit pyramids; then she moved here, to a damp house in the cloudy green Pyrenean meadows, where she was surrounded by white peasants and burly farmers.

461

What did she think as she stared from her kitchen at the goats, listening to their tinkling bells? Did she remember the old gods, Quetzalcoatl and Huitzilopochtli, as she helped to churn the butter? Did she daydream of the skull racks of the eagle warriors, as they brought in the sows for branding?

Over the years Felip had tried to learn as much as he could about this girl, the emperor's daughter, Xipahuatzin Montezuma, not least because of the intriguing legends of a treasure, buried hereabouts. What could it be? The great and secret treasure of Montezuma himself? A cache of marvellous gold and turquoise? Eighty years ago some Germans had apparently rented the sloping fields of Casa Bima and tried to find it, and failed; every so often, every few years, someone else made the long wearying walk from Toloriu, already a remote spot in the mountains, to try to find the same. No one had ever found anything. Of course.

Because it *was* just a legend. And now the house was a saddening sight, and fewer and fewer visitors made the effort to see an old ruin, full of cowpats, vipers and damp cobwebs. Yes, one day soon they would have to decide what to do: probably they would demolish it, maybe build something new. A hotel with a pool. For proper tourists.

Rubbing his hands, Felip finished his sandwich and threw the last piece of crust to the happy dog.

'*Anem hi*, Miro.' He turned, commencing his walk back to Toloriu. His precious day off was being wasted, his wife would be back from Urgell with the grand-children soon enough.

But again he paused at the top of the forest path, and gazed at the tall, notable yellow shrub. This singular morning glory plant grew around Casa Bima, and only around here, on the southeast-facing slope. It was a curiosity in itself. Felip could remember when there were hundreds of these distinctive shrubs on this slope, but they too had dwindled over the years: because of climate change, perhaps? The plants seemed very susceptible to altering conditions – very delicate and fragile.

And then that Scotsman had come here, nearly two years ago; the tall old man with the charming smile – who had picked most of the seeds! Felip remembered the man's agreeable but distracted nature. He had presumed, at the time, that he was an eccentric botanist. If so, he was surely not a very good botanist: by picking all the seeds he seemed to have killed off nearly all the remaining shrubs.

Felip did not, however, especially mind this destruc-tion. The plant was a nuisance. Occasionally one of his cows would stray near the forest, and nibble the leaves and seeds, and then fall sick. So he wasn't upset that the plant was dying out, even if it was rather pretty. And now there was just one plant left.

Why not get rid of it altogether? The farmer nodded to himself. Yes: tomorrow he would get up early and he would come back here, and pull up the last shrub by its roots, get rid of it once and for all: burn the golden flowers and toxic seeds. Then he would do something about the rotten old fencing in the woods.

Calling his dog to heel with a cheerful whistle, Felip Portera continued his stroll along the dappled green path, to his village in the hills. A wind was picking up, and it was time to go home. And as he walked away, the little golden flowers shivered, in the sweet and freshening breeze.

Killer ReadS.com

The one-stop shop for the best in crime and thriller fiction

Be the first to get your hands on the **latest releases**, **exclusive interviews** and **sneak previews** from your favourite authors.

Browse the site and sign up to the newsletter for our pick of the **hottest** articles as well as a chance to **win** our monthly competition!

Writing so good it's criminal